Praise for DOUGLAS MUIR

RED STAR RUN

"THIS ONE TAKES OFF LIKE A DRAG RACER AND
NEVER DECELERATES. HIS MOSCOW SCENES RI-
VAL *GORKY PARK* IN THEIR AUTHENTICITY."

—Oakley Hall
author of *The Downhill Racer*

". . . A BOOK THAT WILL KEEP YOU NAILED TO
YOUR CHAIR. MOVE OVER, TOM CLANCY!"

—Paul Gillette
author of *Play Misty for Me*

TIDES OF WAR

"FAST-PACED . . . IT STARTS WITH A BANG AND
CHARGES HEADLONG TO A SURPRISING CONCLU-
SION."

—T. Jefferson Parker
author of *Laguna Heat*

AMERICAN REICH

"A HUMDINGER OF A THRILLER."

—Channel 7 Eyewitness News
(Seattle)

"FAST-PACED . . . MUIR PULLS IT OFF WITH CON-
SIDERABLE APLOMB."

—*Los Angeles Times*

And now, his newest, most shocking . . . . .

MIDNIGHT ADMIRALS

DOUGLAS MUIR

CHARTER BOOKS, NEW YORK

MIDNIGHT ADMIRALS

A Charter Book / published by arrangement with
the author

PRINTING HISTORY
Charter edition / June 1989

ISBN: 1-55773-203-5

PRINTED IN THE UNITED STATES OF AMERICA

10   9   8   7   6   5   4   3   2   1

ACKNOWLEDGMENTS

The author's thanks to the U.S. Navy, and especially to the crews of the aircraft carriers *Ranger* and *Constellation*.

～～～～～ Prologue

When the boy was born his father was reputed to have said, "Now isn't that an unlucky, homely little sonofabitch for you?"

Ten years later, Roscoe Eisenbinder's appearance hadn't improved a lick. The kid had turned into a freckle-splotched runt with a flat, squashy nose and protruding ears as deformed as oyster shells. The embarrassing ugliness was compounded by a surly, impish manner that seemed to have set in for good. When Roscoe's lips weren't locked in a pout, they seemed formed in a lazy, crooked smile; his small hazel eyes were constantly filled with naughtiness, and the other children in the neighborhood feared him.

Today, as usual, he was alone, except for his Maltese Terrier who answered to the name of Rapunzel. Roscoe climbed off his Schwinn junior bike and surveyed the deserted pond. Canted absurdly over his head of violent red hair was a far-too-large, moth-eaten Navy officer's hat. He tipped the tattered headpiece forward to shield his eyes from the hard-edged sun and stood there for a long time, purposely staring at the water. Suddenly, a short distance away a bullfrog leaped from a lily pad, startling him.

Roscoe regained his composure and edged closer to the pond, glaring down at the expanding ripples caused by the frog's disturbance. Seeing his own scarecrow's face reflecting back from the water, he grimaced and quickly looked away. Roscoe's hate for mirrors of any kind was well-honed, but there was no time to fret over his appearance now.

Already the exciting, vivid pictures had begun to dance in his mind. Accompanying them was the echoing voice of his grandfather, reminding him that this wasn't a mere neighborhood pond at all, that actually it was the legendary river Styx! Roscoe's grandfather, before his death, had taught him all about that hellish place, for the old man loved to read in a book by a poet named Dante.

Savoring the apparition, Roscoe hunched his shoulders and

twitched his nose like a rabbit. He didn't have to work hard on his fantasies at all; the memories, vivid images, and exciting deeds came back to him easily, playfully revolving in his mind like the twinkly mirrors on a carousel. Thanks to *his ingenuity*, the family cat had been the first to be ferried across the Styx's bloody waters. The other bodies he'd consigned to join the souls of the dead didn't count, like the grubby toads deliberately squashed under his bike wheels and the live gerbil consigned to the garbage disposal. They were trifles, experiments of minor symbolic consequence. Any brat kid on the block might try stunts like that.

Roscoe laughed, his usual puckish, self-serving giggle. His grandmother had named the feline Sylvester, after the blundering cartoon character. The cat was really his first test of nerve, and Roscoe had been successful; not once did he flinch or feel even the slightest remorse. Sylvester could have fought back with his claws, but the black and white tabby had been so trusting. *And stupid*. Until the day of its demise, it kept trying to sleep with him at night, pressing in close. *No! Animals or people, Roscoe didn't want anyone to get that close*. Not now, not ever.

At the time he had difficulty deciding between the trash compactor and the clothes dryer, the latter winning out because of the old-fashioned, see-through door. Observing was important in a game of nerves. *Courage needed to be measured*.

Kerplunk, kerplunk, kerplunk, kerplunk. Sylvester clawed frantically at the sides of the revolving drum and stared out at him with terrified umber eyes. *Meeeeyoooooww!*

Roscoe had calmly smiled back, pretending to reassure the animal. Sylvester howled mournfully, and then he was strangely silent. *Or dead*? The thudding noise became more subdued, almost gentle. Perhaps it was the quarter-roll of fabric softener he'd tossed inside to keep the creature company. Roscoe had been so taken up by the grisly horror he let the dryer run another ten minutes just to be sure.

Berblumm, berblumm, berblumm, berblumm. Too bad, pussycat.

His mother had given Sylvester to him as a tiny kitten. Convinced the cat's death was an accident, she'd cried for two days. Or so the once-a-month letter from his mother's nurse at the mental health hospital had claimed. Grandmother Ramona, too, had wept.

Roscoe was glad he truly didn't know how to cry. Oddly, he'd never learned, not even as an infant. And not even later, when his drunken, short-fused father had abused him. All he'd learned to do was keep his awful hate inside, pretend not to hurt, and practice becoming the ultimate actor. The bruises were gone now, as were his mother and father. Living with his grandmother had turned out better than expected.

Roscoe had snuffed the pussycat two years ago. Replaying the incident in his mind brought on a sense of excitement and challenge for the more complicated ritual he would perform today. The other children in the neighborhood who so rigorously avoided him would regret missing this important rite. It really didn't matter, because they'd never understand it. He was far too mature for them; their infantile minds had never been a match for Roscoe Eisenbinder's cunning inventiveness and superior intellect. The others were always bragging about their mothers, something he couldn't do in turn. He'd told them his mother, Felicia, was dead, all too aware of the cruel, terrible time they'd give him if they knew she were in a psychiatric ward for the criminally insane.

How time flies! It was hard to believe he would have another birthday tomorrow. The event, unfortunately, would be infuriatingly predictable. Grandmother Ramona would present Roscoe with her mindless gifts, and, if his father were sober enough, she might grant the man visitation rights for the afternoon. His father might even be allowed to stay for dinner if the two of them didn't start throwing tableware at one another. His father had annoying whiskey breath, but recently—possibly because of the social worker's close monitoring—the man had at least learned to keep his big, destructive hands to himself.

Too bad grandmother Ramona couldn't keep her hands to herself. A drunken fool's breath wasn't nearly as hard for Roscoe to take as a coddling grandma who liked to fuss with his hair, tease his nose, and bury his head between her sandbag tits. His grandmother also smelled strange. She insisted it was because of her diseased kidneys, that she might die soon. What really bothered Roscoe most, however, was that she liked to fondle. Always grabbing and handling! *Why were people forever touching him?*

Roscoe wondered what old Ramona would buy him this time around for his birthday. Last year the doting woman had given him a boy's sailor suit, one of those cute Buster Brown types with a big blue bow. He'd nearly shit in his pants when he saw it and smelled the mothballs. *Barf on you, crazy woman!* What an insult, considering that he'd requested a whaling harpoon or a neat piece of scrimshaw. "Come on, Grandma," he'd warned her, "What else would a brainy kid into nautical stuff want for a gift? And not another ship model, thanks. My room is full of them, some not even finished yet." The advice to the woman had gone unheeded.

The niggling, silly bitch! Damn you, Grandma Ramona! Screw last year's birthday and Ramona's silly, rich-kid's sailor suit! This is the nineteen seventies, not the thirties. For hours after his party he'd fantasized on reaming the old woman with the harpoon he'd desperately wanted but didn't get. Perhaps he'd devise a surprise for her tomorrow, depending on what maddening gift she brought him. It wouldn't take much to trigger his imagination. Tomorrow, however, was a long way off; there were still important things to do today.

Roscoe looked around, checking once more to be sure the area was deserted. Overhead the sky was clear, a perfect translucent blue. The sun was round and fuzzy-hot; a perfect day for taking pictures and preserving the event for posterity. He knew the pictorial effect would be far more stunning at night, but for now high noon would have to suffice. When he was older he'd conduct his rituals at midnight on full moons during the bewitching hours. He'd also know a little more about photography then, especially the camera's flash attachment. And it would also be easier to get away from his watchful grandmother. He wondered how much longer she'd live, how many more years he'd have to put up with her.

Ramona would scold him mercilessly if she knew he was wearing her deceased husband's Navy hat. The headgear was old and the flag officer's scrambled eggs on the bill were torn and badly tarnished. Roscoe's small head was swimming inside it, but that didn't matter; he was still an admiral of the fleet for the day. Ramona had called his grandfather "her mad midnight admiral" because he'd left her, committing suicide by jumping off a ferry boat on a stormy night. Roscoe felt differently about Gerald Eisenbinder. His drowned grandfather was special, a great man who was merely misunderstood.

The pond was nestled in a brush-filled gully just beyond the housing project. Everything Roscoe needed had been crammed into the red wagon and towed behind the bike. The wagon contained the despised sailor suit, a huge cardboard box, some tape, an improvised mast, a sail made from one of Ramona's pillowcases, a can of charcoal lighter, matches, firecrackers, and a Polaroid camera.

Rapunzel watched him as he unloaded the big cardboard box and examined its interior. It was one of the heavily waxed cartons used by supermarkets for poultry, and by carefully taping and retaping the bottom seam, he felt sure it would stay afloat for twenty minutes or more. Ten minutes was all that was really needed. Or so he hoped. *How long was a Viking funeral supposed to take?* His clumsy, improvised ship could have been launched without the sail, but Roscoe wanted a reasonable degree of authenticity. After spending hours researching the matter in the library, he'd traced the Nordic design on the pillowcase sail and carefully painted it in with red and blue tempera colors.

Now that everything was ready, he tucked the ugly sailor suit in the bottom of the cartoon. *Good riddance.* At least it would make a nice bed for the dog. Tail wagging, Rapunzel foolishly jumped inside the box, sitting obediently as her collar was fastened to the mast. *Now it was time for the firecrackers*! Feeling a little stingy, he tossed only half a pack into the improvised boat and saved the rest.

Roscoe ran a dry tongue over his lips as he stood back and surveyed his work. The Viking ship was crude, but it floated steadily enough. *But why shouldn't it?* He'd twice calculated the displacement, just to be sure. The heavy cardboard box with the dog in it drew just over an inch of water, just as he'd estimated. Roscoe glanced up as a couple of black crows cawed overhead. *An omen?* He waited until they disappeared over the hill.

At last the pond was spooky quiet, except for a slight breeze that raked its surface. *Perfect.* Just enough wind to carry the makeshift vessel away from the shore. Roscoe smiled at the bewildered pet. He sprinkled the lighter fluid liberally over the carton, mast, and sail as the dog cocked its head and looked back at him in wonderment.

Roscoe's heart fluttered and his breath came unevenly; he trembled slightly as a shiver of excitement crept slowly up his spine like a restless Tarantula. Roscoe Eisenbinder might only be a pint-sized angel of death, a mere beginner, but none the less, he felt all-powerful. "Bon voyage, Rapunzel," he said firmly. Emptying the rest of the lighter fluid over the dog, he stood back and struck a match.

Whump!

The Polaroid, quick! Hurry it up, dummy, before the inferno dies down! Roscoe frantically struggled with the camera, but the first print turned out a dud. Disgusted, he tried again. This time the floating pyre was perfectly captured on film, and he was delirious with joy. To drown out the dog's piercing wail, he started to sing a sea shanty learned in the fourth grade. His soprano voice ricocheted around the pond.

> *"Blow boys, blow, the sun's drawing water;*
> *Three cheers for the cook, and one for his daughter."*

1

The auxiliary conn on the 08 level was one of the quietest places on the *Abraham Lincoln*—when the nuclear carrier was in port. Captain Swain Bullock once more enjoyed the view and its relative silence. Despite the inconvenience it caused his orderlies, he'd decided to have his breakfast brought up. Solitude was difficult to come by on a warship, and he was determined to enjoy the mood of isolation while he could.

Finishing off his two poached eggs on toast and the front page of the *San Diego Union* at the same time, Bullock took his mug of black coffee over to the open starboard window and peered outside. The autumn air was crisp and pearly with humidity; over a hundred feet below, the slightly ruffled water was barely visible. Up forward, the carrier's bow was completely shrouded in fog. Though Monday morning had brought sunshine just a few miles inland, the entire North Island waterfront was wrapped in a nebulous winter haze—a peculiar, patchy fog that would suddenly lift then close in again rapidly.

Swain Bullock knew, like other seasoned ship commanders, that sporadic fog was the most dangerous kind. Fog killed more ships than typhoons, reefs, and icebergs combined. Fog was like a fickle woman, he reflected. Bullock was glad the *Abraham Lincoln* was secured to the dock bollards, as seemingly puny as they appeared compared to the supercarrier and its mammoth hawsers. To say his warship had a commanding presence would be a gross understatement. Newest and most sophisticated of the Nimitz-class nuclear attack carriers, the *Abraham Lincoln*, also known as the CVN-71, dwarfed its surroundings; wherever it was berthed, the self-contained leviathan appeared restless—as if yearning to be out to sea where it could breathe again.

Bullock was lucky. The vessel had just returned from a lengthy deployment. It would be another two years before the next new supercarrier, the *George Washington*, was commissioned at Newport News, and until then, the *crème de la crème* of the fleet—indeed, the ultimate Navy assignment—was his alone. Bullock knew that although the five-thousand-plus men aboard took fierce pride in their ship, most of them had no abiding affection for their barrel-chested, five-feet-eleven captain. Many, rumor had it, despised him. *Old Sourface. Hardass Bullock. A regular Captain Bligh*, some called him. There were others who probably took a dislike to his vivid red hair. Bullock admitted to being a cold, ruthless taskmaster who ran a supertight ship, so tight that an executive officer who had asked to be transferred had called him emotionally dispossessed, as cold as a deepfreeze, and as unimaginative and petty as a wallet calculator.

Bullock knew he could afford to shrug off such grousing—as long as he maintained a few highly-placed contacts. Getting to the top in peacetime and staying there not only required a strange mix of grit and dream, but it also meant a certain kinship with the *old boy network*—making timely use of his Annapolis ring-knocker pals at the local officer's club.

Gazing out at the fog, Bullock took off his baseball-type command cap and ran a hand through his curly hair. He sipped his coffee, taking no real pleasure in it. At forty-eight his heretofore cast-iron stomach was beginning to protest the four cups a day, and he needed to quit. The after-duty double martinis had to go as well. Five years earlier he'd exorcised his body of a smoking addiction and increased his daily constitutional from two laps around the flight deck to three—when the weather was good. When it rained or flight operations interfered, he used the exercise bike in his day cabin.

Staring into the nothingness beside the carrier, Bullock's nose crinkled in irritation as he once more thought about his too-empty personnel file. *Not enough damned letters of commendation. By now, he should have several more.* Had he cultivated the wrong friends or been too modest? The problem wasn't his, but the dead wood up the line. The fat cats at the Pentagon wouldn't recognize brilliant leadership if it blinded them! Talent too often went unrecognized because of the system. From now on Bullock would flaunt it.

Bullock suddenly flashed on an uncompleted task, something he'd meant to take care of the moment he'd arrived on the bridge this morning. The auxiliary conn jutted out on the starboard side of the bridge, and he could be seen by the duty man and radar maintenance technician. *Not enough privacy here.* The adjoining chart room was deserted, so Bullock went in there and closed the door behind him. He withdrew from his pocket a U.S. passport, glancing briefly one more time at the likeness of an attractive Chinese woman inside its cover. Finding a large metal ashtray, he set the passport afire and watched it burn. When it had turned to a charred, unrecognizable spiral of ash and cooled, he crumbled the remains in his palm and went back out on the bridge. He quickly tossed the powder out into the bay.

Bullock's body stiffened slightly as he heard seven bongs on the intercom. Below him, beneath the fog-shrouded flight deck, a flag officer was coming aboard. It was an unscheduled, unanticipated visit, and Bullock wondered why.

Four minutes later Bullock's immediate supervisor, Rear Admiral Fritz Tanner, head of Carrier Group Seven, stepped out of the elevator and entered the bridge. The staff at North Island and Miramar had nicknamed Tanner "Babe" because of his Oliver Hardy, moon-shaped face, peach-bloom cheeks, and abbreviated black moustache. Given a little more lard around the butt, a derby, and a 1920's flivver, he'd be a dead-ringer for the comedian. But not this morning. The admiral appeared vile-spirited, his face cross-grained and humorless.

He got up on the wrong side of the bed, Bullock thought. Actually, he was envious of Tanner. Where Bullock himself was known as hard-nosed and difficult, Fritz was popular among the men. Indeed, they called Tanner the sailor's admiral, a term that hadn't been heard since World War II and the time of Bill Halsey.

Seeking privacy, the admiral gestured for the armed Petty Officer of the Watch to step briefly outside the bridge. When they were alone, Tanner spoke first. "Swain, I came over here myself rather than let Naval Intelligence bring the bad news."

"You knew I was here instead of at the billet?"

The admiral lowered his head, his pinched face softened as he fussed with his shirtcuff. "Unfortunately, I've already been to your on-base living quarters. And before you ever made port, my wife tipped me off on the pending divorce with Maxine. As sorry as I am about your marriage, there's far worse news that—" Tanner hesitated, his mouth working like a beached fish. Nothing came out.

Bullock started to speak, but Fritz Tanner thrust up his hand like a traffic cop. Bullock stared at the gold braid on his superior's sleeve—one broad stripe surmounted by a single star. *Rear admiral, lower-half*. The overdue promotion for which Bullock himself was still waiting and yearning.

An uncomfortable, metallic silence settled in the bridge.

Tanner rubbed his moustache and exhaled sharply. His eyes

were razors of determination as he pointed to the elevated, leather
command chair. "I think you'd better sit down, Captain."

A half-dozen edgy SPs guarded the homicide site at the officers'
housing just off Quentin Roosevelt Boulevard. From their ashen,
somber faces it was obvious that this wasn't the kind of thing they
expected to do after finishing basic.

Lieutenant Commander Todd Dougherty of the Naval Investigation Service was equally unhappy. He shook his head,
convinced that he'd now seen it all. If parallels could be drawn,
Dougherty was the Navy's equivalent to a first captain of a
homicide squad in a major city, the only difference being he
sometimes had to function in a legal capacity as well. His primary
claim to being a hot-shot detective was a certificate on the wall
testifying to six weeks of special training at the FBI Academy.
Dougherty admitted his real savvy was cutting through Government red tape, the ability and the patience to ease through the
recondite bureaucratic complexities of the Defense Department in
general and the U.S. Navy in particular.

Leaning inside the window of his oxidized-gray, Navy-issue
station wagon, Dougherty replaced the radio mike in its cradle and
let out a wretched sigh. He left the vehicle and retraced his steps
back to the ribbon marking the crime investigation perimeter. One
of the SPs lifted the barrier, permitting Dougherty to cut across the
lawn. A clog of distressed neighbors stared at him, silent
cardboard silhouettes in the fog.

A smartly dressed, attractive woman in her early thirties
stepped off the concrete stoop at one end of the tan stucco duplex
and came up to him. He immediately recognized her. Pamela
Bonner was unsmiling and from her determined step, appeared to
mean business. She surprised Dougherty by reaching up and
straightening the shoulder strap on his navy regulation raincoat.
Noting with interest his new grade insignia, she said with a smile,
"In that much of a hurry this morning, Lieutenant Commander?
Still no wife to straighten your collar?" She winked. "It's been too
long. Needless to say, I'm impressed with your promotion."

He shrugged. "Hello, Pamela. Go for crow, as they say in the
Navy." *Another stripe, so what,* he said to himself. Wait until the
FBI woman sees what confronted them. He secretly wanted to tell
her, *My ass will be grass, the end of the line, if one of us doesn't
break this case quickly.*

She stared at him with hard, disarming eyes. "If my memory's
intact, it's been fourteen months since we last worked together."

"A year and a half, give or take." Dougherty looked back at the bureau special agent, once more pleased with what he saw. Pam Bonner had surprised him before as the consummate professional and she'd probably do it again. She also had an infectious smile and a measure of charm once her initial hard-case, assertive facade was broken. As usual, her emerald eyes sparkled with mischief. Pamela wasn't without ego. Right out of college she'd changed her name from Bonagofski to Bonner. Her pretty Polish face had a timeless, soft-edged quality men liked; the sandy hair was shorter and lighter than he remembered it, and she was too well-tanned for this time of year, even in southern California. Dougherty wondered if Pamela had just returned from vacation in Hawaii. An overworked special agent with a backlog of Government caseloads usually didn't have time to work up a bronze like that.

Pamela extended her hand, her inquisitive eyes continuing to study him. Under less conspicuous circumstances, Dougherty might have ignored the formality and afforded her a decent welcoming hug. He shook her slender, smooth hand instead and said, "Welcome back to the old stomping ground, G-woman."

"How does the song go? Give me one more chance on the midway? Something about another ride on the merry-go-round?"

"You won't be so flip when you see what's inside. Speaking of promotions, I understand the San Diego Rape Crisis Network is hurting, hardly the same since you moved upstairs."

Pamela shivered. "So? Here I am back in the dirty cellar. God, it's cold out here. I've got goosebumps. Please, let's go in."

He grinned at her. "In the Navy we worry about goose barnacles."

"Whatever, but right now I'm cold."

"Fair warning. You'll be far more miserable in there."

"A crime of passion?"

Dougherty exhaled sharply. "I doubt it."

"Your duty-minded assistants have been less than cooperative. I was barred from the bedroom until you returned."

"Sorry. My orders."

They headed up a flagstone walk bordered by neatly manicured bluegrass, still wet from the automatic sprinklers. On-base family living quarters for officers, with its symmetrical, clinical appearance, seldom varied. *Cellblocks*, Dougherty mused. Ubiquitous Spanish tile roofs, perfectly trimmed cedar shrubs framing the entries, regulation kiddie swings or teeter-totters in the back yard. The scattered flower boxes and planters looked like a profusion of

semicolons in the middle of a clunky paragraph. They somehow
didn't belong. The aesthetics aside, for the lucky occupants the
price was right. His own bachelor pad was off base at Mission
Beach, and it cost him an arm and a leg above his housing
allowance.

Dougherty glanced at the two knee-high wire signs beside the
walkway. The first proclaimed that this end of the duplex was
occupied by CAPTAIN SWAIN BULLOCK. The second sign, askew and
staking out some territory of its own nearer the porch, read simply:
AND MAXINE.

The screen door still hadn't been dusted for fingerprints and it
was propped open and red-tagged. As Dougherty led Pamela
through the entry, the lab photographer's flash went off inches
away from his face. Dougherty winced. Every inch of the living
room was being committed to film, and they were in the way. A
roll of white butcher's paper had been spread across the short-
napped green carpet—a yard-wide, antiseptic footpath that led to
the grisly scene in the next room. Pamela stepped softly to keep
her heels from going through the paper. Beside them, vacuuming
the rug meticulously for minutia, was Glen Meadows, one of the
civilian technicians from the local NIS office. Meadows had a
bullet-shaped bald head, along with a boxer's ears and stance. He
was so preoccupied with the carpet he didn't look up.

Another NIS assistant, Sol Steinberg, stepped out of the
bedroom and said to Dougherty, "Sir, the coroner's still inside.
We've left it to Rear Admiral Tanner to break the news to the old
man."

Dougherty scowled at Steinberg.

"Sorry, boss. I meant to say *Captain Bullock*." Tall and slender,
Steinberg had a sharp, beak-like nose and wore silver-framed
Trotsky eyeglasses. The assistant had a nervous habit of stretching
his neck, and he reminded Dougherty of a whooping crane.
Steinberg had brain power and efficiency to spare, but getting
used to his occasional sandpaper manners would take some effort
on Dougherty's part. The man was new to his NIS staff, having
just transferred out to San Diego from the Judge Advocate's
Office at the Pentagon. The pushy assistant continued. "Considering the appearance of that bedroom, I suggest the next-of-kin
identification might better be conducted at the morgue. If you can
get Captain Bullock down there." Steinberg hesitated, eyeing
Dougherty's female companion with uncertainty.

"It's all right, Sol. She's FBI, from Los Angeles. Meet Ms
Pamela Bonner." Dougherty placed an emphasis on the *mizz*.

Steinberg's smile was friendly enough, but Pamela didn't offer her hand. She merely nodded, studying the Navy investigator only briefly. Her eyes darted over the rest of the living room, taking the area in like a falcon considering a new roost.

Dougherty had to nudge the FBI woman to recapture her attention. He couldn't resist teasing her. "Sure you're prepared for this?"

She looked at him with annoyance. "If you're going to play the chauvinist, at least put on a good performance, Lieutenant Commander."

"I'll try to do better. Provided you make an effort to call me Todd."

Pamela shrugged. "Just like before, right? I'll make a note of it." Turning to Steinberg, she said calmly, "Forewarned, forearmed. By your grave look, Mr. Steinberg, shall I assume we have a sex maniac on our hands—one who likes to do a little pre-Thanksgiving carving as well?"

Steinberg replied uneasily, "I defer to the boss."

Dougherty shook his head. "No, even more arcane, I'm afraid. Our quarry binds his victim, takes his erotic pleasure, smothers her with a pillow, then blows the body up. Correction, an important *part* of it."

"Firecrackers," Steinberg added, morosely.

Pamela blanched. Meadows, the technician with the vacuum, gestured for her to step aside so he could probe under the paper runway.

Steinberg held out a handkerchief, carefully cradling an empty 35mm film container and a torn Kodak carton. "Appears our sick friend liked to take pictures—after the fact."

Dougherty said to the assistant, "Fetch the woman and her daughter from next door. They said something earlier about Maxine Bullock owning a dog. A yapping miniature poodle that never shuts up. Ask them to query the other neighbors about the dog's sudden disappearance. And if Captain Bullock shows up, try to keep him outside until we're finished."

Sol Steinberg headed for the door. Dougherty steeled himself for the weight his stomach would again take on, then piloted Pamela into the bedroom.

2

Pamela stood there, arms hanging loosely, her knees growing more rubbery by the minute. She felt like a marionette, her emotions suspended between revulsion and numbness. As a former San Diego police officer, Pam had seen a few seasonal fireworks accidents before, but never the aftermath of their apparent deliberate use in a homicide. She stared at the gore-flecked bedroom walls in disbelief. *Outrageous!* The word was after-the-fact and useless, but it kept repeating itself in her mind. Todd Dougherty was so close by she could feel his warmth. Right now, as stunned as she was by the grotesque scene, she damn well needed it.

The room smelled of spilled cologne, cigarette smoke, and a cloying, coppery smell from the blood-soaked bedding. The assistant coroner had removed the neckties binding the wrists and ankles, but the woman was still spread-eagled across the bed. The victim's name was Maxine Bullock, and she was probably in her early forties. Pamela noted that the woman wore a good deal of makeup and not the usual face cream or who-knows-what mud compound a menopause candidate might use on retiring. The desecrated body was clad in a negligee of lavender satin, cinched up around her waist like a whore in a Lautrec painting. The woman's half-open vermilion lips looked more like a gash than a mouth, and the mascara from her lashes was smeared down swollen cheeks as if she'd been crying. Several false fingernails lay scattered on the queen-sized bed and around the rug, apparently broken off in a struggle. Reluctantly, Pamela ran her eyes over the lower half of the victim's body; she had to fight off nausea, for Maxine Bullock's private parts defied description, unless one were to use the tentative word *missing*.

Pamela felt Todd Dougherty's breath in her ear. He whispered, "Whoever the bastard is, he might just as well have used a quarter-stick of dynamite or a frag grenade."

She looked at him seriously. "You've already decided our Captain Blood is, in fact, a *he*?"

"A woman wouldn't have left pecker tracks on the sheets," he replied with aplomb.

Pam forced herself to smile. Any distraction at all was welcome at this point. It was an odd time to stare at Dougherty, but she needed his comfort. His blue eyes sparkled beneath bushy eyebrows that matched his dishwater blond hair—or was it gray? *Too close to call.* Whatever his age, the lean, flat-bellied naval officer still took very good care of himself—or maybe it was the tailoring of his jacket. She'd always been a sucker for uniforms. Pamela exhaled slowly and forced herself back to reality—back to the abhorrent carnage on the bed.

Dr. Harold Wetherby, the assistant coroner, glanced up from his work. Brandishing a scalpel in one rubber-gloved hand, a glass slide in the other, he ignored her and spoke to Dougherty in a heavy, Moses-like drone. "Unfortunately, this is one corpse that's not about to provide us with a vaginal smear. But we're still lucky. Our man was a dribbler, leaving sperm on the victim's knee. If he's also a secretor, we'll at least have a blood type and enzyme count in a matter of hours." Wetherby glanced over at Pamela, acknowledging her presence as if it were an afterthought.

She smiled back without enthusiasm. "Enough for a genetic fingerprint?"

"All depends on the DNA." The gruff, hard-nosed forensic medicine specialist was a cadaverous individual with a shock of wiry hair that stood out on the sides of his head like Einstein's. But where there'd been a warm gleam in the great scientist's eyes, in Wetherby's there was only a dull, cantankerous glare. Pam knew from previous cases that Wetherby was difficult to get along with, but he knew his business. She saw another familiar face on the opposite side of the bed.

Vic Shapiro, one of her fellow FBI agents, nodded. "Good morning, Pamela."

"Hello Vic." Pam was on a first name basis with both men, having worked before with Dr. Wetherby while on the San Diego force, and Vic Shapiro was a well known technician from the FBI crime lab in Washington. Visiting southern California on other business, Shapiro, like herself, had been pressed into immediate service to help the U.S. Navy. Crimes on military bases are not subject to local police jurisdiction and are a high priority FBI matter. Pamela knew Shapiro's latent-image fingerprint expertise would be a boon to their investigation. The Washington-based special agent was a short, paunchy man in his forties with a colorless piggy face and a prissy manner. Wearing a polyester sportcoat, an open-collar knit shirt, and white brogues, Shapiro looked as if he'd just been interrupted at the golf course.

Pamela looked around the Bullocks' bedroom with its plum-colored walls and gray paisley curtains. The furniture appeared inexpensive but tastefully coordinated. On the nearby bedside table, there was an overturned bottle of Nina Ricci cologne and a princess phone taken off the hook. An oversize, mirror-framed portrait of a uniformed Naval aviator—apparently Swain Bullock when he was younger—glared back at Pamela from the dressing table. There was nothing askew on the dresser or bureau, and the rest of the room and closet appeared undisturbed. The bondage battle, from all appearances, had been confined to the bed. If, in fact, there'd been a struggle. Tacky accusation that it was, Maxine Bullock somehow looked the type who enjoyed kinky scenes. Pam would make a point of nosing through the capacious bookshelf she'd seen in the living room. She was convinced that books said more about a person's taste and habits than a closetful of clothing or accessories. She asked Dougherty, "Doors, windows. Nothing was forced?"

"The neighbors in the other half of the duplex claim Maxine Bullock's dog was kicking up a fuss around eleven-thirty. They think she may have had company arrive then."

"She just *invited* the killer in? Great. Any chance the neighbors would admit to snooping out their window, checking up?"

Dougherty grinned. "No luck. A Commander Margolis, his wife, and their ten-year-old daughter only moved into the place a week ago. They don't strike me as nosey types. Anyway, they were in bed at ten, and the wife only met Maxine Bullock once—very briefly, on the way to the market. It would have been impossible for them to know the captain. Bullock's marriage was on the rocks, and I understand he's slept on the ship since it arrived in port a few days ago."

"Which ship?" Pam asked.

"The *Abraham Lincoln*. It just returned from a lengthy deployment in the southeast Asia area."

"One of the supercarriers—*a nuke*?" Pamela's voice squeaked slightly as she said the word "*nuke*." *God, it seemed eons ago that she'd been a student activist, demonstrating at San Onofre and cheering on the Greenpeace ships every time they made a splash in the headlines*. Having to work for a living had mellowed her out on nuclear power and half a dozen other issues.

Reaching into her handbag, she withdrew a small spiral notebook. She had a good memory but wanted, for Dougherty's sake, to look a little more official. Regarding a week-old memo to pick up a pair of aqua panty hose, she added an exclamation point. She'd try to take care of that errand on the way back to the hotel. Turning to a clean page, she began jotting down facts of a far more serious kind. "This Captain Bullock, what's his first name?"

Dougherty replied smugly, "Swain. It was on the sign out front."

She ignored the gentle barb. "How soon can I see his file?"

Dougherty shrugged. "Whenever you finish here. But I suggest we break for lunch before bugging the Bureau of Personnel. It's going to be a long day for everyone concerned."

"After this scene? Food is the farthest thing from my mind." The fact was, Pam's stomach felt like she'd just stepped off the Shock Wave at Magic Mountain. She looked at her crime team partner seriously, thought for a moment, then asked, "Your staff, Todd. How many? Besides Steinberg here and the silent types outside with the vacuum cleaner and camera?"

Dougherty gave her an annoyed look, as if she were testing him.

She persisted. "Ferrets, gofers, whatever your bluejacket nomenclature. God knows, we'll need help and plenty of it. I can borrow two investigative assistants, maybe three, from the L.A. office and, in a pinch, another agent locally."

"Relax, Ms Bonner. I assure you that with a loathsome incident of this magnitude, the Navy will provide all the manpower I need."

Pamela gently lifted Dougherty's strong, clean-shaven chin. She had a silly hangup on moustaches and beards and couldn't abide them; on that count alone the potential partnership had some points going for it. She said to him, "All the help *we need*, Lieutenant Commander. *We're going to be a team*, remember? I seriously suggest we pool our resources from day one and keep it that way. Agreed?"

"I'd never thought otherwise, my dear."

Before she could respond to Dougherty's smug manner, Vic Shapiro came up to them. He smiled condescendingly and held up a small, zip-seal plastic packet. All Pamela could see inside it was a piece of torn, red and black filigree paper, scorched along the edges.

"Outer wrapping of the firecracker," Shapiro said triumphantly.

"If we don't get a partial print from it, we'll at least learn the manufacturer."

Pamela frowned. "Great. What good to us is a factory in China? We need local sellers and buyers. And this is October, not the Fourth of July when the stands are open."

"Nevertheless, I'd check it out if I were you," Shapiro snapped back. His eyes danced, a trifle mischievously, as they studied her. "We have to start somewhere. Stick around, Pamela, and I'll teach you some time-proven tricks before I retire." Shapiro ambled off to check out the bathroom.

Tricks. I'll bet, she thought with mild annoyance. Rape specialist or not, Pamela Bonner was still a woman in a man's world. Being reasonably attractive had only compounded her problem. Far too many men seemed convinced that the way to manage her was to screw her. Thank god, thus far Todd Dougherty seemed different, a measure less intense than the others. She wondered what his past domestic problems and current hinge of happiness might be. Like the last time they'd met, Dougherty seemed to hold a little of himself in reserve. One good thing, he didn't seem to underestimate her intelligence. At least that had been the case a year and a half back when they'd worked together. She wondered what, if any, sexist myths he might have subscribed to in the meantime. *Scars left an indelible mark on a person's personality.* Pam was convinced that the wrong lay on the wrong day could corrupt a man's judgment for months, sometimes years. A woman's, too, for that matter.

Dougherty stood in the bathroom doorway, continuing to bombard fingerprint expert Shapiro with questions. Pam listened, deciding not to interrupt. She'd let the men talk as long as they wanted; from experience she knew they'd do their homework, and they'd be back, talking again. And of course all the while she'd listen to them carefully, making notes. When appropriate, she'd ask questions and remember the answers.

Beside Pam, Dr. Wetherby continued his shrew-like movements around the room. Using tweezers to pick a gobbet of flesh off a lampshade, the assistant coroner dully explained, "Anterior portion of the vulva."

Gritting her teeth, Pam summoned Dougherty. "Todd, have you started a property list?"

He faced her. "Not until I sit down with the husband. Still may be difficult to figure if anything's missing. It's hard telling what Maxine Bullock bought while hubby was at sea for six months.

Some Navy wives are notorious for pigging out the moment their spouse's ship clears port."

She scowled at him. "I suggest you have one of your men get started on the credit cards and checkbook."

There was a sudden silence in the next room as Meadows turned off his vacuum. The technician stuck his head through the bedroom door. "Lieutenant Commander, I found that 45 RPM adapter for the stereo player. It was behind the sofa and covered with dust."

Dougherty nodded, then shouted to Shapiro in the bathroom. "What about that single on the turntable, Vic? Any prints?"

"Clean as a baby's nipple. Judging from the blurs on everything else, I'm convinced the killer wore rubber gloves the entire time he was inside the house."

Pamela thought for a moment, then shook her head. "I think he put them on somewhere inside. Would you admit a guest who stood outside your door wearing rubber gloves? God, especially at eleven-thirty at night. May I see that record?"

Meadows disappeared back into the living room, returning a few seconds later with a 45 RPM single. The disc had been placed in a glassine sleeve that Pam now held up carefully by the edges. She noted that a double-backed section of tape—apparently punched with a pencil—covered the large hole in the center, adapting it for the Bullocks' stereo turntable. Pamela examined the record label. The title was in both Italian and English, and it was performed by the American rock group, The Midnight Admirals. She said to Dougherty, "The same number on both sides, Part One and Part Two."

He looked over her shoulder and read the label. *"Molte volte al fatto ildir vien meno."* Translated, *"Many a Time the World Comes Short of Thought."* He looked at her and shrugged.

From the doorway, Meadows interjected, "If I remember my literature, it sounds like a line out of Dante's *Inferno*. I'll check it out. Lofty material for a heavy metal group."

Dougherty nodded. "Peculiar in another way. It's the only single disc in the Bullocks' music collection."

"Meaning?"

"In fact, only a dozen or so LP albums in the house; the Bullocks collected *tape cassettes*. But here's the clincher. Meadows found a duplicate of that record in the trash—but it was scratched and unplayable. My guess is both 45s were brought in by the killer. One more thing. The automatic turntable was deliberately left on *repeat*. The cleaning woman found the record playing at 0730 this morning."

"Apparently a part of some sex ritual." Pamela scribbled feverishly on her note pad. "Has our coroner friend here estimated what time the death occurred?"

Harold Wetherby looked like an entomologist on a field trip as he continued to gather up bits of flesh with his tweezers. He looked up with impatience. "The lady suffocated just before midnight. Choked to death."

Vic Shapiro came out of the bathroom holding a couple of pieces of tin foil on a handkerchief. "Found these on the floor by the sink."

"Chewing gum wrappers?" Pamela asked innocently.

"Wrong." Shapiro smiled. "Foil off a couple of suppositories. And I already checked the cabinets; no box of Preparation H anywhere."

Pamela sighed. "So you assume they belonged to the murderer and not the victim?"

Dougherty tapped her on the shoulder. "Two suppositories, not one, Pamela. Looks like a severe case of hemorrhoids. You going to make a note of that?"

She did, with reservation. Considering for a moment, she changed the subject, asking Dougherty, "How about an interview with the cleaning lady?"

"Already talked to her. She's one of those green cards from Tijuana. My Spanish is the pits so I used an interpreter, but it was a dead end, a big zero. The housekeeper came in one day a week, and she'd only been on the job less than a month."

Vic Shapiro was apparently finished with the bedroom. Closing his scuffed, gray Samsonite briefcase and adjusting the sleeves of his sport coat, he swaggered up to Pamela. He said confidently, "Sooner or later the creep will make a mistake. It's inevitable. While we get smarter, he'll get careless." Shapiro exhaled with impatience as he studied her. "Very good, Ms Bonner. I can see those wheels of yours are already clicking like Reno slots." Turning to Dougherty, he added, "Keep pulling her handle, Navy, and you may come up with a winner."

Pamela said icily, "Are you finished, Vic?"

"Not yet. Still have the back porch and kitchen." Reading her annoyed face, he started to leave, but turned back abruptly for one last question. "You think he operates on lunar phases?"

Dougherty passed, letting Pamela respond. "According to the smiling face on my grandfather clock, Mr. Shapiro, we had a quarter-moon last night. Try again." She wasn't even sure if the killer would strike again, but Shapiro seemed to be. *Do men have a better nose for smelling serial or series killers*? Pam thought for a moment, then said to the fingerprint hotshot, "I have a feeling this is going to be bigger than your ordinary full-moon neurotic. Considering the record music—if Meadows is right—there might be a message for us in Dante's *Divine Comedy*—particularly the section on the *Inferno*."

Dougherty slowly shook his head. "You think it's some religious fanatic fulfilling a self-inspired prophecy?"

Pam wasn't ready to buy that. "Playing the role of the returning Messiah is old hat. These days they're more apt to fantasize on playing Dr. Spock, Rambo, or the Red Baron—not to mention a reincarnation of Hitler. Maybe in this case it's one of Dante's heroes—the poet Virgil. On the other hand, it might be something simpler. Like a deranged derelict who strayed away from skid row."

Dr. Wetherby looked up at her. "No," he sourly explained, "we're not in the ghetto here, trying to sew back together society's dirty underbelly. This is officer's country; it takes a decent set of I.D. to get inside the base."

"I'll make a note of that," Pamela sighed. "I suspect, gentlemen, that it's still too early to speculate on precipitate fiendishness." She was beginning to feel anxious and tight. *Get out of here, Pam, go someplace where you can think*. What she needed now was some fresh air—foggy, cold, or whatever; at this point, she wasn't fussy. It would also be an excuse to talk with some of the neighbors ringing the police line.

Dougherty sensed her impatience, but before they could exit, an untimely smell drifted into the bedroom, overpowering the stench of blood and spilled perfume. Curious, Pamela inhaled deeply. *Cooking! Someone in the place was cooking, for God's sake!* They all caught the scent but it was Dougherty who first broke into the the hallway and bounded for the kitchen. Pamela quickly followed.

She sniffed again. *Overcooked roast beef*? But there was a peculiar singed-hair odor as if someone had used a powerful blow dryer too long. The stove and oven however, were cold to the touch and Comet-clean. Pamela heard a soft chime. She and Dougherty turned as one and stared numbly at the shiny black microwave oven on the far wall. Persons unknown had apparently set its automatic timer mechanism the night before, and it had turned on just moments ago, doing its job *ipso facto*. *Breakfast*?

Dougherty shut off the unit and gingerly opened the door. He stood back, his nose crinkling with displeasure.

They could call off the search for the Bullocks' miniature poodle.

The kitchen's miserable silence was broken by an infuriatingly pleasant voice from the doorway. "Where's the body, please?"

Pamela turned. A Jesuit priest stood framed in the entry, a prayer book and purple stole clasped in his hands. He looked young, probably new on the job, and a little confused. Behind him stood Sol Steinberg with a perplexed look of his own.

"*Which* body?" Pamela said to the priest with a tone of defeat. She gestured toward the open microwave.

Dougherty shook his head. He promptly led the clergyman out of the kitchen, back toward the bedroom, but by now Pamela had seen more than enough. She hurried outside. Waiting on the front stoop, she made another cryptic notation on her note pad: the Bullocks are Roman Catholic. At least the captain's wife appeared to be.

Just over the porch on the edge of the roof a covey of pigeons, apparently intimidated by the fog, cocked their heads and watched Pam carefully. She wondered if Maxine Bullock had been the compassionate type to feed crumbs to the birds.

From inside the house Pam could hear the priest's words, "*Ego te absolve . . .*"

3

The Navy fighter settled down at Mach 1.2. Not that speed was critical or even important, for today its two-man crew had all the time in the world. Howard "Squeegee" Liddell and Mitch "Hambone" Greco were both pissed. Along with the rest of the VF-2 squadron, they'd routinely flown their F-14A Tomcat off the *Abraham Lincoln* the day before it made port and returned to their shore base at Miramar Air Station. Under normal circumstances, after a lengthy WESTPAC deployment they'd both be entitled to a decent liberty, but this time their squadron and several others that were a part of the carrier's air complement would rejoin the ship Wednesday after its brief San Diego layover was concluded. The carrier's ultimate destination was the drydock in Bremerton, but on the way up it was scheduled to participate in some brief fleet maneuvers. Enroute the ship would also make one port call in San Francisco as a part of that city's Fleet Week.

Most of the other pilots had been given three days leave in San Diego until the carrier embarked. Thanks to the ship's CO, pilot Squeegee and his radar intercept man Hambone were not among them. With luck, they might yet get away tomorrow.

Squeegee spoke to his cockpit companion on the F-14A's intercom. "You got a range on that damned Texaco yet, Hambone?"

"Less than eight miles. Height about ten thousand. He's on bearing."

Squeegee put the twin-engined Tomcat into a gentle roll. Glancing out the perplex, he watched the F-5 Tiger with their squadron commander in it do the same. He and Hambone hadn't expected their superior to come along and check up; his gnarly reprimand that they needed more practice refueling had seemed insult enough. All because of some purported minor delays they'd caused flight operations back on the *Abraham Lincoln*. Squeegee had no doubts that the air boss had been intimidated by the ship's CO himself, "Hard-Ass" Bullock. The big thunder had resounded to squadron level.

"Sorry, Hambone, I got you into this."

"Hell, it's easier on the old equilibrium than practicing dog fights."

"Yeah. But not as productive." The plane straightened on course. Squeegee looked down at the barren El Cajon desert, then forward and above, watchful for the fuel-laden KA-6D. He cut the twin throttles back and articulated the wings forward for better lift. The Tomcat shuddered down to a snail's pace of 375 knots. Squeegee saw the tanker up ahead and slightly to the left.

"Hambone, you still a soft touch for making bets?"

"Horses, dogs, or fighting off bogies?"

"Negative. None of the above. The radio news this morning."

"Yeah, bad stuff. Understand the skipper's wife took one hell of a beating at North Island. She's dead. What about it?"

"Lay you six-to-one the old man gets pulled from the carrier. Somebody else takes the ship back to the barn."

Squeegee heard heavy breathing on the intercom. He figured Hambone was thinking about Captain Bullock and calculating the odds. The KA-6D loomed closer, unreeling its fuel hose and basket.

Hambone said in the hot mike, "You're on. I say nothing budges that tough bastard off the carrier but his own iron will."

"Ten bucks says you're wrong. And another ten against all that scuttlebutt in the officer's dirty shirt wardroom."

"Come on, man, elucidate. *Which* scuttlebutt?"

"That the skipper's about to get his first star and take over a cushy North Atlantic Fleet job. Maybe even NATO. I say he's all washed up."

"You're about to lose twenty bucks, Squeegee. Bullock never loses."

An angry voice rasped on the intercom: "Knock it off, you blow torch jockeys, and get down to business. Forget the ship's CO, and start worrying over that tanker about to piss in your lap."

For the security guard at the Honolulu warehouse it had been a peaceful, balmy afternoon–until the hooker's outburst.

"Don't give me any of your rat shit!" Penny Sherman screamed at the top of her voice. Hands on her hips, she strutted closer to the gate. She glared at the annoyed watchman and said firmly, "My roommate's been gone for eight days now. You goin' to tell me she came over here and just disappeared into thin air?"

The guard, a shade or two blacker than Penny, signaled a refrigerator truck to move on into the warehouse yard, then turned back to her. He nudged back the bill of his cap, leered at her, and rasped, "Look woman, your girlfriend don't tell you where she's going, that's not my problem. Now get lost. We're busy."

Penny did better than just stand her ground. Jacking up her tits, she inched closer, confronting her adversary eyeball-to-eyeball. They were momentarily alone at the gate, but Transocean Frozen Food Distributors was a beehive of truck traffic, and she'd have to make her point fast. Penny knew that the smirking guard who stood before her did pimping on the side–whenever he could arrange to work the night shift. She was also aware that being a Waikiki tart and working for others, she'd overstepped her territory by venturing into this part of the city. All that didn't matter a lick now, for she was seriously worried over her friend's safety.

Feeling the anger rise within her, Penny said to the guard, "Who you trying to kid, dick-face? I know you were hustling for her on the side, glossin' over the scene with this job. Didi told me all about it."

"Just maybe she was lyin' up a storm, too."

"No way." Penny glanced over the man's shoulder, taking in the long trailer set up just inside the gate that served as a temporary office. Penny knew better. She gestured toward it. "Hell, Dude. You think I don't know how the two of you set 'em up in high-style comfort? Out-call service don't work so good with the military types stationed at Hickam and Pearl, do it? They got to have a place to go, so you give it to them in that trailer when this frozen-food operation shuts down for the night. Tell me, black boy, how many supervisors here you have to cut into the action? The warehouse owner, too, maybe?"

The watchman's eyes turned into daggers of hate. He looked both ways to make sure they were still alone, then snarled, "Listen, slut, you're just jealous I didn't take you on. Lose a little of that lard, and maybe I will. In the meantime, stop jiving me. I don't know any more about that honky bitch than you do. One night she just disappeared." He snapped his fingers. "Pfffft! Just like that, understand? You think that every time Didi took a sailor in that trailer that I asked for his fuckin' I.D. or checked him out?"

Penny waited while two delivery trucks roared through the gate, then replied, "Why not? You probably fleeced their wallets for everything else. Probably even considered blackmailin' the higher rankin' ones."

"Woman, I suggest you get back in that cab out there before your nose gets bent out of shape."

"I'll leave when you tell me what you're goin' to do about Didi. Maybe it's high time somebody talked to the Honolulu Police."

The security man lowered his voice. "You try that, cunt, and I feed you to the crabs—and I don't mean the tiny critters you usually chum around with. I'm talkin' about those big, hungry bastards at the bottom of Pearl Harbor." He paused, then said sharply, "Forget all this, and find yourself someone else to help pay the rent, okay? Plenty of other working ladies in Waikiki."

"Didi was my friend, you asshole."

"Bullshit. She was a fickle, opportunistic whore and a tough one." He pointed to one of the nearby warehouses. "More than once she'd toss a hot and unruly customer into one of them freezer rooms for cooling off. That bitch took better care of herself than I could."

"Yeah? Then *where did she go*?"

"How the hell should I know? Probably fell in love, decided to get out of the business. That's the way they usually do it, sudden-like. No fuckin' explanation at all. Some gullible Navy cocksman probably bought her an airline ticket to Hollywood. California's like a graveyard, baby. Everyone ends up there eventually."

"Remind me never to let you do my pimping." Penny backed slowly away. Her taxi was waiting at the curb, and the meter was still running.

The guard grinned. "No chance of that, fatass. I got a classy waiting list. You ever do come across that bitch, remind her she owes me for that last swabby. Pulling out of the racket's her affair, but I don't take kindly to being screwed out of what's owed me. Say, you don't happen to have any snow on you, do you honey?"

She glared back at him. "You're flybait. What's in that warehouse that needs protecting by an incompetent, part-time pimp?"

"Frozen foods, baby. Tons of it, from the mainland. I make sure it don't melt. Like when I work shift or graveyard, I keep things real cool around here, understand?"

Penny spat on the street and climbed into the taxi.

The guard called after her, "Hey, motor-mouth! Wait up a minute! You're so nosey about frozen foods, how about sucking my Popsicle?"

 4

Todd Dougherty's office just off North Island's Roe Street was Spartan, even by the usual military base measure. Both the interior and exterior of the World War II concrete block structure were overdue for paint, but the building boasted new air conditioning and Dougherty's second-floor window had an unobstructed view of Pier India and San Diego Bay.

The office wa only a stone's throw from the homicide site in the officers' quarters area, and already Dougherty had made three round trips, resifting through evidence and asking questions he'd overlooked before. They'd taken Maxine Bullock's body downtown just moments before her husband had arrived on the scene. The FBI woman had begged off, letting Dougherty drive the steadfastly silent Captain Bullock to the morgue for the official identification. Dougherty now wished he'd let one of his assistants take care of that unpleasant but necessary errand. Less than a dozen words had been uttered by Bullock despite Dougherty's plea for badly needed information.

Oddly, the captain had seemed more concerned with the possibility of his wife's funeral conflicting with his carrier's departure than her sudden and tragic demise. The coroner had finally assured Bullock that the body would be released in time for an early burial rite on Wednesday morning, just hours before the *Abraham Lincoln* was scheduled to sail for the Pacific Northwest.

On the return trip back to the base, Bullock had further surprised Dougherty by requesting that he be let out at the Officer's Club bar. The carrier commander had promised to come by the NIS office later in the afternoon to answer questions, insisting that he needed time alone, a chance to get a proper grip on his emotions and clarify his memory. Dougherty wasn't entirely satisfied with that but decided, for the interim, to buy it. A few minutes ago, he'd used an employee acquaintance at the club to check up on the captain. Apparently Swain Bullock had retired to the solitude of an empty banquet room where he sat alone, chain-smoking and fortifying himself with Canadian VO on the rocks.

Dougherty debated whether he should interfere with Captain Bullock's private emotions, simply go ahead and grab him now before he was completely snockered. A timely, efficient interrogation was imperative for the investigation to move forward.

No, he'd give the captain time and wait until later in the afternoon. Even drag Bullock through a sauna or icy shower if need be. Dougherty had plenty of angles to explore in the meantime. While he'd been at the coroner's with Bullock, Pamela had insisted on going over to the Navy Bureau of Personnel. Dougherty checked his watch, wondering how long she'd be there. It was already a quarter to one, and his stomach was growling. He wondered if she'd changed her mind and gone for chow after all. Heinous crime of the month, year, century, whatever, Dougherty wasn't about to let it dent his appetite or ruin his sleep. He debated whether to continue waiting for the FBI woman or skip out now and grab some junk food at the vending machine downstairs.

Dougherty cleared off his desk and straightened the in-and-out box. As always, the work surface was scrupulously tidy, the way the Navy preferred it. *Neatness*. Dougherty wished he could say the same for his chockablock apartment. The next pay increase, he was determined to get a part-time housekeeper. It suddenly occurred to him that Maxine Bullock's Mexican maid might now be available. He might even look in to the housekeeping matter this month, rather than later. One less meal out a week might make up for the red ink on the budget. Jokes about *penis substitutes* aside, giving up the Porsche would be a minor crisis.

Dougherty mused over the double standard, his meticulous nature here on the base and the way he tended to sluff off a little on the personal side. After the divorce ten years ago, he'd seriously entertained the idea of remaining single forever. It didn't take long for loneliness to set in, however, and he'd soon reevaluated both his short and long-range objectives, among them his continuing to slide downhill with the singles routine. Helping one of his Navy pals coach Little League Soccer stirred hidden urges to have kids himself before it was too late to enjoy them. Outside, his facade might well be aloof and stoic, but inside, Dougherty was an incurable romantic.

As for going by the book and being super-organized on the job, in college back at Kent State his roommates had chided his rigidity for neatness, claiming he was boorish and an insufferable perfectionist. Loosening up had always been difficult for Dougherty. As an undergraduate, he'd studied political science with a minor in chemistry; his grades were good but not spectacular enough to make the dean's list. His real accomplishments at Kent State University had consisted mainly of a keen tennis game and playing his guitar at hayrides and rally bonfires.

Later, studying law at Michigan, scholarship became a priority, and his penchant for orderliness at last paid off. Who ever heard of a *successful* sloppy lawyer?

Dougherty learned quickly enough that the Navy Judge Advocate General Corps program wasn't the place for him, though he'd come out of that officer's school with not only his first cuff stripe but with honors. After a year shuffling papers in a Pentagon legal library, he was bored and hungry for excitement. He found it— more or less—after transferring to the Naval Investigation Service.

Dougherty idly glanced at the daily memo pad on his desk, then up at the calendar on the far wall. He smiled to himself. After all the mulling over his precise nature, the month on the Metropolitan Museum of Art calendar still didn't jive with the day-to-day memo on his desk. When it came down to it, he'd postponed tearing away September because he enjoyed that month's reproduction of Rosseau's *Shepherd and Lion*.

Shrugging, he pushed back his chair and went over to the wall. Belatedly, he folded under the calendar page, at the same time copping a peek at November's art. The year had passed too quickly; it was hard to believe that already the frost was on the pumpkin, and next week would be Halloween. Already, some ghoul had made an early trick or treat call on Maxine Bullock.

Dougherty again glanced at his watch with impatience. He'd give Pamela just five more minutes, then take off. Going back to his desk, he flipped through the next day's appointments. After the news-generating homicide, several administrative matters would definitely have to be put on the back burner. Dougherty idly turned back to the memo for the day before. He liked to make doubly sure all his bases were covered—behind as well as up front. Frowning, he took a pencil and circled one of the previous day's appointments, an uncomfortable meeting that spelled impending trouble. Dougherty recalled the complaint of the crewman from the *Abraham Lincoln*, how the sailor had insisted he'd been assaulted with the subsequent shipboard investigation going unresolved. The peculiar affair had blossomed into an incident that just might shake the Pentagon itself.

Ed "Gecko" Corman. Dougherty again considered the sailor's name and the incident, wondering now if in some way they might relate to last night's homicide. The disgruntled aviation boatswain's mate had filed a criminal complaint, but Captain Bullock, after conducting his own investigation, had disallowed the allegation, claiming Gecko Corman was a troublemaker. Further, the allegations of an attempt on Corman's life were false and frivolous. Oddly, the more Dougherty had pursued the matter, the more the enlisted man had clammed up about the assault, insisting he would only talk with someone of high authority, beyond the Pacific Fleet command. The sailor had even refused to send a red-line chit to the Command Master Chief, the ombudsman of the *Abraham Lincoln*. Nor had he been willing to talk with one of the chaplains. Gecko Corman was very much afraid, and Dougherty was concerned.

Great timing, Captain Bullock. Some men have a knack for neatly disappearing in the military, going low profile and becoming little more than an inconspicuous number. Others, like Swain Trevor Bullock, have a way of repeatedly making waves. Big waves. Nothing wrong with that, as long as a ship is prepared for them. But now two tempests in one week confronted the captain. Dougherty grimaced at what might lie ahead.

The glass-panel door to his office rattled open, interrupting his thoughts and mesmerized stare at the appointment calendar. Looking up, Dougherty made a mental note to have the molding around the frosted glass replaced or tightened. Sooner or later some testy individual would slam the door to drive home a point and shatter the pane.

Pamela hesitated inside the entry. Dougherty noted that her tan suede shoes were greenish-wet around the soles. He guessed she'd been back to the crime site, tramping around in the wet grass. Plopping down in the gray steel, gray naugahyde armchair beside his gray desk, she let out a weary sigh. Pamela's face seemed to have taken on a gray, tired look as well, despite her make up. *Was she ill?* No, it had to be the light from the window bouncing off the office's drab interior decor. Dougherty decided it was time to summon the painters, along with some trendy color swatches.

She gave him a wan smile. "What do you have?"

Dougherty said amiably, "A legal pad full of scribbling. Dates, events, people. Interconnecting lines, a few arrows."

"Scribbling or interesting graffiti?"

"You want to see it?" He shrugged and gestured to the crumbled yellow paper in the nearby wastebasket. "I like to think with a pencil. My own way of cutting through the Gordian knot." Dougherty reached into the desk and withdrew a pack of Carltons. "Mind if I smoke?"

She raised an eyebrow and held it there. "It's your office."

He looked at her askance and tossed the cigs back in his center drawer.

Pamela smiled smartly. "The new me–a reformed nicotine addict. It used to be one and a half packs a day. An ex-boyfriend broke me. Insisted that he was tired of making love to a charcoal briquet and threatened to leave if I didn't give it up."

Dougherty looked at her sympathetically. "I remember him. Leonard, the not-so-prolific writer. Quitting smoking made him happier?"

"No. He left anyway, went to Europe. The last I heard he was sitting in the Piazza San Marco in Venice, fighting off the pigeons, writing postcards, and pretending to read Byron."

Dougherty laughed. "Any excuse to ogle the tourist women. I'm envious. At least the rejection didn't make you go out and get a Joan of Arc haircut."

"Would it bother you?"

Dougherty smiled but kept his silence. He stared at her purse, suddenly aware it was bulging with proprietary photocopies.

Pamela immediately flipped them out on his desk. "Now that

you've been brought up to date on my life history, I suggest you take a look at Captain Bullock's."

"I already have. An exemplary record, do you agree?"

She stared back with impatience. "You might have saved me some time. If you've already checked out the file, when? Obviously you haven't been over to BUPERS since we met at the crime site this morning."

Dougherty smugly explained, "Yesterday, at one in the afternoon, to be specific. Another unrelated incident prompted my involvement. As for saving you the effort, not a chance. If the FBI wants to be a critical part of this investigation, you'll have to do your homework and swim with the rest of us, not just dabble your toes in the water. Besides, I hear you're a winner when it comes to dedicated, tough research. We can use that kind of perseverance."

"Or stubbornness? Nice speech. A bit gooey, but thanks. You're appealing to my vanity, Lieutenant Commander. Could be I like it. Now it's my turn to appeal to yours."

Dougherty leaned forward in his chair. "I threw out my vanity the moment I heard they were sending you down from Los Angeles. So where are you staying?"

"The Hotel del Coronado. I've a weakness for wicker furniture and Victorian verandas. I'd hoped they still had gaslight, but no such luck."

"An incurable romantic, the white-picket-fence type. I figured as much. Your stomach recover enough for lunch?"

She smiled at him engagingly. "Provided we make it a quick one. I intend to talk with those women across the street from Captain Bullock's living quarters. A hunch."

"*Hunches*? You're speculating this early in the game?"

"Why not? I've always been good at it. I also intend to go out to the suburbs and visit the victim's parents. But I'd like some insight into Maxine Bullock's character first. Possibly the neighbor women can help."

Dougherty thought for a moment. He slowly shook his head. "This morning you sounded like you'd already formed some heady opinions regarding the victim's character–or apparent lack of it."

Pamela rose and went over to the window. "A lovely view of the bay." She stood there silently for a long time, then finally turned around to face him. "Sorry, Todd, to burst a few of Naval Aviation's high-flying, sacred balloons. A ship captain's wife or not, I don't need to find a pubic hair in the refrigerator to tell me this particular homicide victim was a sleaze."

Dougherty wasn't prepared for that. Frowning with annoyance, he stashed Bullock's personnel file in his security drawer and locked it. "Forget it for now, okay? Let's go eat."

Whatever Pamela's observations, Dougherty never liked to speculate this early in the investigation–not even on a cut-and-dried homicide, which this one sure as hell wasn't. The dastardly Maxine Bullock murder could be the NIS case of the decade for all he knew at this point. He'd often thought the greatest challenge of a naval investigation career might be probing into a real-life *Caine Mutiny*, or better yet, unraveling the complex factors surrounding a major collision of two ships at sea. Instead, the biggest thing to come down the pike appeared to be a grisly rape-murder that might even portend ominous series or serial possibilities. Dougherty's mind reeled as he went over to grab his raincoat.

"Todd, wake up, for God's sake! You don't need it. The fog lifted long ago, and it's almost seventy degrees out there."

"You're right." He wondered how many more times he'd be forced to say that before Pamela Bonner left town for good. He came up close to her, determined now to share some of the murky, subliminal images batting around in his brain, the odd, uncomfortable feeling that things were going to get worse before they got better. "Pamela, I've a premonition that what's going on here is beyond one, sadistic local homicide. Maxine Bullock, regardless of what you think of her morality, may be just one part of a bigger, more intricate plan."

"Or puzzle." She stared at him, considering.

Dougherty grinned and pulled out a quarter. "Flip you to see who drives?"

Pam agreed and lost. Grabbing her purse, she followed him out of the office, surprising Dougherty by matching his own swift strides down the hallway and stairs. She said to him, "Care to lay odds on what your official Navy psychiatrist friends will tell us?"

"No. And whatever, they're not available until tomorrow morning. Haven't you heard your share of their broken records by now?"

"When it comes to rape, yes."

He kept walking, but glanced at her critically. "Why the sudden silence? I'm waiting for your prognosis, Ms Bonner."

"After lunch, okay? Suffice it to say now that whatever the

matrix, our sick adversary is a bad actor, completely mesmerized by manipulating his victims before the kill."

Dougherty stopped at the bottom of the stairs, turned, and gave the FBI woman a dismal smile. "Fine. Obviously, actors need an audience. Just be sure to ask our shrink consultants this question: Why the hell did this sadistic misfit pick the U.S. Navy for his theatre of pain?"

~~~~~ 5

Whenever he could, Detective Lieutenant Kenny Chi liked to dine out in Macao, where low overhead and cheap family labor kept prices below the usual tab in Hong Kong. He also enjoyed the cuisine here for ancient, symbolic health reasons. For Chi, eating was more than a necessary metabolic bother; it was a rite, and like many Cantonese, he found great adventure in gourmet fare. Like the bowl of live baby mice he'd just consumed for the sake of his ulcers, a forbidden meal that was becoming difficult to find at any price back in the Crown Colony.

Detective Chi prided himself on being a good cop with plenty of experience on the firing line. He'd seen a lot of dirty water pass in and out of Kowloon Bay in twenty years on the force. He'd watched the gaudy signs of the Wanchai fade and weather with age, the Suzie Wongs of yesterday mature into women now pushing forty and fifty. The raucous sailors still came by in droves when a foreign ship was in port, but gone were the heady R and R days of the Vietnam war when entire fleets would arrive for an "anything goes" visit. Now, more often than not, it was the well-heeled Japanese and Korean businessmen who did the tomcatting.

Kenny Chi had taken the forty-five minute jetfoil trip across the channel today for three reasons. First, a periodic hankering for what his superior, Chief Investigator Niles Halliburton, called *uncivilized food*. Chi was not above paying any price to cure his recurring ulcers. Second, he needed a little space, some time out on the bay, a breather away from the congested office of the Royal

Hong Kong Police. Last, and the most important reason, Chi needed to interview the woman owner here at the restaurant where he'd just finished his highly-mobile, curative meal.

Around him, the Cabidela Cafe smelled of saffron and slightly rancid lard. Chi passed up the hundred-year-old duck eggs the waiter offered him to chase the mice, instead asking for green tea and the presence of Madame Twan, the proprietor. Seconds later an emaciated, stooped-over woman came to his table in the back room. Exotic food the likes of which he'd just consumed was never routinely served out front at the Cabidela.

Chi flashed his badge at the frail little woman, not that it really mattered, for the colony I.D. cut no weight in Portuguese Macao. He merely hoped the gesture would convince her of the serious nature of the conversation to come. She touched the badge with her boney fingers, noting the red tab beneath the serial number that indicated he spoke English. He asked her in Cantonese if she could speak it as well. "*Neih wuih mwuih gong ying mahn*?"

She shook her head. "*Deui Miyuh.*"

Chi couldn't get to first base in Portuguese so they proceeded in Cantonese. "Madam Twan, you know why I'm here?"

She shrugged and stared back at him, almond eyes blazing. "Forbidden cuisine, of course."

"Traditions are important, yes. But there is something else I came to discuss. Your *daughter*."

The old woman jerked her head to one side. Her eyes softened and started to moisten. "I have no daughters. One ran away with her father to America. She ignores me. My other daughter in Hong Kong is dead. But then you are from the police and must know about this."

"Yes. I know all about the murder, Madame Twan. A brutish incident, and I'm still investigating."

"My daughter Mai was very wealthy. She had no use for my humble restaurant. She had no use for me in life, and I have no use for her in death. Mai Twan disgraced her ancestry."

Chi thought for a moment, choosing his words carefully. "Family disagreements have their place, but we must still find your daughter's murderer. Madame, I need all the help I can get." Chi hesitated. "Mai was never married and yet she kept an apartment in Victoria Park and drove a Rolls Royce Silver Cloud."

The old woman looked at him suspiciously. Finally she spoke. "No, she never drove herself. There was the chauffeur. He would bring me money, and I would refuse it. Mai had many wealthy

Hong Kong admirers. And she lived with a successful ship builder, a pleasure junk captain, until his untimely death. A very fat man who died of a heart seizure. He left her half his estate."

Kenny Chi frowned. "I don't understand. If she was settled down and financially secure, why would she have hung out in Wanchai? At those pseudo-plush girlie bars?"

Madame Twan looked frightened. She said quickly, "No! Not recently, that was very long ago."

Chi regretted what he had to tell her; the old woman's spirits already appeared shattered. "I'm sorry, we know that she went there recently. Yes, quite often in fact, just before her murder."

"I don't understand. What places? You must be making a mistake."

"In Kowloon, the Bottoms Up on Hankow Road. And the Red Lips, a favorite hangout for well-heeled Japanese and Korean businessmen."

Trembling now, the old woman withdrew a package of English 555 cigarettes from her apron pocket. Chi pushed a metal ashtray across the table. He sipped his tea while she lit up.

"How do you know all this?" she asked seriously in her high-pitched voice. The cigarette shook in her hand.

"An informer for the Hong Kong Police told me. A woman I know only as 'Molly the Mooch.' She runs an expensive escort service and claims your daughter worked for her on occasion. Mai must have made very good money indeed. We found several collector's items of jade in her apartment, and, of course, there was the Rolls Royce in the garage."

"Mai didn't have to work, there was her late boyfriend's inheritance."

"Perhaps she was lonely then? But there are better places to meet people than in a Tsimshatsui gawk bar."

Madame Twan stared into her own cigarette smoke with hollow, cadaverous eyes. She slowly shook her head. "I fear it is a holdover from when Mai was young, restless, and beautiful."

Chi sipped his green tea. "She was still beautiful at the time she was murdered. Thirty-five years old is far too young to die. Madame Twan, you must try to remember. When she came to visit you during the last few months–did she bring men with her over to Macao?"

"She was only here three times this year. After the fat shipbuilder's funeral, with her barrister. A second time during the Dragonboat Festival. Then later, when an American sailor took her to the Casino Lisboa to gamble." The old woman paused.

"She called me on the telephone before returning to Hong Kong. It is expensive to call here from the territories. But she and her boyfriend did not come by to see me then."

"This American–how much did she tell you about him?"

"I'm sorry I cannot be more helpful. She said nothing more— only the words *sailor man*. She was with an American. He was an important *officer*, she said. Also, that she was preoccupied. Mai was so secretive, always preoccupied, with no time for this old woman."

"Thank you, Madame." Chi patted his stomach thoughtfully. "And the baby mice were indeed excellent."

"Would you like one or two more? I have one more litter left."

Chi shook his head and withdrew several patacas from his wallet to pay the bill. He hadn't converted enough money so he paid the balance, along with a generous tip, in Hong Kong dollars. Madame Twan didn't object. Taking one more sip of his tea, Chi rose to leave. The woman shuffled along beside him all the way to the exit. He said to her at the door, "Your other daughter in the United States. What is her name?"

"Yung Liu. My wicked husband took her away ten years ago. For all I know he sold her into slavery."

"I doubt that. Where is she now? What city?"

The old woman shrugged.

Chi frowned. "Does she know of her sister's death?"

"I'm sorry, I have no way of knowing. At times I suspected Mai knew of her younger sister's address, but she would never tell this old woman. It was as if Mai were ashamed of Yung Liu. Now I will forget them both."

"I'm sorry, Madame Twan. Thank you for your help." Chi shook her hand and stepped outside the cafe.

The light monsoon had increased, and the gutters were sloshing full. It was only mid-afternoon, but the sky was dark, and the street stood out in a jungle of garish, winking neon. Chi threw on the transparent plastic raincoat he'd brought along. It might take him a while to find a taxi. Trying to delay venturing out into the maelstrom, Chi hesitated in the protection of a storefront canopy. Withdrawing a small clasp envelope from his coat pocket, he again examined the contents. His associates had been through the Victoria Peak apartment twice with a fine-tooth comb and still the only leads–if they could be called that–were the undetonated firecracker and matchbook.

But there was still the matter of the silver lady hood ornament from Mai's Rolls Royce, the only object the houseman-chauffeur had reported missing after the homicide. Chi figured that the broken-off mascot was probably a dead lead, the work of vandals. As for its monetary value, a stainless steel *Spirit of Ecstasy* with a serial number stamped on it wasn't likely collateral for pawn shops.

Chi flipped the paper matches over in his hand. Possibly this was nothing at all, only a tired bar souvenir. Chi knew the matchbook was manufactured in the United States. Again, he examined the aircraft logo and the cryptic term "*Screwbirds.*" On the flip side were the words, SQUADRON 77–NORTH ISLAND. Chi had already checked out the San Diego-based flight squadron's deployments, discovering that the matches were from the officer's wardroom of the U.S. Carrier *Abraham Lincoln*. It was a new navy ship, and it had yet to pay a visit to Hong Kong.

Chi decided to check out the Casino Lisboa and ask a few questions. He might even stick around for some quick *fan-tan* or *sik-po* before catching the jetfoil back to Hong Kong. Even if he left now, by the time he got back it would be too late to go to the Half Moon fireworks factory. He would go probing around there tomorrow. If only the heinous crime had been committed in the Walled City neighborhood, Chi might have blamed it on the mob and brushed the sordid affair under the table. But not in Victoria Park. The powers that be were alarmed by the rape-murder-mutilation and had made their displeasure known to Chi's superiors in no uncertain terms. If the second powerful firecracker had gone off in the woman's mouth, as the brutish killer had intended, the diabolical disfigurement would have been even worse.

Chi wondered what kind of dementia made a man love and despise women at the same time. He also wondered how long it would take him to solve this case so he could leave on vacation.

6

Todd Dougherty chose the place for lunch, a newly opened oyster bar in Seaport Village. Pamela drove him in her rented Hertz compact. He'd wanted to grab a bite at the nearby Officer's Club so he could check up on Captain Bullock, but she wanted no part of it, insisting they both deserved a sixty-minute break from the gore and grief. Dougherty made up his mind to go after Bullock as soon as they returned to North Island.

They drove across the Coronado Bridge in a disquieting, frosty silence. Pamela was right; the dense fog was history. The sun was sticky-hot, and the entire city sparkled under a clear azure sky. Below them, the high-tech cruiser *Ticonderoga* passed under the bridge. Dougherty glanced briefly at the naval vessel, then stared blankly out at the traffic ahead. For the moment, conversation eluded him. His mind felt like the revolving door in a hotel lobby, disparate thoughts coming and going, never stopping long enough to get a grasp on any one of them. He was also physically uncomfortable. The front seat of the Sentra was pulled up too far and Dougherty's long legs felt cramped. If anything, he would have preferred remaining back at his desk, munching on a sandwich from the machine and jotting down some of his agitated questions on a green legal pad.

When they arrived at Seaport Village, Pamela exercised her woman's prerogative to change her mind. "Sorry, Todd," she apologized. "I don't feel like fighting off the tourists. The place is a zoo."

They dined instead at an uncrowded Mexican restaurant downtown on Fourth Avenue. Dougherty wolfed his way through a pair of good-sized soft tacos, chasing them with a large iced tea without sugar. Pamela only picked at her chicken burrito. Dougherty wondered if she'd ask for a doggy bag and pig out later. "What you need is a double Margarita," he chided.

"A brilliant idea—if I wanted to sleep the rest of the afternoon. I'll take a raincheck on getting stiff for later."

Dougherty felt clunky and restless. Going to lunch with his own staff, there'd have been plenty of detective memos and other doodles on the napkins by now, not to mention a few verbal exchanges of sick humor. None of his men had the slightest qualm about discussing murder and mayhem over a pastrami on rye. *Wasn't that the blasé way they did it in the anatomy labs up at the UC campus?* Dougherty guessed that Pamela Bonagofski Bonner's stony silence protected a squirrely stomach. Trying to force the conversation, he asked, "How long do you plan to stay in San Diego?"

That only brought a narrow gaze. "As long as it takes. I'm at your disposal twenty-four hours a day. No, let me rephrase that. Let's say I put in whatever hours are necessary until we break the case."

"If you're not going to kill that burrito, can we discuss business?" Dougherty grinned, and this time she smiled back.

"Suit yourself." She pushed the plate away and slowly sipped her coke. "While we're setting the record straight on my availability, tomorrow afternoon I have a prior commitment. You might even like to come along for an education."

"Don't tell me you're going shopping for trinkets in Tijuana?"

"Hardly. I'm giving a speech. The San Diego Women's Crisis Unit is hosting a regional conference of psychologists out at La Jolla."

Dougherty wiped the smile off his face and lowered his head. "Your special subject, *rape*, naturally. If you don't mind, Pamela, I'll pass on this one."

"Afraid of being outnumbered?"

"If I showed up and asked questions, your knees would probably be the ones doing the samba. You really want to see this male chauvinist go after some of your feminist totem poles with a chain saw? In front of a crowd, yet?"

She stared at him with withering contempt. "Fuck yourself."

Dougherty rode over the insult. Shrugging, he changed the subject. "Any thoughts on that rock music the killer left on the stereo for us?"

"My mind's still working it over. Pretty depressing stuff."

"I didn't find it that bad. I'm curious. Tell me, any particular piece of music make you happy? I mean *real happy*."

She looked at him. "Definitely. The opening waltz from the musical *Carousel*."

"And sad?"

"What is this, a quiz? Tchaikovsky's sixth, the *Pathetique*. And for your information, I happen to enjoy good rock—not sleaze. Or morbid groups like The Midnight Admirals."

"You've wider taste than I figured."

She smiled triumphantly. "I also drink Bud in the can."

Dougherty sat back, fascinated. She insisted they split the tab, and he didn't argue. They left the restaurant in an upbeat mood.

On the way back to the base, Pamela openly discussed the *Abraham Lincoln's* commanding officer with Dougherty. She brought up several notations in Swain Bullock's personal file, needling Dougherty about their significance to the case. He listened to all this without comment. Although Pamela claimed to be open minded at this point, he could feel her preconceived dislike of the carrier commander. Dougherty finally said sharply, "You want to tag along with me to the Officer's Club?"

She visibly stiffened behind the wheel. "No thanks. I'm far too impatient and intolerant to fake communication with a lush. I'll wait in the wings until Bullock's sober."

"The captain's not a lush. Facts are he seldom drinks anymore. This time I suspect he deserves the binge."

"Fine. You let him run astray, you deserve the job of drying him out."

Dougherty didn't respond. Instead, he stared out at the traffic, thinking, against his better judgment, Godawful, unfair thoughts about the *Abraham Lincoln's* skipper. His mind was working fast now, like Pamela's. He said to himself, *No, Andy, put the idea away. It didn't fit. It would never fit. Why would a man of Bullock's caliber kill his wife and make it look like another madman did the job? What's the motive?* Before the investigation went much farther, he and Pamela would be calling in the specialists for a professional evaluation. Dougherty knew virtually nothing about the twisted byways of the psychopathic brain, but he was willing to learn. He remembered how only last week he'd been fascinated with an article in *Time* magazine, a theorization that series killers were all victims of cerebral damage, some specific part of the brain.

When they arrived back at the NIS office on North Island, it was already after two. Pamela didn't bother to come upstairs with him, deciding instead to return on her own to the crime site. Dougherty didn't object. There was too much to accomplish in a short time; holding hands with her would be gratifying, but not nearly as productive as each of them working alone. He said goodbye and hurried up the stairs alone.

Sol Steinberg and three other investigative assistants in the outer office all sat forward in their seats when Dougherty entered. The motley group looked a little starved for leads—like Boston Celtics fans impatient for a score. Steinberg immediately filled him in. Despite their combined effort, nothing had crystallized for the NIS support staff. They'd made zero progress on the house-to-house interviews; the coroner had called with the preliminaries, and that information was on Dougherty's desk; one man was still working through the yellow pages of several nearby cities, checking on fireworks distributors; base public relations had called twice, asking for an official protocol.

Following Dougherty into the private office, Steinberg took off his metal-rimmed glasses and continued his spiel. "I've already started to work up Maxine Bullock's mail. Nothing significant yet. Oddly, no letters from Captain Bullock while he was away."

Dougherty slumped behind his desk and waved Steinberg into a seat by the door. "A supposition—maybe the skipper's not the letter-writing type. The *Abe Lincoln* has ship-to-shore phones, and rank has its privileges." Dougherty thought for a moment. "Next point. Computer time—how much are we good for?"

"It's all set. Pearson and Baisinger are standing by. Which menus?" Steinberg wiped his glasses with a handkerchief.

Dougherty stared at his desk, noting the manila folder marked PROPRIETARY. He quickly opened it. Dr. Westberg's preliminary report had been phoned in, and Steinberg had already typed it up on a neat blue form. Dougherty quickly read over the coroner's brief memo.

MAXINE BULLOCK DIED OF STRANGULATION—ONE OF THE NECK-TIES. Great, Dougherty already knew that. ASSAILANT DEFINITELY A SECRETOR. BLOOD TYPE O POSITIVE. CURLY RED HAIR, OBVIOUSLY NOT MAXINE BULLOCK'S, FOUND UNDER THE VICTIM'S FINGERNAILS AND ON BEDDING. ONE LAST NOTATION: NOT SURE THE BODY HAS BEEN RAPED. FOLLOW-UP DETAILS FORTHCOMING AFTER AUTOPSY HAS BEEN COMPLETED.

Dougherty looked up at Steinberg. "*Not sure*? What the hell's that supposed to mean?"

"That lower half of the torso was a mess. You'll have to ask Dr. Westberg."

"I intend to. What about Vic Shapiro? Did he have any luck with the fingerprints? How about a handspread on the neck? Gloves on all the time?"

Steinberg shook his head. "Sorry, boss. We're still waiting for his report. He asked for more time, the rest of the afternoon."

Dougherty tilted back in his chair. "The coroner's at least given us a decent start. Not positive evidence but good circumstantial stuff."

"You want me to pull every sailor's name on the base who matches red hair and Type O Positive?"

Dougherty nodded. "And add medical treatment for hemorrhoids to that list. Wait. Do it up right. Prepare an identical cross-check at the last two on-base living assignments for Swain Bullock and his wife." Dougherty glanced quickly at the captain's personnel file. "That's Pensacola and Pearl Harbor."

Steinberg looked at him in amazement. "Christ almighty, that'll take time."

"Get on it. And what about the base gate logs for last night?"

"Duck Harris is checking them out, but so far routine crap. The civilian visitor list after nine o'clock was mostly couples, along with a half-dozen defense-contractor types. North Island Security's working up a list. You want me to put yesterday's civilian employees on the computer, too?"

"No, not yet."

Shifting in his seat, Steinberg put his glasses back on. "Todd, maybe we should call in Captain Bullock's executive officer. I understand Commander Thorndike and his wife have been friends of the skipper for years."

Dougherty smiled vaguely. "*Were friends*. From what I hear, it's strictly business now. Anyway, the XO is out of town until tomorrow."

"Shouldn't we call in Captain Bullock now, instead of later?"

"Shouldn't we be doing a lot of things? Relax, Sol, or you'll wind up prematurely gray. I'm on my way to the Officer's Club now to take care of it myself."

"You want me to tag along?"

"No, that won't be necessary. You've plenty to do here."

"There's also the matter of interviewing the victim's parents. I understand they're somewhat estranged from the captain, and you never know— "

Dougherty nodded with impatience. "Forget it. The FBI woman's on top of that angle."

Steinberg leaned forward. "You want to talk about the Gecko Corman thing?"

"No." Dougherty scowled. The super-efficient Steinberg was like a persistent mosquito, his conversation bolder and more annoying by the minute, A meeting with him was like a ten-round boxing match. Ringing the bell and counting the points meant nothing; he had to be put out forcefully. "Sol, shut up. You need more to do yourself, get me a trace on every toll phone call Maxine Bullock made during the last thirty days. And wangle it out of the phone company by tomorrow morning. That'll be all."

His dignity patently wounded, the gangly assistant backed out of the office. He left the door open.

Dougherty called to him, "Steinberg, close the damned door. And real easy-like, okay?"

His assistant returned, but hesitated. "Lieutenant Commander, sir," he said testily, "in all respect, in case you've forgotten, Captain Bullock happens to have *wavy red hair*."

Dougherty had hardly forgotten, and it wasn't a point he needed to have rubbed in. He looked at Steinberg impatiently. "So do maybe three or four hundred other men among the thousands at North Island and Miramar. Put the *Abe Lincoln's* commanding officer out of your mind, Sol. I can't buy it. Find something viable."

The assistant left and gently closed the door behind him.

Before Dougherty took off to find and sober up the captain, he had an important phone call to make. He was determined to check up on Aviation Boatswain's Mate First Class "Gecko" Corman, the troublemaker who claimed to have life-threatening problems under Bullock's command. Now that Dougherty had stuck out his neck to set up a meeting tomorrow with some flag brass from Washington, he didn't want Corman changing his mind about appearing and instead suddenly taking a powder. Tomorrow's inquiry would be an informal one, but a precedent had been established. Never in Dougherty's career had he seen a sailor's frantic appeal rocket up the line and be answered so swiftly, and he wondered why. He could only speculate that Rear Admiral George Whitney had other reasons to be in the area tomorrow.

Dougherty was still uneasy about the matter, but thus far he was inclined to agree with the original Captain's Mast conducted on Gecko Corman's behalf. According to the ship's log, Swain Bullock had insinuated then that Corman was paranoid and given to hallucinations. The official log entry aside, scuttlebutt had it that fellow shipmates enjoyed Corman's hobby, playing a mean saxophone, but they disliked his verbal bullshit and habit of injustice collecting.

Dougherty placed the call to the Corman family home up in Downey, California and waited for the ring. He now halfway

wished he hadn't promised not to tell anyone where the frightened
sailor was holed up while on liberty. So much for secrecy. He
should have passed the problem on to someone else on his
staff—like Harris or Meadows. Dougherty cursed the inconvenience the complaining aviation boatswain's mate had caused the
NIS; he genuinely disliked pissers and moaners. Too often lately
it seemed he'd been forced to listen to their convoluted complaints. The worst of it was that he just didn't need the pesky
Corman problem on the *Abraham Lincoln* now, not at the same
time as a base homicide that was making Godawful headlines.

No one answered the long distance ring, and he put the phone
down. Dougherty shuddered, wondering if he was being too
skeptical. Supposing the sailor's accusations were true, that an
unidentified officer on the *Abraham Lincoln* did indeed try to
throw Corman off the catwalk into the sea?

7

Over at the base housing area, FBI agent Bonner was getting
nowhere with Maxine Bullock's neighbors. One officer's wife,
directly across the street from the Bullocks' duplex, even refused
to let Pamela in. The woman complained that she'd already been
grilled all morning by one of Dougherty's NIS men. Another
neighbor was too cooperative; obviously on the sauce, she would
have ranted on forever with meaningless psychobabble.

Pamela showed her I.D. to the SP on duty and again strolled
inside the yellow ribbon surrounding the Bullocks' duplex. There
was no answer when she knocked on the door of the neighbors
who shared the other half of the building. Pam glanced at her
notes. The occupant, a Commander Margolis, had probably sent
his family temporarily away from the crime site. She didn't blame
him.

Pam looked up. The birds were still there, observing her from
the roof over the Bullocks' front door. Were they keeping a death
watch? Why hadn't the feathery creatures flown off now that the

pea soup had lifted? *Probably still waiting for a crumb from Maxine.*

On the street a garbage truck was making its rounds. Pam hoped Dougherty's men had thoroughly checked out the containers behind the Bullocks'. She walked around the side of the duplex, observing a chain-link fence, apparently put there to keep in the dog. Pam noted for the first time that the Bullocks' back yard, what there was of it, abutted another duplex. The structure to the rear was even closer than the units on each side. *Women like to chat over backyard fences*, she thought. A chance to get friendly without having to dress or leave their own territory. The wire fence was waist-high, just tall enough to keep a kid's beach ball from rolling too far and Maxine Bullock's dog from digging up the neighbor's dahlias and snapdragons.

Crossing her fingers, Pamela went around to the front of the close-by duplex and knocked at the entry. The door opened on the chain, and a dark face glared out at her. A jet was running up its engines on the nearby base runway so Pam had to raise her voice. "Hello! I'm Pamela Bonner from the FBI! Would you mind answering a few questions?"

No response.

Pamela tried again. "May I please come in?"

The eyes softened, and the door opened the rest of the way. An attractive black woman in a red and white striped housecoat stood poised in the entry. The woman—apparently one of the gawkers outside the ribbon barrier earlier in the morning—recognized Pamela and invited her in. She ignored the extended badge and I.D. and gestured toward the living room.

"I figured you'd come by soon enough. I tried telling those SP boys I had something to say, but all they did was bob their heads and write down my name."

Pamela smiled. "Which is?"

"Sarah Cleveland." Her huge brown eyes sparkled like multi-hued opals. "My better half's Commander Trevor Cleveland. He's squadron CO for the VS-29, the Dragonflies."

At the moment Pam wasn't interested in either Trevor or his Dragonflies, but she nodded politely and withdrew her notepad. "Sarah, I need your help. And I'm going to have to ask you to get a little personal, okay?"

"At least it'll be easier talkin' with you than one of the men investigators."

"What may appear to you to be nothing more than idle gossip

could be a valuable lead. If we're to catch Maxine's killer, we have to check every angle."

"I hear the bastard did in the dog, too."

Pamela nodded uncomfortably. *Sarah Cleveland knew?* They hadn't planned to release that part of it to the press. *The priest had been blabbermouthing.*

The woman offered her a seat on a couch cluttered with dog-eared copies of *People* magazine and the *National Enquirer*. The living room smelled of stale cigarette smoke and talcum powder and there were plastic toddler's toys scattered around the floor. An intrusive television in the kitchen blared a soap opera, but Sarah ignored it. Shaking her head disconsolately, she sat down opposite Pamela in a black Boston rocker. "Bolts on the windows, new lock on the door. Even hold my breath when I answer the phone. I'm plenty scared, Miss— What'd you say your name was?"

"Bonner. Just call me Pamela, okay? Look, how well did you know the Bullock couple?"

"Never met the captain. Lord, not sure I want to, either. According to Maxine, the bastard hadn't come home or set foot in the house for sixteen months, almost a year and a half. Before that—well, folks fret about catfights keeping them up all night? Damnation, you haven't heard a thing until you've heard them two going at it. Course, that was a long time ago."

"Sarah, tell me. Did you talk to Maxine often?"

"Never been inside her house, but we'd chat often enough out back."

Pamela smiled with encouragement. *Admit it, Sarah*, she thought. *Gossip. Don't hold back now; pass it on, please. I need all of it.*

The black woman all too eagerly continued, "She'd let her little poodle come over and play with my oldest. Only thing I ever really talked to Maxine about were the other women on the block and maybe the prices at the Base Exchange. Actually, I didn't have to talk much to get Mrs. Bullock pegged, you know what I mean?"

Pamela eased back on the sofa. "Sorry, I don't. Would you explain?"

"The walls in these base housing units aren't too thick, and we used to hear plenty before old Swain left for good. Like the captain screaming and calling Maxine bad names. Like *fickle, two-timing airhead bitch.*"

"A real gentleman. You heard him call her that?"

"And worse. One night he was out emptying the garbage and bellowing at her that she was useless and had a fried brain. Just for not using plastic bags, mind you. Good God, half the time I even forget to put my kid's diapers in plastic bags before throwing them out."

Pam sighed with impatience. "Back to the captain. Please go on, Sarah."

"Another time, Swain Bullock left the house calling back from the street that she was a two-timing whore. Like I say, that was months back, but my ears are still ringing. My husband and I thought sure they'd divorce before the captain left on another deployment."

"Your squadron commander husband—Trevor? Has he met Bullock?"

"I don't know, ma'am. They're on different ships."

"Call me Pamela, please. Sarah, I'll rephrase the question. Obviously, Trevor *knows of him*. Does he have kind words or otherwise for the carrier commander?"

"Sure. He's heard that Bullock's a goddamned—" Sarah stopped suddenly. "Sorry, I think you'd better talk to Trevor about that."

Pam decided to get to the point. "Did Maxine Bullock date other men while her husband was away?"

The Cleveland woman retreated into an uncomfortable silence. The Boston rocker started to go back and forth.

"Relax, Sarah. Mrs. Bullock is dead. She's hardly in a position to take offense at anything. Do yourself and every woman on the base a favor. Please tell me everything you know."

"Seems to me the refrigerator repair truck spent an awful lot of time at that house. Then there was the bright orange Kawasaki left outside the back door two weekends in a row. I think it's the same bike parked over behind the base exchange all the time. Another instance I found Maxine in her backyard, passed out in a lawn chair, drunk as a skunk. Woo-wee! Other than that, well, I'm not the type to peer in bedroom windows. I'm no snoop, mind you."

"You're sure there's nothing else?"

Sarah stopped rocking. She twisted so hard with the buttons to her robe that one of them came off. "My brother goes to a place called Spanky's Saloon out at Midway. He's seen her there several times with enlisted men."

Pamela sighed. "I'm beginning to think Maxine Bullock took no part whatsoever in the social life of the Navy and had nothing to do with other officers' wives."

"You can say that again. She was too preoccupied to have anything to do with us. All she did was invite trouble in, and she got it. Oh, there's one more thing. Maxine did confide in me that she had an abortion, about a year ago."

Pam scribbled more notes.

Sarah said gloomily, "All I'm worried about now is if this homicidal madman will strike again in the same neighborhood."

"Fifty feet away is a little close by for comfort, but I'd say it's like lightning striking twice in the same spot. Sarah, any idea what kind of music Maxine liked? Did she buy records?"

"Sorry, I haven't the foggiest."

"Any other eccentricities you can think of?"

Sarah sniffled. Pulling a Vicks inhaler from her pocket, she inhaled deeply, then considered for a moment. "Yes. On the back porch. She'd feed the damned dog on her best china plates."

Pamela didn't write that down. Instead she scribbled a note to herself that Maxine appeared to be one of those women who gravitated toward quicksand relationships.

They talked another five minutes, but nothing more of value materialized. Sarah told her that the other half of her own duplex was empty. Pamela sighed with satisfaction. *No interview there. Good. It was time to get moving before the rush hour traffic if she were going to get out to the suburbs and meet the victim's parents.*

Sarah Cleveland walked with Pamela around the building and over to the car. The black woman said goodbye quickly, explaining that she had to hurry home to watch *The Young and the Restless*.

As Pam started to drive off, she saw a newsboy ride up on a bicycle, gaze at the four-inch-wide police barrier ribbon with puzzlement, then toss a folded paper over it to the Bullocks' front porch.

8

Delmonico's gym managed to get them all, thought Assistant Manager Tellie Fisher. She knew from experience that fitness freaks came in all sizes—physically and mentally. Judging from the nervous manner and peculiar appearance of the man who now stood on the opposite side of the counter, it looked like this was going to be one of those off-the-wall afternoons.

Tellie rang up the twelve dollars for the temporary membership card, continuing to eyeball the new patron with reservation. The individual before her had curly, dishwater blond hair thinning at the crown and severely brushed back, pomaded to each side of the head. His splotchy, freckle-covered face looked as if it had been in a head-on auto wreck, and the bones in his roller-coaster nose had never quite come together again. Though the sour-mannered applicant had presented a driver's license and Navy I.D. showing an age of twenty-four, he looked much older, as if he might have been through a war or two. The man's moustache was neatly trimmed, but his lips were thin and colorless over a receding chin that made him look like a sick bird. The new customer told her that he'd recently returned from Hawaii, the Philippines, and China, that he was only in San Diego for a short time before heading north to Bremerton. Tellie might ordinarily have asked a sailor what ship he was from, but this sailor's abrupt manner didn't invite an expanded conversation.

Slouched over the reception counter, the surly man took his time with the simple application form. He wrote precisely, in delicate cursive script much like a woman's, taking as much care with his words as an architect might devote to a finished drawing. After an untidy start, he looked up irritably and asked for a new application.

Tellie glanced with annoyance at the old one before trashing it. "I don't understand. You've changed your name. You wrote down Eisenbinder. *Roscoe W. Eisenbinder.* Your driver's license says Steelbinder. Which is it Roscoe, or can't you remember?"

He glared at her and pursed his lips. "Hmmmm-nnnnn."

Shrugging, she gave him another application. It was the second time he'd made that sound, *hmmmm-nnnnn*. Tellie couldn't decide if the two-tone humming was a silly attempt to imitate a door chime or if he was trying to clear a nasal blockage.

Gazing up at her with obvious malevolence, he said impatiently, "My dear woman, *eisen* is the German word for steel. My name has been legally Anglicized, but I sometimes go back to the traditional, purely on whim." Reaching out, he gently tapped her wrist and asked thickly, "Surely a lovely girl like you sometimes engages in whims? I also detest the name Roscoe. If you must get personal, call me R.W."

Tellie pulled back her hand as if it had been contaminated. Smiling vaguely, she slid a new application across the counter.

Wordlessly, he filled it out, again taking his time.

When he was finished she retrieved the form, tore off the bottom section for his proof of membership for one week, then handed him the key to tanning room number three. She said without enthusiasm, "Will you be wanting a towel and locker as well, Mr. Steelbinder?"

"No, not today." His tone softened measurably. "Just the tanning equipment. I have access to a workout room on the ship."

"Fine. But I suggest you come back and try our sauna and refurbished hot tub while you're in port."

"No, I think not. I'm averse to bathing with strangers."

Tellie stared at him, managing a bleak grin. She quickly changed the subject. "Was the weather pretty gnarly during your Far East mission?" Considering the new customer's muscular build, what she really wanted to ask was *how come you're so damned pale and anemic looking?*

Now Steelbinder seemed to be studying her, smiling broadly for the first time and revealing uneven teeth. His immense olive-colored eyes had a slight twitch that made Tellie uncomfortable. He glanced down at his colorless forearms as if reading Tellie's mind, then abruptly turned away from the counter and headed in the direction of the tanning rooms.

Tellie watched him swagger down the hall. She couldn't help smiling, for Roscoe Steelbinder—or *Eisenbinder*— walked oddly, as if he had an egg in his shorts and was afraid to drop it. Even his name—Roscoe—struck her as peculiar for the nineteen-eighties.

Tellie was glad the newcomer had only taken out a temporary membership, even though the boss had told her to mind her own business when it came to judging character. All that really mattered, her boss insisted, was the color of the customer's money. Still, it was hard not to gawk at someone as odd as Roscoe Steelbinder. The blond, oily-haired sailor wore faded dungarees and a polyester tank shirt with thin straps front and back. His body might be chalky white, but it was obvious that he regularly pressed weights; Steelbinder was the type who liked to call attention to himself by flexing his shoulder muscles as he walked. Tellie couldn't help shuddering as she stared at Steelbinder's back.

The new gym patron must have been reading her thoughts, for suddenly he turned. Tellie quickly composed herself.

Stroking his moustache, Steelbinder said irritably, "You're very pretty. Don't spoil the image by ugly thoughts. Do I set the timer device myself? Or do you come in and instruct me?"

Tellie struggled to hide her annoyance. "If you wish, I'll have the male attendant assist you."

"No. It's quite all right. I'll manage."

Stepping into the cubicle the woman had designated, Steelbinder critically surveyed its furnishings. He hated the closed-in feeling and the redolence of sweat but was determined to make the most of the situation. He'd been in more offensive places, including the workout gym aboard the carrier.

Dominating the small room was a tanning unit that resembled a giant waffle iron. There were also a metal chair, mirror, a set of stereo earphones, and a couple of red ceramic hooks to hang up clothing. Steelbinder undressed quickly, folding his dungarees and tank shirt meticulously over the chair. His hemorrhoids had been bothering him all morning, but this wasn't the time nor the place to worry about that. He had just enough time for a tanning treatment before his drive up to Los Angeles.

He stood there for a moment in front of the mirror in his blue French jockstrap, admiring his pectorals and biceps—miserably pale as they were. No wonder the gym attendant stared at him. As always when confronting a mirror, he avoided gazing at his ill-shapen face, particularly the roller-coaster nose. Once more he murmured to himself, forcing out the words one at a time: *Cosmetics are nothing, Steelbinder!* Say it to yourself again and again. *Mind and muscle are everything. Power.* Think positive enough, and even the ache in your ass will disappear!

Continuing to admire his physique, Steelbinder slowly ran his hands over his forearms and thighs, feeling the stubble. He hadn't shaved his body since taking that cheap room ashore in Hong Kong, and the hair was growing back out rapidly. It was impossible to tend to such personal matters on the ship, where it was like living in a goldfish bowl. Opening the tanning machine, Steelbinder looked over the glass-covered UVA tubes with reservation. He had serious doubts about the mechanism's cleanliness, but thankfully, he'd come prepared. *Be prepared* was the motto of the Boy Scouts, a group he'd always admired as a youth—until he'd been expelled for alleged troublemaking.

Steelbinder withdrew from his dungaree pocket some folded paper towels and the small aerosol can of Lysol disinfectant he always carried with him. Humming softly to himself, he sprayed the top and bottom of the tanning machine, carefully wiped it down, then repeated the procedure for good measure. He decided not to take off the athletic supporter for a nude tan; while he may well have killed off the larger creepy-crawlies, it was the invisible, mutant kind that still concerned him. Steelbinder wasn't about to suffer a setback from venereal disease, herpes, or any disinfectant-resistant microcosm. Who knows what they still might learn about AIDS? He would also leave on his white crew sox, not to guard against athlete's foot fungus, but because he couldn't abide bare feet.

Before donning the stereo headset, Steelbinder sprayed each earpiece with the Lysol, as well as two nickels he withdrew from his pants pocket. He carefully dried the lot with a paper towel. Easing his body under the lamps, he adjusted the earphones, placed a cleaned coin over each eye and pulled down the hinged lid. Steelbinder set the tanning machine timer for twelve minutes and relaxed his body.

～～～～～ 9

Swain Bullock was pie-eyed. Dougherty found he was also a big bastard, and it had been a struggle wrestling him up the flight of steps to the front door. There wasn't time to unfold the sleeper-sofa in the living room, for once inside Dougherty's apartment, the carrier commander crashed on it with all of the grace of a gooney bird at Midway Island.

At first Dougherty had considered taking Bullock back to the ship, but he figured that the captain's name had probably acquired enough question marks after it. Why invite more? What Bullock didn't need right now was a gabby crew or a watch officer with an axe to grind seeing their captain wobbling over the gangway. Dougherty found it difficult enough sneaking Bullock out the back door of that Officer's Club banquet room and into the Porsche.

Already the captain was snoring. Dougherty decided to go into his bedroom to use the phone and catch up on some paperwork. He'd remain there, nursing his impatience while waiting for Bullock to come around. He wanted the captain sober, dead sober, and he was still willing to wait as long as necessary to see him that way.

On the way up to meet the murdered woman's parents, Pamela spotted a large music and video store in a shopping center adjacent to Interstate 5. On impulse, she pulled off the freeway, parked, and hurried inside.

Assisting her at the order desk was an officious, earring-clad youth with hair the color of Neapolitan ice cream. He told Pam that the single 45 record she wanted had been out of rack distribution for at least two years, but that it could probably still be ordered. He did have the Midnight Admirals' spoof on *The Divine Comedy* on cassette, however, and tried to sell her one. She declined and asked to speak to the music store's manager.

Moments later an older, girthy woman with a ludicrous bouffant approached and said archly, "Is something wrong?"

"No. Everything's fine. I need to talk about your policy on special orders."

Pamela took out one of her FBI business cards and handed it to her. The eggbeater hair made the woman look topheavy, and Pam had to resist a temptation to reach out and steady her. After listening to Pamela's request, the woman manager promised to examine the store's orders and check with the employees on the other shifts. If anyone had recently ordered "Many a Time the World Comes Short of Thought," the store would of course cooperate and let the FBI agent know. Pamela had purposely avoided bringing up the North Island homicide, instead claiming to be investigating a possible copyright infringement.

Pamela left the store. She decided to pass the buck on the followup work. One of Dougherty's assistants could do the finger-walking through the yellow pages and check the other retail outlets. It might be a dead end. There was every chance the killer might be a civilian from out of town or a sailor off a visiting ship. The records could have been purchased thousands of miles away.

Pam avoided the freeway and drove her rented sedan north on old Highway 101 toward the Torrey Pines seashore. She sorely missed her own red VW Rabbit convertible, still in for repairs at a garage up north. In her rush to get out of Los Angeles, she'd hopped a plane down to San Diego and rented the Sentra at Lindbergh Field.

Toying with the radio's signal seeker, she was surprised that KLOS, L.A.'s ass-kicking, all-rock station carried this far down the coast. The music, something ancient by the BJ Surfers, throbbed in her ears. The station started fading in and out, and she had to listen carefully to make out the bizarre lyrics. Had she heard right? "I smoke Elvis Presley's toenails when I want to get high." At the conclusion of the number, the D.J. announced the grotesque title: "The Shah Sleeps in Harvey's Grave." Pam winced and turned the radio off, enjoying the silence. With so much on her mind, she'd be better off concentrating on the driving.

The tanning machine wasn't uncomfortable, but Steelbinder grew increasingly restless. Bored with soporific music, he changed the radio from FM to AM, tuning to San Diego's all news station. The homicide at the North Island base topped the local report. Annoyed as he was by the overly-strident woman announcer, Steelbinder paid rapt attention. But after a few moments he'd heard enough.

Angrily, he tore away the earphones and turned off the tanning lamps. *Dunderheads!* What Steelbinder had just heard was incredibly stupid. He took strong umbrage to the dithyrambic namecalling coming from several interviewed bystanders and so-called authorities. *Firecracker Fiend! The Detonator! Cherry Bomber!*

"Cherry Bomber" was the worst, the most galling accusation of all! Steelbinder's mind flashed over the news report. They'd made it sound like he was attacking innocent, pre-pubescent girls. How dare these uninformed, clod-pated news reporters! If only he had time to put these cretins in their place. The depravity was not his, but the perfidious lust of the whore woman! What would his fulsome critics ever know about deserving punishment and the *mortification of the flesh*?

Steelbinder's grandfather had quoted Dante's cantos to him as often as his grandmother had the Bible. Some of the lines from the

Inferno were indelibly etched in his mind. One of them came to him now:

> *Many are the animals that with her wed,*
> *And there shall yet be more, until the hound*
> *Shall come and in her misery strike her dead.*

Pamela found several recreational vehicle parks within a mile-long stretch of coast highway. Windemere Glen was the last one, less pretentious than the others and hidden a little off the road behind a weatherbeaten clapboard fence and funky neon sign over the gate. She drove inside. Cockleburs and dandelions pushed through the cracked asphalt drive, and the speed bumps badly needed repainting. Pamela was surprised to find the park so crowded with RVs in late October. Despite the packed house, the place seemed oddly quiet. It suddenly dawned on her why. *Snowbirds*, come south for the winter. No children in tow.

Everywhere awnings had been extended or big sun umbrellas set out, and from beneath many of them came unfriendly, geriatric stares. *Driving too fast.* She braked, slowing the car to a crawl.

Pam was glad she'd called first and that the three of them would be expecting her. Browne was Maxine Bullock's maiden name. Pam saw Cora and Marvin Browne waiting beside their Winnebago. So was Arthel, the murder victim's grandfather, who had his own Airstream trailer parked right next door. A metal table was set up, and the three of them hunkered around it on flimsy folding chairs, the kind sold at discount drugstores. The woman seemed to be talking at a breakneck pace until her husband held up his hand in protest and pointed toward Pamela's car. The trio confronting her wore the bored expression of the retired, comfortably well-off, and lonely. Pamela smiled at them from inside the Sentra, but they didn't smile back.

Maxine Bullock's father was clad in the RV park's apparent uniform of the day—a billed, breathe-through cap and full-cut polyester print shirt left outside his pants to cover a considerable paunch. He had a florid face with excess baggage under the eyes and chin and wore glasses with hinged shades, now tilted up. Pam couldn't pin down Marvin Browne's age, but guessed there was a working man's air about him, and that he'd retired prematurely to sit on his ass and enjoy the American Dream.

Marvin's flat chested, gabby wife Cora looked older despite her outrageous apricot-colored hair and pasty makeup. She had orange pencil lines instead of brows, and her eyes were shot with red—probably from crying. Pam smiled inwardly at Cora's hair; she'd seen that color dye job often in Beverly Hills, and invariably there'd been a matching poodle in tow. Not this time. Somehow, the trio confronting her didn't appear to be animal-lover types.

Father and son checked Pam out like hungry buzzards as she stepped out of the car. Not bothering to get up, their rheumy eyes conveyed only undisguised contempt as she stepped forward. The old man spoke first. "B'fore you set your head about asking 'barressing questions, let's just see the color of your badge."

Pam stared at him. Arthel Browne was of medium height but scrawny and wore a soiled T-shirt over Levis. His arms hung to his sides like hairy breadsticks, and his eyebrows looked like they hadn't been trimmed since the dust storms of the thirties. Arthel's eyes seemed ratlike and sharply pronounced, while the skin of his face was as formless as a pricked balloon and layered all the way down to his adam's apple. Pam guessed that the old crank couldn't be hurting for money, not with that new, aerodynamic aluminum trailer. She wondered why he dressed like a cracker.

Pam went up to Arthel, obliging him by flashing her badge. He sneered at it and pushed her hand aside.

Marvin Browne stirred with effort. The rivets in his folding seat creaked in protest as he shifted his bulk. "Never you mind, Grandpa. Cora and I intend to take care of this."

"Bullshit, Marvin. I say let's save time. Tell her right out what Maxine told us. 'Bout how she suspected Swain had a fling with some Chinese woman up in Frisco."

Cora looked embarrassed. "You hush, Grandpa. It doesn't do no good now bringing up gossip that can't be proved." She grabbed another metal chair and dragged it up to the table.

Cora didn't bother to brush the dried birdshit off the seat, so Pam did it herself and sat down gingerly. Pulling out her note pad, she tried to explain as politely as possible why it was necessary to intrude on their period of mourning and ask disquieting questions about their murdered offspring. She studied their faces one at a time. The old geezer still wasn't buying it.

Cora Browne wiped her eyes and sat forward. "Stop scowling, Gramps, and listen to the woman." She turned to Pamela. "Don't mind Arthel. Back home he's what we call 'sot in his ways.'" Cora went on to explain home was West Virginia, and that her daughter had moved south for secretarial work. First to Atlanta, then to Florida, and that Maxine had met Swain Bullock when he was going through naval aviation training at Pensacola.

Pamela listened carefully, jotting down few notes. She already knew most of this.

Cora went on to explain in a grief-filled voice that the Bullocks had been married fourteen years, that it was only the last three that had gone sour.

Beyond the agitated woman, Arthel cursed repeatedly. He wasn't about to be put off. "I got more to say. A lot more. But not to an FBI woman. They run out of gritty men agents?"

Pam sighed with impatience. Marvin Browne sat forward, raising the back of his hand to the old man in a threatening gesture. Arthel obediently shut up. Marvin asked his wife, "What time do you have, Cora?"

The cowed woman squinted at her watch, a man's Timex with a big silver dial. "Three-thirty, why?"

Marvin looked disappointed. "Too early to offer our guest a serious drink, but you'd better bring out a pitcher of lemonade." He glanced at Pamela and said brusquely, "You rather have tea?"

"No. Lemonade is fine."

Cora padded across an eight-by-eight-feet square of yellowing crabgrass and disappeared into the Winnebago.

Marvin said to Pamela, "Martini time never starts until five around here, we're sticklers on that one. Wouldn't want to acquire a hollow leg, no way."

Arthel grunted. "I don't drink with troublemakers."

Pam watched the cantankerous Arthel get up, straighten with difficulty, and shuffle arthritically back to his own trailer. He plopped down with considerable effort on the Airstream's metal steps and continued to stare at Pamela as if he wanted to tear out her heart. She glared back, unintimidated. Pam wanted to say, *Get off my case, Grandpa.* If Arthel were younger and the timing of her visit were different, she'd flip him off with her finger.

Making no effort to apologize for his father, Marvin Browne looked at Pam smugly. His wife was still inside the Winnebago. "You have nice legs, Ms Bonner. My daughter had a nice body, too. Maxine was a full ten years younger than Swain, you know. You look young, very young to be a detective."

"Thank you, Mr. Browne. I wonder if we might . . ."

"How'd you come by an FBI career?" Marvin interjected. Shaking his head, he added, "Pretty woman should have better things to do with her life than get involved with the bloodsucking government. You get your fancy education with one of those Federal student loans?"

Pam was taken aback. *Combative bastard!* At least the annoying oaf had stopped drooling over her legs. "I'm sorry, Mr. Browne, that's none of your business." She glanced nervously over at Arthel, aware now that they were two peas from the same pod. Their unkind words had clung to her like sticky, smashed bugs on a clean windshield. She sat up straight and said defiantly, "Whether you like me or not isn't important, Marvin. I still intend to do my job."

He was staring at her body again. "Pretty figure like yours, next thing you'll tell me is that you work out with that Jane Fonda program."

She sighed with impatience. "I have in the past, yes."

"Hollywood liberals. New dealers. Future dealers. The coons and the Commies are enough to drive reasonable, good American stock like us right to drink."

Pam looked at him. "Good American stock?" She wondered what next gem of wisdom would come from her carping hosts. She didn't have to wait long.

Arthel shouted from his trailer, "Hell, ask her smack-dab, Son, or I sure will. *Bonner*—that your real name, Miss?"

Marvin grinned, baring his teeth. "Mind your manners, Arthel."

Cora had arrived with a tray of lemonade. Her tears had dried, and she now wore a silly stewardess smile. She said quietly to Pam, "They're wondering if you're Jewish."

"No, I'm not." She turned, glaring irritably at the old man. "Third generation Polish. The family name is Bonagofski. Does that get your hackles up as well?"

Arthel grunted, "Hummph! You still look too uppity to pee off the back porch. Just like that smart-ass Annap'lis grad, Swain Bullock."

"Sorry about Pa," Cora clucked. "No offense intended." She poured pink lemonade into four unmatched glasses—the kind that had previously contained jelly or peanut butter.

Marvin raised his lemonade in a mock toast. "Well then, young lady, what is it you want from us?"

Pam was surprised by the sudden deferential tone. She took in a quick breath. "If we're to find your daughter's killer, I need your cooperation."

"Then stop lollygaggin' around here," Arthel said quickly. Curiously, this time the old codger's voice was less strident, almost pleading. "If you're really a cop, get yourself aboard that aircraft carrier and arrest the captain. My kids here are too damned polite for their own good. Swain's guilty, sure as shit. You don't hang him, I'm goin' after the sonofabitch myself with a shotgun."

Marvin Browne winked at Pamela. "Pa's eyes being what they are, he's not going hunting for anyone. But like you see, he's pretty upset. Anyone lets out a contract on the captain, it sure's hell would be Arthel. If only I had the courage, I'd take care of the matter myself with my Colt pistol."

Pamela tried to think of something dramatic to say, at least a warning for them to remain out of it. The harsh spirit of the Old Testament came to mind, and she wondered if the Brownes were into religion. The only fish on the back of their RV was a decal of an arched rainbow trout. Pam thought about the *lex talonis*, the biblical version of punishment from Exodus 21, "an eye for an eye, a tooth for a tooth." She also considered the counterpoint, "vengeance is mine, sayeth the Lord."

The three of them waited, staring at her. Instead of giving them a sermon or timely quote from the criminal codes, Pam decided to continue the interrogation. She looked at Marvin seriously. "What makes you so sure Captain Bullock killed his own wife?"

While Pam waited a lizard darted past her chair, pausing briefly to gaze up at her. On the other side of the table, Cora lowered her head and started to sniffle. The old man by the Airstream, thankfully, had retreated into silence. Marvin leaned forward, apparently ready to use the momentary silence to fire off another salvo. Cora put a hand on her husband's forearm, restraining him.

Cora said apologetically to Pam, "We all know it. The captain's prone to violence. I'm surprised he wasn't booted out of the military years ago."

"I'm sorry, Mrs. Browne. The facts appear to the contrary. The U.S. Navy seems quite pleased with Swain Bullock's performance. I've seen his file, and it bulges with commendations."

Cora didn't like that. She glanced nervously at her Timex, then at her empty lemonade glass. Rattling the ice cubes, she looked imploringly toward Marvin. "Under the circumstances, couldn't we make an exception?"

Marvin smiled vaguely at Pamela. "Cora likes to advance cocktail time whenever she finds a decent excuse." Turning to his wife, he gestured with his thumb toward the Winnebago's entry. Cora shoved her lemonade glass aside and took off like a happy retriever. She returned moments later with a black-lacquered tray containing a fifth of Bombay gin, some dry vermouth, and a bucket of ice.

Pam declined a cocktail, sticking with her lemonade. Cora perked up considerably while mixing drinks for herself and the others. Booze was obviously number one on the Brownes' list of priorities. Primping at her apricot hair, Cora sat back with her double martini and unwound. She started to talk—slowly at first, then nonstop. She continued to tear into Swain Bullock, at the same time heaping praise on her dead daughter. Pamela only vaguely heard the woman; she was thinking about Maxine. And an old song from the sixties was replaying in her mind:

> *She doesn't love me now*
> *She's made it clear enough,*
> *It ain't no good to pine.*
> *Mrs. Brown, you've got a lovely daughter . . .*

~~~~~ 10

Dougherty checked his watch. It was after six o'clock, and in the other room the *Abraham Lincoln's* intoxicated skipper had slept over two hours without awakening. Dougherty wondered why the FBI woman hadn't called him with a report. He didn't expect anything earth-shaking to come out of the interview with the victim's parents up by Torrey Pines, but Pamela had insisted on the on-site interrogation, and he was curious. Left to Dougherty, the preliminary questioning would have been handled by telephone, just as he was about to do now with Swain Bullock's mother, a widow who resided up at Lake Tahoe.

Earlier, he'd left the bedroom door open just a crack so he could hear the captain if he came around. Dougherty now closed it firmly and placed a call to the Squaw Valley exchange he'd gleaned off Bullock's personnel file. From Dougherty's homework, he knew that Abigail Bullock was a deeply religious, older widow. He wondered why she'd want to live alone up in the California Sierras.

He had his answer moments later after she picked up the ring. Bullock's mother turned out to be surprisingly alert, independent, and tough mannered. After a few minutes of feisty conversation with her, Dougherty wondered if she might be related to any of the rugged Donner Party survivors. Abigail Bullock explained that the dogs barking in the background were show stock, that she raised blue-ribbon cocker spaniels. She also told Dougherty that she was prepared for a call from the Naval Investigation Service and was especially pleased that her interrogator had the rank of lieutenant commander.

Dougherty listened patiently for a while, then said quietly to her, "Mrs. Bullock, I'm with your son now, but he's not in much shape to talk to you. It's been a rough day for him."

"Liquor. I figured as much. God forgive him. He called me immediately after he learned of the murder, claiming he was going for a drink then. Will he be all right?"

"I suspect so. Whether the captain will sail with the ship on Wednesday, I can't answer at this point. Do you plan to come down to San Diego for Maxine's funeral?"

"I'm trying to make arrangements. This couldn't have happened at a worse time. Still, it's the Lord's will."

"Personal problems up there, Mrs. Bullock?"

"Yes. One of my dogs is pregnant and overdue. Another is scheduled for stud service."

Dougherty smiled to himself. Abigail's mountain life might be drab, consecrated only to God and cocker spaniels, but it appeared to have more sex in it than his own humdrum existence. He said quickly over the line, "I have a favor to ask when you arrive in San Diego Wednesday. I'd like you to come by my office without the captain knowing, if possible. I have some items to show you and a few questions. I promise to be brief."

"Well, I really don't think I can be of much help. I haven't been in touch with Maxine for almost two years. Just a polite exchange of Christmas cards."

Dougherty's bedroom door suddenly opened. Swain Bullock stood there, big as life, red-eyed, and a little unsteady. He looked at Dougherty curiously.

Trying to ignore him, Dougherty said warily into the phone, "Please, Mrs. Bullock. What I requested is important."

"All right, I'll be there, but—" In the background her dogs were barking again, and she screamed to shut them up.

Swain Bullock strode into the bedroom and snatched the phone out of Dougherty's hand. Guardedly, he said into the mouthpiece, "Mother? Why are you speaking with the lieutenant commander?" He listened for several seconds, all the while rubbing the back of his neck. Finally he replied, "I'm fine. On my way back to the ship. You just stay out of this, and don't fret over a thing."

Dougherty waited while the captain listened again, apparently getting an earful. Finally Bullock said sharply, "I don't want to talk about it now. Get a damn babysitter for your dogs, and I'll see you tomorrow at noon. No, I don't intend to meet you in San Francisco. Come down here. How would it look if you didn't show up at your daughter-in-law's funeral? I have to go now. Good night." Bullock hung up the phone, shook his head, and made an effort to smile. "Okay, Lieutenant Commander. Let's back up. For the official record, cancel out anything I might have blathered earlier. I'm stone sober now."

Dougherty grinned. "Facts are you've been remarkably silent, not even a snore. I've been able to catch up on my work."

Bullock's amiable expression faded. He took on a stony stare. "Why did it happen at my house? My wife? You have clues or not?"

"Don't I wish. Captain, before we get too palsy-walsy, I need some serious questions answered. You may find them uncomfortable. I'm not pointing any fingers, mind you, just trying to get at some bare-bones, investigative facts. Shall I begin?"

"Sure, why not?" Bullock shrugged. "Info the computer can get a decent *bite* on, right?"

Dougherty ignored the pun. "Call my probing what you will." He tried to study Bullock, but all he saw now was an expressionless face conveying nothing but the sickly pallor of a hangover. "Captain, where did you go last night?" Dougherty wanted to come off like a friendly doctor questioning a patient, but it didn't work; already he was sounding accusative. He suddenly flashed, *The hell with it, the hell with big mogul ship commanders*. Just do your job. Fire the main battery at once, and get it over with. "Captain, the watch officer logged you off the ship at 2100. You didn't return until long after midnight."

"One-fifteen in the morning, to be precise," Bullock snorted. He held Dougherty's gaze without batting an eyelash. "I went to a movie, a fourplex in La Mesa. Afterward, I was a little bored. I drove down to Coronado Cays and Mission Beach looking for some action." He pondered a moment, then continued evenly, "Checked out one place, but the crowd was too young. At another, the parking lot was so jammed I couldn't get in. I finally gave up and went back to the ship. Anything else?"

"Yes. Anyone see you at the theatre? What were the names of these clubs? Were they bars, dancehalls, what?"

"Look, Lieutenant Commander, I appreciate the little rescue this afternoon and the use of your pad." Bullock stiffened. He was pissed and his staccato voice let it show. "But if the tab for your hospitality is a series of goddamn slap-in-the-face insults, you, the NIS, and your Judge Advocate legal buddies can shove it up your asses."

Dougherty backpedaled. "Relax, Captain. I'm only trying to keep things reasonably informal. You prefer to answer questions before some hardass Board of Inquiry?"

"Aggrandizement. And bad manners. You're interrogating the wrong man, Dougherty. And you're forgetting your rank."

"I'm sorry, sir. Would you like a belated salute?"

"Fuck yourself."

Bullock stomped back into the living room. Dougherty followed at his heels. The captain's eyes flashed around the apartment, searching for something. *His hat*; Dougherty had left it on the seat of the Porsche.

"You want me to take you back to the ship now, Captain? Or will you let me send out for a pizza so we can talk some more?"

"I've nothing to say. I may have had some differences with my wife, but I'm as appalled as you about what happened. It was horrible, unbelievable."

"You'd have been more appalled had we permitted you to venture into that bedroom."

"Look, Commander, I don't need to hear about it again. All I want is to get my carrier back out to sea and get on with my job. I still have a deployment to complete." Bullock hesitated. Small beads of perspiration began to form on his forehead as he glared at Dougherty. "Your work is important to you, mine's important to me. But I think if you were to ask the Pentagon brass whose work is more important, they'd nod my way. Get the picture?"

"Not really." Dougherty kept his cool. "Admiral Whitney from the Judge Advocate's Office is coming in from Washington tomorrow. You'll have the opportunity to ask him that question yourself, Captain. There's nothing else you have to say to me tonight?"

Bullock lowered his head in thought, then looked up abruptly and pushed out his chin. "Yes. I need this case solved as much as you do, Lieutenant Commander. Even more so. So I'll give you a tip. Stop trying to do everything yourself. Get tough with your subordinates. Use them. You'll solve this crime by exacting the same kind of discipline I get on my ship. Don't be afraid to get pushy, you know what I mean? Peak performance won't be good enough; you'll have to go beyond that. This killer sounds clever, so we'll all have to go him one better, right? How about it, Dougherty? Do you think you're clever enough?"

"Don't fret over it, Captain. A challenging investigation to me is like a history-making flight to Lindbergh."

Bullock stood there, nodding to himself. "You don't say. A substitute on your part, a fantasizing for naval pilot's wings, possibly?"

"Maybe. But your eager carrier birds average ten years in the service before burn-out sets in. I'm bent on a long-term career and a comfortable retirement."

"Climbing for the stars, then."

Dougherty shrugged. "Down the road, why not? What about yourself? I assume you're about due."

"Assume? We don't assume anything in this man's Navy." Bullock looked at him sideways. "No, I'll take that back. You can correctly *assume* that nothing's going to come between me and that promotion to rear admiral lower-half. Not you, not this ill-timed homicide, and certainly not any rabble-rousing sailor named Gecko Corman. Do we understand each other, Lieutenant Commander?"

Dougherty felt dismayed and irritated at the same time. He still had a sea bag full of questions to put to Bullock, but obviously this wasn't the time and place. The captain would only continue to blow smoke.

"Damn it, where's my cover?" Bullock barked the question as he straightened his tie.

Dougherty gestured toward the door. "In the car. I'll drive you back to the base. Captain, you haven't asked about your dog."

"Fuck the dog."

~~~~~~11

Aviation Boatswain's Mate First Class Eddie "Gecko" Corman didn't particularly like his lizard-like nickname, but it had caught on in junior high, and he'd been unable to shake it. Even his parents insisted on calling him Gecko. Sitting at the family dining table, for the first time the young sailor was unable to enjoy his mother's home cooking.

No one had exchanged a word for the past five minutes, not even his usually talkative little sister. Gecko didn't question the rest of the family's silence; he merely used the interlude to reflect on the escalating problems that brought him running home. He thought about his alto saxophone, now at the bottom of the sea, and he thought about life aboard the *Abraham Lincoln*. Even with the cable television, library, workout facilities, and the assortment of war games in the crew's lounge, there was a frustrating, gray quality about carrier duty. Gecko was glad he had some musical ability with the horn; it made life aboard the ship a little easier and more pleasurable, not only for himself, but for anyone else who liked jazz.

Apart from the music, Corman worked long hours on the flight deck and had made few friends. He readily admitted to a habit of embellishing stories, and because of this, most of the other sailors avoided him, calling him a bullshitter. Gecko had also been in a little trouble with drugs at one time, and his superiors were still suspicious of him. Twice he'd been called before Captain's Mast, the last incident resulting in a Summary Court-Martial and probation.

Gecko enjoyed playing his sax in groups, solo, or whenever; he wasn't a virtuoso, but he wasn't a slouch either. There were plenty of guitars aboard the carrier, but his horn was different; it had a haunting, romantic quality the sailors and flight crews liked. All, apparently, except one individual who hated not only the sound but Corman himself. Gecko was positive the attempt on his life had not been mistaken identity. Nor was it just a *goddamn drunken stunt*, as the ship's master-at-arms had implied. No, there was far more to it than that. Gecko felt trapped.

He recalled the terror-filled incident clearly enough; he'd damn-well remember it the rest of his life. He'd sought out his favorite place on the carrier to practice his horn, a small catwalk-like extension that hung out over the stern of the ship two levels below the cantilevered flight deck. Finding spare hours to play music wasn't easy for a yellow shirt. When the ear-splitting, acutely dangerous work of playing musical chairs with aircraft on deck was concluded, all most sane crewmen wanted to do was crash in the sack. Gecko handled his built-up tension in another way—music. Until that night he'd almost been hurled overboard with his saxophone.

It had been just after eleven on an overcast, moonless night, the kind even the gung-ho fighter pilots dreaded. The *Abraham Lincoln* was bound for San Diego, some four hundred miles out of Pearl Harbor when the trouble occurred back on the stern. Gecko had been playing "Sentimental Baby" in the style of Frankie Trumbauer, staring moodily out into the darkness at the ship's churning, phosphorescent wake.

First there'd been the odd, uncomfortable feeling that he was no longer alone on the catwalk, that he had company nearby in the pitch blackness. An uncomfortable premonition told him to stop playing. Dropping the sax on its sling, he turned. He heard slurred words: "You blackmailing, two-faced, son-of-a-bitch." Gecko jumped sideways as a wooden object—apparently a baseball bat or a cane—clunked into the bulkhead where he'd been standing a moment before. The weapon was swung again, this time clipping him on the shoulder before striking the railing.

Gecko was confused and frightened, but he immediately fought back with a fury of a gamecock. His adversary, who reeked of alcohol, was muscular and very strong. The saxophone was torn away from Gecko's neck and hurled overboard, then he, too, was wrestled up and partially over the rail. Only by cursing and kicking his angry assailant in the groin was he able to gain a precious moment of time and a better footing on deck. Gecko had fought to maintain his precarious purchase on the rail with one hand, while clawing at the attacker's neck and shirt with the other. When he tore a section of collar away, a piece of metal came with it—an officer's rank insignia! A *silver bird!* Before Gecko managed to recover from his amazement, he'd heard voices approaching from a nearby companionway. The blurred form who had nearly overpowered him suddenly let go and stumbled off in the darkness.

"Why are you sweating, Gecko?" His mother's voice from across the dinner table. She added firmly, "And what's that in your hand?"

Very slowly, one finger at a time, he opened his clenched fist. A week had passed and he still carried the memento everywhere. *The evidence!* Everyone at the table stared at the polished silver eagle with its outstretched wings. *Go for crow, set your goals high,* they told him when he enlisted in the Navy. Gecko felt a twinge of anger. His stern-faced father, who sat opposite him, gestured impatiently with his open hand. Gecko reluctantly handed Barney Corman the metal insignia.

The two other family members at the candlelit table looked on in stupefied silence. His mother Naomi wore her inevitable halo of innocence, while sister Meg seemed lost in some distant reverie. Gecko wondered again why it had taken a dozen years for his parents to have a second child. With a span of only five or six years, Meg might have been a useful pal instead of an annoying little gnat.

Gecko watched his grim-faced father turn the grade insignia over in his hands. Barney Corman was a hulk of a man, a truck owner-operator who took immense pride in his heavily-chromed and polished rig. He'd never encouraged Gecko to join the Navy, but he hadn't objected, either. Skyrocketing insurance rates, higher maintenance costs, and increasing competition made the highway freight business shakier than ever and he wasn't sure if that's what he wanted for his son twenty years down the road or not. Gecko's four years in the Navy would give father and son both room to breathe and think about the future.

Barney Corman was six-three with biceps the size of cantaloupes. He was an ox of a man, the kind who monopolized elevators and in crowds was like a boulder splitting rapids. Gecko had always resented turning out to be such a runt by comparison. For years he'd wondered if he were adopted, despite the birth certificate his doting mother repeatedly flashed in his face. He and the old man did have one thing in common: elongated ears. From the front they both looked a little like basset hounds.

Gecko stared at the food on his plate that had turned cold. He now wondered if he'd done the right thing, bringing his parents into his troubles. Especially since he couldn't tell them the *entire story*, certainly not what happened in Hong Kong. He really hadn't wanted to come running home for sanctuary, but there was no place else to go.

Across the table, his father grunted and shook his head in disbelief. The familiar high color consuming those chunky cheeks meant an angry lecture was forthcoming. Gecko wondered how far he could trust his father. Would the short-fused Barney Corman compound an already difficult problem by doing something crazy? Maybe Gecko shouldn't have rented the car and driven up to Downey after all; he might have been better off hiding out in some remote desert fleabag. Anything, even digs like that creepy Bates Motel in *Psycho* would feel downright comfy and safer than another night aboard the ship.

Naomi Corman sighed and said to her husband. "Barney, please. Your blood pressure doesn't need this kind of excitement."

"Look at this," the big man sputtered, holding up the metal

eagle to the candlelight. "You tell me I should relax when my kid is assaulted by some goddam Navy brass? For Christ's sake, you know what this rank means? Probably the carrier's skipper, that's what."

Gecko lowered his head. "I can't be positive."

"What the hell you sniveling about, can't be positive? You lying to me again, you little bastard?"

Gecko shook his head. The only sound in the room was his mother's foot nervously tapping under the table. She said impatiently, "Barney, watch your language in front of Meg."

Gecko looked at his little sister, the only one at the table to have cleaned her plate. Despite the intrigue and ominous nature of the conversation since his arrival, she appeared to be suffering pangs of boredom. Abruptly, she asked, "What's for dessert, Mom?"

Naomi paid her no attention. Barney looked at his wife with impatience then turned back to Gecko. "Look, kid, let's backtrack a minute. You claim they had some kind of kangaroo court on the ship, and they laughed at you?"

"No. Not exactly. They call it a Captain's Mast. The CO suggested I was hallucinating again."

"What's the skipper's name?"

"Bullock. Captain Swain Bullock. And the XO fell into line, backing him up. They thought I was spaced out on dope."

Gecko tried to avoid his father's scowl. His mother sipped her wine, gazing at him critically over the top of the glass. "I don't understand this *hallucinating again*."

"I do," Barney interjected. "The old marijuana charge keeps rearing its ugly head, that's what." He turned back to Gecko. "I told you when you went in, I told you when they first called you on the summary, and I'm telling you again now. Keep your nose clean. No coke, no grass, understand? What do I have to do? Run you down with my Mack to get it to sink in?"

Meg giggled and tapped Gecko's arm. She gloated, "My teacher says people who take dope are lower than the stripes on the highway."

"Not funny, Meg. Dry up, okay?" Gecko suddenly felt infected by a kamikaze anger. The family wasn't helping; instead they were smothering him with nasty *old business*, an uncomfortable past that hung as heavy on him as a pea coat in the tropics. He looked from one parent to the other. "Listen to me! You're both treating me like a damned delinquent. I wasn't hallucinating, okay? They gave me a urine test, and I came out clean. I'm off the drugs, and I've lived up to the terms of the summary's probation."

His father stared one more time at the cast metal bird in his hand, then flipped it back across the table. "Tell all that to that visiting bigwig admiral tomorrow. *Jesus Christ*. What did the ship's commander say when you confronted him face-to-face with this assault crap?"

"I didn't accuse him specifically. Just said it was one of the officers. After that, Bullock called me a funkoff."

Gecko's mother looked at him. "A what?"

Barney interjected, "Probably an officer's candyass way of saying *fuck off*. Forget that. What did this Bullock say about the eagle?"

"I didn't bring up the rank insignia. No way. At the time, there were three men on board entitled to wear a bird. The skipper, the executive officer, and a visiting air boss. All *captains*. I was scared shitless. That's why I waited until I reached port and went in to the NIS office."

Meg looked up at him benignly. "Don't you like the skipper, Gecko?"

His father bobbed his head in agreement. "Wipe that smile off your face, kid. I was about to ask the same question."

Gecko felt cornered. He didn't dare tell his parents everything he knew about Bullock; he'd incriminate himself. Gecko decided to generalize. "The captain's a hotshot pilot turned ship jockey. He might know how to get a big nuke carrier from point A to point B without running aground, but when it comes to managing people, he's out to lunch. Most of the crew think he's a tyrant. To me, he's just an asshole."

Barney Corman leaned forward, resting both his hairy forearms on the table. "Yeah? How do you know all the men feel that way? Maybe it's just you. Like you're as disgruntled as ever."

"I just know, okay? I spent a day chauffeuring Bullock around Hong Kong." Gecko hesitated, staring at his dinner plate. "Never mind, just take my word for it. Look, I just know the sonofabitch has flipped out—like some kind of psycho, understand? All I can tell you is that I'm convinced he wants me dead. And I'm scared shitless."

It was his mother's turn to say something, anything, but all Naomi Corman could do was start to cry. Fussing with several strands of her hair, she mumbled, "Why, why?"

Barney glared at her. "No scenes, understand? If it's true, we got to find out the motivation, what's gone wrong. Let's hope the kid gets it all worked out tomorrow. If he doesn't, I sure as hell will." He turned to Gecko. "This time you show that damned eagle insignia to the top brass, understand?"

Gecko nodded.

"Good. What time's your meeting?"

"One in the afternoon."

His father sat straight up. "I'm going with you."

"Pop, don't embarrass me. Besides, it's impossible. Navy regulations."

"How much leave time do you have left?"

"Forty hours. The carrier pulls out again Wednesday."

His mother asked quietly, "Surely you're not going back to sea on the same boat?"

"*Ship*," Gecko corrected. Shrugging, he thought for a moment. "It's my job to roll with the doughnuts, but not if that bastard Bullock remains in command. I'll ask for a reassignment or risk U.A.—unauthorized absence."

Across from Gecko, the big trucker pushed back his chair. The floor trembled as he lumbered to his feet. "Tell them anything. Your mother's sick, and you need shore duty close-by. And don't take any Government red-tape bullshit. As for tomorrow, when you finish testifying, I want you to get your ass down to my brother's condo in Del Mar."

"Why can't I come back here? Uncle Freddy's a screaming queen."

"You may have a determined enemy on your tail, that's why. A wacko. Listen to me, kid. The first place your opponent will check out if you're on liberty or leave is right here. Take my word for it, you've got to disappear. Now that I think about it, you'd better get down to Del Mar tonight. As for Uncle Fred, he's out of town, so relax. Just make sure nobody but your mother and I know where you're holed up, okay?"

Gecko grumbled as he mulled over his options.

His father grinned for the first time. "Look, pal—if it'll help you unwind, I'll loan you my new set of golf clubs. Fred's condo is near the course. You'll love it."

Gecko felt panicky. No matter what he did the next two days, it would probably be the wrong move, especially as far as the U.S. Navy was concerned. An inner voice shouted, *this isn't the time to think about Navy careers, it's time to think about self preservation, staying alive! Get with it, nerd!* All he'd lost thus far was the alto sax, but if he made the wrong move in the wrong direction, the stakes were much higher.

Gecko climbed to his feet and looked wearily at his father. "All right, I'll go along with it. Now do me a favor, and let's change the subject for a few minutes?"

Naomi Corman heaved a sigh of relief. "I'd love to," she beamed.

He smiled back at her. "Let's adjourn to the other room. I brought some gifts back from China."

The presents—Chinese embroidered silk robes for his mother and sister and a Rolls Royce *Spirit of Ecstasy* hood ornament for his father's automobile mascot collection—at least put an upbeat mood to the evening. His father opened the glass cabinet in the den and put the new mascot on the shelf in a place of prominence. The dusty collection, Gecko noticed, hadn't grown at all since he'd joined the service. He wondered if his father had tired of the hobby.

"Wanted one of these silver ladies for years," the older man finally acknowledged. "When I started collecting mascots, the kleptomaniacs were all convinced the Rolls hood ornaments were made of genuine sterling silver."

"No such luck, Pop. Stainless steel. I've been reading up on the company."

"Fine. But where'd you get it?" Barney asked sharply.

Gecko avoided his father's eyes. "Easy, man. A sailor acquaintance on the ship—I traded my portable radio." The lie had rolled out easily enough.

"You didn't question him regarding its source, I suppose?"

"*Source*? Oh yeah, sure. He told me a fabulous yarn about the mascot."

Both parents stared at him with impatience.

Gecko slowly went on: "*Spirit of Ecstasy* is Rolls Royce's greatest asset. A dude named Charles Sykes designed it, using a kinky lady friend as a model. Word has it she hated to wear clothes."

Naomi pirouetted in her new Chinese robe. "How convenient for the automaker. Always a woman behind a talented man." She giggled.

Gecko sneered. "Uh-huh, sure. She drowned during the war. A passenger on a British ship torpedoed by a U-boat."

His mother stopped prancing, the delight vanishing from her face like a snuffed match.

The family meeting finally dispersed, and Gecko was glad to seek out the privacy of his old bedroom. He showered, changed into fresh civilian clothing and a pair of comfortable Reeboks, then took time out to peruse a new musical instrument catalog. An hour later he was ready for the road.

Gecko loaded his duffel along with his father's golf clubs into the car trunk, then went back to the front porch to bid his parents goodbye. They all lingered on the steps.

"Call us as soon as you get away from those investigators," Barney growled. Gecko's mother kissed him three times, but his little sister quickly disappeared back into the TV room.

Feeling a little down, Gecko walked down the familiar cracked sidewalk to where he'd left the rental Chevy in the street. He stumbled in the darkness at curbside, once more cursing the city for its lack of adequate street lighting in the neighborhood. As a kid he'd sprained an ankle on the same curb. Starting the car, he glanced back to the porch one more time, but his parents had turned off the porch light and gone inside.

Gecko wondered if he was doing the right thing, leaving here and holing up in his uncle's condo in Del Mar. It was a two hour plus drive, and he'd get in late, but at least he'd be closer to his appointment tomorrow out at North Island. All Gecko could do now was keep his fingers crossed and hope the Pentagon people would show up for the hearing. Lieutenant Commander Dougherty had warned that flag officer schedules were unpredictable and subject to sudden change. At least when the ordeal was over, Gecko could lose himself on the golf course.

The Old River School Road was dimly lit, and the traffic was sparse. Gecko decided to pull over and use the rental sedan's overhead light to check out the freeway map his father had given him. He was familiar enough with southbound I-5, but he needed to make sure of the Del Mar offramp outside San Diego. Gecko edged the car over to the apron, braked, and shoved the Chevy's automatic transmission into park.

He was about to reach for the glove compartment when he was surprised by a sudden blur, a thin object hurtling down over his head. At the same instant there was a shifting noise in the back seat. It was impossible to determine what was happening, no time for anything at all! Before he cry out, a length of thin nylon rope had quickly closed around his throat. Two powerful hands cinched it tighter and tighter, then twisted at the base of his neck.

Gecko felt himself pulled back, downward, his spine burrowing into the foam rubber seat. His hands flailed uselessly and his Reeboks chattered on the floorboards. He could feel his eyes bulging from their sockets, and he needed air desperately. Then he wanted to vomit. Finally, in his last seconds of consciousness, he realized he'd never again perform either of those functions. The garrot was all too lethal.

~~~~~~ 12

The floors squeaked and the view from her veranda didn't favor the ocean and the famed Point Loma sunsets, but Pamela was blissfully content. Her room faced east and looked out on a panorama of city lights mirrored on San Diego Bay. Pamela didn't care if the accommodations were second or third best, she still felt sure this was paradise. The Hotel del Coronado had cast its fabled spell on her. She'd paid the difference beyond her official Government per diem allowance to book a room at this Victorian palace, convinced the visit would be worth every last penny. To stay here was a dream she'd had since adolescence, an on-again, off-again fantasy out of *The Great Gatsby*. Still, it didn't seem quite right holing up here alone with only a briefcase full of FBI paperwork for company. It would have been nice to share the experience.

Staring out at the night skyline, Pam tried to avoid thinking of the naval base murder, the investigation that would now keep her in this city longer than she'd intended. She missed this balmy-weathered, kicked-back place and the six years she'd remained here after graduating from college. Somehow home really wasn't Los Angeles, the urban stress of the Westwood area and her anthill apartment building within walking distance of UCLA. Home was still her parents' fireplace hearth back in Teaneck, New Jersey. But that was stretching it a long way back. Reflecting on her cross-country transition, it seemed to have taken forever to stop rolling the damned r's. Last Christmas in Teaneck her plumber-father was convinced she sounded like a foreigner—"Like one of those slick guides at Universal Studios or Disneyland." She wasn't quite sure what he meant by that. The family had damn near disowned her when she'd changed her name from Bonagofski to Bonner.

Pamela wondered about her cat back in Los Angeles, how it

would survive the neighbor's care during her extended absence. The intelligent, good-humored Abyssinian had cost her an arm and a leg, and she prayed it didn't go bonkers from loneliness.

Inevitably, as she knew it would, Pam's mind returned to the North Island homicide and what little she'd accomplished in the investigation thus far. *How many hours had it been?* Rape was supposed to be her specialty, but that element in the crime had yet to be resolved. As for the interviews, the neighbors had provided some interesting leads that bore checking out. Marvin and Arthel Browne, however, had proved more murderously annoying than productive. At least the booze had loosened up Cora's tongue.

Pam smiled to herself, thinking that if Maxine Bullock were still alive, her ears would be ringing. The most curious statement to bubble out of Cora Browne was a reference to her daughter having an abortion last year. This was odd, since Todd Dougherty had learned earlier that the Bullocks wanted children but were unable during some thirteen years to conceive.

The tale of Maxine's loneliness that Pamela had gleaned from Cora Browne was probably typical of many Navy wives. For a score of years Maxine Bullock had followed her husband around the world, meeting him whenever possible at whatever port he put into long enough for liberty. Rio, Hong Kong, Naples, Honolulu no longer meant anything to her. Instead of trailing her fingers in the waters of the Blue Grotto or reading romance novels in front of the Moana in Waikiki, Maxine apparently found deja-vu in the bottle and encounter sex. A woman could explore just so many flea markets while waiting for her husband to get off work in a foreign city.

Pamela had been glad to get away from the Windemere Glen RV Park. The Browne family, like many red-necks, was self-serving, paranoid, and completely void of compassion. Toward the end of the interview, Cora had begun alternating back and forth between crying jags and cursing her son-in-law. Her profanity and compulsive tippling had given Pam a twinge of anxiety. Pamela put the late-afternoon encounter out of her mind.

Stepping away from the hotel window, she went to the phone and tried Todd Dougherty's Mission Beach number again. Still no answer. She tried the office, and a Navy answering exchange took her message. "No, it's not an emergency, operator. Just have him call me when it's convenient."

Pam headed for a high-back wicker armchair, plopped on its blue paisley cushion, and opened her memo pad. Before she could begin reviewing the day's notations, the phone rang. She was on top of it right away but let it finish a third ring before picking up the receiver.

"Pamela? This is Todd."

"Good. I've been trying to reach you."

"Sorry, I was playing chauffeur. Our obdurate skipper friend needed a lift back to his ship."

"He's sober now?"

"Yes, thank God. I'm downstairs on the lobby phone. You had chow yet?"

"An hour ago. I stopped at a drive-in."

"You mind having company up there? We need to talk."

Pam hesitated. "It can't wait until morning? I'm a little bushed."

There was a long, uncomfortable silence. Pamela hated it when people left silent gaps in phone conversations; dead air had an awkward ambiguity and made her squirm. "Todd, are you there?"

"Yes. At least let me buy you a nightcap."

"I'm not thirsty."

"Loosen up, working girl. Sometimes it's good for the spirit to dance in the rain."

Pam exhaled sharply. "Look, I don't need advice. One drink, all right? I'll meet you downstairs in the bar. Give me ten minutes."

He hung up. She genuinely liked Dougherty. Beyond his initial iciness and aloof manner, there was a tenacious enthusiasm about the handsome lieutenant commander. No, *capricious* enthusiasm was a better term. Todd was caught up in Navy bureaucracy and up to his ears in pursuing gold stripes, but he also had a rebellious, independent streak she liked. He appeared to be the kind of guy who put his own personal touch on things, regardless of the ever-present, convoluted regulations. *The book*, as most Navy men called it. As an FBI agent and Government employee herself, she had plenty of her own red tape to wade through.

She wondered what kind of people—female and male—the closed-mouthed Dougherty hung out with in his off time. At least the hibernation following his divorce appeared to be over. She'd met him three times before this case but had never been to his apartment or met any of his cronies. He'd made a play once, but at the time she'd been seeing the would-be writer, Leonard, on a steady basis.

All Todd Dougherty had told her then was that he collected art—etchings, no doubt—and played a halfway serious game of golf. Like another auto freak she'd known, Dougherty had taken his Porsche 944 up to Bob Benderon's track in northern California to learn high-speed driving, but he'd never tried competitive racing or played around with the car rally crowd. He was five years older now. She idly wondered what difference five years would make in how a man treated his toys—women included.

They found a quiet table in the corner of the Prince of Whales Room. Dougherty was hungry. The kitchen was still open so he ordered a chicken pasta salad and a glass of blush wine. The waiter came back almost immediately with both, praising the house wine a little pompously. Pamela didn't catch the brand name; she could care less about gourmet fare tonight. Dougherty did talk her into a coffee laced with Grand Marnier. She sipped it slowly and watched him eat.

He smiled back at her enigmatically. "Have you changed your opinion of the late Mrs. Bullock?"

"I was brought up to discuss *pleasant* things at the table. If etiquette's not a good enough reason to bypass the subject, consider the Latin phrase, *Mortius nii nisi bonum*."

Dougherty gave her a quizzical look. A spiral of rigatoni dangled from the fork he held in midair.

Pam smiled and explained softly, "Say nothing but good about the dead." She purposely steered the conversation to the very much alive Captain Bullock, and they began comparing notes on his background. Unfortunately—perhaps unavoidably—the dialogue kept drifting back to the captain's wife. Pamela put her squeamishness aside and told Dougherty everything he wanted to know about her research on the dead woman.

He was surprised to hear about Maxine's abortion and took his time explaining why. "The captain wanted kids. At least that's what he told his executive officer, a Captain Thorndike. Bullock once also complained that his wife couldn't conceive. Apparently, from what Cora Browne told you, that's a bold-faced lie. And Bullock's medical records tend to back up Cora's story."

Pam raised an eyebrow. "I haven't had a chance to go over the medical end of it."

"You want the nitty-gritty now?"

"I've given up on table manners. If it's pertinent, proceed."

Dougherty wiped his lips with a napkin and fortified himself with a long sip of wine. "Six years ago, when Bullock was still wearing oak leaves, he had a benign tumor removed from his testicles." Dougherty reached for the paper coaster under her drink. "Loan me your pen and I'll draw you a picture."

"That won't be necessary, Todd. Just keep talking."

"Bullock recovered from the surgery and was given thyroid extract for general glandular stimulation. Apparently there was no improvement in the viability of his sperm so we can assume the tumor did permanent damage. Right?"

"Not necessarily. What about mental stress, emotional disturbance as underlying factors?"

Dougherty shook his head. "If he consulted a psychiatrist, it's not in the record. He'd have done so outside the Navy."

Pamela thought for a moment. "I think you should know that the Bullocks did have arguments over impotence. They apparently blamed each other."

"Maxine's parents told you that?"

"No. One of her neighbors. Maxine liked to gab over the backyard fence."

"What does all this prove? We're still in the pits."

"Todd, the carrier's executive officer—this Captain Thorndike—did he say anything else?"

"That among the men Bullock is a needler, first class. He sweats perfection and demands the same or better from others. More often than not he avoids Officer's Mess, preferring to eat alone. On the bridge he's often petty, and he seems to purposely keep his subordinates from getting to know him."

"A loveable type." Pamela exhaled slowly and sipped her spiked coffee. "And when all this perversity is compounded, it makes cramped shipboard living even more unbearable, correct?"

"Sailors get used to physical discomfort. One more thing. Although the XO considers Bullock an odd duck and unpredictable, curiously enough, he'd still give up an arm for him."

"So much for loyalty being blind. I'm surprised Thorndike talked to you."

"Pam, I suggest you forget Bullock. You're barking up the wrong tree. The factors that do fit are flukes."

She smiled at him. "We can analyze statistics later. Acute paranoids operate on fear and emotion, Todd. Their positions are arrived at independent of logic, no matter how formidable the data."

They were both talking so fast Dougherty had difficulty finishing his salad. When he almost choked on a piece of chicken breast, Pamela pushed a water goblet toward him. He took the drink, swallowed quickly, and said to her, "Captain Bullock might be paranoid, and he may even be an unbearable egocentric, but I'll stake my career that he's not a cold-blooded killer."

"Ahhhh. A rush to judgment." Pam shrugged. "If you're

making a case for the Navy, Commander, I suggest you hold off until our facts are better documented. If it's Swain Bullock you're defending, are you admitting that the killing was a one-time incident, just a crazed act of passion? What if this is only part of the picture, one in a series of killings? I may come off like a jaded old broad, but my scare index on this one is high. Very high."

He looked at her seriously. "Fine, Ms Bonner. You're so keen on *what ifs*. Similar crime patterns can be *traced*. That's the FBI's job, not mine."

"We've already begun. I'll have the domestic end of it by noon tomorrow. Our contact with Interpol is shaky, so that trace will take time. But I intend to check out every port the *Abraham Lincoln* has visited since Bullock took over the command."

"That was the day the carrier was commissioned." Dougherty pushed away his plate of salad. The chicken and broccoli were gone, but half the pasta remained. He checked his watch then stared at her expectantly.

She quickly asked, "The conversation's spoiled your appetite?"

Dougherty looked at her coolly. "No, I'm trying to cut back." He signaled the waiter for the check.

Pamela nodded approvingly. She liked men who watched their waist. "Maybe we're lucky this kind of thing doesn't happen more often."

"What's that supposed to mean?" He looked at her dubiously.

She shrugged. "Well, think of it. A planetary patina of trillions of cells, billions of years old. The few that go astray, screw up, to this extent seem minutely insignificant."

Dougherty stared at her as if she'd suddenly cracked. "Unless you're the unlucky victim." He reached into his jacket pocket. "You need something to read before hitting the pillow tonight?" He handed her a pocket book with a shiny, explicit cover featuring a scantily-clad dominitrix and a coil of rope.

Startled, Pam stared at the title. *Frauleins in Bondage*.

Dougherty grinned and explained, "It's evidence from the crime site, so you'll have to return it tomorrow. Don't worry, we've already documented two sets of prints from the cover. One set belonged to the victim, Maxine Bullock."

Her pulse quickened. *Another lead*. "Stop jacking me around, Todd. Where did you find it?" She noted that on the inside of the cover someone had scribbled PROPERTY OF P. J.

"It was under the bloody mattress."

Pamela stared numbly at Dougherty as he got up from the table. He said to her, "Sorry, I'm a little bushed. If you're not inviting me up to spend the night, I'll go crash at home. I not only have this confusing case to face tomorrow, but a crotchety Admiral from the Pentagon to confront as well."

After bidding Dougherty good night, Pam took the porno paperback up to her room. How viable a lead was it? If Captain Bullock in fact slayed his wife, why all these grim theatrics? The record on the turntable, the powerful firecracker mutilation— nothing made sense yet, but Pam had a feeling there was a well-conceived, deliberate plan. Most rapists and serial murderers don't just choose their victims at random.

Pamela finally crawled into bed—not with the crudely illustrated paperback Dougherty had given her, but with a handful of three-by-five memo cards she planned to use for her upcoming lecture tomorrow at UC La Jolla. She'd given the same speech to a women's group several months earlier, but some modifications were now in order, especially after today's screaming headlines about the North Island murder-mutilation and her involvement in the investigation. Pam made some quick memos on several of the cards then reviewed them all again. She finally put the speech aside and dozed off.

Several hours later a nightmare brought Pamela bolt upright in bed. In the frightening dream, she'd gone to select wallpaper for her L.A. apartment only to find every page in the sample book smeared with blood. In the identical gory pattern she'd seen spattered across the walls of Maxine Bullock's bedroom!

Pam tried to get back to sleep but couldn't. Tossing fitfully, a thought came to her. She turned on the lamp beside the bed and without bothering to check the time, phoned Todd Dougherty. After a dozen rings he answered in a sleepy, unfriendly voice. "Yeah?"

"Todd, we need to talk."

"At this hour? Go back to sleep."

"No. I have an idea."

"I'm impressed, Ms Bonner, but tell me about it in the morning." A couple of coughs, followed by, "For God's sake, it's a quarter to four."

"That's it, don't you understand?" She sat back against the pillow. "It's what I want to tell you. In Scandinavia, they speak of the *hours of the wolf*. It's the wee time of the morning—after midnight."

"Pamela, what the hell are you talking about? You on loco weed?"

"In folklore, it's the time when your phobias sneak up on your subconscious dreads. When the ghosts of the past wreck your sleep. Listen, Todd, I have some thoughts. The record left at the crime site . . ."

"Pam!"

"The lyrics to the music were based on the wild imaginings of the *Inferno*. The Midnight Admirals rendition may have been a put-on, but the killer had to find a message there."

"Pamela, I'm too sleepy for a medieval lecture. Save it until tomorrow morning."

Ignoring him, she went on. "Dante's been called a long-faced poet of the graveyard, but there's a definite structure to his work. I think we should pursue it." Pam pressed an ear to the receiver, waiting for Dougherty's reaction. She listened a long time before deciding that he'd hung up and gone back to sleep.

 13

The trunk of the rented Chevette was too small, so Corman's body had to be crammed behind the front seat. Steelbinder drove the twelve miles from Downey to Long Beach very carefully, keeping under the speed limit. He'd schemed too long to have everything spoiled now by a minor traffic violation. Steelbinder knew the area well enough, for he'd lived in Long Beach with his grandmother when she'd moved here from Baltimore. *After his mother had been committed for the final time*.

He shivered, not from anxiety or fear of being apprehended, but because the night had turned out surprisingly cool. He'd forgotten how crisp southern California nights could occasionally be in the fall.

Steelbinder suddenly remembered Gecko's small duffel in the back seat. Deciding to check it out for a sweater or jacket, he pulled off into a shopping center and drove around the back of a supermarket. He parked in the darkness by a trash bin, turned on the maplight, and rifled through Corman's bag, carefully noting the contents. Discovering a Navy regulation undershirt and pair of shorts with Corman's name in indelible ink, Steelbinder quickly tore off the markings; he'd flush these scraps of cloth down a toilet later. He also found a familiar, incriminating photo, which he promptly tucked in his shirt pocket. Nothing else in the small duffel interested him except for the folded, bleached-out Levi jacket. He noted that it, too, following Navy regulations, was name-tagged with bold, indelible ink. *Relax, Steelbinder. Put the damn thing on.* Just wear it back to the ship, and leave it in Corman's locker. You have the key. The jacket was too tight for his muscular shoulders, but at least he stopped shivering.

Steelbinder had almost forgotten the golf clubs. He couldn't leave them in the car. The expensive, handsomely-matched set sorely tempted him, but he flung them into the dumpster, along with what remained in Corman's duffel. He hid the items from prying eyes with some spoiled produce and several cartons.

Steelbinder climbed back into the car and drove the remaining two miles to the funeral parlor where he'd worked part-time during his senior year in high school. Levin Brothers Mortuary did a lot of advertising on billboards and the back of city buses. Big on cremations and budget-priced burials at sea, the stucco-fenced facility occupied almost half a block in an industrial area just off Long Beach Boulevard.

Steelbinder checked his watch under the glare of the beach city's distinctive yellow street lights. It was almost ten-thirty, and he knew the only one on duty at the mortuary at this hour would be a live-in college student who doubled as guard, telephone monitor, and companion to the current inventory of deceased.

Gecko Corman's body had to disappear quickly and permanently. Had there been more time, Steelbinder might have ventured out to a remote spot in the Mojave Desert and let the scavenger birds, coyotes, and ants work the corpse over. But time was a luxury he couldn't afford; he needed to return to San Diego, get back aboard the *Abraham Lincoln*, proceed with his plans. Gecko Corman was just a minor, annoying part of a grander scheme. Adolf Hitler had his supercilious master race; Petty Officer Second Class R. W. Steelbinder had a supereminent *master plan* with his own brilliant vision of the universe. Genius has its proper time and can never be denied. Indeed, his was a natural, ongoing force that could never be stopped.

Steelbinder smiled to himself. It wasn't just a matter of defeating one's enemies, but a matter of technique—*how they were defeated*. And the all-important timing! Crassus, Napoleon, Bismarck, several of our own Civil War generals, yes, even Vietnam's Westmoreland, should have recognized that, but they didn't. They weren't military geniuses at all but mere gambler-warriors. *Blunderers, buffoons*! Steelbinder had read avidly about them all, and he had been amused, though he'd found more satisfaction in watching old videotapes of the Keystone Kops.

Again he thought of Swain Bullock. The commander of the *Abraham Lincoln* had made a grave, unforgiveable error in bringing him up before Captain's Mast at the same time as Gecko Corman. Such an insult! The supercarrier captain was no leader, but a *punchinello*, just like the other military blunderers. Steelbinder was sure about that. Wasn't it the Peter Principle, where a man got promoted to the level of his own incompetence and mediocrity? Bullock was a mediocre, insecure individual who had learned to rely on a Captain Bligh facade. And Petty Officer Second Class R. W. Steelbinder, of all people, should know. As one of the ship's quartermasters, he'd observed the carrier commander often enough at close range on the bridge. *Too close.* How ironic that they should have it in for each other.

Once more Steelbinder recalled the Navy placement tests taken at the time of his enlistment, how he'd passed the ASVAB with flying colors. *Imbeciles! Why shouldn't he have*? It was more than a matter of brains; he was clairvoyant, a seer. Test scores were important to a sailor's career, and Steelbinder had specific goals. He quickly found there were only three ways to achieve them: one, become a hospital corpsman—he rather enjoyed the sight of blood. Two, be a quartermaster or navigator, taking advantage of his photographic memory and knack for numbers. Or three, try for an officer's commission through the BOOST program—an option that would mean longer military service.

Leaving the Navy with officer's stripes might mean better career opportunities in civilian life, but Steelbinder wasn't interested in long-range planning. Why should he be? He had bitten the bullet on a four-year hitch and was very close to achieving his goals. The attorneys had given him a choice: according to his mother's will, all he had to do to collect his late mother's estate was finish college or complete a hitch in the Navy. He had made a fleeting attempt at the former and been kicked out in his sophomore year, a scandal involving a rattlesnake in a women's dormitory. He was doing much better suffering through this Navy thing, with just under a year to go. It was a stupid legacy, and he detested its provisions, but he had no choice. He would endure if his emotions didn't win out over his intellect. And if his grandfather remained in his grave where he belonged and left him alone.

Steelbinder thought about his half-ass relatives, how they'd insisted his institutionalized mother had been mad to the very end and that her will was invalid. He had threatened, cajoled, and fought for its provisions, and he had won. The others, wisely, had backed off because they were afraid of him. The legacy wasn't a fortune, but it would be a building block for the future. The two-hundred-thousand-dollar bond portfolio would be R. W. Steelbinder's alone, and his only penance was four years of *imprisonment* in the Navy.

Not such a bad sentence, he reasoned. Any man should be able to wear a hairshirt for at least four years. In the beginning, Steelbinder had hoped the military might make some unique use of his genius. It didn't work out that way at all, for they seemed afraid of his brilliance—every last one of them.

All of his Navy assignments presented no challenge and bored him. It wasn't the work Steelbinder hated so much, but the agonizing social end of it. The constant pretending, the supercilious smiles, the never-ending protocols, all tried his patience. He preferred to be silent and think, and on board a busy warship this was not always possible. His fatuous shipmates seemed to be forever running off at the mouth, either bragging or asking silly questions. Steelbinder spent countless hours in the carrier's library to avoid them. Lately, he'd turned to the classics for solace. The books were perfect company.

The rating of quartermaster called for applicants who were good at figures and level-headed. Unfortunately, the term *level-headed* to Steelbinder meant *dullard*. He was beyond level-headed, of course. Beneath his veneer of calmness there was a caldron of boiling energy; there was also a creative genius with a consummate skill for drama.

Performance! Steelbinder knew that the best actors were adept at turning theatrics on and off without anyone the wiser. *Actors are the cleverest people on earth*. They understand the magic of manipulation better than any other human being. Only a fool should trust them. So warned Grandfather Gerald some eighteen years ago. It still made wonderful sense.

R. W. Steelbinder and the captain were both dependent on facades but in different ways. Swain Bullock's facade, however, was about to undergo a major facelift. Their hair being a different color had at first presented a problem, but Steelbinder had overcome that hurdle easily enough. A little stumbling and fast sleight-of-hand while at the ship's barber at the same time as Bullock remedied that situation. He didn't have many strands of the captain's curly red hair stored away in the plastic box, but there was enough for what lay ahead.

Steelbinder put Swain Bullock out of his mind and glanced at the body in the back seat, wondering how long it took for rigor mortis to set in. It was a shame that Gecko Corman had to die, for he had talent; his soothing saxophone had a narcotic effect on the carrier's crew. It was unfortunate the meddlesome aviation boat-swain's mate knew so much and had complicated matters. Corman might have been coerced into keeping silent for the rest of his Navy hitch, possibly even for years afterward, but eventually he'd make a slip of the tongue or purposely confess everything— possibly in some fit of remorse. No, Steelbinder didn't dare take the chance. Too much was at stake.

The mortuary was on a side street, and it was deserted. Steelbinder climbed out of the car and hurried up to the familiar pink stucco building. A service door, tucked inside a Spanish portico, was well lit and equipped with a buzzer and speaker-phone. When he nudged the button, a fuzzy voice answered his summons immediately. "Yes? Who's there?"

Steelbinder didn't recognize the voice. He wasn't even sure if the sibilant query came from a man or a woman. Leaning close to the speaker, he said with mock authority, "Oak Hills Mortuary. I'm a little early, but you should be notified by phone shortly. One of our clients changed her mind and wants her late husband handled in your shop."

"What? You've got a hearse out there?"

He thought a moment, then continued to fabricate: "Yes. And I'll need help bringing the merchandise inside."

Moments later the door opened. Steelbinder no longer stood on the stoop with an air of expectancy. Now he was pressed against the stucco wall, close beside the entry.

The night attendant was new, a woman he'd never seen before. Steelbinder was surprised and felt cheated; he also felt a strange, unexplainable anger. He brought the tire iron down on the unsuspecting woman's skull with a special vehemence. The sound was like a door slamming on a carton of eggs.

He didn't wince, having honed himself to this kind of objec-tivity and emotional indifference a long time ago. He promptly dragged the victim inside the building, closed the door, and rolled her over. Curious, he checked for a pulse. Zero, nothing. The woman was young but grossly unattractive, with spindly legs, undeveloped breasts, and stringy hair that needed washing. Blood ran in rivulets from her scalp, sullying the Spanish tile floor.

Steelbinder wondered what kind of man would want to screw a mud duck like this. He stood there, staring at the body for a full minute, cursing the additional inconvenience the dead woman had caused him. The original plan had been to merely sap, bind, then toss the mortuary attendant in a closet. In his haste, he'd been overzealous, and now additional arrangements would be necessary.

Quickly, Steelbinder checked out the rest of the funeral home to make sure the attendant was alone. There was a television turned down low in her room, but the rest of the familiar building was deserted and uncomfortably silent. In one of the darkened viewing alcoves, several small votive lights burned beside a closed casket.

Roscoe moved on. He found a gurney in the undertaking area and rolled it outside to retrieve Corman's body. The street was still clear in both directions.

He pushed his victim around to the rear of the building, keeping to the shadows of a long, colonnaded porch. He hurried to a separate structure set back from the others. Fumbling with several keys on the attendant's ring, he finally found the right one. Steelbinder rolled the gurney inside the crematorium chamber, turned on the overhead light, and surveyed his surroundings. The modern, spotless facility didn't look foreboding at all, but he suddenly felt like a trustee at Auschwitz. Roscoe smiled to himself. It wasn't an entirely unpleasant feeling.

How difficult would it be to operate a crematorium furnace himself? It had been several years since he'd watched the mortuary's technicians perform the task. Would he remember? The room, lined with light blue industrial tile, had two brick-encased ovens along the end wall. Steelbinder examined them methodically; he knew the modern retort and pulverizing process would take around three hours to turn Corman's body to dust. There was even a viewing port to monitor the results if he wished. No, he didn't have time to wait around.

Opening the cast-iron door, he studied the gas jets along the sides of the furnace. Thankfully, the ignition, temperature controls, and timer mechanism were automatic. There were several coffin-like cardboard boxes nearby, and he struggled to dump Corman's body inside one of them. He rolled it into the oven, slid the box off the gurney, then hesitated.

"Hmmmm-nnnnn." The mud duck—was he better off having her discovered at the entry, making the intrusion look like a robbery attempt, or should she, too, conveniently disappear off the face of the earth? *Neatness, R.W.! Always keep it neat.* His grandfather's voice. Steelbinder went to retrieve the other body.

It took less than a minute to get a powerful blaze going in both furnaces. The gas nozzles gave off a deep, throaty roar. The chamber had been cool when he first entered but now it had warmed up considerably. "Goodbye, Gecko. Goodbye, Mud Duck!" he said quietly. Steelbinder smirked as he rubbed his hands before one of the ovens and stared in the viewing port. All he needed was a wingback chair, a good book, and a friendly Irish setter to complete the hearthside scene!

A dog! Peeking through one of the furnace doors at the Dante's inferno inside, his mind backtracked fifteen years. It seemed like only yesterday. Everyone called him Roscoe then. Again he saw the blazing cardboard boat on the pond, and he heard Rapunzel's wail as vividly as though the animal were before him now, inside the furnace with his enemies.

Steelbinder shook his head and backed away from the fiery orifice. As a rule he didn't like to reminisce over his childhood. Not when he was awake. The nightmares of his growing years came often enough when he was asleep.

"Don't be squeamish, Roscoe. Remember the words of Dante." Again, his grandfather's voice. Steelbinder forced himself to think about *The Divine Comedy,* trying to recall how Dante Alighieri might describe this fiery spectacle. The section of his allegory called *The Inferno* was his favorite.

"New punishment must needs by me be dirged . . ."

It was time to leave. The furnaces would turn themselves off and cool automatically. The Levin Brothers attendants would be in for a surprise when they arrived in the morning, but that surprise—mounds of ashes and a few small bone fragments— would not be traceable.

Steelbinder left the crematorium and went back to the main building. He cleaned the blood off the entry hall floor then carefully retraced his movements in the mortuary, wiping any fingerprints from everything he'd touched. Finally he turned out the lights and relocked the door.

Driving back to San Diego proved the most dangerous part of the entire operation, for Steelbinder could barely stay awake. Two and a half cups of coffee and two and half hours later he arrived at Lindbergh field and parked the Chevette in one of the rental return spaces. The airport lobby was deserted at this hour, and no one saw him drop the keys and auto rental contract into one of the express return slots. The job at last finished, he headed for the terminal entrance and grabbed a taxi.

He felt completely satisfied. It would now appear that a panicky Gecko Corman did in fact return to the San Diego area, then chickened out of appearing at this morning's inquiry at North Island. It would look like Corman had returned his rental car and taken a plane under an assumed name to destinations unknown. Flown the coop. AWOL—or in the current jargon, UA. And with this convenient disappearance, the charges the sailor was about to make against the *Abraham Lincoln's* skipper would never surface. They'd be forgotten, as well as R. W. Steelbinder's involvement.

At last Steelbinder was in his bunk on the supercarrier, dismissing the evening's events as easily as he had every other hurdle in his lifetime. The much-despised loudmouths who usually shared his compartment were on shore leave and he had the four-bunk alcove to himself. Turning on the light over his pillow, he took his time examining the photo he'd found earlier in Gecko's duffel bag.

The likeness was of his arch-enemy, Captain Bullock, with an arm around that Chinese woman in Hong Kong. *Mai Twan!* Steelbinder would never forget her name, or her expensively furnished apartment up on Victoria Peak. In fact, he felt a perverse shiver of excitement merely looking at Mai's likeness in the photo. By far, she was the prettiest and classiest of the whore-creatures. Unlike the other prostitutes, Mai Twan had put up no battle at all; she was already dead when Steelbinder had approached her. The wildcat Bullock woman was a different matter. At first Maxine had even played along with the bondage scene—until she'd discovered his true intentions. The Honolulu tart was feisty, but she'd been a pushover in the end. The incidents in New York, Los Angeles, and Miami were too long ago to remain vivid in his mind.

Steelbinder tried to focus back on the Hong Kong affair again, particularly the firecracker part, but he was too tired to get aroused. He needed to forget the past and think about the rich opportunities for the future. Turning out the bunk light, he chuckled quietly at what he had in mind for Swain Bullock and the U.S. Navy. Soon it would be time to put the photograph of the captain and the Chinese bitch to good use. Timing would be everything. The picture was like a wild card; tossing it into play would be as good as feeding Bullock to the sharks.

Steelbinder didn't ponder long about the matter, for it had been a busy day and sleep came quickly.

14

Tuesday morning broke clear and crisp at the nation's capital. Vice Admiral "Biff" McCracken glanced briefly out the bathroom window to check the weather, then mounted his exercise bike and started pedaling. He usually tried to avoid thinking about the office during his workouts, but this morning it couldn't be helped. McCracken figured his job as Deputy Chief of Naval Operations had to be one of the cushier slots in Washington—except for the two or three times a year when the public affairs staff slipped up and the shit hit the fan. Case in point, the last two days out on the West Coast—all the trouble brewing around the *Abraham Lincoln*. If ever McCracken felt like a dog-robbing flunky, the past forty-eight hours was it.

A bone was stuck in the Navy's throat, and, unfortunately, the job to remove it was McCracken's. "A potential embarrassment to the entire U.S. military," the Chief of Naval Operations had insisted. "Send a legal officer out to San Diego immediately to take care of it. No second-rater down the line; a man of ability." *Bullshit*, McCracken reflected. The CNO had continued: "Take care of it before some ambitious Congressman or junior Senator brings the embarrassing matter to the attention of the Defense Secretary."

Biff McCracken was no fool; he liked to avoid irate memos from either the Defense chief or the Secretary of the Navy. He had another pay scale to hurdle, and it was too close to retirement. There was double-trouble out on the West Coast, and if both incidents weren't brought under control immediately, they could be unmercifully exploited by the media. The local San Diego press was already making mincemeat of the North Island base homicide. The U.S. Navy didn't need a scandal aboard a supercarrier as well.

Being a part of the Pentagon brass had its compensations for McCracken, but having to face inquisitive, persistent newshounds wasn't one of them. For the entire Naval Operations staff, too often the press was an enemy task force, a formidable armada either to be circumvented or treated with a degree of respect. McCracken was glad the Navy had the agile frigate birds down at Public Affairs to run interference and set up the requisite smoke screens when necessary.

McCracken pedaled faster, glancing sideways into the full-length mirror on the bathroom wall. His scalp glistened with perspiration through his neatly trimmed, iron-gray crewcut. The Harvard Athletic Department sweat shirt felt clammy inside, and his fingers trembled slightly on the exercise bike's handlegrips, but his heart thumped as powerfully and steadily as if it were on cruise control. McCracken glanced at the digital readout. The extra two miles had been an effort, but he was determined to work off the brandy stinger he'd consumed the night before with his dessert. At last he stepped off the bike and let out a lungful of air. The machine was the latest state of the art and expensive, but it beat pounding the streets of Georgetown alongside the weirdos.

The extension phone on the wall rang before he could slip into the shower.

Activating the hands-free speaker unit, he said crisply, "Good morning. McCracken here!"

"Biff, this is George. Thank God I caught you before you left for the office."

McCracken wiped the sweat from his brow and listened expectantly. The buoyant voice on the line belonged to Rear Admiral lower-half George Whitney, from the Judge Advocate's Office. Whitney was the Navy's top trouble-shooting lawyer, McCracken's frequent golf partner, and the man he'd picked to rush out to San Diego to handle the Captain Bullock affair.

McCracken slipped out of his sweat suit and turned on the massage shower head over the tub. "Carry on, George. I'm listening. You already at the airport?" Turning up the volume of the speakerphone, he stepped inside the bronzed glass slider.

"No, I'm not."

"Anything wrong?"

George Whitney's metallic voice boomed in the tile-lined enclosure. "Have you had a chance to read the morning papers? The Post did an update on the North Island homicide."

"Not yet. What I saw last night on the network news is still sinking in. *Uncomfortably,* I might add."

"That's not why I called you, Biff. It's about my flight this morning. Sorry, but DOD has vetoed the trip. Something important has come up. You'll have to find someone else. What can I say?"

McCracken sobered. "You crawfishing on me, Admiral?"

"No. The chairman of the Joint Chiefs is calling me in on another matter."

"What's more pressing than the murder of a ship commander's wife? In the Navy's backyard, to boot."

He heard Whitney clear his throat at the other end of the line. The judge advocate finally said, "I'm a lawyer, not a detective. That NIS office on North Island is one of the most competent in the service. Mind if I ask why your sudden personal concern with the homicide? Yesterday your main reason for me making the trip was that mare's mess aboard the *Abraham Lincoln*."

McCracken's eyes were closed, his head covered with blue anti-dandruff shampoo. He sputtered, "Violence on shore, purported violence at sea. The CNO insists we look into both. My opinion is that the murder was merely one of those wrong person, wrong place, wrong time incidents. A quirk of fate."

"Sorry, Admiral, but I'm not much of a believer in either luck or fate."

McCracken wasn't listening. He blithely continued, "And as for that incident aboard the CVN-71 and the temerity of that sailor's complaint—I doubt whether I'd have given it a second glance but for the old man's insistence. The CNO runs a little scared. Me, I happen to trust Swain Bullock. Implicitly."

What McCracken should have said to Whitney, but instead purposely postponed mentioning, was that Captain Bullock was his own hand-picked man for the job on the *Abraham Lincoln*; that there wasn't a snowman's chance in hell that the skipper could have fucked up and not responded properly to a crewman's assault complaint. Or so McCracken hoped, for if he'd *miscalculated* in recommending the red-haired, hardened ship commander in glowing terms, it would be a splotch on his own judgment. Now, as Deputy CNO, he wondered if in the hours and days ahead he'd have to justify that endorsement—or would he have to do what he could to salvage Bullock's career? McCracken hoped this Aircraft Boatswain's Mate First Class Gecko Corman was hallucinating as Bullock had apparently claimed.

The speakerphone crackled again. "What's that, Admiral? All I hear is water!"

McCracken raised his voice. "I said Bullock is a tough bastard, but I trust him! Whitney, our NIS field man in San Diego. What's this honcho's name again?"

"Lieutenant Commander Dougherty. First name is Todd. On the surface, a rather arid, distant chap, but he's damned efficient. Who do you want to go out in my place, Biff?"

"I'm still thinking."

McCracken struggled to reach his feet with the bar of soap. The exercise bike might be working wonders for his ticker, but so far it had done nothing for his arthritic knees.

Whitney's voice again echoed in the bathroom. "Biff? You still there?"

"No. I was just sucked down the drain. Good sea-lawyer like you should have one of these toilet phones, Whitney. Great timesaver." McCracken thought for a moment, then again shouted above the sound of the shower. "This case, Admiral! Something about Corman's accusation baffles me. Has to be a mistake. Swain Bullock's reported to be one of the best, no holds barred. Outstanding grease marks all down the line, and he's overdue for his first star. Fact of the matter, after he delivers the *Abe Lincoln* to dry dock in Bremerton, he'll be up for battle group commander. His next step is NATO, if the Defense Secretary approves. Damn it to hell, why? Now, of all times, right out of the blue, we get this double-wammy."

"Naval Operations has its problems, I've got mine. Hell, I could have been a red-hot corporate lawyer in civilian life, owning the best part of Philly or Baltimore by now."

"We all might have done things different. Especially Captain Bullock's wife, by not answering her goddamn door in the middle of the night. Have you heard anything from the FBI? Any leads at all?"

"Easy, throttle back, Biff. Give them and the NIS some time. The body's still warm. Maybe we can postpone that San Diego hearing a couple of days until I can get away."

"The carrier goes back out to sea tomorrow," McCracken said sharply. He turned off the shower, grabbed a towel, and rubbed briskly. "Whitney, this bird who's pointing the finger—Gecko Corman. Where's he now? Still aboard the ship?"

"No. Understand he'd gone to ground, hiding out somewhere."

"*Hiding out?* What kind of military bearing is that?" McCracken grimaced and swore under his breath. "Admiral, have your secretary change that air reservation to my name. I'm going out to San Diego myself."

"That's big of you, Biff."

"Not that big. I have four days leave coming, and southern California's as good a place to spend it as here in Washington. My wife can grab a later flight and meet me in Indian Wells."

Dougherty woke earlier than usual—for the second time. First it had been Pamela disturbing him, now it was the birds. The clock radio wasn't scheduled to go off for another forty-five minutes. Dougherty stretched like a cat, sat up, and slowly shook his head. Looking outside, he saw that a *kaffe klatch* of screaming seagulls had taken over the apartment lawn. Living just off the beach had its advantages and disadvantages. Instead of setting the snooze alarm, he decided to get up and face the day early. Once awake, he liked to stay that way.

Dougherty showered and shaved, then went into the kitchen and prepared a cup of decaffeinated instant coffee. He made up his mind that if Ms. Pamela Bonagofski Bonner ever again spuriously called him at four in the morning he'd feed her piecemeal to the sharks over at Sea World. Dougherty listened to the KSDO news and traffic report as he cut an orange in quarters and poured himself a bowl of Cheerios with low-fat milk. He finished breakfast then slipped back into the bedroom and dressed in clean khakis. His shoes were already spit-shined from the night before. Dougherty's morning routine seldom varied; habitually he was out of the apartment and turning the ignition key of the Porsche less than thirty-five minutes after rolling out of the sack.

He'd almost forgotten how much additional time had been added to this schedule when there'd been a significant other to fret over. It seemed like his ex-wife had moved out light years ago and that he'd spent the better part of his life in the fast-lane singles scene. With plenty of extra time on his hands this morning, Dougherty took the long way to the base at North Island. He crept along in the Porsche but still arrived at the office a half-hour earlier than usual. He spent the time cleaning up his in-and-out box, going over yesterday's neglected mail.

At eight sharp his investigative staff and the FBI crew working on the Maxine Bullock homicide assembled in the outer office. Everyone sipped coffee. Half the group sat on top of their desks, the others in swivel chairs. Noting that the FBI woman was missing, Dougherty wondered if she'd overslept. Sol Steinberg, too, appeared to be late. Dougherty checked his watch. Annoyed, he decided to teach them both a lesson in Navy punctuality by beginning on the button without them.

Dougherty looked around the room, measuring his assembled task force for size. The team wasn't large, but each member knew well enough how to build up an information network, extend contacts, get the branches and feeder roots out there working. Meadows, the bald lab specialist, had worked with Dougherty the longest. Then there were the field operatives: Chief Warrant Tim Kelly was short and wiry with alert Irish eyes and a quick sense of humor. He and Dougherty were the only ones on the staff who wore uniforms, for NIS was primarily an undercover civilian operation. Quincy Petrich was a bulky, red-cheeked Slav who forever claimed to be on a diet but his waistline never seemed to show it. The towering, barrel-chested black man, "Duck" Harris, was a former Green Beret who could menace his adversaries by size alone.

On the FBI side, fingerprint specialist Vic Shapiro had delayed his departure back to Washington at Pamela's request. Walt Courtney, the crewcut preppie from the San Diego bureau office was new on the job and obviously eager to make a name for himself. And then there was the missing Pamela, if and when she showed her face. Dougherty felt a twang of annoyance at her tardiness.

The NIS office had one more staff member, a civilian secretary, but she wouldn't be in until nine. Myra Horn had logistical problems with a babysitter, so Dougherty had fixed it for her to work an hour later at night. Her late shift worked out well for everyone.

After Dougherty's introductory small talk, the first parry from the assembled brainstormers came from Tim Kelly. "Sir, what frail ends we do come up with point squarely at Captain Bullock. Somehow, it's almost too perfect."

"Glad we both agree." Dougherty was surprised to see Kelly without pastry in his face at this hour. Ever since they'd met, the chief warrant seemed addicted to bear claws.

Kelly continued, "I don't think any of us are ready to point a finger yet, Lieutenant Commander. But it would help if you'd fill us in on your interview with the skipper."

Dougherty thought for a moment, then decided to lay his lousy cards on the table face up. "Sorry to report that Captain Bullock's been less than cooperative. Yesterday, he had three sheets in the storm until early evening. Following that, for a hangover he had a disposition that could curdle milk. I'm trying to interrogate him, but it's not easy. The man's got a glacier-like facade that's tough to penetrate. I intend to try again today."

Quincy Petrich leaned forward. "Maybe we should let the FBI woman try to soften him up, melt that ice pack."

Dougherty shook his head. "Let her hear you talking like that and she'll soften you up." Impatiently checking his watch, he added, "Where the devil's Steinberg? Unlike Sol to be late."

Glen Meadows looked up from his coffee. "He called in from the base exchange before you convened the meeting."

"Helluva time to buy toothpaste when I call a task force together."

Duck Harris leaned forward. "I took the call. Sol said it was important, a lead involving the case." The black man withdrew a note-covered business envelope from an inside suit pocket.

Dougherty noted the new gun in Duck's waistband. The rest of the men generally carried standard service thirty-eights, but Harris preferred a .45. *A sign of the times?*

Reading his notations, Harris said, "It's only a start, but the empty black and white film carton found on the bedroom floor definitely came from a numbered lot at the BX. I figured as much when I found one of their developing envelopes in the Bullocks' garbage. The short end of it is that the film could have been purchased any time in the past six months."

Dougherty nodded to Harris. "Keep on it. What about a 35mm camera? Did one show up in the household inventory?"

"No. Only a Polaroid. An old one at that, still loaded and ready to go."

Dougherty considered this. "Photo buffs who work in black and white aren't that common. Have to be a pro or at least an advanced amateur. Keep pushing the base exchange, find a customer with a darkroom. Stay on it, Duck."

Harris shrugged. "Guns, sophisticated weapons I know like my face in the mirror, but when it comes to hobbies and creative stuff, I'm a little green. Especially photography. Maybe you want this Bonner woman to check into it. I hear she likes cameras."

Dougherty gave him an irritated look. "Maybe later. Wherever Pamela goes she kicks up a wake of little whirlwinds. Leave her out of this one for now."

FBI agent Vic Shapiro cleared his throat. "I trust, Lieutenant Commander, that's not meant as a put-down of the bureau?"

Walt Courtney looked as if he'd been about to ask the same question.

Dougherty applied a little balm. "Only being expedient, gentlemen. A matter of assignments since your fellow agent has yet to arrive. No reflection on the bureau's expertise." Dougherty heard a soft cough.

"Sorry, all of you, to be late." Smiling enigmatically, Pamela stood in the doorway. She was dressed in a forest green business suit with a beige blouse, and her hair was brushed sexily to one side, almost covering one eye. The men looked at her as she crossed the room and took the empty seat by the window.

Dougherty exhaled impatiently and turned back to Shapiro. "Now that the FBI's one hundred percent in attendance, you can begin your report, Mr. Shapiro." The fingerprint wizard wore spotless white slacks and his appearance reminded Dougherty of Rodney Dangerfield in *Caddyshack*. Dougherty had to work hard to stifle that impression and take the casually dressed investigator on a deadly serious basis.

Shapiro smiled at Pamela, ambled across the room, and tossed a manila folder on Dougherty's desk. "It's all here—the latents, the red powder report. The entire ball of wax." He returned to his seat, checking it first as if he were wary of a whoopee cushion or chewing gum. Spreading out, Shapiro let his eyes flicker back and forth between Pamela and Dougherty. "What can I say? If that porno book we found under the mattress is relevant, we're on first base; if not, we're batting zero. The records and stereo player were clean. No prints in the bedroom, not even on the spilled cologne bottle. The killer apparently kept the damned rubber gloves on all the time he was raping her. *If he raped her*, according to the forensics people. The firecracker messed up the evidence in that department." Shapiro shook his head. "Whatever, the bozo's a real flip-top. He doesn't wear a condom but screws with rubber gloves on his mitts."

Pamela shrugged with impatience, but Dougherty waited, eager for more input from Shapiro. More of what, he wasn't sure, but at this point, every last bit of fingerprint data was critical. As for speculation on the rape end of it, he wasn't about to question the expertise of the pathologists at the coroner's office. Not yet.

The FBI print specialist continued in a bland voice. "The only time he gook off the gloves was when he grabbed the struggling dog. There's a blurred partial on the collar tag and one of the valleys may give us a comparison, but it's too insignificant to hold up in court. As for the microwave, it was wiped clean. Sorry I can't be more productive."

Pamela said to her fellow agent, "Nice try, Vic."

Dougherty frowned. So much for expertise from out of town. One by one, he studied the others in the room. "Any of you ever use the sobriquet 'Cherry Bomber' with the press or any of Bullock's neighbors at the crime site?"

They all shook their heads.

Dougherty continued, "If it's speculation on the part of one reporter, that's one thing, but this is precisely the kind of investigation detail we intended to withhold. How the hell did the fact our killer plays around with fireworks leak out?"

Pamela sat forward. "The priest talked about the dog. He could have let the fireworks factor slip as well."

Dougherty saw red. "Meadows. Dammit, you were supposed to read him that clause on hardnose silence."

Glen Meadows rubbed his shiny bald head as he glanced nervously at Pamela, then back to Dougherty. "Sorry, Lieutenant Commander. No excuse. When I saw Ms Bonner talking to the clergyman in the front yard, I just figured, well, with her intensive manner and all, she was laying it on strong enough."

Pamela grinned. "Mr. Meadows, please. I think you're a lousy judge of when I'm laying it on strong. In the words of Mae West, *come up and see me sometime*. Maybe I'll show you then."

There were titters and suppressed laughter. The black man openly giggled. Fellow FBI agent Courtney said bravely, "Atta girl, Pam. Give 'em hell."

Observing the youngest member of the team, Dougherty said condescendingly, "Glad to have you aboard, Walt." Dougherty took in the others, one at a time. The chief warrant sat numbly, as if forgotten. Shapiro looked restless. Petrich vacantly stared out the window. Only Harris sat attentively. Dougherty tapped the desk with his knuckle. "No more leaks, agreed? From now on, nothing but *no comment* from anyone but myself, the base commander, or COMNAVAIRPAC Public Affairs. The gag's on, so keep it tight." Dougherty looked at Pamela. "Sorry, Pam. I hope a muzzle won't smear your lipstick."

Glaring back at him, she folded her arms in a dramatic gesture and changed the subject. "What about the refrigerator service truck and the orange Kawasaki?"

Dougherty replied, "I asked Steinberg to work on the bike angle."

Quincy Petrich suddenly came to life. Raising a finger, he

announced, "We found the refrig fixit man. If he was porking her, he didn't do it that night. He has a family, and his alibi sticks. What's more, the repairman has straight black hair."

While Dougherty pondered for a moment, Pamela asked Petrich, "How about cross-leads, mutual acquaintances?"

"Nothing. He and Maxine apparently never went out of her house. No parties, either. Just three or four afternoon quickies."

"Pretty thin," Dougherty summarized. "Next topic. Who's on top of the fireworks?"

Walt Courtney's eyes sparkled. "I'm working on that end. It was a big mother, the kind outlawed in California. An off-brand called Half-Moon. The glitch is, the product is popular in the Far East, but not ordinarily distributed in this country."

Everyone took down the fireworks manufacturer's name except Pamela, who looked like she had something to say. Dougherty nodded to her. "Go ahead, let's have it."

"I know the firecracker element has potential, but I've a hunch the two 45 RPM records are more timely leads. That Midnight Admirals release is now a special order. How many people carry around with them two identical discs—maybe even more—of a no-longer-popular record? With an obscure Italian title to boot?"

Shapiro shifted in his seat and straightened the pleat on his white linen slacks. "Hell, the sonofabitch could have a warehouse full of them for all we know. He could be a disgruntled member of the band." Shapiro looked at Pamela. "And I've got news for you. I never heard of the group."

"You've probably never heard of the Rolling Stones, Vic." With a crafty grin, she added, "The Midnight Admirals are into heavy metal. They peaked four years ago, and the word is they're trying to make a comeback. Their grotesque concerts make Ozzie Osborne look like a saint."

Meadows grunted incredulously. "I remember the outfit— with considerable distaste."

Dougherty said, "Thanks, Pam. You're doing fine. Stay with it." He looked up as the door to the outer hallway burst open. Sol Steinberg, his tan corduroy suit jacket flapping open, entered quickly with a shit-eating grin on his face. All eyes turned to him.

Steinberg said, "Pay dirt, folks. I set up a little ambush and found the man with the 90cc orange Kawasaki. His initials just happen to be P.J." Steinberg turned to Shapiro. "And he's got a set of prints that match what you picked up on that sleazy paperback."

Vic Shapiro suddenly looked a shade less grim. Pamela and Dougherty rose to their feet at the same time.

Steinberg adjusted his glasses. He read their looks of disbelief and immediately extrapolated, "A flaky character named Pip Jacobsen—a civilian worker at the Base Exchange. He was picked up late last night by the Armed Services Police. Tried to go through the barrier ribbon and sneak inside the Bullocks' living quarters—with his own key."

"Why?" Several voices at once. Pamela's was the loudest.

Steinberg went over to his own desk, its littered surface now occupied by Duck Harris's ass. Instead of rising, the black man only shrugged and slid over. Steinberg sat beside him and calmly continued, "The prisoner was booked for disturbing evidence at a crime site. Not sure if we can make breaking and entering stick since he insists Maxine Bullock sent him his own key. Jacobsen claims he has a note at home to prove it."

Dougherty had nursed his patience long enough. "Great, Sol. Good work. But did he continue talking after you read him the Miranda?"

"I couldn't shut the sleaze-ball up."

Pamela frowned with concern. "Unusual, don't you think?"

Steinberg shrugged. "The guy's a born motor-mouth. Insisted he'd only banged Maxine a couple of times, that she took him in temporarily when he had squabbles with his wife."

Pamela asked sarcastically, "Did you also ask him if he had hemorrhoids?"

Steinberg glared at her. "No. I forgot. But there's plenty of time. You want to ask him yourself?"

Dougherty grimly interjected, "Why did he go back into the house? And don't give me that *murderer always returns to the scene* bullshit."

"Jacobsen panicked when he read about the murder in the newspapers. It all ties in. Said he went back after a couple of incriminating items that belonged to him." Steinberg stiffened. "One of them, obviously, was the kinky hardcore literature with his initials boldly scrawled inside the front cover."

Dougherty asked, "And the other?"

"A pair of Nike running shoes. We apparently missed them, assuming any men's furnishings in the place belonged to Swain Bullock."

Vic Shapiro sat back, unimpressed. "Fine. What color hair does this Pip what's-his-face happen to have?"

Steinberg hesitated. Smiling awkwardly, he flipped his wrist back and forth. "It's a dirty blond, but *definitely* on the reddish side. And not exactly straight."

Dougherty nodded without enthusiasm. "Okay, Pamela and I will talk to him. The next problem is to get a blood test—*legally*."

"I've already got it. The lab will call when it's ready."

Pamela looked surprised. "Coercion, Mr. Steinberg?"

"Unnecessary. I told you—sleazy character or not, the guy was a gem when it came to cooperation."

Bullshit, mused Dougherty. For a suspect, this Pip Jacobsen was being entirely too cooperative. *It didn't fit.*

Steinberg took off his glasses and nervously polished the lens with his handkerchief. "You have to admit things are looking up—for the skipper specifically and the U.S. Navy in general."

Pamela said sourly, "That's your opinion, for what it's worth, Sol. In my book, old hell-on-the-water Swain Bullock is still prime suspect number one." Her statement hung in the room like a clothesline of tattered underwear.

The men all looked at each other uncomfortably.

Dougherty looked at her with annoyance. "Going out on the limb a little early, aren't you?"

Pamela momentarily smiled, but her face turned serious when she spoke. "Why not? And please don't get any ideas about sawing it off."

"You're wrong, lady detective, dead wrong. This character with the Kawasaki may or may not be our man, but I could spend the rest of the day coming up with reasons why Captain Bullock shouldn't be a suspect. You want me to begin now?"

Pamela backpedaled. "Lieutenant Commander, please. We're wasting time. If it will make you happier, I apologize and withdraw the precipitate personal opinion."

Dougherty felt an impotent kind of anger and he wasn't ready to put it away, not quite yet. Especially in front of a staff that was gung-ho Navy and whose teamwork he needed. Right this moment he could care less about the trio of outsiders from the FBI. He looked at Pamela sharply. "Do me a favor? Please. Just listen to me for a minute. Sit back down, Harris, you can use this, too. The meeting's not over."

They all stared at Dougherty, waiting. He turned back to Pam and said firmly, "Consider these arguments carefully, for what they're worth, okay? Line officers of the Navy are one of the few classes of people who must constantly demonstrate their fitness to hold their jobs. You know what that means, Ms Bonner? I'll tell you. Every pay grade up the ladder, every nit-picking inspection,

each damned efficiency test along the line gets *tougher*, not easier.
I know this, because I've been there, through the gauntlet. Get the
picture? Too much eyeballing, too many opportunities for observation, too many know-it-better critics, too many people that
understand and respect Captain Bullock. All that counts for
something."

Pamela stared back at Dougherty. She said acidly, "A lot of
people knew and respected actor John Wilkes Booth, too, but he
killed Lincoln."

The telephone rang, interrupting what might have been a
prolonged, interesting argument. Dougherty picked it up and
identified himself. He listened intently, scribbling a few notes on
his desk memo pad and occasionally glancing over at Sol
Steinberg with a look of disapproval. Dougherty finally hung up
the phone and said to the assistant, "Your prime suspect's blood
test came back. No wonder this Jacobsen is singing like a bird. It's
Type A—Positive. Forget any trumped-up *disturbing evidence*
charge and let him go."

~~~~~ 16

Steelbinder finished shaving his body, then briskly wiped himself down with Aqua Velva. Feeling much better, he put on his
clothes.

The fenced-in storage facility was located in one of the seedier
parts of National City and Steelbinder had taken a bus to get there
from downtown San Diego. He'd rented the ten-by-twenty-feet
unit when he'd first joined the Navy, and, though it cost him a
chunk of his monthly allotment, it was worth every penny. Sadly,
this hidden-away, unglamorous dustbin was the only viable
privacy he had left in the world. While many sailors kept a small
locker ashore, Steelbinder prided himself in maintaining a mini-
warehouse.

Removing the plastic dustcover from his grandmother's favorite
wing-back chair, he slumped down in it, sighed, and once more
surveyed his accumulated treasure. As usual when the door was

closed, the inside of the storage unit was warm. Steelbinder sometimes left the corrugated aluminum garage door up to let in fresh air and daylight, but, when he did, other storage park patrons would happen by and want to get friendly—especially the older retired types with time on their hands. As a rule, Steelbinder liked to go out of his way to befriend older, lonely people, for he genuinely felt sorry for their lot. But not today. His mind was preoccupied.

Steelbinder stared fixedly at his 35mm Minolta hanging from its strap by the door. Once more considering the incriminating exposures the camera contained, he rose and went over to it. It was time, he decided, to change his *modus operandi*. Quickly, before sentiment caught up with him, he unloaded the black and white film from the camera, stripped it in the light, and tossed it in a wastebasket. A still-photo replay of his little quest at North Island would be electrifying, but the lingering evidence would be too dangerous. Moreover, he had no running water here in the storage unit, and there was no guarantee of privacy when using the ship's darkroom. The thrill of a replay was no longer worth the risk.

Steelbinder put the Minolta away, gazed around the drywall-enclosed, musty chamber and sniffed the air. The storage unit smelled of mildew and building insulation, and there was little he could do about it. Once he'd tried hanging sachets or rose fragrance on the wall, but they'd melted away immediately in the closed-in heat. The dust was everywhere, but that could be remedied with the shop vacuum. During his last visit he'd forgotten to cover the ornate, gold-framed portrait of his mother that hung high on the rear wall. The painting of Felicia Eisenbinder, a set of Bing and Grondahl china, and the first few pages of the family album were the only mementos of the woman that remained. He'd purposely sold or given away the rest, for too many mementos of the woman were dangerous; they might contaminate him. Steelbinder wasn't about to chance coming down with the same mental disorder that had afflicted Felicia. He was still convinced that there was more to out-of-body projection than met the eye.

Steelbinder crawled over several stacks of old magazines—*National Geographic, Omni, Guns and Ammo, Soldier of Fortune,* and *Popular Mechanics*. Reaching the far wall, he tore the dusty bedsheet away from his workbench. The counter surface was spotlessly clean, and above it all his tools were neatly arranged, just as he'd left them a year earlier. But next to the workbench, his grandmother Ramona's easel—the one she'd used to paint Felicia's portrait—had toppled over. Nearby, a moth-ravaged deer head had fallen from the wall. He stared at both objects with conjecture, wondering if San Diego had experienced a strong earthquake during his absence at sea.

Surveying the rest of the storage unit, he debated whether to restack several cartons to get at the upright player piano beneath them. *No, not this visit, R.W.* Don't waste your time until it's properly tuned. In fact, the time-weary instrument hadn't been touched since his grandmother's funeral. Steelbinder remembered the somber wake, how his neighbors had glowered at him for threading up the music rolls of "Five Foot Two," "The Sheik of Araby," and "Ramona." His grandmother's name was Ramona. What could have been more appropriate?

Steelbinder picked up the tooled-leather family album—or what was left of it. He'd burned most of its contents, including all the photographs of his childhood in Baltimore, Oakland, and Long Beach. All that remained of the album were two dog-eared pages with one picture each of his father, mother, and grandparents. Of the lot, the only one he missed or cared about was his infamous grandfather, Gerald Eisenbinder, even though it had been grand-mother who had worked so hard to bring little Roscoe up in his mother's absence.

Again, he thought of the doting old woman who had raised him. Grandmother Ramona had usually oozed affection, but once, in a fit of anger, she'd exclaimed that Roscoe was the one who had driven his mother to insanity—that his drunken, abusive father had really only compounded a *pre-existing problem*. Aside from this one-time accusation, the old woman had tolerated Roscoe's impish nature, often coddling him and praising his eccentricity. Ramona loved *interesting* people, that was her way.

When his grandmother had been on her deathbed, Steelbinder had briefly considered telling her the truth—the main reason his mother had wound up in the mental hospital. At the time, he'd sat all day beside Ramona, waiting for her to die. Right up to the moment of the old woman's death rattle he'd wanted to blurt out his long-kept secret: it wasn't his anger-wrought, neurotic mother who had wrapped the curtain cord around his baby brother's neck and choked him. It had actually been innocent little Roscoe, and he'd cleverly managed to fix the blame on Felicia. The incident was his first attempt at framing an innocent person and the challenge excited him then as it did now.

After his infant brother's death, Felicia Eisenbinder had repeatedly proclaimed her innocence, but with her well-known, fiery temperament and an earlier incident of child neglect, no one listened. Felicia's mental health rapidly deteriorated. Once she'd gone into a seizure and moaned for hours, begging that her dead baby be returned to her in a pickle jar so she could keep an eye on it! At the time, Roscoe had retreated into a closet and giggled.

Looking back, Steelbinder was glad he'd withheld the truth of that mischief from his dying grandmother. Who knows? The asylum panjandrums might have released Felicia and let her come home, possibly *committing him* instead! He erased that warped recollection from his mind and instead recalled his mother's lonely funeral almost a year to the day after grandmother Ramona's death. No one had attended except himself and a couple of dour-faced attendants from the hospital.

Maximum Security Howard Hall, St. Elizabeth's Federal Mental Hospital for the Criminally Insane. Steelbinder wanted to forget the name of that somber, green-halled place that had been his mother's prison. He'd worked hard, very hard, to erase the past and forget. Changing his name from Eisenbinder and obtaining a new Social Security card had been a part of the strategy. The U.S. Navy knew him only as Roscoe W. Steelbinder, and he was determined to keep it that way.

Certainly nothing must ever appear in his personnel file about feisty Gerald B. Eisenbinder. His deceased grandfather had stubbornly persisted on calling himself a rear admiral after he'd been reprimanded and demoted to commodore. During World War II as a naval flag rank officer, Eisenbinder had been one of the scapegoats at Pearl Harbor; he'd been court-martialed, booted downstairs, pardoned, and quietly ushered out of the Navy all in less than nine months. After that—at least according to Grandmother Ramona—Gerald Eisenbinder's days seemed numbered and he'd spent time alternating between dejection and weaving scatological sea tales.

His grandfather eventually committed suicide while visiting New York City. Weighting down his body, he'd jumped off the Staten Island Ferry the night after Franklin Roosevelt died. Roscoe was young at the time of his grandfather's passing, but old enough to read the lurid newspaper stories. After the incident, neither his mother nor grandmother had kind words for the man. It baffled Steelbinder why they so suddenly and soundly disowned him. Both considered Grandpa Gerald a disgrace, especially to the Navy. Steelbinder took offense to that, for he'd read the official accounting at Pearl Harbor and was convinced his grandfather was a brave, intelligent man and had merely been railroaded. *A scapegoat.*

Grandmother Ramona had insisted her husband had become irrational after being booted from the Navy. Steelbinder had found this difficult to swallow; he knew better. What might be considered slightly abnormal behavior forty years ago wouldn't qualify for hospital internment today. Now even couch therapy was becoming old hat; psychotropic drugs were the fashionable thing. He knew a little himself about modern psychiatry. Several cartons in the storage room were filled with textbooks on the subject, and he'd prowled through them on more than one occasion.

Steelbinder opened one of the nearest cartons. On top was the handsomely bound edition of *The Divine Comedy* that Grandfather Gerald had treasured. Steelbinder gently removed the volume from its protective leather sleeve and thumbed through several pages. The book, printed as a limited edition in 1932 by Officina Bodoni in Italy, was a valuable collector's item. It had been a while since he'd read from it. He needed to devour the book again, savor its tortures, and make absolutely sure he understood all the secret messages the valuable work held for him. Going back to the wing-back chair, he sat down and read several cantos.

Pamela wasn't in the mood to answer questions. All she wanted to do was roll up her sleeves and go to work. Dougherty felt the same way, so they had to draw straws to decide who would handle the morning press briefing over at the COMNAVAIRPAC Public Affairs Office. Losing the flip, Dougherty took Sol Steinberg and the San Diego FBI man, Walt Courtney, along with him for backup. *Moral support*, Pamela mused. She knew full well the three men had gone over to the confrontation empty-handed.

Dougherty loaned her his office in the interim, and she'd begun immediately on the phone, helping Duck Harris with his long list of record stores. They quickly discovered that "Many a Time the World Comes Short of Thought" wasn't available anywhere in the San Diego area. A couple of music outlets agreed that the recording had to be specially ordered from Ecstasy Distributing, a Hollywood-based music supplier. Pamela pulled Harris off the phone, putting him to work on other leads while she called Ecstasy herself to badger their shipping department.

She was in luck. The shipping clerk told her the few 45 RPM records by the Midnight Admirals they had left were gathering dust in the warehouse; moreover, only one store had submitted an order for the past year. The young man at Ecstasy recalled the consignment, because the music dealer in Honolulu had requested it be sent out immediately by air, overnight express mail.

Pamela's pulse quickened. "When did the record go out? And the name of the outlet?"

She heard papers rattling at the other end of the line followed by the sibilant voice of the shipping clerk. "Not one record, lady. *A dozen*. We sent them to Honolulu two weeks ago. Just a minute. Here it is, Watanabe Music in Waikiki. You want their address and the invoice number?"

"No. Just the telephone number."

He gave it to her. A few minutes later she had the store's owner on the transpacific line. He told Pam that he didn't know what customer had placed the special order because the woman clerk who handled the transaction just left on vacation for two weeks on the mainland.

Pam jotted down when the special request was made and the day the dozen records were picked up. She thanked the music store owner, hung up, and called Hawaii again, this time to the office of her FBI counterpart.

Sean Farley of the Honolulu office assured her he'd start a local trace on the vacationing music store clerk right away. "I'll check the woman's relatives, friends, and neighbors. With luck, they might come up with a mainland itinerary, possibly a visit to relatives in California."

Pamela said goodbye to Farley and stared out the window. She hoped they found the vacationing sales clerk; the investigation couldn't wait until the music store employee returned. The question kept turning over in her mind: Who would buy twelve single discs of the same recording and why? *Maxine Bullock's killer*, for one.

Pamela summoned Duck Harris back into Dougherty's office. The black man hesitated in the frame of the doorway, his halfback shoulders almost filling it. She smiled. "Mr. Harris, I may have a lead. How long will it take you to come up with the exact dates the *Abraham Lincoln* was berthed at Pearl Harbor?"

Harris grinned. "Hellfire, I thought you were going to pass a tough one. Give me two minutes." He disappeared outside and returned almost immediately. Harris smiled at her and read quickly from a scrap of paper. "The carrier made a four-day layover in Honolulu with rotating liberties. Arrived September 28, departed October first. You need the time and tide too?"

"No, that's enough." Pamela examined her notes, comparing

the dates with the time period of the music store transaction. They matched. "Duck, do me a big favor?"

"I'll sure try."

"Does Dougherty still intend to go directly from the press conference to that flag officer hearing?"

Harris nodded, but he looked puzzled. "From the frying pan into the fire, as I see it. Why do you ask?"

"I can't wait for his return. Will your NIS credentials get us *anywhere* on the base? Aboard any ship?"

"Sure. Unless there's some proprietary need-to-know, top secret activity in progress." Harris hunched his shoulders. "Uh-uh, wait a minute. I smell trouble. What's going on inside that pretty head of yours?"

Pamela glanced at her watch. There was still plenty of time before Swain Bullock himself left for the Gecko Corman hearing. "I want to go aboard the *Abraham Lincoln*—immediately. I intend to talk to the captain, and I'd like to arrive unannounced. Can you get me aboard?"

Harris shrugged. "No problem, but the boss might not like it. Sure you don't want to wait until Dougherty's free a little later?"

"No." She looked at him narrowly. "And I'd like you to come along."

"Might be less intimidating if you talk to Bullock alone."

"I'd rather not. The captain appears to be a peculiar artifact and might blurt out anything. I may need a witness."

Harris giggled. "Hell, you sure you're not afraid of that son of a bitch?"

Pamela thought for a moment. "Maybe I am."

After a half hour, Steelbinder became restless. He placed *The Divine Comedy* aside and went back to exploring the storage unit's memorabilia. In another carton he found Grandfather Eisenbinder's tired old admiral's hat, carefully protected in a zip-lock plastic bag. Steelbinder decided to take the hat and Dante's book back to the ship with him. He wondered why his grandmother saved the flag-rank hat with its bill of tarnished scrambled eggs her dead husband no longer deserved. *Misplaced sentiment?*

Steelbinder despised the word sentimental, considering it a false compassion. Indeed, during childhood, his grandmother's cosseting had sickened him. Early on, Ramona had wanted him to become a musician, writer, or artist and leave something behind for posterity. She'd insisted that under no circumstances should he make a career of the Navy like her deceased husband.

Steelbinder didn't smile often, but now he smiled to himself. He would leave something for posterity, all right, his grandmother could rest assured. He recalled how Ramona on her deathbed had insisted, "Use your talent, Roscoe. Go out there and invent. *Create* something." When he'd laughed at her admonition, she'd suddenly gasped for air and wagged a trembling finger at him. "Roscoe, come closer!" she'd cried. Oddly, her very last words were, "Always remember, it is not Goethe who creates Faust, but Faust which creates Goethe." At the time Steelbinder had been impressed, until later when he'd discovered that the woman's final croaking was not original thinking but rather the thoughts of an analytical Swiss psychiatrist named Jung. All her life Ramona had been quoting cobwebby stuff from *The Farmer's Almanac* or the Bible, but, on her deathbed, she quoted a shrink!

Steelbinder shook his head and put the uncomfortable rememberings away. He went over to the workbench and the large cardboard box beside it that contained the ship models he'd collected from childhood. Though he'd built over two dozen boat models over the years, most of them had been donated to a children's home when he joined the Navy. Placing a radio-controlled sailboat aside, he withdrew from the carton a twenty-inch-long speedboat hull with a miniature gas engine. The hydroplane model was his favorite, and he smiled. The boat was too small to be taken seriously, too fast and dangerous to be considered a toy or given to children. Aboard the carrier he'd been reading in a hobby magazine how to modify the hull and make it go even faster. The new concept challenged him.

Opening the cupboard doors on top of the workbench, Steelbinder examined his tools. In a prominent position at the top of the cupboard was the claw hammer from his childhood. It was the same one his mother kept in the closet to protect herself from a violent marriage during those years before the flame of her madness ignited. The hammer reminded him of his own protective device—all the terrible times he'd slept with a baseball bat in his bed, though he'd always been afraid to use it, no matter how abusive his father had been. The drunken man had finally wandered off and never returned. Steelbinder idly wondered if his missing father might now be dead.

Suddenly he heard an inner voice crying out, *enough, it's time to stop ruminating over deceased relatives*. The collectibles in the storage unit inevitably did this to him each time he returned from a long voyage. He made up his mind to think instead about his last hours of shore liberty. Today was a time to unwind, a time of exemption when he was released from the pressure and stress of the *Abraham Lincoln's* bridge. Actually, Steelbinder had been in a pleasant state of equanimity all morning. After breakfast, he'd worked out in the ship's gym, once more crafting his biceps, deltoids, and lats to a pitch of perfection. Even the sordid affair the night before at the Long Beach mortuary had been erased from his thoughts.

Now if only he could find the extra balsa wood and marine glue for modifying the speedboat. Continuing to rummage among the stacked belongings, he came across a wooden box; he handled it more carefully than the cardboard containers, aware that it contained a half-dozen hand grenades and several sticks of dynamite. Musing over this clandestine little armory, Steelbinder likened its potential to his own nature. Especially the hand grenades. *Once the pin has been pulled, there's no turning back. You're committed, Steelbinder.* Continue to strike whenever, wherever you can.

The fact that his acts might look like hurricanes of pleasure to others was unimportant. His critics were ignorant, unaware that developing one's animal self was as important as nourishing the intellect. The Navy could never be expected to understand his needs. Not ever. Only the poet Virgil, Dante himself, or his grandfather could truly understand.

Steelbinder gloated. His requirements had been sharply polarized from the outset, but now they were coming into even sharper focus. *Beware, harlots.* Like a Pied Piper, he would lead the wanton women of the world on a tour through hell, passing through all nine rings of misery!

Steelbinder wondered how he might put the hand grenades and dynamite to propitious use. Thus far, in every port of call, the performance of the giant firecrackers was exceeding his wildest expectations. The grenades were bulky and impractical, but sneaking at least one of them past the sergeant-at-arms at the top of the gangway and sewing it within his bunk mattress wouldn't be difficult. It might come in handy as a little insurance policy.

He kept digging through his treasure until he found the spare balsa wood and bottle of marine glue. Taking them back to the workbench, he whistled softly as he went to work on the hull of the speedboat. If he finished quickly, there would still be time today to take the model over to one of the Mission Bay ponds for a sea trial.

Pamela raised her voice. "Captain, after what I've just explained, you're still committed to finishing the deployment?"

Swain Bullock nodded without reservation.

She stared at him. "How can you possibly keep the original embarkation schedule if there's a murderer on your ship? We need time to investigate."

"What's that famous line? Time and tide wait for no man."

"Please be serious, Captain."

Bullock looked concerned but unimpressed. "I don't cut the orders; I merely execute them and to the best of my ability. This carrier is due in Bremerton by November 6. And before that, we have sea maneuvers to accomplish along the coast plus a goodwill call in San Francisco during Fleet Week." He paused, staring at her. "You feel otherwise about the tight schedule, I suggest you take it up down the street with COMELEVEN or the CNO in Washington."

Pamela shifted in the white, Herman Miller contour chair and straightened her skirt. Bullock's formal office-stateroom four stories beneath the supercarrier's bridge was larger and more tastefully furnished than she'd expected. Ships in general made her claustrophobic, and the rest of the *Abraham Lincoln's* white and gray labyrinth interior was no exception. But Captain Bullock's accommodations, forward of the command officer's dining room, were comfortable and surprisingly plush. She'd been surprised when he told her most of the furnishings were installed to his own specifications. The walls were done in dark cherry paneling that matched Bullock's broad, angular desk. A handsome contemporary brass lamp with twin shades hung over the center of the desk, casting harsh shadows across his face. Behind the captain's leather chair and off to one side was an eighteen-inch illuminated world globe. The close-cut, royal blue carpet looked expensive, though it appeared they'd skimped on the padding.

Sitting in silence beside Pamela in a chair that looked too small for him was Duck Harris. His eyes were watchful and expectant, his hands clasped awkwardly between his knees. Swain Bullock sat stonily, turned sideways from his executive desk.

"Captain, your composure astounds me," she said in an even, solicitous tone. "In your position after a family tragedy, I'd have needed a short leave. No, correct that—I'd have asked for a nice, long one."

"You're a woman. I can appreciate that."

Pam lowered her head to hide her expression of contempt. "Captain Bullock, are you patronizing me?"

"Sorry. I only meant to imply that Navy business has to go on as usual. My personal loss, my emotions, are irrelevant."

"Let's hope your superiors feel differently about that."

Bullock spread his hands. "They can afford to be sentimental. I can't. If I make a mistake or lose this command, I fall off the promotion ladder."

She studied his face. "We're not at war, Captain. What's your hurry? There's plenty of time to pause and smell the roses. As for my riding you today, consider it the Bureau's job to keep the garden tidy. If we're to pull out the loco weeds, we need your help. *I* need your help."

Bullock grinned at that. "If you're telling me you want an undercover man to come aboard the carrier and go over it with a fine-tooth comb, he's more than welcome. But it'll have to be done while we're underway."

Duck Harris had a twinkle in his eye as he spoke up. "Maybe you'd have quicker results, Captain, if we sent in a passive probe. Like a pretty woman." He nodded toward Pamela.

Bullock grumbled. "Your humor doesn't become you, Mr. Harris."

Pamela sat forward. "Really, Captain? Don't be so hard on our NIS friend." If not for its kernel of truth, she would have found Duck's remark offensive. She continued, "Captain, there's a human time-bomb aboard this ship. All you have to do is delay your departure a few days. I'm sure you can influence Naval Operations."

"I could, but I wouldn't. If the problem individual is aboard this carrier—which I seriously doubt—I'll resolve the matter myself. It's part of my job to shoulder risks, Ms. Bonner."

"Including the Gecko Corman matter?"

He ignored that.

She tried another tack. "You're obviously a gambler."

Bullock leaned back in his chair. "We all calculate risks and go ahead with life anyway. Often out of necessity." He winked at her. "And sometimes—yes, Ms. Bonner, we take serious gambles. Often just for the fun of it. Why else do we draw to inside straights, knowing the odds against filling one are eleven to one? Have you ever gambled?"

Irritated, Pam shook her head. She still couldn't believe the icy individual confronting her was the same man who had just lost his wife through an awful act of violence. *Unless*—

Bullock didn't pursue his point. He seemed to be gloating as he waited for her next thrust.

Pam shifted uncomfortably. There's something hawklike and impenetrable about this individual, she thought. An acute awareness in the eyes and an archlike, arrogant pose that bespoke possible cruelty. She felt sure Swain Bullock was hiding something. Or was it her imagination, a lingering, preconceived suspicion of his guilt that tinted her vision? She said to him, "You're a most complex person, Captain."

He stared back at her and said seriously, "I suspect you wonder about me because of my late wife's suicidal, Dionysian nature. I assure you, Ms. Bonner, that I'm quite different. Calm, collected, rational; as stable as this carrier in a moderate sea. Ask Mr. Harris here about my demeanor. On behalf of the NIS, he's been on a ship with me before. Two years ago, the *Kitty Hawk*. Isn't that right, Mr. Harris?"

The big man nodded. "Yes, sir." Harris turned to Pamela and explained, "The skipper was a tough-as-nails XO back then. I helped him put down some awkward racial incidents."

Bullock squinted and leaned forward. He said intensely, "We made big waves and put out the fire, didn't we, Harris? Hell of a fight, but I came out on top. Always do. As I saw it then, and still do, the problem with the American melting pot is that it's being stirred too often—with a knife. I use a spoon and stir carefully and only when necessary."

Pamela stared at Bullock. The captain was like the ram that bellowed the most but gave the least wool! *Damn his bragging*. She hadn't come aboard the *Abraham Lincoln* to bolster the man's vanity; nor was she here for an education on putting down gang warfare. She said to him in a tired voice, "I know, Captain. I've heard all about the so-called melting pot before, how it's unavoidable that a few get banged up in the simmering process. We've listened to your pontifications. Now it's our turn for speeches. And questions."

Sensing Pamela's impatience, Duck Harris reached into his

jacket pocket and withdrew four badly wrinkled neckties. Boldly, he held them out toward Bullock. "You recognize any of these, Captain?"

"All of them. Part of the wardrobe I left at the house." He frowned with annoyance. "Thoughtful of you to take such good care of that Thai silk."

Pamela said quietly, "If they're kinked and knotted, Captain, it's from a little sex scene called bondage. Not from being crammed in Duck's pocket."

Harris folded the neckties as best he could and left them on the corner of the desk. "Sorry we couldn't get them pressed."

Bored with Swain Bullock's posturing, Pam put aside the diplomatic niceties and asked abruptly, "Captain, do you own a camera?"

He stared at her with stark befuddlement. "Yes. Who doesn't?"

"Let me be more specific. What kind? And is photography an avid pastime?"

Bullock shrugged and pointed to a nearby wall and four framed black and white enlargements.

Pamela took them in, one at a time. A pelican at sunset. Street traffic in Hong Kong. A flirtatious Hawaiian hula girl. A towering California redwood.

The captain said to her, "Just purchased a new Nikon. Sure, I enjoy the hobby. On occasion, I even use the ship's darkroom. Why do you ask?"

Pamela thought for a moment, then gestured toward the wall photos. "Very nice work."

Bullock appeared to soften; she'd hit the right nerve. She decided to parry quickly while he was still malleable. "Captain Bullock, this ship seems to mean everything to you. I mean, without it—"

"Ms. Bonner," he cut her off, "I'm not a sentimental man, but the answer to your question is yes. The *Abraham Lincoln* is my life. Melville had his whale. Faulkner had his damned bear. Who knows? Someday I may write about my *affair* with a nuke supercarrier."

Pamela got to her feet and began strolling around the royal blue carpet. Harris, obviously eager to finish up and get back to Dougherty's office, gave her an impatient look. Bullock began shuffling some papers on his desk.

Pam studied the photographs on the wall, admitting to herself that they had a surprisingly creative flair. She turned to find Bullock watching her. He was smiling, a little derisively. She said to him, "In your estimation, Captain, what kind of sicko commits such vile acts? Disfigurements of the kind that happened in your wife's homicide? Tell me how it's possible for such a misfit to slip through, somehow become an obscure part of the Navy's fabric."

"I assume you're indirectly asking me *what kind* of men serve under my command." Bullock frowned and thought for a long moment. He looked at the fidgeting Harris then back to Pamela. "Sit down, please. Your pacing is making your partner nervous." Some of the starch seemed to seep out of Bullock's voice as he explained, "God knows where the madman you're after is coming from. We try to filter out the psychopaths, of course. Still, there's plenty of left-outs aboard the *Abraham Lincoln*—or any of our fleet warships. Social misfits given a new lease on life, a new promise, by a military career. In the civilian job market, they're discards. Here, they help run the show. These are men with low self-esteem, still undervaluing themselves because nobody until now praised their work, told them they were someone special."

Pamela sat back down. "Do you tell them this, Captain?"

"As a group, when they first come aboard, I get into it, yes. And intermittently, when I have time. You'll have to remember this is a huge ship, virtually a city at sea. Basically, it's a leadership job that's passed along the line; that's what capable junior officers are for."

"I understand." It was a lie; she still didn't understand Bullock's attitude at all. Pam remembered too well the words of his detractors who insisted he was aloof, stand-offish, and too often uncommunicative with his underlings. Pamela's mind gathered momentum. She wanted desperately to spend some time aboard the ship and probe from stem to stern. "Captain Bullock, I'd like to sail with you when the carrier pulls out. At least partway up the coast, just as far as San Francisco."

Bullock was stunned and let it show. His mouth dropped measurably, and the diamond-like quality of his gaze grew even harder and more derisive. Across from the captain, Duck Harris seemed to be wiping off a smirk, as if he knew all too well what was coming next. Pamela stiffened.

Swain Bullock shook his head. "Regretfully, I can't permit such an embarkation." He looked at her directly. "Of course you can go over my head if you choose, but I'm sure the Pentagon would only refer the matter back to me. Such a request is always at the discretion of the ship's commander."

"May I ask why you disapprove?"

He smiled secretly. "I have enough problems when attractive

female tech reps come aboard. Five thousand men to one or two women is an uncomfortable logistical arrangement, no matter how temporary."

"I assure you, not for me, Captain."

"A nuclear carrier is a warship, Ms. Bonner. Believe me, it's a dangerous place fraught with accidents waiting to happen. We're crowded. Single accommodations are at a premium, held in readiness for admirals and other VIPs flying on and off with little or no notice."

"You're pontificating again, Captain. So I will, too. Your Navy laws objectifying women—written and unwritten—are incredibly archaic."

"Ms. Bonner, please."

"For starters, call me Pamela."

"Pamela, if all this means so much to you, I suggest you do a little feminist research. You'll find the Navy has made tremendous strides since 1971."

Pam didn't know whether to laugh or see red. "Save it, please, Captain Bullock. What you call strides, modern women call petty tokenism. Yes, you now let us serve on auxiliary tenders, research, and rescue vessels. But rugged hand-to-hand combat, if it comes, is more apt to take place on a smaller vessel at some remote place. Why do Coast Guard vessels set out, possibly to face armed dope runners and other dangerous pirates, with a mixed complement of men and women? Is the Navy's precious electronic, nuclear world really more dangerous? Or are you merely trying to preserve the image of carrier life being more macho?"

Duck Harris squirmed with embarrassment. He wanted to leave and let it show. "Pamela, I think we'd better—"

"I haven't finished. You don't want me aboard your ship, Captain. But apparently I'm not alone. I've heard you don't even want your own female commissioned officers. Is it true that an Army or Air Force woman pilot can land on this carrier to make a delivery but not her Navy counterpart?"

Bullock stiffened and made a pretense of checking his watch. "Pamela, please. Are you investigating a homicide or grandstanding for some feminist cause? I'm afraid I don't understand your operative pigeonhole. You're making both of our jobs difficult. If one of Lieutenant Commander Dougherty's men comes along with us on the deployment, I'm sure he'll do an adequate job for you. Harris here, for example."

The black man shook his head. "Please don't make a recommendation, Captain. My wife's due to have a kid at any time, and I'd like to stick around the base. Besides, I'm too big and getting too stiff to go prowling around in some of those tight spaces below the waterline."

Bullock turned back to Pamela. He made a show of checking his Rolex. "Sorry, you'll have to excuse me now. You did come unannounced, and I have a relative to meet at the airport."

Pam wasn't disappointed; the conversation had grown lamer by the moment. Gathering up her purse and notebook, she started for the door. Harris loped along behind her.

Bullock made no effort to placate her irritability. He calmly rose, picked up the phone, and summoned an orderly to escort them to the dock. He said to her while they waited, "I'm getting the impression, Pamela, that you're an impatient, most impetuous type."

"Right now, I'll answer that with an unqualified yes. Time means everything to me." She exhaled sharply. "When it comes to this case, I feel like I'm stuck, like driving behind some fatso riding a bicycle on a narrow road. With or *without* your help, Captain, I intend to move out and shift into high gear. Supposing that firecracker was only an obscene warning, just the beginning? God knows what will happen when this madman's poison reaches the meltdown point."

She and Harris left the compartment escorted by an orderly. As they walked down the corridor, Bullock remained poised at the entry to his cabin. Pam didn't turn around, but she could feel his eyes linger on her.

~~~~~~ **18**

Dougherty was a little disappointed that it was only a hearing to air both sides of the Gecko Corman matter. A formal inquiry going before a flag board with an actual, *prima facie* case would be more productive, and Dougherty would look better in the long run, but that kind of show would also take time to prepare. So

much for short notice and bad luck. A career officer bucking for
silver oak leaves couldn't expect everything to go his way.

Dougherty had arranged to use the court-martial room in the
COMNAVAIRPAC Building. His own NIS office might have
been a more kicked-back setting, but with Vice Admiral Biff
McCracken himself in town, Dougherty didn't feel it was appropriate. He was surprised that Rear Admiral Whitney had cancelled
out at the last moment. Whatever the reason, the appearance of the
Deputy Chief of Naval Operations instead gave Corman's troubles
a higher priority. Minutes earlier an aide had told Dougherty that
Admiral McCracken had other business on the base and was
anxious to get the *Abraham Lincoln* crewman's complaint dis-
posed of as expeditiously as possible.

Biff McCracken had a reputation as a tough disciplinarian.
Dougherty himself wasn't that eager to punish anyone—all he
wanted to hear was the clang of truth. He felt genuinely sorry for
Corman, who was badly frightened and felt cornered.

The long hallway outside the hearing room had two oak benches
at each end of its polished parquet floor. Dougherty had already
gone over to greet Captain Bullock, who sat perusing a recent
Naval Institute magazine and seemed as stoic as ever. Beside
Bullock sat the *Abraham Lincoln's* Protestant chaplain, a soft-
spoken, shambling character who hadn't impressed Dougherty
when they'd talked earlier on the phone. The carrier's chubby
Master Chief had shown up too, but he'd wandered out to the
vending machine for a quick cup of Java. There was still a little
time before the hearing began. Everyone had come in twenty
minutes early except for Gecko Corman.

Dougherty anxiously checked his watch. Five minutes to go.
He now wondered if he'd told Corman that Captain Bullock and
his aides would present their side of it first while the aviation
boatswain's mate waited outside the hearing room. If so, was the
sailor deliberately planning to slip in late to avoid confronting the
skipper? Dougherty's spirits began to fail him as the minutes
ticked by and still no Gecko. Irritated, he sent Chief Warrant Kelly
outside to check over the parking lot.

At the prescribed time, Dougherty reluctantly shuffled into the
hearing room with the others. The chamber was pleasant enough;
varnished oak tables for the prosecution and defense, a flag behind
the elevated bench, and opened windows to admit the gentle
breeze off San Diego Bay. Vice Admiral Biff McCracken entered
with an assistant, a young, gangly lieutenant who walked stiffly
and carried a small tape recorder and table mike. The crewcut,

somber-faced McCracken deliberately avoided the bench on the dais, instead pulling up a chair at one of the long wooden tables.

The admiral gestured for Bullock, Dougherty and the others to sit across from him. The aide had difficulty with the recorder but finally managed to get it started. McCracken ran both hands over his gray hair, sat forward, and put on a pair of gold-framed bifocals. He took his time sifting through several papers then finally looked up and focused on Dougherty. He said sternly, "Lieutenant Commander, I'm ready if you are. Please proceed with your presentation."

Dougherty swallowed back the bile in his throat. "Admiral, I'm embarrassed to say that after all the effort we've expended to provide Boatswain's Mate Corman this appeal hearing, he's done us the discourtesy of being late."

Captain Bullock looked on with a crafty, Achilles smile. "Typical. The man has a reputation as a slaggard."

"Sir," Dougherty started to protest.

Vice Admiral McCracken stared at Dougherty frostily then turned to Bullock. "Captain, do you wish to file a cross-complaint on this matter? I have your prior log reports on this crewman in front of me, but there's nothing about this recent assault charge."

Bullock sat up straight. "That's correct, sir. I'd fully expected to conduct my own inquiry with the Command Master Chief and Chaplain assisting. I thought it best we discuss the purported incident again before committing myself in a letter to the NIS office. I'm sorry, Admiral McCracken, that one of my men has troubled you with this far-fetched accusation. I respectfully submit that—" He paused, glanced at Dougherty, then said firmly, "Aviation Boatswain's Mate First Class Corman is suffering from some kind of hallucination. He'd already been on probation for using drugs last year."

Dougherty stared pointedly at Bullock. "Do you personally dislike Corman and his saxophone, Captain?"

"I resent that allegation. Preposterous. And while we're at it, Lieutenant Commander, I resent your persistent, abusive interrogations."

Dougherty spread his hands. "I'm only doing my job, Captain."

Bullock shifted in his chair. "Even my personal stateroom is no sanctuary away from your intrusive staff."

Dougherty was genuinely puzzled. "Sir? I've sent no one over to the carrier to badger you."

Bullock nodded satirically. "Then you'd better put a leash on Mr. Harris and this Pamela Bonner."

The chaplain beckoned to Bullock and whispered in his ear.

Admiral McCracken looked genuinely offended as he waited.

Dougherty wiggled uncomfortably in his chair and said to Bullock, "Captain, I think we'd all benefit if you start from the beginning. You apparently have strong convictions on this matter. Why do you believe that one of your men was in fact *not attacked*, that in reality *no attempt* whatsoever was made to throw him overboard?"

The maligned expression on Bullock's face did not go away. He nodded to the Command Master Chief, who took the cue and immediately proceeded to read from prepared notes.

Biff McCracken irritably shook his head and slapped the table with an open hand. Reaching for his aide's portable recorder, he switched it off. "Sorry, gentlemen, but I detest wasting time. What kind of farce is this? Captain Bullock, just where the hell is this Corman now? He's still under your command, isn't that correct?"

"Yes, sir, but unfortunately, until tomorrow morning, not under my immediate control. He's on shore leave."

"Who assumed the responsibility for getting him here?"

Dougherty flushed. "I did, Admiral. I'm as disappointed by this tardiness as anyone else."

McCracken worked his eyebrows. "Under the circumstances, it's irrelevant to proceed. If I'm going to listen to galley yarns, I insist on hearing from both sides of the table in open confrontation. I want all the principals in the room at the same time. Accordingly, gentlemen, this hearing is recessed for thirty minutes." McCracken's chair squeaked with protest as he pushed it back and climbed to his feet. Putting away his glasses, he withdrew a packet of cigars and turned to Dougherty. "When it's time to continue, bring in all your principals or don't come back at all."

"Yes, sir," Dougherty replied with chagrin. He was obviously dismissed. Bullock and the others solemnly followed McCracken out of the chamber.

In the outer hallway, Dougherty ignored Bullock and hurried up to Chief Warrant Officer Kelly, who hovered by the exit. "Any sign of Corman?"

"Negative, sir." Kelly checked his watch. "You want me to call the kid's parents' house up in Downey?"

"Never mind. I'll do it myself."

• • •

A half-hour later, events had stumbled from the proverbial rock to a hard place for Dougherty. He'd not only been soundly reprimanded, but Gecko Corman was history, as far as the Deputy Chief of Staff was concerned. Dougherty was pissed. He stood in the hearing room, feeling like he had no place to go; misplaced luggage without a tag. Admiral McCracken had left in a huff, demanding that Dougherty and Bullock resolve their differences with no further rattling of cages at either the CNO or Inspector General level. Before returning to Washington, however, the vice admiral did insist on a briefing regarding the North Island homicide. But later, after a scheduled three o'clock nine holes of golf.

Dougherty hurried to a pay phone booth. There was worse news yet to come from Corman's alarmed parents up in Downey. Dougherty's heart jumped when he heard Barney Corman bellow over the wire that not only had some fellow crewman tried to do his son in, but that he was sure the attempt had been made by an officer with the *rank of captain*!

Dougherty's mind felt like it was swimming—in water over his head. *Why hadn't the aviation boatswain's mate told him that part earlier?* Small wonder the panicky kid had insisted on talking to someone at flag level. *An eagle collar emblem*; Gecko's father insisted he'd seen the evidence himself. Dougherty listened carefully and made notes, making sure he had the correct address of the uncle's Del Mar condo and the rental car agency. He'd assign an agent to get on top of both leads immediately. Corman's father was still screaming on the phone—something incoherent about a new set of golf clubs—when Dougherty said goodbye and hung up.

He and Kelly walked the short distance from the COM-NAVAIRPAC Building to their own NIS facility. Dougherty stomped up the stairs to the second floor office like a man ready for a fight, but, unfortunately, he couldn't decide how and where to vent his anger. Swain Bullock, for being so combative? Gecko Corman, for running away from the battle? Pamela and Duck for interference? Or the damned Cherry Bomber for disrupting Dougherty's little corner of the Navy in the first place? *Cherry Bomber*. He'd reprimanded the press for coining that term, and now he was using it himself.

Entering the outer office, he was at least buoyed by the industriousness of the rest of the crew. On the surface at least, it looked like they were making headway. The room was filled with the sound of clicking computer keyboards and phone conversations—not the thick, ugly silence that signified a stymied staff of investigators about to give up the ghost.

Pamela stood in the doorway of his office, beckoning to him with a thumbs up salute. Fine, what the hell did that mean? Right now, in his current mood, he'd like to give her his middle finger—right between the legs. Steinberg and Meadows were trying to grab his attention as well, but they could wait. At this moment beauty and the beast needed an immediate meeting of minds.

When he came up to Pamela, he could smell cordite on her clothing. "You been in a range war or street fight that I should know about?" He pulled her into his inner office and closed the door.

"No such exciting luck. Practicing at the shooting range. Duck took me over after we left the *Abraham Lincoln*. Weekly workouts are the only way I'll earn the L.A. Bureau's sharpshooter medal."

"You should have told me you were going to see Bullock." His voice had thawed more than he'd intended, but anger was still on his mind.

"Rules! Your rules. Inside that hard-boiled, Navy-issue shell of yours, Lieutenant Commander, there's an emotional being I'd like to know. Or at least understand."

"You? Understand me? Sometimes I have a difficult enough time grappling with my feelings myself."

She smiled grittily. "So you go through life playing Mr. Closed-mouth?"

"Part of the career facade. Now, about Bullock—"

Pamela silenced him with a gently placed finger on the lips. "Don't be offended, Todd. Progress always exacts its price. I have news, the kind with all the right odds. I'm positive the killer's assigned to the *Abraham Lincoln*."

Dougherty looked at her noncommittally. "I'm waiting. Proceed."

"The record stores, the distributor, they all tie together. Someone purchased a dozen copies of the Midnight Admirals' record in Hawaii. During the same period the ship was in port at Pearl."

He blinked at that, admitting to himself that it might be the best lead so far. Dougherty went behind his desk and slumped into a chair. He was dying for a cigarette, but would wait until she left the room. Additional friction he didn't need at the moment.

Pamela sat on the corner of his desk. "There's more. Captain Bullock knows how to use a darkroom."

"I already figured that."

She stared at him, pretty lips turned slack-mouthed. "How?"

Dougherty smiled. "In the hallway in the Bullocks' duplex. A couple of custom black and white enlargements of high-performance racing cars. Not the kind of macho stuff Maxine would go for."

Pamela shrugged. "Great. I thought I was making a discovery when he showed me his work in his carrier cabin."

Dougherty gestured toward the door. "Better open it before the wolves blow it down."

She did, and Sol Steinberg stood outside with a mildly pleased look. He pushed his glasses higher on his nose, entered, and tossed a lengthy teletype down on Dougherty's desk. "The FBI sent its feelers out to Interpol for comps. Nothing in the European area. But look what we pulled up in the opposite direction. *Voila.*"

Dougherty picked up the communiqué, noting the dateline and city. The Royal Hong Kong Police were still in the process of investigating a mutilation murder involving the use of fireworks and were more than eager to trade data. Dougherty's pulse quickened. He sat up straight and read the particulars twice with Pamela looking over his shoulder. Whistling softly, he turned to Sol. "What about these dates? They jive with the CVN-71's visit to Hong Kong?"

Steinberg shook his head. "Sorry, Commander. The *Abraham Lincoln* didn't stop at the Crown Colony on its Far East deployment."

Dougherty exhaled wearily and looked at Pamela. "You still convinced your nefarious Captain Bullock is a suspect?"

She shrugged. "He had an elegant Chinese chest in his stateroom. Where did he get it?"

"Come now, where do you think? Chinatown. San Francisco. L.A. New York. Vancouver. You want me to go on with possibilities?"

Steinberg added, "The carrier commander's been in the Navy forever. Odds are he's been to Hong Kong sometime."

Dougherty waved the telegram. "But not *recently*, when this crime was committed."

"Could be you're wrong, boss." The challenge came from Duck Harris, who had entered quietly and now towered behind

Pamela and Steinberg. "I heard where you're all coming from. So happens I have two friends on the *Abe Lincoln*. When the carrier got stuck in Subic Bay in the Philippines for twelve days to repair an elevator, the morale officer chartered two quick round trips to Hong Kong. Apparently some three hundred officers and men jumped at the cheap group fare and spent part of their liberty there."

A wary look clouded everyone's face except for Pamela, who eagerly went up to Harris. "Duck, what about the captain? Did he go along?"

Harris shrugged. "I didn't ask."

Dougherty said pointedly, "I suggest you get on it, fast."

~~~~~~~ **19**

Steelbinder took a taxi from the storage unit out to Mission Bay. He rode in silence, the speedboat model and radio control unit carefully cradled in his lap. The cab driver, confessing that he, too, was an avid model-maker, tried unsuccessfully to get a dialogue going.

"Hmmmm-nnnnn. That's interesting," Steelbinder replied before retreating into an impervious silence. Though the cabbie—who said he was a part-time college student—was clean-cut and pleasant enough, Steelbinder had more important things on his mind than contrived conversation. He'd asked the youthful driver to take San Diego's surface routes despite the higher tab on the meter, for he hated southern California's freeways. *Concrete. Metal. Too coldly impersonal. Too often, gridlock. Everywhere motorized fatheads and noise.* The stressful cacophony was almost as bad as the busy flight deck of an aircraft carrier. He liked city streets where he could observe people; especially pedestrians waiting for the crossing signal, when he could parry with their eyes.

As the taxi entered the downtown area and paused at Sampson Street for the light, Steelbinder saw a woman in short, sequined pants who looked like a prostitute. In high school he had appalled a prim English teacher by writing an essay on the World's Oldest Profession and couching it with four-letter words. He couldn't remember when the phobia began, but now he felt only a seething contempt for prostitutes. The mere mention of the word sometimes set his blood boiling. They were parasites—feeding and surviving on greed and lust—little more than dirty receptacles of phallic fantasy! Indeed, if harlots were not eliminated from society, their numbers would multiply as fast as uncontrolled rats at a dumpsite. Steelbinder couldn't possibly eradicate all of them but he might be able to frighten vast numbers out of the trade. If somebody, somewhere, had to make a dent in their ranks, why shouldn't it be R.W. Steelbinder? He recalled the *Divine Comedy* line:

> *Not without cause this going is allowed;*
> *Thus it is willed above where St. Michael*
> *Wrought vengeance for the dead of whoredom.*

Steelbinder stared at the sexpot on the sidewalk, and she smiled back. The meretricious woman on the San Diego street looked familiar; she reminded him of the tart in Honolulu. He'd made a mistake during that incident, running out of the freezer compartment *before* the firecracker detonated. He should have waited to make sure it was a good fuse. But he was back on track now, and next time he wouldn't panic. He'd be much more careful, take his time. In the future, his intellect would rule the day, not his hormones or knee-jerk emotion.

Steelbinder looked forward to the upcoming departure of the *Abraham Lincoln* and its impending calls in San Francisco and Bremerton. Each new liberty was an exhilarating plunge into a different environment—a new challenge. Thanks to the gullible U.S. Navy, Steelbinder was like a rolling stone and could carry on his considerable crusade on a global scale if necessary. He was only one man against seemingly impossible odds, but he would cut out these cancers in the soft underbelly of society as best he could. Even if he only scratched the surface of the problem, his point would be made in a spectacular, mind-boggling way.

> *And out of every city shall he thrust*
> *That beast, until he drive her back to Hell*
> *Whence she was first let loose by envious lust.*

As the taxi skirted Balboa Park, Steelbinder thought about the nearby zoo. He briefly considered stopping to see if there were any new colorful birds in the aviary. He liked to observe and photograph animals and exotic birds, though preferably at a distance. Once his grandmother had given him a cockatoo, but it had made the mistake of biting his finger instead of the pencil he'd playfully inserted in its cage. He had exacted immediate retribution by wringing its neck.

The zoo would be fun, but to do it right would take the rest of the day. Besides, he'd left his camera behind. Smiling to himself, Steelbinder looked down at the raceboat model in his lap then back out the cab window. It had been a long time since he'd taken pictures of the dog monkeys and baboons masturbating. No. Not today, R.W.! *Bad timing.* He decided to plan a full day's photo safari the next time he came to town.

Steelbinder instructed the taxi driver to take him to Vacation Island on Mission Bay. The cabbie apparently knew the area on North Cove, for he insisted the spot was reserved for sailboats, that it would be impossible to launch a gas-powered, model hydroplane today. Steelbinder shrugged with indifference and ignored the driver's warning. He wasn't about to be intimidated by overgrown children with sailboats.

It was a gorgeous day, and, as the cab went over the North Point bridge, he could see the water was calm with only a slight ripple disrupting its surface. Perfect for the improved performance he expected from the modified boat model. The taxi appeared to have a bad bearing in its right rear wheel, and he was glad to get out, pay the fare, and be rid of the abrasive, high-pitched moan. He left a seventy-five cent tip and watched the driver examine it with contempt.

Strolling down to the water's edge, Steelbinder felt a familiar charge of excitement. There were several sailboat models on the water, just as the cab driver had predicted. He counted just over a dozen sleek craft with masts ranging from two to three feet tall. Several adults—not children—controlled their individual boats by radio from the beach. The miniature sloops and yawls were gaily painted with painstakingly detailed deckwork and white sails numbered for ease in identification. Nearby on the beach a banner over a folding table proclaimed that the hobbyists belonged to the MISSION BAY MODEL YACHT CLUB.

A swarthy teenager in a tank shirt and cutoff Levis ambled up to Steelbinder, his eyes full of admiration for the sleek hydroplane. The boy was about to speak, when Steelbinder glared back at him icily and stepped away.

Steelbinder felt a sudden constriction in his chest and a slight pounding in his head. It was always the first sign. *The screaming devils were there, clamoring pitchmen trying to get in.* Not now, Virgil, let me be! Rescue me, grandfather!

Instead of dissipating, the annoyance grew. Steelbinder wanted to be by himself, and the people from the model sailboat regatta were in the way! Walking farther along the beach, he tried to fend off the terrible noise in his head by gently humming to himself.

Finally alone, he put the speedboat in the water and primed the engine with the gasoline he'd brought along in a small plastic bottle. He set the hydroplane's rudder for straight ahead and cranked the engine. It started immediately with an ear-shattering roar that drowned out the plutonian shouting in his brain. Steelbinder released the model, and it tore off in the opposite direction from the sailboats, out toward the main channel.

He quickly extended the radio unit's antenna and flicked the rudder control switch. The little hydroplane responded perfectly. *Five degrees to the left.*

Steelbinder smiled. The adjustments he'd made on the hull back at his workbench were working! The sponsons rode higher, and the model cut across the water faster than he'd dreamed possible. *Circle around, come back this way, little one.* Perfect! The boat performed even better than he'd hoped.

Though he prudently let the model circle some distance out, the regatta people were not placated. The noise was disruptive, and they found the water on the bay suddenly ruffled and unpredictable. Several of them glared his way and pointed to a nearby sign on the beach. Steelbinder didn't bother to read it. *Rules were for fools.*

One of the bigger men began shouting at him, using profanity. Coming up beside the bruiser, a woman with peroxided hair and an absurdly fat ass threatened Steelbinder with an upraised fist. He remained silent, only glaring back at her. Screaming profanities was bad enough, he reflected, but a physical threat was inexcusable. His mind began calculating, and the voice in his head became louder. Instead of urging restraint, his grandfather was urging him on! Steelbinder once more cursed Gerald Eisenbinder and tried to think clearly. There had to be an expedient way to shut up these beach troublemakers once and for all.

He had planned to take the speedboat model back to the ship, possibly even use it for target practice off the carrier's stern if the opportunity presented itself. After all, it was only an adult toy and expendable. All of his toys were expendable. *Life itself was expendable*. The people on the beach who threatened him were expendable.

Even from the distance, the sound of the hydroplane model shattered the air. Steelbinder made up his mind. *Why not*? The glorious scene he had in mind would be worth pruning a few weeks off the life of the miniature speedboat. But first he'd need a margin of safety for himself. He stepped down the sand several yards, ignoring the beefy man in the form-fitting T-shirt who continued to shout threats at him. Steelbinder was thankful that the brute's hands—the size of big honeydews—were preoccupied with his own radio control unit.

Steelbinder narrowed his eyes and stared at his circling hydroplane while it made two more passes, then glanced at the minute hand on his watch. The boat should be running low on fuel. He waited until it was in the near turn, then brought it up on the beach.

Steelbinder pulled out a package of Life Savers, peeled away the foil and discarded several before deciding on pineapple. Drawing comfort from the candy's sweetness, he strolled around a small bend in the beach until he was out of sight of the others. He climbed a slight knoll behind a park storage shed then peered around it to make sure he could still see all of the sailboat course. *Good. A perfect vantage*. It took him only seconds to refuel the model.

He smiled to himself and for one last time examined and admired the speedboat model he'd created with his own hands. The miniature hydroplane could use some new paint on the bow and one of the number decals was flaking away, but otherwise it was good as new. *Say goodbye quickly, R.W.*! It was only a model, a toy undeserving of lingering sentiment. He could build another, bigger and better.

His breath came faster as he again compulsively stumbled into the strange, hell-fired cauldron that had tracked him since childhood. He flashed on that blurry fragment of the past, the time he'd attempted to recreate a Viking funeral. At least on that early imprimatur he'd had the foresight to bring along one of the jumbo firecrackers. Fireworks made such magnificent statements! Too bad he didn't have a few with him now as he attacked the enemy sailboat armada. No matter, even without them, he'd make a spectacular impression. Glancing up at the afternoon sun, Steelbinder wiped the perspiration from his forehead. He put the miniature hydroplane in the water and again turned over the engine. It took off, straight out.

A moment later he was back on the knoll, behind the shed, feeling like a secret puppeteer gathering up his strings to go to work. "Hmmmm-nnnnn," he said softly to himself. The actors a short distance up the beach and the colorful props scattered across the water were all about to obediently dance to his command. The coarse individuals who outnumbered and dared to threaten him would now be taught a lesson. There was no stopping R.W. Steelbinder once he'd made up his mind. Only fools built sand forts against the tide. They'd learn, like the others, that he was invincible.

Steelbinder first sent the hydrofoil out in a wide arc, carefully lining it up at right angles to the projected course of the sailboats. Strangely, the words of the *Abraham Lincoln's* captain and navigator as they hovered over the plotting board echoed in Steelbinder's ears . . . instructions he'd heard often enough while standing behind the carrier's helm.

"What's the course to the entry channel?"

"Two-twenty, sir."

"Too close to that outbound shipping, Steelbinder. Take her around, and we'll approach from one-ninety."

The little speedboat was out in Fisherman's Channel now, circling just this side of the bridge. Steelbinder worked the joy stick on the radio control, maneuvering it back toward the cove and the model sailboat regatta. The two-cylinder aircraft engine he'd adapted to the model's hull split the air, shrieking like a banshee. Another two, maybe three degrees will do it. *Nudge the control gingerly, R.W., very lightly.*

Steelbinder chuckled. It was a shame there were no swimmers in the water. The hydroplane was small, but it had wonderfully lethal possibilities. Riding its sponsons, it bore relentlessly on, roiling the placid surface of the bay. On the North Cove beach, the sailboat crowd stared at it, stupefied that this time the racing model had not veered away.

Closer, closer. Steelbinder's heart thumped joyously in his chest.

A gently bobbing sloop was first in his path. The roaring speedboat cut through its hollow balsa wood hull like butter, lifted slightly in the air to plow through the rigging of a second sailboat, then went on to lodge in the side of a third boat with such a fury that the two hulls cartwheeled across the water for thirty feet. The hydroplane's engine died only when the model slipped, belly-up, under the water. The three sloops followed it to the bottom.

Steelbinder grinned and said aloud, *"Take that to the bank, fools."*

The discord fell away to a strange, uncomfortable silence. From where Steelbinder hovered, the others in the cove couldn't hear him, but he started to sing to them anyway. His postured voice was off-key, but it hardly mattered. He hadn't sung the words since childhood:

> *Then blow, my bullies, all together.*
> *Blow my boys, for better weather.*
> *Blow my bullies, blow!*

Steelbinder felt not the slightest remorse, only a bubbling kind of amusement. What he'd just accomplished was like kicking over an anthill and watching the havoc. As much as he wanted to continue observing the disruption up the beach, it was too chancy. Descretion was in order now. *Get away while you can.* Hurrying over to a nearby dumpster, he carefully wiped his fingerprints off the radio transmitter and was about to bury it in the trash when he heard a small voice from behind him.

"What you did was awesome, mister. Can you do it again?"

Steelbinder turned. Confronted by a waist-high boy with a freckle-splotched face, he thought quickly. "No, I'm afraid not. That was my last boat."

"Your song was cool, too. Will you teach me the words?"

Steelbinder patted the kid on the head and tossed him the rest of the roll of Life Savers. "Sorry pal, I don't have time. You planning on building a boat model someday?"

The boy nodded eagerly.

Steelbinder handed him the radio-control unit. "Good. Then you'll have use for this." Giving the wide-eyed youth a smile and a salute, he immediately left the area, double-timing it to the other side of the island.

The afternoon had been productive after all, he mused. He'd also worked up a voracious appetite. Before going back to the naval base, he decided to find a place to order a hot dog, some fries, and possibly a beer. He also needed to pick up an evening paper, for he was curious to learn what headway, if any, the incompetent authorities were making on the Maxine Bullock homicide case. He wondered how long it would take before Captain Bullock would be considered the prime suspect.

～～～～～ 20

The Navy shrink tried, unsuccessfully, to keep a straight face. "Three years ago I counseled a destroyer commander who liked to wear women's panties."

Pamela smiled. "I'd say the key to that one is *how often*. Doesn't everyone have a minor private perversity hidden behind everyday convention?"

Dr. Reisman looked at her. He said with trepidation, "Suffice it to say we drummed him out of the Navy when he wore them in the hallway outside the officers' shower."

Dougherty grimaced. He remembered working on the bizarre case himself two years earlier.

The meeting had been underway for half an hour, and although Dougherty found Bernie Reisman and Clarence Ogden pleasant enough, both psychiatrists seemed to be taking their own sweet time about getting to the point. Pamela, too, looked impatient. Dougherty hadn't looked forward to calling in the Navy shrinks, but it was a matter of official routine; there'd be hell to pay from his superiors if he didn't tie down the Freudian paradigms early on. Too often it seemed the purportedly brilliant specialists from Balboa Naval Hospital represented a world that eroded Dougherty's common sense and ability to make conclusive decisions on matters he considered cut and dried. The fantastically conceited analysts had equivocated in the past, and they seemed to be doing the same thing today. At least it was two on two. He and Pamela weren't outnumbered.

Both consultants had M.D. Diplomates from the American Board of Psychiatry and Neurology as well as full commander's stripes. Dr. Bernie Reisman, who sat near the window, was on the stout side, a squat-down man with an anemic oval face that reminded Dougherty of a hospital bedpan. Dr. Clarence Ogden, who worked hard at holding in his gut and stood posture-perfect by the wall, was tall, blue-eyed, and strikingly handsome. Ogden, however, seemed more preoccupied with Pamela's form-fitting dress than the task at hand.

The two naval doctors had debated among themselves for half an hour, but now Reisman seemed to control the conversation. The portly psychiatrist liked to stare out the window when he spoke, often in monosyllables. Dougherty didn't blame Reisman for being distracted. It was a great view, far more pleasant to look at than the lab photographs of the mutilation murder that were spread out on his desk.

Reisman continued to postulate: "Aboard a warship, time stretches, and it can squeeze a sailor in strange ways. The Code of Spartacus often binds a man to solve his own problems in silence. *Internal passion*, if you please." The psychiatrist looked and sounded a little weary, but he kept clunking along like some knight in rusty armour. "Sociopaths tend to resist classical conditioning—they just don't digest and internalize rules as well as others. Who knows? Perhaps our recruiting efforts might be served better by the laws of natural selection, rather than deceptive achievement profiles and—"

"Doctor Reisman, please," Pamela interrupted, "spare us the messy empirical realities, and be more specific." She peered at him through heavy eyelids and nervously tapped a pencil on a notepad. So far she only had a half page of notes. "Could we get back to the pressures of command and how lengthy missions might erode a marriage?"

Dougherty shifted uncomfortably. He wasn't about to get into that; they'd be here the rest of the damned afternoon. "Pamela, do you mind? Captain Bullock's connubial misery—as fascinating as you might find it—is not the point here."

Reisman held up his hand. "Ms Bonner is entitled to an answer. Bullock has taken every prescribed physical and mental exam incident to Academy entrance, graduation, commissioning, flight school, and promotional review. And he's passed them all with flying colors. Seven years ago he and his wife were approved by a local adoption board in Florida. Several children were recommended to them but they could never agree. A year later they withdrew their request. I'm not implying any significance to this, but Maxine Bullock claimed that she was unable to bear children."

Dougherty sat forward. "Dr. Reisman, Dr. Ogden, forget Bullock for the moment. I need a more definitive crime profile, some cubbyholes I can explore. Let's talk about the killer's motivation." Dougherty gestured toward the slate board on the far wall. "Forgive me for being a little thick-headed, but the last time you were here you gave a little chalk talk I readily understood. Would you mind resorting to illustration again?"

Clarence Ogden glanced at his colleague, then ventured across the room to the board. He erased some old scratching that was one of Dougherty's shopping lists then quickly divided the slate into four even-spaced columns. He scribbled something in Latin at the top of each, allowing his continuing silence to work on their nerves.

Dougherty waited.

Hands folded over his chest, Ogden said, "Diagnosticians, scientists—like everyone else—see the world through the distorting lens of deeply held biases. Truth, unfortunately, is a sort of slippery thing." The psychiatrist paused to slash several x's over the divider lines between the headings. "These borderline situations are the tough ones. I'll try to explain."

Pamela sighed. "I trust, Doctor, that you'll go a few steps beyond the usual lack-of-self-esteem routine. It's already obvious that our gruesome friend is wrestling with a terrible demon, some form of battered self-disgust."

Ogden cast a swift, professional glance at her. "I'll try to oblige you, Ms Bonner." He turned to the window and Dr. Reisman. "And my trusty colleague here can interrupt if he disagrees."

Reisman sat back in his chair and nodded.

Inhaling vigorously, Ogden raised an index finger. "A key question is whether our killer has been violent in the past. In this current heinous situation, such a verification will be difficult, most probably impossible. Often, however, both serial and series killers confide to others somewhere along the line, telling them that they hear voices commanding them to act in antisocial ways."

"*Command hallucinations*," Reisman murmured, as if his colleague's words required a proper footnote.

"If these people hear voices and dismiss them, the risk is low," Dr. Ogden continued. "A temporal lobe epileptic, for example, might hear Christ commanding him to do something, but at the same time *know* it was really his own cuckoo. The key is evasiveness. Psychotics tend to spill the beans on everything; paranoids are mostly guarded and evasive."

Dougherty pointed to the chalkboard. "Your interesting graffiti, doctor. What does it mean?"

"Yes, I was getting to that. Let me finish up on the paranoia. If your man is an acute schizo-paranoid, I suspect you'll know it soon enough. Keep him hooked, but give him lots of line. And room to run with it. You get in too close, and you're in big trouble with paranoids. They're slippery. Of course, it's an understatement that our mysterious friend *hates women*. He's obviously a mysogynist." Ogden looked at the photographs on the desk, then over to Pamela, for the first time their eyes mating in complete understanding. He warned, "You're going to have to be very careful when you bait the hook."

Dougherty glanced at the second psychiatrist, who still sat still as a potted plant by the window. Bernie Reisman had retreated into silence, except for occasionally clearing his throat as if it were a social activity. Across from Dougherty, Pamela was taking down copious notes again. He wondered why the hell she didn't use his cassette recorder.

Dougherty waited impatiently while Dr. Ogden wrote several categorical sub-types within the columns he'd drawn on the chalkboard. The posture-conscious physician explained, "*Religious Obsession*—the maniac who thinks he's the saviour returned." Ogden drew a fish and wrote the word JESUS. The chalk squeaked and Pamela grimaced. Ogden raised his voice: "Next, *Special Powers*—the killer who believes he's a messenger of either God or the Devil. Or anyone else for that matter; maybe even Johnny Carson, Moamar Quadaffi, or the President." The psychiatrist moved to the next column, underscored the words *Retribution—Special Powers*, and continued, "Now, the debt-owed cases, where our misfit is convinced everyone or someone special is out to get him, and retribution is the only escape. And finally, the *Outside Control* situation, where a mad hatter might be manipulated by some alien technology or extra-sensory power only he understands. This gypsy-like individual is keen on out-of-body experience and ESP. Superstition's a way of life." Ogden looked at them. "Have you heard enough?"

Dougherty nodded. He knew statistics were the bread of life for a mental care specialist, and he didn't want to get into them any deeper. Not now; there wasn't time. The categories were enough.

Pamela pretended to glance through her notes. Looking up, she said sullenly, "One moment you're crystal clear, doctor. The next you're as abstract as a Beethoven scherzo. Considering all the confusion, I hope I've learned something. I do have one more important question."

Ogden smiled with caution. "Perhaps I should defer to my colleague. If he's quiet any longer, he's apt to nod off."

Pamela nodded. "Fine. I've often missed some good music by not listening to the flip side. Dr. Reisman, why the record repeating itself and the killer going to such lengths to obtain it? And apparently in *quantity*?"

The second psychiatrist grinned. "So thoughtful of you to field the tough ones in my direction, Ms Bonner. I wish I had a clinical answer to apply to your queries, but unfortunately, we'll need more clues, additional behavioral patterns. Reward and punishment, something that happened in childhood, there has to be a factor. Who knows? The secret may even be locked in the romance ballad's lyrics."

"Romance ballad? No way," admonished Dougherty. "Sorry, it's not that kind of music. The Midnight Admirals are into heavy metal—the sleazy variety."

"Oh." Reisman thought for a moment. "Whatever the extent of the music's heinousness, I suggest we examine the lyrics. We need to study them as well as a profile of this recording group and any significant publicity they may have generated over the years."

Dougherty jotted down a memo to himself. He said, "It'll take time, but I promise you'll get the information."

Reisman checked his watch. "I'm sorry. We've overstayed our allotted time. Both of us have to get back to the hospital." He rose from his chair and turned to Pamela. "Before leaving, however, I'd like to ask a question of the FBI woman."

Pamela leaned forward expectantly. "Please do, doctor."

"You're making quite a name for yourself with these regional lectures on rape and violence, Ms Bonner. Might we encourage you to write an article for the *Journal of Abnormal Psychology*? Your personal investigative experiences, possibly a piece on macho veneer, its generative effect on turbulent sexual encounters?"

"Doctor, as much as I'm intrigued, I'm afraid the answer is no. My bureau job is like a jealous mistress; there're just not enough hours in the day." She hesitated, then said pertly, "To be honest, what damned few free moments I have left I enjoy letting my hair down."

Dougherty smiled to himself, weighing her words against what he'd seen so far. He wondered when and where he might get the opportunity to enjoy some of this kicked-back, hair-down company.

The two doctors laughed. Dougherty knew that he'd have to be good to Bernie Reisman and Clarence Ogden. Later they'd both probably be professional witnesses for the prosecution—when and if this homicide case was brought to court. They now stood nervously by the door, anxious to leave but aware that neither

Dougherty nor the woman had officially dismissed them or said goodbye.

Dougherty smiled and said to them, "I assume we've covered everything, gentlemen." Pausing, Dougherty drummed a pencil on his desk. "But I do have one more difficult question. The *Abraham Lincoln* leaves tomorrow for San Francisco then the Pacific Northwest. Supposing—let's assume the worst—that our killer stalks victims each time he steps off the ship. What are your thoughts on imposing a protective quarantine on the ship's personnel in San Francisco, forbidding them to go ashore until the vessel reaches Bremerton?"

The naval doctors stared at each other, then back at Dougherty. They looked uncomfortable. So did Pamela.

Dr. Reisman cleared his throat again, this time with considerable emphasis. "Lieutenant Commander Dougherty, your suggestion, as well-intentioned as it is, surprises me."

"It'll surprise the hell out of Captain Bullock and his crew as well. But both the NIS and FBI are desperate; we need to buy valuable time."

"At the expense of four or five thousand officers and men who don't deserve being brought up for a round turn? Withholding shore liberty on a deployment is a tough reprimand. And especially during Fleet Week in San Francisco. It's a punishment the crew doesn't deserve."

Dougherty passed on that.

Pamela said quietly, "Besides, the killer doesn't strike at every port. It appears he missed Honolulu."

"His hemorrhoids may have kept him under the weather," Dougherty quipped.

Pam wasn't amused.

Ignoring the remark, Dr. Ogden shook his head. "I have to agree with my colleague. You can't withhold shore leave—even though the alternative might mean going aboard myself and spending every waking hour doing psychological profiles on the entire ship's complement. God forbid, the time element would be staggering!"

Dougherty chuckled. "Don't stick your neck out too far, doctor. It just may come down to that. Unfortunately, I'm less interested in reconstructing the killer's past fantasies as I am quickly identifying him on hard evidence and getting a conviction. That's why I intend to ship out with that carrier myself."

Pamela dropped her pen and stared at him.

When the two medical officers had left the office, Dougherty shrugged. "You were impressed, I take it?"

She grinned. "Dazzled. I think." The sparkle disappeared from her eyes as she said seriously, "Todd, I want to go along on the mission."

"No, and no again. Even if Bullock were to okay it, a tour of duty on a fleet carrier is too intense. It's like taking a drink from a fire hose." Dougherty braced himself, waiting for the static he knew would surely come.

Pam retreated into silence instead, glaring at him long and hard. He met her prolonged stare, and finally she got up and hurried out of his office.

 **21**

At first the growing hostile forces only amused Steelbinder, but now he was concerned, especially over the woman FBI agent. Pamela Bonner was like an annoying gnat, and the thoughts of retribution were difficult to resist. He might do something about it before the ship left San Diego tomorrow, but infinite caution would be in order. Thus far, his carefully laid plan to consign that draggle-tail Maxine Bullock to hell and punish her husband was working flawlessly. No glitches and he needed to keep it that way.

Steelbinder wondered why the FBI had assigned a female to help the Navy's investigation team. Women had clever, intuitive natures, and this could be dangerous for him. How clever was this one? He once more perused the three-column newspaper story on Pamela Bonner. He read the news caption then again studied the photograph, committing her features to memory. It was apparently an old newsphoto, taken of her at a speaker's podium during some earlier feminist clambake in San Diego. She was a pretty woman with a pleasing body, but her eyes, staring out from the newspaper, vexed Steelbinder.

He thought about this new opposition, as well as the officer from the NIS. Todd Dougherty appeared to be the silent type, but he had an intelligent, single-minded, and big-hearted face. He would be little or no threat. The FBI wench, on the other hand, had an unusually intense, never-give-up look about her. It was as if those eyes had some personal message just for R. W. Steelbinder. Had he seen that fixed gaze somewhere before?

It suddenly came to him: *his mother, Felicia!* Back on the wall of his storage unit, the painting with the intense, discomfiting stare. The faces were dissimilar, but this FBI woman's eyes were almost identical to his dead mother's.

Steelbinder shivered. Pamela Bonner would be dangerous to him; he could sense it already. *Fear*—he needed to make her afraid, shatter her composure and self-confidence. Perhaps he should find a way to eliminate her completely. He would give it some thought. Perhaps, like a cat postponing its dinner, it would be an interesting diversion to play with her first. He read the caption on the newspaper story:

FBI WOMAN HERE TO SPEAK ON RAPE

"Hmmmm-nnnn," he mumbled absently. He noted with interest that the Bonner woman was due to lecture within a couple of hours out at the UC-La Jolla campus. *Why not?* There was time if he hurried. The FBI creature had chosen to become his enemy, a grave mistake. He didn't need a clever feminist making things difficult; not now, when events were going so beautifully!

Steelbinder made up his mind. He took a bus downtown, found a convenient car rental agency and flipped his seldom-used Mastercard on the counter. Ten minutes later he sat behind the wheel of a Ford Escort headed back toward National City and the mini-warehouse that was his personal hope chest.

Steelbinder needed several things to complete the wardrobe for his upcoming masquerade out at La Jolla. He found them in a dust-covered carry-on bag hanging on the storage unit's back wall: a cheerful tartan patterned sports jacket, a button-down pale yellow shirt, and a handsome tie that was a little too wide but otherwise harmonized nicely with the coat. He hoped the jacket wasn't too conspicuous. The shoes and slacks he already wore would complete the ensemble. Steelbinder dressed quickly then examined himself in the full-length mirror he'd installed on the inside of the storage unit's door.

"Hmmmm-nnnn. Too slick, not quite the right image," he said quietly. He looked too much like one of those actors from the *The Young and the Restless*. With a pair of eyeglasses he'd look more the part of the scholar. Where were his grandmother's bifocals? Once before he'd worn them to successfully alter his appearance.

Steelbinder rummaged through a carton marked PERSONAL

EFFECTS and found three old pairs. He selected the funky round ones with tarnished silver frames and put them on. He again came across his grandfather's admiral's hat in its protective plastic bag. Beneath it in a small jewelry box was a pair of slightly tarnished stars. *Rear Admiral's stars*. This time he would make it a point to take the hat and rank insignia back to the ship with him.

One more thing. He needed one of the psychiatry textbooks to carry along with him to the Bonner woman's lecture. A prop would do wonders for his credibility.

Pamela was pleased. Her speech, thus far, had been received with rapt attention by an audience that was made up primarily of women. A few of them she recognized. She knew that most of those present, including the dozen or so men, were practicing psychologists, family counselors, and social workers.

Pam checked her watch. It was getting late. Sipping from a glass of water, she continued in an even, energetic voice: "The new laws recognize the realities confronting potential and actual rape victims and acknowledge more fully that rape is a crime of violence, not an act of sexual passion. The California Supreme Court has unanimously affirmed a linchpin of that reform effort— a 1980 state law saying victims do not, I repeat, *do not* have to show that they physically resisted attack. As I said earlier, we have to deal with the possibility of serious harm in resisting a deranged rapist. It's been my experience that many women have been brutalized even more severely than by the rape itself because they tried to fight off their attackers."

Pamela wound up the speech by praising the State Supreme Court again while tossing in a few pet concepts of her own. Finally, she commended the San Diego area's new rape hotline.

She bowed to the applause and began answering the inevitable barrage of questions. There were too many, and she went beyond her allotted time.

At last the session was concluded. Pam shook hands with the other speakers on the platform, gathered up her notes, and started to leave. Her shoes were too tight, and her feet were killing her; all she wanted to do now was get back to the hotel, take off her clothes, and flop.

A stout, older woman with frizzy curls, orange-tinted glasses, and a pompous manner came up and introduced herself as the head of the social ecology program at another UC campus. She held Pamela's arm, preventing her from moving up the aisle. "Ms. Bonner, one last question, please. This rape-murder incident at the naval base that's getting all the sordid headlines. It seems you studiously avoided discussing it tonight."

Pam smiled back at the woman without enthusiasm. "Wouldn't you remain silent as well, if the facts were still sketchy and incoherent?"

"Thank God, it's a freak, one-of-a-kind incident."

Pamela stiffened. "I only wish. Your hopeful words, not mine. I'm afraid this may not be an isolated incident."

The woman took off her glasses. "I don't understand."

"There appears to have been an identical crime in Hong Kong. We suspect our killer has two long-running grudges. The Navy in general and women in particular. I'm sorry, but now I have to run along."

The older woman politely retreated, and Pamela made a break for the door. She managed to get less than six feet, for now one of the male members of the audience blocked her way. He was a massive-shouldered individual with slicked-back, curly dark blond hair, granny eyeglasses, and a sport coat that belonged on a Del Mar quarterhorse. The poor man's face looked as if it had tailgated a semi-trailer. Pam had seen him previously, arriving late and taking a seat near the rear. Somehow, he didn't fit the image of the professional type.

"Ms Bonner? Or is it *Doctor Bonner?*"

She looked at him warily. "Please don't flatter me. I'm very tired. If you read the program, you'll see I'm just a government detective without a terminal degree."

"Hmmmm-nnnnn. Then you could have fooled me. I thought your speech was brilliant. Yes indeed. *Quite academic.*"

Pamela sighed with impatience. "Thank you." She noted that the stranger had a book with him he kept nervously exchanging from hand to hand. She couldn't resist reaching out to steady the text, at the same time examining the title. Startled, he handed it to her then stepped back slightly.

Pam read the title aloud: "*The Mask of Sanity*, by Harvey Cleckley?"

He smiled at her. "Yes, indeed. Allow me to introduce myself. I'm Dr. Mueller. *Hans Mueller*. I have a psychological counseling practice up in Beverly Hills and came down here for the convention." He winked at her. "And your speech, of course, Ms Bonner."

"I noticed. You came in late."

"Sorry. I had an important call from a patient."

Pamela bought everything except the twinkling, nervous eyes.

Was the toady little bastard trying to pick her up? "Dr. Mueller, I must—"

"Call me Hans, please. And do you mind if I call you Pamela?" He pointed to the book. "It's yours. I think it's important you have it for your work."

She smiled. "I don't understand."

"You will soon enough. The Maxine Bullock homicide. The author has some excellent ideas on pyschopathy—like theories on dealing not with a complete man but with something that suggests a subtly-constructed reflex machine—a potentially dangerous machine."

Pamela turned the book over in her hands. She opened it, noting that *Hans Mueller* had been brazen enough to write a short dedication to her.

FOR PAMELA: TO UNRAVELING THE SECRETS OF DR. JEKYLL AND MR. HYDE? MAY WE BOTH LEARN ALL THE SECRETS OF CRIME AND HUMAN NATURE. BEST REGARDS, DR. HANS MUELLER.

Pam looked back up at him, still not sure if she saw guile or not.

"Please," he said in a strangely soft voice. "Could you spare a moment? There is something I must tell you in absolute confidence." He ran a hand over his slicked down curly hair and gestured toward a nearby row of chairs.

Feeling repelled and strangely attracted to Mueller at the same time, she took a seat. *At least it would take the pressure off her chafed bunions.* Mueller plopped down in the next row and faced her.

"I have a patient," he said bluntly, "who, of course, must remain anonymous. Suffice it to say he's in the military and of extremely high rank. The man is having difficulty coping."

Pamela frowned and exhaled wearily. *Patient confidentiality.* If Hans were legitimate, she'd have to phrase her questions carefully. "Considering professional ethics, why are you telling me this?"

"Two reasons. I liked your speech, of course. And I want to see you make some progress on the North Island homicide investigation."

Pam stiffened. She stared at him, and he nervously held her gaze. There was something unsettling about Mueller's eyes behind the studious, metal-rimmed glasses. She asked, "I take it your client is relevant to our investigation?"

He nodded, a trifle smugly.

Pamela thought for a moment. "You realize, of course, that you may be incriminating your patient?"

"*Former patient*. Yes, I'm keenly aware of that." Mueller smiled. "But justice must be served, yes? There are too many men involved."

"Men? Not women?"

"A slip of the tongue. Both. I believe you said earlier, '*the Navy in general, women in particular*.' Am I correct?"

Pamela shrugged. "But not in my speech. You were eavesdropping when I spoke to that woman a moment ago."

"Sorry. I was fascinated by your conversation."

"You first mentioned a military leader. Now you've narrowed it down to the Navy. You've perked my interest, Dr. Mueller. Please go on."

"*Hans, please*," he admonished. He watched her take out a note pad and waited until she'd finished writing down this name before continuing. "Hmmmm-nnnnn. I did give away the branch of the service, didn't I? My, my. Perhaps I should approach this matter differently. Why don't *you* pose the questions, and I'll first screen them, answering only the germane ones."

"Stop beating around the bush, Hans. What's going on? If you have a patient who specifically avowed that he intended to kill Maxine Bullock, you have legal obligations, so speak up. We're dealing with a ruthless butcher." Pam waited while the psychologist loosened his collar.

He said to her airily, "Here piety lives on in pity dead. Who is the greater reprobate than one that grieves at doom decline?"

Pam stared back, unimpressed and unwilling to ask where the quote originated. The absurd man was trying to act dignified, and it wasn't working.

Mueller's forehead was sweating slightly, and he looked uncomfortable, but when he spoke again his voice was surprisingly calm and collected. "To proceed, Pamela. I've been keeping a journal, and what it contains is not only a professional challenge, but rather frightening—depending how you look at it. My notes completely disprove the myth that disturbed people can't sustain a facade and function in high positions. Indeed, in many cases, great disturbances and turmoil can be shrewdly hidden."

"I'm not prepared to dispute that. And I'm sympathetic to the therapist's 'duty to inform' problem. Please go on."

"Like most of my colleagues, I'm not accurate at predicting future violence. But you must believe me. I was able to predict Maxine Bullock's violent murder. You see, it's all written down in my journal."

Pamela's pulse quickened. She'd expected a few red herrings at best, but not for Dr. Mueller to go way out on a limb. She needed to reason with him. "The time, place, and circumstances? You actually have them all written down?"

Mueller chortled. "Mind-boggling, isn't it? There are other women's names as well. And locations. Other cities."

Pam froze. She leaned forward, lowering her voice. "Listen to me, Dr. Mueller—*I'm sorry, Hans*. It's imperative that you tell me. Specifically, what other places?"

"Hong Kong and . . ." Mueller didn't finish the sentence, scolding her with his finger instead.

Pam's heart beat erratically. He was toying with her, feeding her a tidbit at a time, but she had no choice but to play his game. "How old would you estimate our killer suspect to be, Hans?"

Incongruously, Mueller laughed. It was a bitter, suffering laugh, and it made her squirm. Alarmed at his outburst, Pamela edged back gingerly. "I asked you a question, Dr. Mueller."

"Almost caught me, didn't you? I don't have to *estimate*. No, not at all. I possess the patient's birthdate, remember? You'll have to work a little harder than that. Nothing should come facilely in life, should it, Pamela?" Mueller's eyes danced with an uncomfortable, malevolent delight.

"Whatever you say, Hans." Had he not brought up Hong Kong out of the blue, Pamela would have told the annoying psychologist to kiss off and go cure himself.

He said to her, "Hmmmmm-nnnn. Patience, my dear. Perhaps some hints are in order." Mueller's eyes sparkled zestfully. "Let's see how clever you are. Tell me, what body type do you think this murderer might be?"

"What?"

"Endomorph, mesomorph, or ectomorph?"

"You're over my head. Stop toying with me, or I'll leave now."

"A person's physique or *somatotype*, Pamela. In simplistic terms, is the suspect's build most similar to a Parkerhouse roll, a chunk of firewood, or a wire clothes hanger?"

Puzzled and annoyed as Pam was, all she could do was stare at him. Then she replied angrily, "Physique doesn't cause crime, nor is it an inevitable correlate. You should know that, Doctor. Next thing you'll try to feed me is that our killer may be one in a thousand with an XYY chromosome configuration."

Again, a sly, enigmatic smile. "A convenient way to fix the blame, but in this case no. XYY types are purported to have a *deficit in intelligence*. The man you're after has a very acute mind.

He is, in fact, a polymath; a man of great learning in varied fields. He's a *genius*, Pamela. You need to understand that."

"Why is he doing this?"

Mueller shrugged and looked away. "Can you explain why some people prefer vanilla ice cream and others chocolate?"

"That's not good enough. You know more than you're telling me. At least you struck a chord on the Hong Kong information. We need to talk more about this journal of yours, Hans, and obviously, this isn't the place. I'd like you to come by the NIS office at North Island in the morning."

Pamela knew she had to get to Dougherty; with two of them going at Mueller the odds would improve, and they might get somewhere. The man confronting her was loony, but what shrink wasn't to a degree? Whatever, he had information they badly needed. She had to chance it. Hans Mueller also appeared to be more than an angry member of the profession out after some surefire publicity.

"I'd like that, Pamela. I really would. But I have to get back up to Beverly Hills tonight. There are appointments in the morning I can't afford to break."

Pam nodded. *At Rodeo-Drive-going-rates, she could understand why*. She thought fast, trying to come up with a game plan to keep him around just a little longer.

He smiled at her and pursed his lips. "I'll tell you what. Yes, we do need to parley. There's a bar down the road in La Jolla—the Fantasia. Why don't the two of us go there now? We can have a libation in a quiet booth, and you can take all the notes you like."

Pamela needed to pinch herself to slow down. She'd come close to blurting out *why not*? They were both fishing, but this time she'd nearly played into his hands, swallowing the bait—hook, line and sinker. The shrewd Hans Mueller had information for her, but he was also coming off like a slippery troll. Something wasn't quite right, and she couldn't put her finger on it. But what if this character were halfway sincere? A bar was reasonably safe, and he obviously had information she needed now, before the *Abraham Lincoln* pulled out at noon tomorrow.

Reading the apprehension on her face, Mueller reached inside his pocket and withdrew a small photo. He thrust it at her with an air of triumph. "I assume you recognize the uniformed Navy officer?"

Pamela swallowed hard. She sure did. It was Captain Bullock, accompanied by an attractive Chinese woman. They were leaning on the front of a vintage Rolls Royce.

"Interesting, yes?" Mueller asked. "You may keep the photo. Pamela? You look annoyed with me."

"It's your creeping candor." Pam's head was swimming. "All right, Hans. I'm convinced. Go on ahead to this Fantasia. I have to call a friend to explain I'll be late. I'll take my own wheels and meet you at the bar." *God, please. At least let the creep buy the transportation arrangements.*

The banquet room had finally emptied, and they were alone.

Mueller glowered and shook his head. "Negative; that's not satisfactory. I insist on waiting. If we can't go together, I'll follow you there."

Again, the fisherman was drawing her in! Why was he so damned insistent on doing it his way? Pam rose to her feet and stepped back, putting a few inches between herself and the hissing quicksand. *Your imagination's getting the best of you, Ms Bonner. Shape up. There's a gun in your purse. Just get on with the job.* She looked at him critically. "Fine, Hans. But wait until I complete my phone call. I'll be right back." She hurried out of the banquet room and found a pay phone in a lobby alcove.

Several anxious seconds later she had Dougherty on his home line. "Todd, I need help."

"A place to stay or a bail-out?"

"Neither one. Hold on to your hat. I've got a weird psychologist in tow who claims to know Maxine Bullock's killer. He insists the maniac we're after is one of his clients."

"Sure. I'll bet. Paltry shreds of information that later turn out to be worthless. I'll wager you ten to one the guy's a crafty reporter playing games."

"No, I think he's legitimate. But you may be halfway right about the games. He may be interested in the *personal kind*—with me."

She heard laughter in the receiver. "Come on now, liberated woman. What happened to the big girl trying to earn the FBI sharpshooter's medal?"

"Get off it, Todd. He won't open up unless I go with him to the Fantasia Bar."

"Fine, but what's he have to offer?"

"Hong Kong! He knows about that first homicide. I think he's ready to spill the beans about Swain Bullock." She waited through interminable seconds of silence. When Dougherty spoke again he sounded like he'd just stepped out of a cold shower. "Okay, where are you now?"

"The Student Union building on the UC campus."

"Stay there. I'm on my way. Give me twenty minutes. Find an excuse to delay him."

"Todd, he won't buy it. Too skittish. He's already suspicious over why I went to the phone."

"Okay, then follow him over to that watering hole, and I'll meet you there. The Fantasia?"

"Yes. In La Jolla."

"I know the place. Be careful. He's probably harmless but it's still an odd hour and strange place to talk business."

Pamela agreed. Hanging up, she went back to find Dr. Mueller. She looked all around the banquet room, the hallway, the student lounge, even waited outside the men's room for ten minutes. No luck. He'd disappeared. Her spirits sagged.

"Shit!" she finally said aloud. Leaving the building, Pam tramped to the parking lot, keeping close to a cluster of students.

She drove the short distance to the Fantasia, hoping her signals with the elusive psychologist had somehow been crossed, that possibly he'd gone ahead to meet her after all. She found the establishment's parking area virtually empty and parked her car near the side door. She quickly went inside.

The half-empty Fantasia was overdone in mid-eighties art deco kitsch, the inevitable pink and turquoise, copied and recopied. Pam checked the counter and booths to be sure; still no infuriatingly mysterious Hans Mueller. He'd disappeared, and Pamela felt strangely abandoned. And annoyed. It was the first time she'd ever been stood up. Seated alone at the bar, she nursed her irritation with a brandy stinger. A boastful, licentious computer salesman three stools away made advances, and she worked hard to ignore him.

Finally Todd Dougherty walked in and rescued her. Pam waited while he ordered a draft beer and a package of honey-dipped peanuts, then she explained what had happened and handed over the incriminating photo. They talked in hushed tones for several minutes while Dougherty finished his beer, then they left the bar, driving off in different directions. Pamela headed back to her hotel.

They'd both agreed there was nothing more she could do about Dr. Hans Mueller until morning. Damn his elusiveness! Like it or not, the elusive, oddball psychologist was going to have one of his costly Beverly Hills therapy sessions interrupted by a phone call. She'd make a note not to forget to ask Mueller about his client's possible interest in rock music and Dante's *Divine Comedy*. Also, whether or not the shrink's mystery patient was troubled with hemorrhoids.

Pamela felt mixed emotions as she drove alone back to the Hotel del Coronado. The sky was clear and picked out in stars, and she'd rolled down the Sentra's window, hoping the night air would clear her mind. At the top of the bay bridge, she slowed the car and glanced over toward the Navy pier. The lights of the *Abraham Lincoln* reflected up off the water like a jeweler's diamond display case, for swing shift crew was at work, loading and preparing the nuke supercarrier for its impending departure, now less than a dozen hours away.

Here today, gone tomorrow, Pam mused. She suddenly found herself wondering about the rootlessness of Navy life, what it must be like for a woman in the military. She wondered what route her own life might have taken had she joined one of the armed services to see the world. *Too late now*. Hanging out around a workaholic like Lieutenant Commander Dougherty the past few days had taught her how important the ascendant years of a career could be. Go, go, go. Before the mainspring runs down.

Pamela knew she had a long way to go. She certainly didn't feel old. She'd never been the type, like some of her women pals, to linger over ads for mud spas and cosmetic surgery. *Not yet*. It was just being constantly surrounded by all the eighteen and nineteen-year-old recruits aboard the ship and around North Island that had suddenly, oddly taken a toll on her. It was a confused dichotomy, one where she felt genuinely flattered and accepted one moment, slightly decrepit and completely out of it the next. Appearance-wise, she may not have boggled the swabbies, but at least their heads had turned. Or, God forbid, did anything with tits get a sailor's eyes dancing?

After the holidays, she was determined to mellow out and make some heady resolutions for the new year. In the past, special agent Pamela Bonner, her career aside, had been too reckless with life, toying with time as though it were meaningless. A change in attitude was definitely in order. Next year she'd devote as much time to personal relationships as she did to her damned government career. Too many times when out on the town and alone in some singles haunt, Pam had told the little white lies that she was a research consultant and not the truth that she was a G-woman. The one-night stands had to end. AIDS, VD, herpes. Everyone else was reevaluating encounter affairs, and it made perfect sense.

Pam wondered if the big move to Los Angeles and her subsequent nefarious singles life had been a mistake. She'd always been a small town gal at heart. San Diego, a town where everyone seemed to know everyone else, had been good to her. So had old Teaneck, New Jersey.

Stop blaming life in the express lane, Pamela baby. Look at yourself. Is there a stranger in the mirror? If you want to settle down, do it, but stop mooning over the months and years dropping off the calendar like dry leaves in a tempest.

Arriving at the Coronado, Pam let the lot attendant park her car. She hurried through the Victorian portico into the lobby. Her feet hurt badly, and she considered taking off her shoes to go barefoot on the handsome carpet. *Sorry, feet. Wrong ambience!*

Finding no messages at the front desk, Pam smiled to herself, half-pleased. Good, at least the phones weren't ringing off the hook back at the Los Angeles office. The bureau manager there probably figured—for once correctly—that she had her hands full down here in San Diego. Earlier in the day, on the phone, she'd broached her boss on the possibility of forcing the issue with Captain Bullock by insisting, on behalf of the FBI Director himself, that she be permitted to go along on the nuke carrier at least as far as San Francisco. Predictably, regional supervisor Norm Gillespie—hard nut that he was to break for *unnecessary travel*—slapped her down with a firm no. The super wasn't about to make waves by getting into a policy dispute with the Pentagon. It was back to zero where she'd started. Bullock won the first round. The carrier's commander seemed to be the Navy's final say on that matter.

Todd Dougherty, lucky stiff that he was, would have to investigate the crew of the *Abraham Lincoln* on his own. There was no doubt in Pam's mind that the percussive Bullock would be pleased that she'd remain behind on shore.

There was one consolation—or token. Dougherty intended to place her "nominally in charge" of his San Diego investigative staff during his absence. She still didn't know whether to thank him for that or not.

Alone, she felt like a caged bird in the hotel's wire-enclosed elevator. The antiquated lift finally opened on her floor, and Pam stepped down the corridor, her heels sinking into the plush red and beige carpet. When she came to her room, she was startled to find what appeared to be a designer shoe box propped against her door. *Something the chambermaid had forgotten? A gift from the hotel?*

As she turned the room key and eased open the door, the top of the box slid off. Pam noted for the first time that it bore her name in neat, ball-point ink lettering almost an inch high.

FOR PAMELA.

Her mind raced over a list of possible gift-givers but drew a blank. It had to be a joke. No one in their right mind would leave anything of value in a hotel hallway. As for a bomb, to her knowledge none of her avowed enemies were out of prison yet. And she hadn't made any new foes recently—or had she?

Putting away her paranoia, Pam nudged with her toe at the white tissue covering the small carton's contents. She squinted, then bent over the box for a closer look.

Good god!

Fear, like a hairy centipede, crawled up her spine and clung there. Pam drew back, anxiously looking down the hallway in both directions. She refused to go into the room. Instead, she eased the door closed and threw the key back in her purse.

Inside the shoebox was a limp rubber chicken, the grotesque kind sold in joke stores and favored by stand-up comedians. But the bogus poultry alone wasn't what had started Pam's heart palpitating.

A slit had been cut between the scrawny bird's legs, and protruding from it was the largest firecracker Pamela had ever seen—and this time it was intact. The red and black wrapping around it was an Oriental design identical to that on the fragments of charred paper they'd found at the Maxine Bullock mutilation site.

Pamela stared at the shoe box, trying to cope with her escalating fear. Glancing down the hallway, she saw an older couple come out of their room. They smiled cordially at her. *Get out of here now, Pamela. Join them. They may not need company, but you sure as hell do. The evidence. Don't forget the evidence, ninny!* Gingerly picking up the shoe box, Pam tucked it under her arm and scuttled off toward the man and woman, following them into the elevator. Pam's fear intensified as she descended to the lobby.

Less than a minute later she clumsily fished in her purse, trying to find a quarter for the pay phone. The booth was warm, adding to the suffocation she already felt; her usually calm emotions were suddenly choking her, filling her with mindless panic. Twice she fumbled with coins and dropped them. When she finally managed to deposit a quarter, she got the wrong number. The second time around she had Todd Dougherty on the line after several rings.

Before identifying herself, her mind flashed that it was the second time she'd rung his firebell in one night. They shouted at each other for two minutes before she finally settled down enough to speak calmly. While speaking into the receiver, she re-examined the rubber chicken and unexploded firecracker in her lap. "I just don't need this kind of comic invention, Todd."

"I doubt whether our bizarre friend is trying to be funny. The gift is obviously an implied threat."

"Thanks. I needed that affirmation. Wait a minute. There's something else here I didn't see before—a note." Unfolding the sheet of light blue paper, Pam was shocked to discover it was a piece of interdepartmental computer stationery from the *Abraham Lincoln*. The typed message came from a dot-matrix printer.

Dougherty's impatient voice echoed in her ear. "Pam? You still there? Read the fucking message!"

"You won't believe this. 'SINCE ALL IS WELL, KEEP IT SO. WAKE NOT THE SLEEPING WOLF. HE IS ALSO THE REINCARNATION OF ST. MICHAEL, THE GUARDIAN ARCHANGEL. HE IS THE CONQUEROR OF SATAN. LEAVE HIM BE.'" Pam thought for a moment, then sighed. "Sorry, Todd, I'm afraid it's confession time. I've chased down psychos before, but this one spooks me in a different way."

"Don't tell me you're losing some of that famous Bonner equanimity."

She ignored him, anxiously studying the lobby through the etched glass door of the phone booth. The first floor of the hotel was quiet and virtually empty. "Todd, if you want the truth, I'm scared. This guy's pushing hard on my nerves, and I can't think clearly. I need to get back into my room and pick up my bags. Then I intend to change hotels and register under an assumed name."

"Look, I have a better idea. Stay over here."

"No."

"Why not?"

"I like my own pad."

"Listen to me. If your theory holds any water at all, the killer's pulling out at noon tomorrow aboard the carrier. *With me*. If Bullock's still your suspect, I'll be the one to find out the facts soon enough. While I'm gone, you can stay here as long as you water my plants. A deal?"

Her head hurt as she turned the idea over. *Didn't he have a pad at the beach? Privacy.* The proposal had its merits. "And what about tonight?" she asked warily. "You have an extra bed in that bachelor pad?"

"Picky, picky. Pamela dear, for you, anything. Just get out here now. Don't go back upstairs to your room. Forget the luggage. I'll send one of my men over to pick it up in the morning. You think you can make it out to Mission Beach on your own?"

"I might sound a little spooked, but I'm not stupid."

"Take down my address."

Pam wrote on the top of the shoe box, listening carefully as Dougherty gave street directions.

He asked, "You have to go out to the hotel parking lot alone to get to the car?"

"No. I can get the doorman to take care of it." She hesitated. "Todd?"

"Yeah?"

"I think I now know how a canary must feel when there's a huge cat just outside the cage twitching its tail and licking its chops."

"Then get yourself over here, Tweetie-boid, and granny will take care of you. Just keep an eye on the rear-view mirror to make sure no stray alleycats decide to follow along."

"No sweat there. Any problems, I'll get a couple of my old buddies in the S.D. police to ride escort." *Escort, bullshit, Pamela.* Anyone who follows would have to be the killer you're after. It's your damned job to bring that maniac in!

Nothing that fortunate or dramatic occurred on the way out to Mission Beach. She did, however, put on a spectacular performance at the wheel, driving far too fast and running one red light. Pam stopped once at an all-night 7-Eleven for a tooth brush, stick of Tussy deodorant, and a sample-sized bottle of hair conditioner she'd been meaning to try. If her Navy officer rescuer had a bed and breakfast to offer her, he could at least provide the shampoo.

Dougherty stood waiting at his doorway as Pam scaled the steps of the split-level, Spanish fourplex. His flat was on the top, right side front, with an ocean view, and although it was dark and the beach couldn't be seen in the blackness, she sensed it was close by from the sound of the surf. Shrugging, she immediately handed over the shoe box that she'd carefully cradled in a handkerchief. "You think it's worth dusting for prints?"

"I doubt it, but we'll give it a go. So far, our quarry hasn't been the type to be so sloppy."

• • •

Dougherty still didn't know what to think. Closing the door to his apartment, he took Pam's handkerchief and held up the rubber chicken by the neck. A four-inch-long firecracker fell out and dropped to the floor. He picked it up by the fuse and examined it carefully, then turned back to Pamela. Preoccupied, her critical eyes carefully surveyed his living room.

Dougherty had already pulled out the sofa bed and made it up. He put the bizarre evidence down on the coffee table and spread his hands in a helpless gesture. "It's only a one bedroom, but it does the job for a bachelor."

Pamela smiled infectiously. "Thanks for taking me in, you lovable old geezer."

"You're losing points fast. That kind of talk and you're on your way *out*. Since when does age thirty-six qualify as a geriatric case?"

"Sorry. It's that hint of gray in your sideburns that makes you look so mature. Don't fret. I happen to like mature men in their desperate years."

"I'll try and remember that. You look like you could use a drink to unwind."

"No thanks. All I'd like to do is crash."

Dougherty watched her fling herself down in an overstuffed chair, kick off her shoes, and study his eclectic decor. Her eyes roamed over his reproductions—the large El Greco above the fireplace and a cluster arrangement of Gericault sketches on the opposite wall. She seemed most impressed with the pen and ink treatment of the *Raft of Medusa*.

Pamela smiled thinly. "Looks like you've finished the place out of the Smithsonian and Metropolitan Museum mail order catalogues." She hunched her shoulders and shivered. "One thing about the traditional look. It's always in vogue."

"Lord Beaverbrook said to buy *old masters*. They fetch a better price than *old mistresses*. I really can't afford either. Everything's a copy."

Shrugging, she said softly, "Personally, I prefer David Hockney to Rembrandt."

Dougherty went over to the stereo while she stared at him. He smiled and turned up the volume on a middle-of-the-road FM station. "And Twisted Sister to elevator music?"

She nodded. "Except for this not-so-friendly group called the Midnight Admirals. Todd, would you object if a woman changes her mind?"

"About music?"

"No, a nightcap. With your heavy interior decor, I think I need that drink after all."

"Settle for a Dry Sack instead of redoing the apartment?"

"Perfect."

Dougherty shuffled out to the kitchen and dug through the cupboard. He only had two brandy snifters and one was half full of dusty gummy bears. Emptying the candy into the trash, he wiped both glasses with a soft towel and poured the Dry Sack. Before returning to the living room, he grabbed a giant white flannel shirt from the hall closet and draped it over one arm like a waiter. When he rejoined Pamela she was squatting, yoga fashion, on the foldout bed. Dougherty laid out the nightshirt beside her. She read the SKI PURGATORY logo on it and winked.

Dougherty explained, "A souvenir. When I was younger—a hotdog skiier with plenty of piss and vinegar. Sorry I can't offer you a pair of silk pajamas." Dougherty sat across from her and they nursed their drinks in an embarrassed, extended silence. Clearing his throat, he grinned and abruptly asked, "You want me to put on an X-rated video? Under the circumstances, we could both use a little distraction tonight."

"From an X-rated homicide case?" Pamela shook her head. "Sorry, porno films bore me."

"I thought that there was a little bit of voyeur in all of us."

She sipped her drink. "Only men are voyeurs. Women are *exhibitors*."

"Okay, at least I tried. So we change the subject. You rather tell me about that speech you gave up in La Jolla?"

She looked at him wearily. "You actually in the mood for one of my man-needs-lust, woman-needs-trust lectures?"

"Not really."

"Good, neither am I. One lecture a day is enough." She smiled. "I really like your decor. Incidentally, this is a new experience for me."

"How so?"

"I've never been alone with a high-ranking, bachelor Naval officer before."

"Relax. The experience will grow on you. And I'm not that high ranking."

She nodded. "A lieutenant commander officer and a gentleman will do any day, thank you."

"I'm flattered." Dougherty sipped his drink.

"Why did you get the divorce, Todd?"

"The standard cop-out—irreconcilable differences. My ex-wife was only passionate over cats, gummy-bears, and race car drivers. She eventually ran off with one of the latter. I got stuck with a white Persian named Mozart. He was a finicky eater and liked to pee on my jogging shoes."

"I like cats." She looked around her. "Did I hear the past tense *was*?"

"Mozart got run over by a diaper service truck two months back." Dougherty hunched his shoulders. "You win some, you lose some."

Pamela frowned. "I'm sorry. Getting back to your ill-fated marriage—"

"After the divorce was settled without alimony, I inherited twenty grand from a generous aunt. I bought myself a used Porsche as a consolation for the marriage breakup. My airhead ex-wife damned near came back when she saw it. Thank God, the Navy transferred me out here to San Diego."

"Her loss, your gain." Pamela put away the last of her Dry Sack. "Sorry, Todd, I'm too tired to be good company. Mind if I nod off?"

Dougherty rose slowly and padded to the hallway. "Make yourself at home. I put some towels in the bath you might like. Brocaded stuff my mother sent me for Christmas. Too frilly for my taste."

"Good night, Mr. Macho."

He grinned mischievously at her. "If you find that foldout bed too lumpy, there's something firmer in the bedroom."

"I'll bet there is."

"A king-sized, *orthopedic mattress*, Pamela. Just in case you get lonely."

"Pragmatist that I am, who knows? I might consider it. After I get to know you better."

"Cute. Does that mean I should leave the door open?"

"Suit yourself."

Dougherty shook his head. *Prick tease*, he said to himself. He retired to his room and turned on the port and starboard brass lamps beside the bed. He undressed quickly and slipped nude under the thick satin quilt. After his earlier hot bath, the clean pastel sheets and a good book might ordinarily hit the spot, but tonight the real prize would be Pamela Bonner's company. *The hell with it*. He'd read another two or three chapters of *Red Storm Rising* before turning off the light. It seemed everyone in the Navy had read the popular novel three years earlier, and now he'd finally come around to it himself. Dougherty was that way about movies and plays, too, seldom catching them until the rebound. He wanted to be sure they were winners in the long haul. Trendy things tended to turn him off. Dougherty put on the weak reading glasses he'd acquired nine months earlier and tried to concentrate on the novel.

It didn't work. Pamela's clunking around in the bathroom just down the hallway distracted him. He'd almost forgotten how much time a good-looking woman liked to spend puttering around in the can.

Twenty minutes later Pamela surprised him by boldly venturing down the hallway and into his bedroom. Dougherty blinked in disbelief, then broke into a laugh.

She was wearing the baggy flannel nightshirt, and under it she'd crammed a pillow over her back. Stooped over, she held up the grotesque rubber chicken by one leg. "I'm home, master. The evening foraging was only partially productive."

Grinning, Dougherty put down his book and bellowed back in mock sternness, "You're late. If you can't be on time, I'm going to keep you in at night. No more stomping on graves!"

They both laughed. Pamela came over to the edge of the bed, sat , and said to him, "Nice try. Your calmness amazes me. Have you ever in all your life done anything kinky?"

"I let you into the house tonight."

"I'm serious."

Dougherty shrugged. "Maybe, when I get tired of playing war games and retire from the Navy, I'll take up Zen."

"What else? How about marriage, settling down again?"

"Who knows?"

She pushed the reading glasses back a fraction on Dougherty's nose and stared at him seriously.

He stared back. "Mind if I ask why the sudden intense look, Ms Bonner?"

"A sudden flash. Wondering what that odd Dr. Hans Mueller looked like without his bifocals."

"Don't worry about that tonight." Dougherty tossed his reading glasses aside and let his fingers dance softly on Pamela's shoulders. He whispered in her ear, "That reminds me, I have a ninety-year-old grandmother who still doesn't use glasses. She drinks right out of the bottle."

Pam clouted him with a pillow and they scuffled on the bed.

Five minutes later Dougherty pulled a packet of Sheiks from the nightstand and they made love.

23

Decisions! Steelbinder had to decide which car to booby trap, the FBI woman's Sentra or Dougherty's Porsche. Although he'd brought along several sticks of dynamite and plenty of duct tape, there was only one detonator.

Hovering in the shadows beside the beach apartment complex, Steelbinder studied the street. Traffic was negligible, but the FBI woman had complicated matters by parking the Sentra directly under a street light. From practicing with his watch, Steelbinder knew it would take him only ten to twelve minutes to install the explosive device, but he didn't relish the idea of working in a brightly-illuminated area. One never knew when a nearby neighbor, caught up with insomnia, might be peering out from one of those darkened apartment windows. Steelbinder decided against Pamela's Sentra.

He went instead to Dougherty's enclosed carport behind the apartment. A single light burned overhead, but he reached up with his handkerchief and unscrewed the globe without difficulty. The naval officer's sports car was covered and faced out into the alley. Excellent. With the tail lamps by the back wall, he'd be able to work undetected and easily hide if anyone entered the area.

Steelbinder gently lifted the fitted cover on the driver's side and examined the inside of the 944. It was an older model but still must have set Dougherty back some big bucks. He wondered how Dougherty cut it on an officer's salary. Two tiny red lights blinked intermittently back at Steelbinder from the console between the seats. He firmly nudged the side of the vehicle. Nothing happened. Thankfully, no vibration alarm. The system was either door lock or ignition-activated. Steelbinder smiled to himself. So far, it was a piece of cake.

Dropping the protective cover, he reached the back of the Porsche in three strides, crouching in the darkness, and quietly unfolded his small packet of tools. Lack of light would be no hindrance, for what he was about to do was simple enough:

remove two Phillips screws, disengage the tail-light assembly, then attach the dynamite cap connection to the lamp wires. He would use the circuit tester to avoid the brake light, for he needed to make sure the explosion took place tomorrow night, *after* the *Abraham Lincoln* left San Diego, not before. When the driver of the ill-fated Porsche turned on the headlights.

The knotty part of the job was crawling on his back, reaching under the Porsche, running the lightweight igniter line, and securely taping three sticks of dynamite to the frame just under the driver's seat. Several times he had to flick on his small penlight to accomplish this.

Before he was finished, a curious cat peered under the car from the opposite side, startling him. Steelbinder worked faster. In a few minutes the charge was securely in place, and he climbed to his feet, satisfied. If this didn't put an inconvenient crimp in the investigation, nothing would!

Wrapping his tools, Steelbinder headed down the alley to the next block where he'd left his rented car.

The clock radio was set for six forty-five, but Pamela's restive tossing jarred Dougherty awake almost a full hour earlier. Unable to get back to sleep, he rolled over, propped himself up on an elbow, and stared at her. He very much liked what he saw, but he also liked sleep. Pamela ignored him, continuing to stare meditatively at the ceiling. Tapping her shoulder, he asked brusquely, "So what gives now? This waking me up at ungodly hours is getting to be an annoying habit." Feeling her toes meet his under the covers, Dougherty grinned, and his voice mellowed. "On second thought, I could learn to like it. You're the greatest. You think making love again would cure your insomnia?"

She kissed his ear, neck, and shoulder. "Love to. Maybe after breakfast? Provided you do me a big favor?"

"Strings attached. I suspected as much."

"A heavyweight naval investigator of your stature can make waves—I've seen you do it before, Todd. Pull some clout and get me aboard that carrier. At least for a part of the trip."

Dougherty let out a sigh, heaved himself out of bed, and tossed on a turquoise terrycloth robe with a sailboat embroidered on the breast pocket. "Sorry, Pam. That kind of bureaucratic, political boot-licking takes time to set up, which I don't have. The *Abraham Lincoln* sails at one o'clock. Besides, you'd never get to first base on the ship. Captain Bullock's got you pegged as a civilian adversary."

Pamela sat up in bed. "You know why? Your hardass skipper friend doesn't like to be inconvenienced. And he can't handle pain; it's opposed to his nature. I'm on to his type, and he knows it. He's afraid, Todd, I can feel it. For Bullock pain is something to be given, not received." She thought for a moment, then exhaled and said with exasperation, "Yesterday morning I obviously upset his biorhythms."

Dougherty shook his head. "Forget it. While I'm grabbing a shower, you've got a choice. Go back to sleep for an hour or start coffee, and we'll continue the debate over an early breakfast." He held her gaze briefly then headed for the bathroom.

"Todd, wait."

He turned in the doorway. "Yes?"

"Why are *you* going along on the cruise?"

"Not a cruise. We call them *deployments*. I intend to find this killer before he strikes again. And in the process prove that Swain Bullock is innocent, despite all the disfavorable cards falling into place that seem to indicate otherwise."

She glared at him. "You're one of his acolytes."

"Bullshit."

"Come off it, Lieutenant Commander. You don't see Bullock as a dangerous, chameleon-like personality at all. You're afraid that by not supporting him, you'll be drummed out of the inner circle."

Ignoring her, Dougherty hastily retreated down the hallway to the bathroom and stepped into the shower. The hot water felt good on his body, and he stood under it a long time. Dougherty smiled to himself. At least Pam hadn't followed him into the john to prolong the argument as his ex-wife had liked to do. It suddenly occurred to him what was missing in his life—perky little discussions in personal places like the bedroom, bathroom or over the stove in the kitchen. Domesticity and all its nuances.

Pamela was testing him, putting out feelers, and thus far he had to admit to liking it. God, was he old enough for a mid-life crisis? No, it had to be some minor, silly phase he was going through. Whatever, a week or so at sea away from her would test both of their emotions. Dougherty rinsed off the suds, wondering if Pamela was the type to help whip up breakfast or if she'd shrug it off, opting instead for a quick stop at McDonald's for an egg muffin on the run.

He hurriedly dried himself, shaved, and combed his hair. Shuffling down to the kitchen, he paused in the doorway and sniffed. The coffee maker was already dripping, and Pamela had found a box of Swedish pancake mix in the cupboard he'd long forgotten. She added water and an egg, briskly stirring the batter by hand. Pamela's hair was headed in a dozen directions, and she still looked like a rag doll in the rumpled skier's nightshirt, but Dougherty liked the scene. He liked it a lot.

Beaming with pleasure, he showed her the lay of the kitchen and together they put out a breakfast fit for the lord of a country manor. Pam showered while Dougherty patiently nursed the foot-wide pancakes along one at a time, keeping them warm in the oven with the sausages and blueberry muffins. When everything was ready, they moved into the dining room, eating off the blue Wedgwood plates and the red linen placemats he'd bought on sale at the May Company. Had it not been a weekday with a grinding work schedule ahead for both of them, Dougherty would have insisted on brut champagne.

As they lingered over coffee, Pam turned serious. "Todd, I've been thinking about Captain Bullock's impending promotion. All this adversity. Will it kill his chances of getting advanced to rear admiral?"

"I doubt it. The promotion momentum was set up months ago at the Bureau of Personnel. At worst, there may be a delay. Flag officers who make recommendations for a new member of the club don't like to own up to mistakes. If the old boys in the network are clever enough, they never have to."

She grinned at that then said seriously, "How does it go— young men fight wars that old men make in lieu of their failing manhood?"

Dougherty frowned. "That was a mouthful the Navy didn't deserve." He winked at her. "Caught up under your spell as I am, I'll overlook it. Finish your coffee."

"Damn your redundance, Todd Dougherty. All you think about is the Navy, Navy, Navy."

He grinned. "And why shouldn't I? What else is there?"

"I can think of plenty of reasons." Pamela's eyes flashed. "For starters, your precious strutting admirals didn't make this country great. *Thinkers* like Ben Franklin and Thomas Jefferson did it."

"Are you for real?"

"Try me."

Dougherty smiled to hide his mild annoyance. "You're going to spoil that beautiful breakfast for me. Ms. Bonner, for your information, the will of the Continental Congress was fought for by John Paul Jones. Ever hear of him? The politics of Jefferson, Adams, and Madison were *defended* on the seas by Hull, McDonough, Lawrence, and Perry. Farragut fought to maintain the Union under Lincoln. Shall I continue, or do you need time to catch up? Have you heard enough?"

"You needn't bother," she replied in a huff. "I know, the U.S. Navy did the job when Kennedy confronted the Russians over Cuba. Let's change the subject, okay? I'm bored. For the moment, I'm obviously outgunned."

"You're cute when you get your back up against the wall." He watched her blot her lips with a paper napkin then idly fold it into an origami bird.

"A crane," Pamela whispered. "The Japanese love cranes."

Dougherty shrugged. "So do the Russians."

She looked at him. "Interesting thought. Any possibility this homicide might be a smoke screen to cover some espionage hanky-panky? A traitor along the line who's playing footsies with Ivan?"

"At this point, no. Just an over-the-line paranoid out on a rampage. In my opinion, it's probably a madman with a string of defeats or rejections. That's why I can't seriously believe a success-oriented individual like Swain Bullock should be a suspect."

"I disagree. I've learned not to underestimate human cunning. Why should Bullock be above suspicion? What's it going to take to convince you?"

Dougherty looked at her with impatience, then snapped, "Catching him in the act, a confession, a witness. Not circumstantial evidence alone. In other words, fingerprinting, not fingerpointing." Determined to change the subject, Dougherty thought for a moment. *Firearms—as good a topic as any.* Besides, he was genuinely interested in what a woman detective yearning to be a sharpshooter thought about them. He asked her, "Have you ever used an automatic rifle?"

"Yes. At the FBI Firing Range."

They talked about American, Israeli, and Russian machine weapons, then Dougherty changed the topic to handguns. She told him that for her own personal use she preferred a small, easily concealed 9mm Biretta or an Erma Excam .22.

As they lingered over a second cup of cinnamon coffee, it was Pamela's turn to switch the subject. She told Dougherty about one of her favorite pastimes—improvisational theatre. He promised to go along with her when he returned to port. They stared at each other for several seconds. Smiling and synchronizing their watches, they wandered back to the bedroom, allowing themselves forty-five minutes for another toss in the sack.

24

Dougherty's bags were already packed from the night before. Since he'd be leaving directly for the carrier from his office, he decided to keep the 944 garaged and let Pamela drive him to North Island in her rental car.·

Enroute, he said to her, "Make you a deal. Stay at my place, feed and talk to my plants while I'm gone, and you can drive the Porsche. Dump this rental, and have some fun."

She shook her head. "Too much responsibility."

"Don't be silly." Dougherty figured he'd better exaggerate. "You want it to just sit there, have my valves get gummed up from disuse?"

"I'll think about it. Depending on when they want me back in Los Angeles."

They drove the rest of the way in silence except for an early morning all-news program on the radio. Dougherty was thinking about the investigation and figured that she was, too.

Gecko Corman's father was waiting when they arrived at the NIS office at twenty minutes after eight. Alarmed by his sailor-son's sudden disappearance, Barney Corman had driven down to San Diego the night before and grabbed a motel. He claimed to have already done some nosing around at the car rental agencies and airline counters over at Lindbergh Field. As an individual citizen, he'd gotten nowhere with his queries over his son. Corman was pissed and bellowed that it was time for the Navy to lend a hand.

Dougherty tried to assure him that checking the outgoing flight manifests would be fruitless; if his son Gecko were intent on a permanent UA status and disappearing, he wouldn't have purchased a ticket using his own name. Pamela concurred.

The beefy, foul-tempered truck driver wore too much cologne or toilet water, Dougherty reflected. He could smell it five feet away. Barney Corman continued to growl back at them, "Fine. You tell me how Gecko could kiss off the Navy, his own parents as well, with less than a hundred bucks in his pocket? This on top of the hefty cash deposit he simply left behind at that car rental agency? Bullshit."

Dougherty spread his hands. The scenario didn't make sense to him, either. Outside his office window, a foghorn sounded somewhere out on the bay; it was another socked-in morning on the San Diego waterfront. Pamela asked Dougherty to be excused, insisting that she wanted to get a head start on some important leads of her own.

Dougherty struggled to find words that would appease Gecko's father. "Mr. Corman, I'm sympathetic with everything you've said. My staff is working on it, I assure you."

"Sure, sure. If that carrier pulls out today without my kid aboard, he's in hot water, right? Discipline may be all the Navy gives a shit about, but me and the wife have more important concerns. Like maybe Gecko's in danger. Life-threatening stuff, as I see it. The kid fully intended to show up at that hearing yesterday, Lieutenant Commander. He promised me."

"Sit down, Mr. Corman, you look uncomfortable. How about some coffee?"

"Jesus Christ, I am uncomfortable. The hell with the coffee. Like I told you on the telephone, some sonofabitch bird-rank officer on the *Abe Lincoln* tried to kill my boy! What more do you want?"

"A dangerous assertion that we can't exactly prove. Not yet."

"Yeah? Find my son. He'll tell you. He's still got the torn-off collar insignia with him. Wished to hell now he'd left that damned eagle with me instead of a goddam car hood ornament."

Dougherty sat forward. Something clicked in his mind—a photo he'd all too recently studied under a magnifying glass and a conversation with Pamela. "Look, Mr. Corman. Do you mind if I call you Barney? Tell me about this automobile hood ornament. It wasn't, by chance, a damaged mascot ripped off a Rolls Royce?"

Corman looked sandbagged. He sat forward. "Hell, how'd you know that? But don't get the wrong idea, see? Gecko didn't steal it. The kid's been clean for years. He told me he traded the mascot for a portable radio."

Dougherty thought for a moment. "Think, Barney. Who did your son do the swapping with?"

"He just said one of the men on the ship. No name."

Dougherty grimaced. He said impatiently, "Depending on the

mission, there are five to six thousand men on that carrier. Narrow it down, please."

Barney Corman's belligerence had faded considerably. "I don't know, dammit. It was a gift. I didn't want to pry into the kid's business. And he never mentioned his friends, not once. Only thing he ever talked about was his damned saxophone or how dangerous his job was up on the flight deck."

Dougherty rose from his desk, went to the doorway, and called out to Pamela.

She stepped back into the room with a look of expectation. Dougherty winked at her then turned back to Corman. "Barney, we need your help badly. I have to leave at noon on that carrier. There isn't time for you to go home and retrieve that Rolls Royce hood ornament—what did you call it?"

"A car hood mascot. I collect them. Have over twenty now. This one's called *The Spirit of Ecstasy*. Some Rolls owners refer to it as the *Silver Lady*."

Dougherty looked at Pamela. "Mascot by mascot, piece by piece, Ms Bonner—the puzzle inevitably comes together. The evidence is out there if we're all patient enough."

She smiled. "Get to the point, Todd."

"All right, here's the plan. Barney, I'd like you to go back up to Downey, package up that trinket and send it to us, express overnight mail. Pamela here will make sure it's forwarded out to the carrier in one of the pony express pouches. She'll also stay in touch with you while I'm gone." Dougherty checked his watch and shouted toward the doorway. "Steinberg! I need you in here!"

Dougherty drummed his fingers on his desk as he waited. Barney and Pamela continued to stare at him in puzzlement. The bespectacled NIS assistant joined them in the inner sanctum. Dougherty said quickly, "Steinberg, take Gecko's father here under your wing. I want the two of you to check out gift catalogues, go over to the base exchange, do whatever's necessary, but come up with a photo, at least an illustration of Gecko's portable radio. I'll need it to take with me."

Steinberg looked bewildered.

Dougherty turned to the equally dumbfounded trucker, "You will recognize the model, I trust?"

"Sure. I was with the kid when he bought it. Less than a year ago."

Dougherty glanced up at Pamela. Hovering close by Barney Corman, she was sniffing his cologne and obviously not liking it. She said suddenly, "Why the concern over a portable radio?"

"A small lead. Trust me," Dougherty replied. "Sol, work fast."
Steinberg nodded. "Anything else?"

"No, get on it, or you'll miss the embark." Dougherty faced
Corman and extended a hand. "Goodbye, Barney. Pamela and Sol
will keep you posted. We'll do everything possible to find your
son."

For the moment pacified, the burly truck driver shuffled out of
the room behind Steinberg.

Pamela smiled at Dougherty. "Rolls Royce—*The Spirit of
Ecstasy*? I'm impressed."

"And forgetful?" He reached into his desk drawer and withdrew
the photo she'd given to him at the Fantasia Bar just the night
before—the interesting snapshot that the remote Dr. Hans Mueller
had provided her following the La Jolla conference.

Dougherty looked over Pam's shoulder as she took her time
examining it again. Captain Bullock in his dress whites, an
attractive Chinese woman in her late thirties in a silk dress split at
the knee. Behind them, a shiny, older model Rolls Royce.
Dougherty told Pam to look closer and she did. "The car's
distinctive hood ornament. It's missing." Dougherty wasn't about
to say more. His stubborn defense of Swain Bullock had already
begun to scratch away at her equanimity; no sense making things
worse.

Pamela thought for a moment. "Todd, what's your point?"

"Obviously, the mascot was removed prior to the time this
picture was taken. And does the captain look the type to run off
with souvenier trinkets?"

"Sentiment then. She could have given it to him."

"Don't be absurd." Dougherty stiffened. "Next thing you'll tell
me is that the captain does away with women in some kind of
protective delusional scheme. All this, of course, compensated by
unbearable feelings of inadequacy."

"A mouthful, but now that you put it that way, it's worth
considering. Todd, before either of us gets carried away, I suggest
we take care of some basic footwork. Like getting that photo off
to Hong Kong on the FAX transmitter. I'd like this enterprising
Lieutenant Chi to run a trace and find out who that Chinese
woman is. I still intend to call Dr. Mueller, but after his eccentric
behavior last night, my expectations are zilch."

Dougherty frowned. "You'll be running the show here. Do
what you like."

"And your next move?"

"Among my priorities, when the time is ripe on the ship, I'll ask Bullock about the photo."

"Good." Pam leaned over his desk. "But before you pull out, run the Hong Kong trace with this Kenny Chi, okay? And one more thing. That 45 RPM record in the evidence file—I suspect you're taking it with you?"

"Yes, why?"

"No problem—provided you let me make a tape cassette first. I'd like the rest of the staff to start thinking about those lyrics."

Pamela stepped briskly from Dougherty's office and found an empty desk with a phone. She called Los Angeles information. "Western area, please. The number of a Dr. Hans Mueller. I believe it's a psychiatric office in Beverly Hills." She waited impatiently. "What? Well, try the Los Angeles central or Santa Monica area."

Again, a similar response—no such listing. Pamela put down the phone, pulled a small notebook from her purse, and called a number the FBI often used for "hot line" information: the American Psychiatric Society in Los Angeles. When the representative there told her there was no physician named Hans Mueller practicing in southern California, a sudden intuition—almost a certainty—struck Pamela.

Her conversation the evening before with the muscular, homely individual known as Hans Mueller had been intriguing but at the same time unsettling. The shrink seemed knowledgeable and articulate enough, but he'd also been oddly evasive, his staring, intense eyes making her squirm with discomfort. Now it appeared that the self-proclaimed psychologist or psychiatrist had no practice or even patients. There was still the remote possibility that he was on some university medical school staff. No, that didn't wash. The man said distinctly that he had a *very busy* Beverly Hills practice. Pam thought briefly. Something else bothered her about that Delphic conversation—the intimate, familiar way Mueller had talked about his killer-client. Was it fantasy or reality? What if this were a combined madness, with Mueller and his client somehow working together?

A notion germinated in Pam's mind. Her thoughts reverted to Captain Bullock, who hardly seemed the type to pussyfoot down hotel corridors late at night with fake chickens in a shoe box. On the other hand, something like that might be right down the alley for a quaint, embittered romantic like Dr. Hans Mueller. *If, in fact, that was his real name.*

25

Rear Admiral Fritz Tanner looked around at the shipboard accommodations he would occupy for the next week. Tanner loved Naval Aviation and everything about it. Even the unpleasant riding it often gave him for not trimming down his own ballast. He'd tried, unsuccessfully, to convince his superiors that his Oliver Hardy girth was not entirely his own doing. Tanner's northern Italian wife was the world's *numero uno* chef, and he liked to boast that there were only two answers to his weight problem. Divorce the woman or stay out at sea as often as possible. At least that's the story he encouraged his superiors and the hard-asses at the Bureau of Personnel to believe. The real reasons he liked to go to sea were boredom with his North Island desk and an eagerness—after some twenty-one years—to escape his wife's nagging, not her cooking.

Tanner wished only that he could still fly, but he knew a man had to give something up with encroaching age and a fast climb up the ladder. Tanner's son was Navy to the gills as well, a cadet and football player at Annapolis. If Fritz had his way, any future grandson would follow right down the line. The U.S. Navy was a good life, a proud one, and it built fine men.

Dropping his carry-on bag beside the heavier luggage the orderlies had brought aboard the *Abraham Lincoln* earlier, Tanner noted that the carpet in the handsomely appointed flag-rank cabin was more expensive than that found in the *Kitty Hawk*, his last assignment. The flag suite was near Captain Bullock's on the 03 level. Tanner was especially impressed that these same quarters had been used by the President of the United States during the supercarrier's commissioning ceremony on Chesapeake Bay.

The upcoming deployment, unfortunately, was a short one. He'd sail with the *Abraham Lincoln* to the Pacific Northwest and see it safely into drydock, stopping briefly enroute in the Bay Area. Between ports, they'd conduct two anti-sub warfare maneuvers, testing the advanced SU-22 Osprey tilt-rotor aircraft.

When the ASW mission was wrapped, Tanner intended to fly back to San Diego with Captain Bullock.

Tanner was startled by a voice calling out from the cabin's open doorway behind him. "Sorry for such a short-term, damp-weather assignment, Admiral. Next time we'll do better."

Tanner turned to discover the Deputy Chief of Naval Operations himself, Vice Admiral Biff McCracken, standing in the entry. McCracken smiled and continued, "Halloween in San Francisco. Veteran's Day at Bremerton. Back home in time for Thanksgiving. Not so bad, Fritz. You could have drawn worse." McCracken sauntered across the cabin and took a seat in front of the handsome desk Tanner was just about ready to try on for size.

Tanner glanced at his watch and said quickly, "Glad to have you aboard, sir. You're a little early."

McCracken nodded. "They still call you 'Babe'?"

"Doesn't sound right coming from you, sir. Let's make it Fritz."

"And I hope you'll remember to call me Biff. You're satisfied with the fleet complement?"

Slipping into his new swivel chair, Tanner didn't lean back but sat stiffly. He thought for a moment. Smiling, he replied, "One carrier, a supply ship, an outdated attack sub, and two frigates are smaller than my usual support complement. That's not a complaint mind you, just an observation."

The vice admiral opposite him leaned forward, the spikes of his silver crewcut pointing at Tanner like a bed of nails. "The Commander of the Pacific Fleet told me of your concern over Bullock shipping out on this one. Fritz, I think you're unduly alarmed. As far as the captain's concerned, the Pentagon's position is that we trust him." McCracken paused to pull out a Van Dyke panatela and roll it between his fingers.

"Mind if I smoke?"

"Not at all. I may join you with my pipe."

McCracken unwrapped and lit the cigar with a flourish. "Understand the men in the Pacific Fleet call you the 'Sailor's Admiral.' What the hell does that mean in peacetime?"

"Sorry, I don't know, sir."

Both of them smiled. McCracken puffed his cigar and examined his watch at the same time. "What time's the captain due back from his wife's funeral?"

"I left the graveside service an hour ago. Afterward, Bullock intended to put his mother back on an airplane."

The Deputy CNO exhaled a column of blue smoke toward the

ceiling. "To get back to the point of my visit. I think you're reading Swain Bullock wrong, Fritz. You think he's got no soul. Well, maybe not. Just one hellishly efficient left side of the brain—a computer-like brain that seldom makes mistakes. Cold. Statistical. Mathematically precise. But for the Navy, at least, superbly efficient."

Tanner had to look away to hide his annoyance. He waited for the vice admiral to continue.

McCracken did, his voice harsh. "Relax, Admiral. I came aboard to get your candid opinion. You're the one who has to go to sea with the man. If you have serious reservations about our red-haired boy Bullock, I want to hear them now before heading back to the Pentagon. Not a month from now in retrospect, or from the Bureau of Naval Personnel."

Tanner cleared his throat as quietly as possible then said what was on his mind. "After what happened, even Superman would deserve a leave. We owe Bullock a few days' privacy." Tanner shifted in his chair. "Unfortunately, Personnel tried and failed. And I talked with the captain again last night. The prideful, gung-ho bastard won't hear of it. He's a goddamn workaholic."

McCracken nodded. "I understand Dr. Reisman from the Navy hospital interviewed Bullock early this morning. Apparently the bereaved captain is calmer than any of us. When's his next scheduled physical?"

"He just had one five months ago. We'll send him in again after the carrier gets settled at Bremerton. Do you buy Reisman's professional evaluation, that as of now Bullock's emotional status is A-OK?"

"Without question. Your ship couldn't be in better hands."

Tired of watching Biff McCracken blow smoke rings toward the air conditioner outlet, Tanner pulled out his briar and a plastic pouch of Bond Street. He nervously filled the pipe, all the while admitting to the Deputy CNO, "The captain's a friend of mine. Supposing we ship out together and he winds up with a case of delayed stress syndrome? Damned if I want to be the first superior officer to write up a negative performance report on Bullock. I'm still not sure we're handling this right, Biff."

McCracken leaned forward. "I'm listening. Go ahead, get it all off your chest."

Off limits. Steelbinder knew the rules well enough. Taking unsanctioned short-cuts through the ship could get a sailor into trouble. The blue curtains with the large silver star on each panel were a reminder that the 03 level companionway, from this point on, was admiral's territory. Enlisted ranks were not to use it except for authorized business. Actually, if a man watched his feet, the flag barriers were superfluous, for most of the corridor linoleum throughout the aircraft carrier was brightly coded— green for routine ship's business, blue for officer's country.

Ignoring the possibility of disciplinary action, Steelbinder made sure he was alone, then parted the curtains and padded along the blue-tiled corridor. He knew both admirals had headed down this way minutes earlier. Since Captain Bullock still hadn't reported back to the ship, the bigwig from the Pentagon must have gone to Rear Admiral Tanner's quarters.

Steelbinder found the flag officer's cabin he wanted and paused in the corridor. First checking in both directions, he nudged up against the entry. There were raised voices coming from within, but he couldn't make out the conversation. He pressed his ear against the aluminum honeycomb door and the words became clearer.

He smiled to himself. Inside the cabin, just as he wanted, the rat's antennae were twitching, sensing trouble. *Perfect.*

Vice Admiral McCracken's eyes narrowed. "You've made an interesting argument, Fritz. But are you prepared, in less than an hour and a half before this carrier leaves, to prepare the paperwork to change Bullock's orders?"

Tanner said quietly, "We might consider replacing him when the ship gets to San Francisco."

McCracken shook his head. "We do anything that could be construed as panic now, and we'll both get laughed out of the military. A serious mistake, a faulty accusation, and we could even get *drummed* out."

Tanner, now at a loss for words, stared at the ceiling. The ball, unfortunately, was back in his court. He said in a subdued voice, "Fine. You have my cooperation. No knee-jerk reactions. But I suggest we slow down, at least take our time with his impending promotion." Tanner got up and started pacing.

Bill McCracken dourly shook his head. "I tell you this. Drag our feet and the CNO won't like it. The old man's got his neck stuck out a mile recommending the captain for his first star and that tactical fleet command at NATO."

Tanner ended his pacing. His back to the Deputy CNO, he slowly shook his head and stared at a photo of the Secretary of the Navy on the wall. He said dully, "There's the petty stuff, too. The captain's former XO claims that Bullock only partially trusts his crew. That he's nervy and short-tempered with his officers during important sea maneuvers." Tanner faced McCracken.

The vice admiral waved his cigar like a field marshal's baton. "Easy, Fritz. For Chrissakes, you're making the man sound like an ogre."

"Sorry, Biff, but we can't ignore the facts. Even before the homicide, Bullock appeared to have a sea locker full of connubial miseries to worry over. I mean, we're talking about major distractions here. A man's personal life gone bonkers. In my opinion, where there's smoke, there's fire. God knows, if there's a sweet smell of success, and it seems there is, what about the scent of failure?" Tanner's words hung uncomfortably in the air, and he wondered if his comments had come off like cheap shots.

Disagreement seemed to have an explosive effect on the Deputy CNO, but McCracken merely continued to puff on his cigar. He finally leaned forward and gestured for Tanner to sit down. "We can't overlook Bullock's performance. Both as an administrator, aviator, and master seaman. Let's not forget that he was at the top of his class at the Naval War College. And need I run through his decorations to refresh your memory?"

"That won't be necessary." Tanner shook his head. "Look, Biff. No one's questioning the record. It's just that genius has its dark side, and there's no arguing that our man's a very complex, somewhat unorthodox individual."

McCracken apparently didn't buy that. "Complex? I'd say Bullock's the opposite. Simple and direct. I'll tell you something about *simplicity*, Fritz. Consider a sailor's duffel bag. The damned thing's a heap of clutter, right?" McCracken gestured toward Tanner's still unpacked luggage by the door. "Your flight bags aren't much better, Admiral." He held up his cigar to make a point. "Ah! But the French *portmanteau*, on the other hand, is folded in the right places, highly organized, and superbly efficient as a piece of luggage. Perhaps our minds should travel as lightly, and as certainly and practically, as Swain Bullock's. I say give the bastard a chance to prove himself."

Tanner stared at the cigar-chomping McCracken. "Baggage? I'm afraid I missed the corollary, Admiral."

McCracken glared at him. "The naval aviator matrix. Think about it a minute. Our top gun pilots, fliers like Bullock promoted to carrier commanders or air bosses, are highly structured, *neat* people. Those wings on your chest. You're an airdale yourself, Admiral. Everything from the frigging aircraft cockpit to your bunk to the ship's bridge is part of an orderly, efficient system. Absolutely no winging it. Step-by-step, no nonsense orderliness that's hard to shake, it becomes ingrained in you. You do it to stay alive in a multi-million dollar airplane that's unforgiving of sloppiness and mistakes. *Straight-forward simplicity*. Bullock epitomizes this." McCracken cannily winked, then continued. "So why pick on him alone? Some of our best pilots are, as you put it, *too precise*, unbending, and sometimes anti-social. Believe me, this old surface sailor is jealous. I just don't see Bullock as a crisis situation."

Tanner knew now he was standing on weak ground. "Then I rest my case. In fact, our line concerns may damn well be irrelevant, with the Naval Investigation Service breathing so hard on Bullock's neck. Instead of the usual NIS civilian gumshoe aboard, this trip out we'll be hosting a ferret with a bit of rank. Lieutenant Commander Todd Dougherty."

McCracken frowned. "I met the man yesterday for the first time. He set up a wild goose chase of a hearing without a goddamn plaintiff. I'm beginning to think this Dougherty couldn't find his ass in a mirrored commode."

Disgruntled over what he'd just overheard in the flag cabin, Steelbinder shook his head. So the NIS lieutenant commander himself was coming along on the mission, leaving with them within the hour. This when there was a wonderful surprise waiting for him when he drove his Porsche later in the day! Steelbinder cursed his lack of foresight. He thought he'd figured it perfectly, that tonight Dougherty would either take Pamela Bonner out to dinner or take her back to his Mission Bay apartment. Steelbinder wondered where the Porsche was at now. He suddenly heard an unwelcome noise, footsteps in the corridor. The corridor in which he didn't belong.

"Sailor, you eavesdropping or do you have business here?" The booming voice belonged to an officer with bronze oak leaves on his collar, a big, bearish man Steelbinder recognized as one of the landing signal officers from Air Wing Two. He knew the lieutenant commander was also one of the top guns, a hotshot instructor-pilot with plenty of hours in both Tomcats and Skyhawks.

The tension in the corridor was immediate and suffocating. Steelbinder nimbly stepped away from the admiral's doorway. He wore no cover so a salute was unnecessary. In haste, he explained, "I'm Quartermaster Steelbinder, sir." The rest he fabricated: "Authorized visit. Out to wind the ship's clocks. I didn't want to interrupt the admiral if he was in a conference." Steelbinder was assigned to the helm and not clock winding, but the brownshoe confronting him might not know the difference. Or so he hoped.

Seeming to buy it, the LSO nodded and hunkered off down the companionway; but at the blue curtain divider he paused to look back, apparently still suspicious. He stood there until Steelbinder moved on.

Steelbinder promptly headed back to a corridor with the more hospitable green linoleum tile. He hoped, with the thousands of men aboard the carrier, that the naval flier would soon forget his face.

Vice Admiral McCracken asked Tanner, "Captain Bullock, is he aware that Dougherty's coming aboard?"

Tanner nodded. "Regardless of what he thinks of the NIS detective, Bullock wants his wife's killer found. I'm afraid Dougherty is halfass convinced Maxine Bullock's butcher is assigned aboard this carrier."

McCracken shook his head impatiently. "Better forget my own impatience with Dougherty, Fritz. Under the circumstances, I suggest you and Bullock make sure his investigation is given top priority. Short of interfering with your mission schedule, of course. And as for that aviation boatswain's mate who missed the hearing—his complaint remains on the books?"

"Gecko Corman? I believe so, sir. But the issue may be irrelevant. That jellyfish not only stood you up, now it appears he's gone UA. I suspect Captain Bullock's contempt for Corman's reliability is justified."

"Admiral Tanner, for the record, I trust someone along the line kicks ass hard for me on this matter." McCracken rose, sniffed the air, and came over to Tanner's desk. "The center drawer; see if there's a decent set of scissors inside."

Tanner found a pair and handed them over. For McCracken, the smoke in the cabin had apparently reached the saturation point. The crewcut vice admiral whacked off the smouldering end of his cigar and saved the rest, tucking it into his shirt pocket. Tanner, taking the cue, snuffed out his pipe.

McCracken appeared restive. "Fritz, I'm leaving it up to you. If you feel it's necessary to reevaluate Swain Bullock's suitability for continuing command of the ship, make your move. When and where necessary."

Tanner nodded. The Deputy Chief of Naval Operations was passing the buck.

Smiling secretly, McCracken added, "Right now I have to get to the airport. But before leaving I'd like to eyeball that new backup system for the flight deck elevators."

The meeting was over and Tanner felt a genuine sense of relief. He got up and accompanied Biff McCracken out into the corridor. On the way to the hangar deck, Tanner couldn't resist asking the Deputy CNO the question that had been bothering him for the past two weeks. "A new warship, the latest from the drawing boards, and you still call us back to the drydock for a need-to-know refit? I feel left out, Admiral."

McCracken smiled and without breaking his stride up the ladder, replied, "No longer a secret. Minor changes in the carrier's primary coolant pumps. The smart-ass upgrading we put in the CVN-71 and CVN-72 hasn't performed to expectations." McCracken glanced over his shoulder at Tanner and said jovially, "Relax, Admiral. The *Abraham Lincoln* will be out of service for less than sixty days."

After a lengthy inspection of the aft elevator on the starboard side, Tanner bade farewell to the visiting brass from the Pentagon. A Sikorsky Sea King was waiting on the flight deck, its engines revving. Biff McCracken climbed quickly aboard and the helicopter left the ship.

~~~~~~ 26

Goodbye and good riddance, Tanner mused. Biff McCracken, at this point, wasn't needed at all; the vice admiral was like an awesome lightning display over an already stormy sea. Tanner would be glad when the Deputy Chief of Naval Operations headed back to the Pentagon where he belonged.

Tanner made up his mind to stop worrying about the possibilities of the captain coming down with delayed stress syndrome. As long as the feisty Swain Bullock changed his socks every day, kept the *Abe Lincoln* on even keel, and performed decently at the brief fleet exercises COMNAVAIRPAC had ordered, everything would be peachy-keen. As for Todd Dougherty's ongoing murder investigation, this was an unpleasant inconvenience that the carrier commander would just have to suffer through. Tanner was no philosopher, but he'd learned early on in his Navy career not to get upset about foul weather he could do nothing about. Still, he knew he'd have to gird himself for the barrage of questions Dougherty was sure to field his way. Some of the probing would be uncomfortable. What a man did in his own time was none of Tanner's business, and discussing Captain Bullock's personal life had never entered his mind even before the terrible headlines in the San Diego newspapers.

Strolling over to the oval opening in the side of the hangar deck, Tanner gazed out at the pre-departure activity on the dock below. The ship had already been cleared of visitors. A twenty-piece band, its brass instruments glittering in the midday sun, gathered itself together in front of a fenced-off area that held back hundreds of parents, wives, sweethearts, restless children, and even a couple of barking dogs. Tanner sniffed the air, once more taking in the distinct smell of a Navy vessel coming to life: fresh vegetables, women's perfume, flowers, hemp, and diesel fumes from the tugs. Above the signal bridge, fluttering from one of the halyards, a blue flag with a white square center—the Blue Peter—proclaimed the *Abraham Lincoln's* intention to sail.

Tanner watched a Navy station wagon approach and a tall lieutenant commander step out, accompanied by a blonde civilian woman. She handed her companion a sheaf of documents, then they kissed goodbye. The officer stepped briskly across the pier, carrying his own bags. Both were bulging blue duffels with yellow stripes; not *portmanteaus*, reflected Tanner. He recognized Todd Dougherty as he climbed the gangway and disappeared into the bowels of the ship.

An auto horn sounded in the distance. Tanner again glanced down the pier. Outside the wire perimeter fence an approaching taxi tried to bulldoze its way through the spectators. When the driver gave up, one of the cab's doors burst open and Captain Bullock, impatient as ever, quickly emerged. Dismissing the taxi, Bullock elbowed his way through the crowd, smiling back every now and then at well-wishers as if Navy regulations required the gesture. He hurried across the dock and took the stairs to the gangway two at a time, then, just before entering the ship, Bullock glanced along the hangar deck as if by premonition he knew he was being watched. Spotting Tanner, he smiled vaguely. Tanner nodded back; both of them were too far apart for conversation. One of the minor inconveniences about supercarriers, Tanner mused, was that measurements came in football-stadium increments. *Three* football fields, in fact, would fit on the *Abe Lincoln's* flight deck.

Tanner thought seriously about Bullock. Too bad that the ship's captain had missed the spirited encounter earlier with the Deputy CNO, and how McCracken had so staunchly defended him.

So much for backstage posturing and murky glimpses of Swain Bullock, discomfiting preview that it was. For the next week Tanner would be confronted with the real thing. When the carrier pulled out, both he and the captain would shake off the entanglements of the shore, only to assume complications of another form. Tanner's gabby wife, with all her ready clichés, might have intoned, "Out of the skillet and into the fire."

•

Steelbinder hovered on the narrow catwalk just below the flight deck, feeling uncommonly euphoric as he gazed down at the departure activity on the dock below. Watching the *Abraham Lincoln's* captain step briskly up the gangway, he took secret pleasure at the delicious complications he'd personally brought upon Bullock's Navy career and personal life. In an abstract way, Steelbinder admired the skipper and the way he valiantly fought to stay afloat. In the end Bullock would drown in his own misery. The captain undoubtedly believed that with his wife's burial, the worst was over; that emotionally, he'd survived the most terrible disaster that could happen to him. *Wrong*. Little did Bullock realize that his curve of destiny was still inclining downward, not up.

There would be roadblocks ahead, but Steelbinder knew that he could easily hurdle them. Like Lieutenant Commander Dougherty coming aboard for the deployment instead of sending one of his minions. No matter; if the chief headhunter from NIS gets too close, it will be a minor thing to arrange one of those unfortunate shipboard accidents. The first thing a recruit learns when assigned to a carrier is that the warship is in fact an *accident waiting to happen*. Even without enemies on board, a crewman needs eyes in the back of his head. Vigilance is crucial to survival.

Steelbinder thought again about Pamela Bonner, who seemed to have something romantic going on the side with Dougherty. It would have been far more exciting having the FBI woman along on the deployment. Perhaps she'd help herself to the naval officer's beautiful red Porsche during his absence. He still gloated over the FBI woman's nervous confoundment the night before when he'd masqueraded as a psychologist, putting on the bravo performance as Hans Mueller. Indeed, he would remember that name and use it along with the granny glasses whenever necessary. He'd also remember the look of desperation and fear on Pamela's face when he'd observed her in the Hotel del Coronado phone booth following the rubber chicken incident. Her panic had profoundly excited him.

Terror in the woman's eyes was indescribably satisfying. If the explosive charge in the Porsche didn't do the meddlesome woman investigator in, she'd probably be waiting for Dougherty when the carrier made port in San Francisco. Fine! If necessary, Steelbinder would enjoy playing games with her again. Pamela Bonner's budding affair with the NIS officer would be short-lived.

Beneath him, out on the dock, the Navy band began to play. He stared at it and spit over the catwalk, expressing in the gesture all the feelings he could muster just now for the Navy, the captain, and his current tedious assignment at the *Abraham Lincoln's* helm. *Patience, R.W., it's just a matter of time.* In less than a year—ten months from now—you'll be a civilian, free to pursue your real passions full time. Indeed, these women dedicated to evil incarnate could be eradicated much more quickly and efficiently once he was out of the service. His pulse quickened as he envisaged the splendid tableau: the violent bursts of flame and flesh—like lava, red and hot. *Volcanic vulvas!* The River Styx running with blood! There were simply too many deserving punishment to contemplate. Often the magnitude of the task he'd undertaken kept him awake with insomnia.

Captain Bullock had chosen an unfortunate, inconvenient time to become Steelbinder's enemy. It was clear now. His own unnecessary persecution and torment were not unlike what the Navy had done to his grandfather! An ultimate retribution was definitely in order, revenge against Bullock and the abhorrent system that created men like him.

The Navy had seen fit to chastise his grandfather during World War II. The court-martial and demotion might just as well have been death by firing squad, for the eventual suicide proved just as odious—both for Gerald Eisenbinder's family and the government. *Slacken up, R.W.* This isn't the time to dwell on the incident! File the maddening memories away.

Steelbinder tried to concentrate on the band music and the crowd on the pier, but he couldn't be rid of the persistent past, the bygone family injustices. *Retribution.* He had to have sweet, splendid retribution for his grandfather! There was no other way out. Only then could he blaze forward with his own mission with a clear conscience and unobstructed mind.

Steelbinder shuddered. He needed to calm himself before these emotional undercurrents took over his whole being and he made a silly blunder. Tomorrow Petty Officer Second Class Steelbinder was assigned to the dogwatch up on the bridge—where he could observe and consolidate his plans. It would be time to go through the mock-heroic motions again at the *Abraham Lincoln's* helm. Where he could closely observe Swain Bullock.

~~~~~~ 27

After seeing Dougherty off down at Pier L, Pamela spent the rest of the afternoon tying down loose ends in his NIS office. Although she and Dougherty had divided their responsibilities, Pam felt like she was walking a tightrope alone—one of those situations where moving too hastily in the wrong direction would send her plunging.

Rather than breaking ground on new leads, she decided to spend the rest of the afternoon going over what they already had. She also fired off another telegram to Detective Lieutenant Chi in Hong Kong, requesting more specific details on the firecracker homicide there. Proprietary FAX documents were also forwarded to her criminal investigation counterparts in Bremerton and San Francisco, alerting them to the possibility of trouble when the *Abraham Lincoln* came calling. Goodwill visit during Fleet Week in the Bay Area aside, she wanted the local police to be ready for the worst that might happen.

Pam again turned to Dougherty's miniature tape player and dropped in the Midnight Admirals cassette. She would listen to "Many a Time the World Turns Short of Thought" one more time to make absolutely sure she'd written down the exact words to the lyrics. Again, she winced at the morbidity. The parody on the *Inferno* was completely off the wall, something only a ghoul would appreciate.

> *The one-eyed ox sees all,*
> *The rings of hell will call;*
> *Come with me, my love,*
> *To a place where men howl like wolves,*
> *Where the sun casts no shadow.*
> *The fox and spider women abound,*
> *And gryphons, sirens sound.*

Then came the equally morbid chorus. This part was stolen straight from Dante and barely comprehensible above the beat of the drums:

> *My sage guide leads me by another way*
> *Forth from the still air to the tremulous;*
> *And now I come where shines no light of day.*

Pam considered the lyrics carefully, each line at a time. Still nothing made sense to her. She wondered if it would help showing the transcript to a cryptographic specialist or possibly some self-proclaimed expert on the occult. Why had the killer brought the record along to the crime site? Pam figured it had to be one of three reasons: a bizarre part of the murder ritual, a deliberate, subtle message for the investigation team, or a stunt to throw them off into an unproductive witch hunt.

Duck Harris entered Dougherty's inner office and slumped down in a chair opposite Pam. Already the desk's surface was littered with files and notes, a far cry from the usual tidiness confronting Dougherty's staff. Harris looked at the disorder and smiled. "You wanted to see me?"

Pam slid the legal pad with the music lyrics aside. "Duck, the telephone logs for Maxine Bullock. You were right; they didn't reveal a thing. I think she was smarter than we're giving her credit for. I'd like to go further back."

"How far? Six, maybe eight months?"

"No, even more. Try a year and a half earlier, *before* the couple's estrangement. All outgoing calls during the time Swain Bullock was still living in the house."

Harris's face lit up. "I'll get on it right away."

She gave him a cool, inquiring look. "And what about the list of *Abe Lincoln* personnel who flew out of the Philippines for that Hong Kong R and R?"

"Sorry, not today. The carrier's XO was too preoccupied

getting the ship underway. He promised to give the roster to Dougherty tomorrow."

Pam said in a placating tone, "Let's hope that list breaks down to less than a dozen redheads. They can't all be Type-O Positive and have hemorrhoids."

Harris blew out a breath of air. "Incidentally, the coroner is bothered about those strands of curly red hair on the bed. He wonders about the location and why there weren't more. What do you think?"

"Your boss already insinuated that the hair might have been planted. Far-fetched, but a possibility. What's more, if the killer was so meticulous about rubber gloves, he could have worn a cap."

The black man frowned with disapproval. "Sure, sure. I suppose one of those dark blue stocking jobs we like to wear down in the ghetto?"

"Excuse me, Ms Bonner." Dougherty's secretary stood in the doorway holding a red and white Purolator courier box. "I thought you'd want this right away." She put it on the desk and left the room.

Pamela eyeballed the package then nudged it toward Harris. "It's from Gecko Corman's father. Do you mind? I just glued on new fingernails this morning." She watched the NIS agent grab the package in his paws and easily tear it open. The Rolls hood ornament dropped on the desk with a thud. Pam winced, glad the *Spirit of Ecstasy* wasn't made of Lalique crystal like some other exotic automobile mascots she'd heard about. Harris retrieved the hood ornament and handed it to her. Pam carefully examined it.

"Look at the bottom," Harris said to her, "broken threads. It's been forcibly removed."

Pam nodded. She opened the right side drawer of Dougherty's desk, stared at the shiny mascot a moment longer, then gently placed it inside. She closed the drawer and keyed the lock. "When the photo lab opens in the morning I want the mascot photographed and a facsimile sent off to the Hong Kong police."

Pam stood up, glancing out the window at the setting sun. The day had gone by too quickly, and there was still plenty to be accomplished. She looked at her watch, suddenly aware she still hadn't found time to take the Sentra back to the rental agency. "Duck, you in a big hurry to get out of here tonight?"

"In this business, I get home when I get home." He stared at her with big brown eyes, hard and dark as pine knots. "What do you have in mind? I'm not sure my pregnant wife would 'ppreciate the two of us having a candlelight dinner without her. You being all alone, you're welcome to come over to our place."

Pam smiled. "You're a dear, but that wasn't what I had in mind. I have some logistic problems with transportation. I'll be staying out at Todd's and need help exchanging wheels. You mind coming along to his apartment with me to pick up his Porsche, then follow me with it back to Hertz?"

Harris chortled. "A chance to drive the old man's 944?" He climbed to his feet. "Wouldn't miss it. Consider the job done, lady."

Outside the frozen food warehouse, the Honolulu temperature was seventy-one degrees, but inside the forklift operators wore Eddie Bauer Arctic jackets to ward off pneumonia. Foreman Casey Rodriguez knew well enough that operational overhead could make or break the wholesale frozen food distribution business; if it wasn't the electricity bill to run the sub-zero refrigeration equipment for hours on end, it was the maintenance factor. Or disgruntled employees who deliberately took their time at shifting the merchandise.

Like the current to-do in Storage Room Three. A critical coolant pump part hadn't arrived from the mainland and it was necessary for the warehouse crew to transfer a dozen three-tiered pallets of peas, broccoli, and assorted frozen dinners to an adjoining building. It was a time consuming task, and the forklift operators wanted to postpone it until morning just in case the delayed refrigeration component finally arrived. Unwilling to gamble on possible spoilage, Rodriguez disagreed. At the end of the shift, the job was still incomplete, so he moved in on his own to cut down on the overtime.

Rodriguez deftly wheeled the battery-operated forklift up against the last pallet of cases along the back wall. The cartons were marked FROZEN BROCCOLI. Chewing gum, Rodriguez looked like a busy locomotive as the frigid air caused little puffs of steam to constantly emerge from his mouth. As Rodriguez eased the Towmotor backwards, carefully tilting the load on its twin tines, he heard a loud thud.

Rodriguez cursed at clumsiness. He was good at his job, and it had been six months since he'd dropped a load or even creased one of the boxes. Climbing off the forklift, he ambled around to the other side to investigate.

Frost hung heavily in the air and glimmered on the ceiling-high stacked cartons, but Rodriguez could see clearly enough. He gasped aloud and accidentally swallowed his gum. Rodriguez's knees almost gave out as he stood there, staring down at the frozen configuration of a young woman. She was nude, except for a torn-away brassiere, some gaudy plastic earrings, and what looked like a tampon protruding from her vagina.

The frozen body was ramrod straight; it had apparently been crammed upright into the space between the wall and the stacked pallets, toppling over like a bowling pin when Rodriguez moved the stack. The forklift operator wanted to cry out, to summon help, but his voice caught in his throat; even his breath had momentarily ceased to frost the air. Rodriguez bent closer, determined to make sure this wasn't an apparition. Possibly someone was playing a joke on him. *A department store dummy?* He nudged the icy form with his foot. The body was real enough.

The woman was a hideous white, almost blue, except for her nipples, which had turned purple. The death mask of her face was covered with a layer of ice, so it was difficult making out her features or age. Rodriguez's eyes were again drawn to the strange object between the woman's legs. He stared in disbelief. It wasn't a protruding tampon at all, as he'd originally thought, but a large firecracker! It had a charred fuse that appeared to have fizzled out halfway along its length.

It was nine in the morning Hong Kong time when Detective Kenny Chi received the cable from San Diego. The FBI woman had sent him a barrage of questions, and for most of them he still didn't have an intelligent reply. But toward the end of the wire, Pamela Bonner communicated information that marginally boosted his spirits. She advised that two photographs—one of an American naval officer and Chinese woman posing in front of a Rolls Royce, the other a close-up detail of a *Silver Lady* hood ornament—would be placed on the facsimile and transmitted via satellite first thing in the morning. *California time*, Chi reflected, looking up at the clock on the wall.

For what seemed the hundredth time, Chi opened the two-inch thick file on the Mai Twan homicide. Many of the documents had become dog-eared from repeated handling by a half-dozen other members of the investigative staff, and the folder sleeve itself was stained with tea.

He thought about the similarity of the crimes. The *modus operandi* in the United States was identical, especially as far as the final act of disfigurement and brand of firecracker were concerned. The genital mutilation aside, the actual cause of death had differed slightly. Here, the coroner insisted the Victoria Peak woman had died from strangulation, but her brain appeared to have been damaged by an earlier concussion. Mai Twan's body was also badly bruised as if she'd been in a terrible fight, auto accident, or serious fall. She'd apparently been badly hurt *before* her sadistic killer began toying with fireworks. In San Diego, according to the FBI, death was by strangulation at approximately the same time as the disfiguring explosion. The most important thing Chi had to go on was that the firecracker was the same brand—Half Moon—and the same size.

Kenny Chi found himself wondering if a trip to southern California was in the offing. He wouldn't mind that at all. San Diego had its famous Sea World and zoo, and the city was close to Disneyland and Hollywood. He'd never been to America before.

Shuffling through the Mai Twan investigation documents, Chi reflected on the interviews he'd conducted just two days earlier. Mai's mother had contributed nothing of value, so that page in the file was virtually blank. The Macao gambling casino manager hadn't promised anything, but he'd indicated a willingness to look at photographs of American sailors—in case an actual likeness jogged his memory on the two men who had last accompanied Mai to his establishment.

Also in the file was the deposition of Mai's driver-houseboy, who had insisted he was given leave for three days to visit his ailing mother in Kowloon. His alibi had checked out. When Sam Loo had returned, his employer's body had already been in the morgue twenty-four hours.

Both Mai Twan's apartment and the Rolls Royce had been wiped clean of fingerprints. No one had heard a disturbance. Chi again examined the testimony from the neighbors. The Victoria Peak apartment was in a congested area where it would have been virtually impossible to keep tabs on the comings and goings of visitors. No one remembered seeing an American serviceman—at least not one in uniform. A day before the murder, a street flower vendor a block away did recall delivering two dozen roses to Mai's apartment. The blooms had been paid for by a young caucasian man, but he didn't have red hair. Chi frowned. For some reason the woman FBI agent in San Diego was primarily interested in suspects with red hair.

Chi had already gone over all the overseas shipping schedules at the time of the homicide. This included the week prior and the week after. Two U.S. destroyers from the Sixth Fleet had come into port just briefly for fuel and provisions, but there had been no shore liberty; both had already visited Hong Kong just the month before.

Chi noted that a Victoria Peak postman had recalled that over a six-month period he'd delivered several letters to Mai Twan's address that had a San Francisco FPO return. If they were love letters or fan mail from a U.S. serviceman, Mai hadn't kept them around out of sentiment.

Chi again read over the notations from his interrogation of the apartment building's owner—a Tong Woo. The landlord mentioned that six months before the homicide the victim had abruptly left on a trip, being away for three weeks. She'd told him her destination was Singapore and Bangkok, and although he'd taken care of her canaries during the absence, he'd received no foreign postcards as he'd requested. Landlord Woo, an avid stamp collector, was still annoyed by Mai's ingratitude.

Mai Twan's sudden vacation still bothered Chi, for there had been no record of visas nor any entry or exit stamps in her Crown Colony passport. And Chi himself had checked the airlines for that time period. Again, he pulled the woman's passport out of the homicide file.

He slowly thumbed through it. The American law enforcement people wanted all the victim's vital statistics. Date of birth, birthplace, parents' names, personal description and health data. Chi decided to make a photocopy of the passport and send it out express mail.

Chi once more closely studied the Hong Kong passport. Two items on the vital statistics page captured his attention.

MAI BETH TWAN. Twan was a popular name, almost as common as Smith in America. Her middle name, Beth, however, was unique, at least among the Cantonese. Chi remembered his dead end inquiries at the airlines. In any given week hundreds of Twans are booked on passenger flights, many with the first initial "M." The Beth part might make the difference, especially if—Chi studied the travel document again and bit his lip. Of course! He hadn't thought about it before, but now this identical case inquiry from San Diego prodded him to consider even the remotest possibilities.

Mai Beth Twan was born in Honolulu, Hawaii, where her parents had gone temporarily on extended business. That meant she could have dual citizenship and be eligible for an American passport. Mai was smart, wealthy, worldly-wise, why not? Dual travel documents would be to her advantage. But no American passport turned up in her Victoria Peak apartment. If the killer had run off with a Rolls Royce hood ornament, perhaps he also black-marketed in other items—like stolen identification. Or had he destroyed the passport, for fear the entry and exit stamps it contained might incriminate him?

Chi hated himself for not thinking of these possibilities earlier. Instead of checking on eastbound travel itineraries, he needed to go through the manifests of flights in the other direction, *to the United States*. And he needed to look under the name *Beth Twan*. Chi also would make an important visit to the American Legation. He hoped the U.S. State Department kept passport applications on a computer for quick access.

28

Pamela missed the traffic signal and had to wait. Duck Harris, ahead of her in Dougherty's Porsche, roared on ahead and was already halfway up the block. It didn't matter, for they'd arranged to meet shortly near Lindbergh Field at the Hertz rental lot. Pam had never driven a Porsche before and was halfway looking forward to slipping behind the wheel of the borrowed car. Thank God, the 944 was an automatic.

While waiting for the light to change, she glanced down at the seat beside her and the ominous note they'd found moments earlier in Dougherty's garage. It had been tucked under the Porsche's windshield wiper and had probably been there since morning or even the night before. Pam picked it up and again read the threatening message she assumed was meant for Dougherty. The note was folded in half, on ship's stationery identical to that used for the message she'd received back at the Hotel del Coronado. But this time the missive was hand-written in a delicate, rounded script that might be a woman's. With consternation, Pam again read the words:

Those who dare to wake the sleeping wolf must pay the consequences. There is nothing, absolutely nothing, you

can do about my machinations. Each time I strike it is
because of an even stronger, irresistible will. Your per-
sistence only amuses me, for I am a clown of God.

The red light changed to green. Pamela placed the note aside
and stepped on the gas, still thinking hard about the warning.
She'd heard that last phrase before on a recent cable TV movie. It
was a quote from the greatest Russian dancer of them all,
Nijinsky, after he'd gone mad and been committed. Most curious
of all, the message didn't sound like it came from the Swain
Bullock she'd met on the ship. Pam had seen Bullock's handwrit-
ing before, and it puzzled her that this scribbling was different and
definitely on the feminine side. Tomorrow, if there was time,
she'd consult with a graphologist.

Pam tramped on the accelerator in an effort to catch up with
Duck Harris; she didn't know why, perhaps it was some suppressed competitive nature. It was silly, for the Sentra was no
match for the Porsche. The sun had already dropped over the
horizon and here and there the facing traffic began turning on
headlights. Winter in southern California really wasn't winter in
the harsh sense at all, and often the only reminder that it had
arrived was the shorter day and driving home from work in the
dark. Up ahead she saw Harris, obviously high on the Porsche and
feeling his oats. Dodging the pack at a signal, he set out ahead of
the others, navigating up a moderate incline. Pam knew that on the
other side of the hill was the on-ramp to I-5, the fastest route into
the city center.

Pamela saw the tail lights on the 944 come on only briefly
before a brilliant flash blinded her eyes. She suddenly went rigid,
causing both feet to involuntarily jam forward. The right one,
luckily, hit the brakes, and the Sentra screeched to a sideways stop
in the fast lane. The deafening explosion hurt her ears.

Pamela also felt sick; she opened her mouth and breathed as
deeply as she could, trying to quell the impending upchuck. Her
car was a good block away but the resounding whump had still
thrown her shoulders and neck back against the seat. The
concussion also caused a station wagon two car lengths in front of
the Porsche to go out of control, crashing into a nearby light
standard.

Awestruck and numbed, for several seconds Pam couldn't
move. The fireball blast had been brighter than high noon and
what was left of the sports car and Harris was scattered for
hundreds of feet. The area reeked of burnt cordite. The largest

remaining part of the Porsche—a charred forward section of the frame—had careened off at an angle, sliding to a halt across the expressway. Two intact wheels, blown off by the blast, came hurtling back down the hill, rolling at high speed past Pamela. A plume of black smoke rose from the spot in the pavement where gasoline still burned from a small section of the 944's cockpit. For hundreds of feet in all directions the roadway was littered with charred debris, flesh, and bits of cloth, little of it recognizable.

Pamela shivered as she stared at the scene. When her trance finally lifted, she felt a sudden, awful case of guilt. Harris's death could have been avoided; she'd asked him to do her a simple favor, and this was the outcome. Pam could have driven the Porsche herself, but he'd eyed it like an envious teenager. Lowering her head on the Sentra's steering wheel, she swore softly. The tears would come later.

The stakes were getting higher. Their deranged adversary, instead of fading into the woodwork after his North Island crime, was going high profile and considerably out of his way to make a point. Or vent his anger. Revenge had to be a critical factor in this madman's personality.

Pam's mind gathered speed. She'd planned on a quick diet dinner alone then going back to the NIS office to continue work. Food now was out of the question, and her other plans would have to wait, for the case had suddenly and literally exploded beyond the federal confines of the naval base. Out of necessity, the investigation's reins would now have to be shared. For the next few hours she'd be up to her neck answering questions from her old friends at San Diego Police Homicide Division.

Forty miles off the coast of California, the *Abraham Lincoln* headed north at sixteen knots through moderate swells that only gently rocked the carrier. Dougherty had taken his Dramamine before the vessel had left San Diego harbor just to be on the safe side. Now, with the grim priority communication from Pamela Bonner, he was glad he had. If ever there was a proper moment to be ill, this was it.

The only way to ease the burden Dougherty felt from Duck Harris's death would be to work harder, dedicate himself to solving the case quickly. The easy-going black giant had not only been one of his best field men but a close friend. Dougherty had briefly considered flying off the carrier and returning to San Diego, but that would mean closing down the inquiry here and losing valuable time. Time was everything before the killer struck again.

Pamela was capable. He'd trust her to tie down that end of the investigation while he bit the bullet here and carried on as planned. He would offer his condolences to Duck's family by ship-to-shore telephone and meet with them as soon as he returned.

Dougherty prayed that the booby trap in the Porsche—*the sports car had been a cherry but wheels were replaceable*—had in fact been planted prior to the ship's departure. He didn't want to think of the other possibility—he'd be the complete fool if it turned out the killer were still wandering around on shore back in San Diego. *Keeping Pamela company.*

Dougherty's glum mood was a stark contrast to the rest of the carrier's crewmen who seemed high-spirited and looking forward to extended shore leaves once their ship was delivered to the Bremerton drydock. Many of them would also get to spend Halloween in San Francisco. All were glad that this was a short-term deployment, not one of those vague missions to God-knew-what new trouble spot on the globe. Sailors and flyers were like everyone else; their morale was highest when they were kept informed.

Dougherty unpacked his things and crammed them into the wide drawer beneath his bunk. The two-man cabin, like most of the interior of the ship, was painted off-white. It was located on the third deck, just above the *Abe Lincoln's* waterline, close to the forward passenger escalator. Dougherty would be sharing the cabin with a tech rep from the Wang Computer Company.

Initially, the ship's Executive Officer had suggested that Dougherty team up with the regular investigator on board, a civilian named Fuller who had been assigned to the carrier from the NIS office at Pearl Harbor. Dougherty had declined that arrangement, insisting the key to his snooping success depended on anonymity—at least at the beginning. Above all, he didn't want to panic the entire carrier with word getting out that a psychotic killer was on board. To get the cooperation he needed, the ship's key operational officers would have to be cognizant of Dougherty's authority but not his mission. Of course, a few would need to know exactly why he was here and what he was after—the XO, Rear Admiral Tanner, and Captain Bullock himself would be enlisted in the manhunt from the beginning.

Swain Bullock, Dougherty flashed. Now that the ship had cleared port, taken aboard most of its flight complement, and settled into a cruise routine, it was time to pay a call on the bridge. The captain would want to know what happened to Dougherty's assistant back in San Diego. *Or would he?* Whatever, the two of them had some other things to talk about—like Hong Kong, photography, and music. Dougherty knew Bullock had a stereo player in his cabin, and that was as good a place as any to get him to listen to the lyrics on the Midnight Admirals' 45 RPM record.

Dougherty didn't climb up to the island directly. He took his time, on the way stopped off on the 03 level to introduce himself to the carrier's medical officer. At the dispensary, a Commander Herb Bellows invited him into his private office and closed the door. From all appearances, Dougherty had been expected. Bullock must have tipped Bellows off.

"Welcome aboard, Lieutenant Commander."

"I won't keep you long, sir," Dougherty apologized. "Not on this visit, at least. Later in the deployment, I expect to make a regular pest of myself."

Dougherty expected Bellows's private office to smell faintly of Phisohex, but instead he caught the distinct odor of Juicy Fruit. Across from him, the commander-doctor spit a wad of gum into a scrap of paper that he quickly crumbled and tossed in the waste basket. He replied to Dougherty, "Your prerogative, I'm sure. That ugly incident back in San Diego demands top priority. Anything I can do to be of help." Dr. Bellows was a soft-spoken, unimposing individual with receding, wavy gray hair, plumpish, owl-like cheeks, and blue eyes. He had an easy-going, prairie manner as he said calmly, "From what they tell me, you're just the man to resolve the matter."

Dougherty managed a grin. *"They?"*

Bellows smiled. "Do you have a profile of the killer?"

"Damned little, I'm afraid. Except that the man is a paroxysm of violence and cunning." Dougherty stopped there. He'd be here all day if he told Bellows now about what had happened to Harris in his Porsche. Let him read it in the paper.

The Navy physician sighed. "Well, I wish you luck."

"Thank you, sir. I'll need it. To begin, I'll need to go through a stack of medical records. Officers and enlisted men alike. Any of the data on a computer?"

"Some of them. Most are still in individual folders." Commander Bellows looked at him. "As for the computer, what'll the menu be? Allergies? Mononucleosis? Herpes? Gonorrhea?"

Dougherty thought for a moment. "What about *hemorrhoids*?"

Bellows grinned again. "Perhaps I shouldn't laugh; you look serious."

"Deadly serious."

"Sorry. Only the treating physician's written memorandum regarding the case. In the patient's individual file. We've never kept statistics in that area."

Dougherty frowned. "Fine. But how do I find out who's been treated for hemorrhoids in the past six months?"

Bellows's face twitched. "My God, you might as well ask how many men on the ship have a double chin, hazel eyes, or red hair."

"Yeah. Matter of fact, I was coming to that."

"Sorry, Lieutenant Commander. The only way is to examine the individual files of five thousand plus men, one at a time. Unless the patient you seek was treated recently, and the doctor involved has a photographic memory."

"Okay, Dr. Bellows, forget the sore assholes. Here's an easy one. I need the names of all personnel on the *Abraham Lincoln* who have blood type O Positive."

"Much better. I can have a printout for you in a couple of hours." The MD cannily winked. "Mind giving an old Agatha Christie fan a hint as to what you're after?"

Dougherty smiled. "It's our best circumstantial evidence to date. The forensics people claim the killer left some sperm at the scene of the crime and he's a secretor." Dougherty added in a lowered voice, "One more thing. I know this sounds crazy, but is there any way crew members could find out that the carrier's commander had a blood type of O Positive?"

Bellows was astonished and tried not to let it show. He stared at the air for several seconds, then smiled. "Not unless the crewmen worked on my medical staff."

"That's a beginning, at least. I'll need a list of everyone in your department with that kind of access."

"Whatever you need, Lieutenant Commander. But I haven't finished; there may be more." Bellows hesitated. "On our last trip to the Orient, there were several members of the *Abe Lincoln's* crew who were privy to that blood type information."

Dougherty narrowed his eyes and became more attentive. "Mind elaborating?"

"On the way out, off Guam, we had a nasty catapult accident. One of the yellow shirts lost a lot of blood. Internal, external bleeding. The call went out on the ship's master P.A. for donors. *Type O Positive*. Over two dozen men showed up. Captain Bullock was among the first waiting in line to donate."

Dougherty finished up as quickly as he could with Bellows, requesting a return visit later to pick up the blood type data. He liked the Navy doctor's easy-going, straightforward manner and looked forward to establishing a possible friendship during the cruise. Life aboard an aircraft carrier, Dougherty had been warned, was a lonely enough proposition; surviving a deployment was supposed to be difficult, if not impossible, without friends.

Dougherty ascended several ladders to the 08 level, all the while carefully rehearsing in his mind how much or how little he was about to tell Captain Bullock. Their last meeting had developed into an uncomfortable confrontation; this time Dougherty intended to keep the dialogue as cordial as possible. Bullock was, after all, master of the ship, a virtual god to all who sailed under him. Dougherty wasn't a part of the *Abraham Lincoln's* operational complement; he was a guest on board, extra baggage. Accordingly, he'd be obliged to watch his manners.

Dougherty didn't get beyond the corridor outside the port side entry to the bridge. The Officer of the Day, a lean-faced young lieutenant with a sharply protruding chin and soft-spoken manner, stopped him. Dougherty returned the OD's crisp salute.

The lieutenant said abruptly, "Sorry, sir. The captain sends his regrets. I was about to send a runner down with a message."

"Which is?"

"The CO is unavoidably detained, sir. Off the record, he's about to conduct a Captain's Mast for a problem crewman. Right after the change of watch. But he definitely wants to meet with you later, Lieutenant Commander."

Dougherty tipped back his cap and leaned against the bulkhead. "Fine. Did he give you a time that would be convenient? An hour from now? Later? When, specifically?"

"Sir, Captain Bullock's dining with Rear Admiral Tanner this evening, but he wants you to join him tomorrow night for dinner. The Captain's private mess is served at eighteen hundred hours."

Dougherty smarted. "*Tomorrow night*? What makes him think what I have to say will keep until then?"

"Sir?" The lieutenant looked at him querulously.

"Forget it." Dougherty gestured beyond the young OD's shoulder to the door leading into the bridge. "This Captain's Mast—does he always conduct it on the bridge instead of in his sea cabin?"

"Apparently so, Lieutenant Commander. Especially if it involves bridge personnel. Captain Bullock is fond of *setting an example*, sir."

Dougherty could feel the duty-minded officer's attitude stiffen against him. He said to the lieutenant, "Supposing I don't approach the CO, just step inside and quietly observe the proceedings? Any objections?"

The OD looked surprised and turned a little pink in the cheeks. Contracting his eyebrows, he stoutly replied, "I have my orders, sir." He paused, considering Dougherty. "If you'll wait here, I'll go relay your request."

The young officer started for the bridge entry, but Dougherty called him back. "Lieutenant, never mind. Tell the captain I'll take him up on the dinner invitation." Dougherty hesitated, then said icily, "Tomorrow night."

The OD moved off, but Dougherty stood there for a long time at the rail feeling the wind in his face. From the island's 08 level, the carrier spread out before him in three directions. This was the best part of being a senior line officer—the view from the bridge. The *Abraham Lincoln* was huge, over three acres of floating airport. It was also a city of support services, but everywhere there was the intense, sinister look of a fleet warship, a look of strength that admitted no purpose but fighting sea and air battles.

Dougherty had been aboard a carrier before, many times, but still he had to shake his head in amazement that this steel monster even floated. The size of the ship was beyond superlatives. Dougherty slowly shook his head, wondering about the skills of marine architects. Were we really any better today than the great shipbuilders of the past? They bragged, too, of the state of the art. The *Great Eastern* was supposedly too wide to roll over. The German battleship *Bismarck* was absolutely unstoppable. The modern *Titanic* was too compartmentalized to sink. The *Abraham Lincoln* was so big it could carry everything necessary to make it an impossible target. Dougherty smiled to himself, thinking that every object, every person, had to go someday; a matter of mathematics, if nothing else. It was just beating the odds until the wrecker's torch. If some enemy didn't vaporize this new carrier with a direct nuclear hit, there was always the possibility of a monstrous wave condition like the once-in-twenty-years stress encounter that might do the job.

Still, Dougherty was awed by this monster of a ship. And he was envious of the line officers aboard. This was the real Navy.

Steelbinder had a knack for sensing impending trouble. He first felt the premonition halfway through his watch at the carrier's helm. Now, with only minutes to go before the duty change, he was sure that the less-than-benevolent mood on the bridge meant a conflict was brewing. Captain Bullock, in his raised, gray leather throne on the port side, had been unusually sour and tight-lipped ever since they'd finished taking on the carrier's aircraft complement. Several times Steelbinder had sneaked a look in his direction, and Bullock, studying him, had glared back as if having difficulty maintaining his composure. The captain appeared to be biding his time, a ticking bomb waiting to detonate. Steelbinder wondered what or who it would be this time to set him off. It wasn't his own performance at the helm, he was sure of that; the carrier was true on course, its wake arrow-straight.

As if to confirm Steelbinder's premonition of impending trouble, the ship's Command Master Chief and the head Chaplain quietly entered the bridge as if prearranged and stood stiffly off to one side, waiting in silence. *Witnesses.* Everyone on the bridge exchanged glances of concern. It was obvious now that Bullock was about to set up a Captain's Mast. *The bastard gets to play God again*—right here before the entire watch.

Steelbinder's feet were planted comfortably apart on the deck and both hands gripped the spoked stainless-steel wheel as he looked from the compass to the sea that lay beyond the rectangular windows then back to the instruments. Captain Bullock had ordered a course of 340 degrees magnetic, almost due north. As the ranking helmsman on the ship, Steelbinder took pride in his ability to concentrate and hold a true course; he enjoyed setting an example for the others. Most of the other quartermasters were younger, a few of them mere teenagers whose eyes and minds were prone to wander. *No discipline.* A weaving wake behind the ship was grounds for transfer or demotion. If the ship's CO were about to call Steelbinder on the carpet, it wouldn't be for dereliction of duty at the wheel.

From out of the corner of his eye, he saw the captain slip down from his chair. Bullock stretched, walked over, and glanced at the reading at the wheel then stepped through the open doorway that led into the adjacent chartroom. Steelbinder heard him conversing in muffled tones with the navigation officer, but it was impossible to make out their dialogue.

When the watch ended and the relief crew took over, Steelbinder was the first man to head for the exit. Lieutenant Spooner, the skinny, hatchet-faced assistant navigator, blocked his way. "Hold on a minute, sailor. The Captain wants to see you in the chartroom." Spooner nodded to the Chaplain, Command Master Chief, and the petty officer assigned to keep the log, indicating that they should all follow along as he escorted Steelbinder into the adjoining compartment to confront Bullock.

The carrier commander stood at the other side of the plotting table in his usual hard-ass stance. Steelbinder wasn't sure, but he thought he detected a slight smile or smirk in the corner of Bullock's mouth.

Swain Bullock's face reddened as he said sourly, "You're intelligent, highly capable at the helm, Steelbinder. Why the hell are you prone to trouble the minute you leave the bridge? If you're wondering what I was reading a half hour ago while seated in my command chair, it was your personnel file." Bullock turned to the petty officer with the clipboard. "Make an official note for the log. I'm calling this Captain's Mast in the presence of the Master Chief, the Chaplain, and the Assistant Navigator." Bullock glanced at his watch, unnecessarily, for the brass clock on the wall to his left bonged loudly. "Note the time."

"Sir?" Steelbinder blurted out. He was completely unafraid but genuinely curious. "I don't understand."

Bullock stared back, his mouth pressed into an icy vise that bordered on a smirk. After a few seconds, he said, "What I'm still trying to figure out is how the hell you ever made petty officer third class, let alone second. Minding the helm to the proper degree is only part of your job, Quartermaster. That naval uniform demands a little more of you. Like personal character."

Steelbinder didn't bat an eyebrow.

Bullock said gruffly, "The issue before us is veracity. You know the definition of the word?"

"Yes, sir." Steelbinder's puzzlement slowly gave way to anger, but he didn't dare show it. *Not yet.* He merely stiffened and bit his lip. Prick-face Bullock had a head of steam, and all he could do was let it dissipate. Steelbinder glanced over at his own superior, Lieutenant Spooner, but the assistant navigator only stood by impassively.

Bullock continued in a less strident voice. "This is the second time you've been called before Mast, Steelbinder. Do you remember what I said at the last one, just after we left Subic Bay? Or have you forgotten?"

"Yes, sir. I mean, no, sir, I haven't forgotten. You didn't want to see me in a reprimand situation again."

"That's right. What else did I say?"

Steelbinder thought for a moment. "That you loathed liars. But again, I'd like to remind the captain that regarding the Hong Kong situation, I wasn't lying. It was a matter of *forgetfulness*."

Bullock shook his head like a disagreeable pit bull. "Forgetting, my ass. You weren't on shore leave but officially on duty. Assigned to drive the car, when and where needed. You failed to show. Either drunk or asleep."

Steelbinder avoided Bullock's eyes. He remembered the incident all too well and didn't want to be hit over the head with it all over again. He hadn't been eligible for the R and R charter trip, so he'd volunteered for the extra duty in order to see Hong Kong. He'd first driven the admiral, then Captain Bullock as well, in a car furnished by the military aide at the American Legation. His only crime had been picking up Bullock at his hotel two hours late. The skipper had trounced on him unmercifully.

At the time Steelbinder claimed to have had a car breakdown in heavy traffic, and Bullock had insisted he prove it, which he'd been unable to do. He didn't have an auto malfunction, nor was he drunk or asleep. Far from any of these, Steelbinder had been purposely preoccupied, and time had escaped him. To complicate matters, he hadn't allowed for the choking Hong Kong traffic. Little did he realize at the time the extent to which he'd be reprimanded and punished for the tardiness.

He knew now that there was far more to it than that. The entire stay in the colony flashed before him like shuffled cards: Aviation Boatswain's Mate Gecko Corman suddenly being called in to replace him as Bullock's personal chauffeur; Steelbinder's anger and the game of cat and mouse that followed; the tangled, secret affair he'd stumbled upon; the beginnings of a wonderfully perfect scheme; all this followed by the undeserved, embarrassing Captain's Mast later, back on the ship. Now the nervy, two-faced Bullock was daring to crucify him again.

The captain was shouting at him, trying to get his undivided attention. "Steelbinder, eyes front when I'm talking to you! Have you forgotten the punishment for my last reprimand?"

"Reprimand or retribution, sir?"

Bullock's face took on a waxen, concentration camp look. "Don't get flip with me, Steelbinder. You dare to try my patience?"

"I'm sorry, sir. I just felt the award was a little iron-bound and undeserved."

"A hundred and fifty dollar fine? You were lucky. Might as well have swatted you with a goosefeather pillow. A man could be given a reduction in rate, even put on probation or tossed out of the Navy for dereliction of duty. Your prior superior performance on the bridge saved your ass." Bullock paused to frown at a half-page, handwritten memorandum in front of him. "This time I may not be so lenient."

The chartroom was confining, too confining for the angry electricity that charged the air. The other officers shifted uncomfortably. None of them were consulted or given leave to speak, and apparently none saw fit to interfere with Bullock's tirade. For Steelbinder the proceedings had all the markings of a kangaroo court.

"Now then." The captain's finger jabbed in the air, pointing in his direction. "Have you ever met or would you recognize Lieutenant Commander Gromacki, the air wing's landing officer?"

"No, sir."

"Well, that's unimportant. He's recognized you, and described you to a 'T.' Moreover, he's discussed your job assignment with the navigator who in turn has come to me. And I don't like what I hear, Roscoe. Not at all."

"Respectfully, sir, may I be included in all this derogatory *hearsay*?"

"God damned right you can. You've been spinning sea yarns again, Steelbinder. Mistruths, and I want to know why. Before we left the pier in San Diego, you were caught eavesdropping outside Admiral Tanner's cabin. At the time you told Lieutenant Commander Gromacki that you had official business in flag country."

Steelbinder inhaled deeply, trying to buy a few seconds to compose himself and think. *Damn that hotshot pilot. Fucking, nosey brownshoe airedale! Think quickly, R.W.* "No, sir. I mean, that's not exactly true."

Bullock's wrath continued to ricochet around the walls. "The air wing officer said you told him you were winding clocks, just waiting to go inside the admiral's cabin. He said you were listening at the door."

Steelbinder's mouth was stripped of moisture. He glanced around the room, taking quick inventory of everyone present. "Where is this lieutenant commander now, sir?"

"Flying with one of the squadrons, but he'll be back soon enough. You want to deny the charges to his face? That's easily enough arranged. Suit yourself, but I have his deposition right here."

Steelbinder stared at the floor.

"Well, sailor, I'm waiting."

"Sir, I'm sure he misread something I said about *looking* for one of the other quartermasters, one of the men assigned to the clock-winding detail." Steelbinder shifted his feet. "I'm sorry, sir. I confess to taking a short-cut through that blue-floor area. I didn't realize the flag staff had already come aboard."

"You're lying, Steelbinder. One of the things a captain learns to do real fast when he takes command of a ship is to smell out fog, storms, and sea-lawyers. You may be smart enough to know some quartermaster ranks get assigned to the clock-winding detail, but obviously you've never had the duty yourself aboard the *Abraham Lincoln*. Had you performed the job, you'd know that the clock in the admiral's quarters, as well as the one in my own cabin, is electric." Bullock gestured to the brass instrument on the nearby wall. "This is a new carrier, and there are only three traditional ship's clocks on board, none of them below the 05 level. I want to know why you were prowling around in flag country, Steelbinder. Why the eavesdropping at Admiral Tanner's door?"

"Sir, I told you I was negligent. I'm not a snoop."

Bullock contracted his eyebrows. "Quartermaster, off the record, okay? You dislike me, don't you? Ever since we left Hong Kong, correct?"

"No, sir." Steelbinder lied splendidly. "That's not true."

"I believe your precise words were that you think I'm a son-of-a-bitch, a *first class prick*, isn't that right?"

He swallowed hard. Late one night on the way back from Honolulu, he'd whispered those exact words to one of the other duty sailors on the bridge. At the time, Steelbinder had assumed the captain had been in his sea cabin, out of earshot.

The chart room grew deadly silent as Bullock stubbornly waited for an answer. Steelbinder looked around him, then back to

Bullock. "Captain, would it be possible for me to discuss this matter with you privately?"

The protruding artery just below Bullock's jawline quivered. "So you could hatch more lies later? Without witnesses around to back either of us up? Absolutely not."

The Chaplain and Command Master Chief exchanged odd glances.

Steelbinder said quickly to Bullock, "Sir, I'm in a difficult spot. It looks bad, but these charges aren't true." *Fake it, R.W. You're the consummate actor, remember?* Pretend to squirm a little. That's what the bastard wants more than anything else. Pretend to dance to the strings and don't fight him. Behind the scenes, you're the one in command, and that's what counts. Bullock might enjoy the smell of his own farts now, but he'll be taken down several notches and wake up to reality soon enough.

The captain smiled wanly. "All right, Steelbinder. You've got your reasons for withholding the truth, I have mine for wanting men on the bridge with me I can trust. One of the nice things about being captain, I always get my way. As of now, you're at the bottom of my shit list. If we needed clock-winders, I'd give you that job, since you apparently enjoy playing the role. But we don't."

Bullock turned to the assistant navigator, Lieutenant Spooner. "I want this man pulled from the bridge crew and sent to duty in the aft emergency steering compartment." Bullock vented what was left of his anger on Steelbinder. "As of now, you're on probation for the rest of the deployment. You make trouble one more time, I promise I'll do more than award you a work station close to the bilge. Another step out of line and you'll get a reduction in rate, and it'll be two days in the brig with bread and water. You've got less than a year to go on your hitch, sailor, so don't tempt me beyond that. And stop scowling. Dismissed."

A glut of resentment once more pushed up in Steelbinder's throat. He heard a distant voice: "*Why prolong it, Roscoe?* Forget the rest of your plans, blurt it all out now. *Fucker.* Spit out everything you know about Hong Kong! Go ahead, rain on Bullock's parade now, right here in the chartroom while you have plenty of witnesses." The harsh words in the back of Steelbinder's brain seemed to be coming from underwater. "*Destroy the bastard!*" He recognized the voice of his grandfather summoning him from the bottom of New York Bay.

Steelbinder stiffened. No, this time Gerald Eisenbinder was too impatient. He was wrong and had no business interfering! Forty years ago the rear admiral's mistakes had cost him a demotion, and he'd been ushered out of the Navy. R.W. Steelbinder would not commit a similar mistake. Everything would continue according to plan. Why torpedo Captain Bullock now when in a matter of days Steelbinder would have the pleasure of watching him die slowly and more painfully—in far greater disrepute?

He gave Bullock a mock salute, then turned and hurriedly left the bridge. The chaplain followed him all the way down to the aft mess deck, but Steelbinder ignored the officer's repeated overtures to talk. Shrugging, the chaplain retired to his own office next to the ship's library, a place commonly known as Trouble Central. Steelbinder proceeded down the corridor. He didn't need anyone's advice; all he wanted now was to be alone, let his temper cool, and think. He didn't like the idea of being pulled away from the helm duty on the bridge, but under the circumstances, he would find a way to make it work to his advantage. With events coming closer and closer to fruition, it might even be a blessing being out from under Bullock's close scrutiny.

 **30**

The telephone had been ringing off the hook ever since yesterday's car bomb incident, but now it was strangely quiet. Sitting at Dougherty's desk and nursing her exhaustion, Pamela knew that she faced far more than she could handle alone. Her fellow bureau agent, Walt Courtney, had been called out of town on an emergency assignment. *Lucky for him.* She was glad for the competent, hard-working crew the NIS had provided to help pull her through the crisis. It was now going on six-thirty, and she'd just sent them home to their families, for Steinberg, Meadows, Kelly, and Petrich would have worked all night had she let them. The same with Dougherty's secretary, Myra. That fierce determination to apprehend a cop killer was the same everywhere. The NIS staff was angry and fired up, for they'd all been close to the good-natured, hard-working Duck Harris.

The hushed office was lonely without the others. Pamela felt no lingering fear from the bomb attempt on either her own or the lieutenant commander's life, only an awful guilt over the mistaken victim. For lack of better evidence, she was still halfway convinced the culprit was Swain Bullock, and he was now miles away at sea. The dynamite had to have been planted before the carrier departed.

Aside from private comments to Dougherty, Pam made up her mind to keep this Jekyll and Hyde accusation to herself and not influence the rest of the NIS staff; she needed their absolute objectivity. Circumstantial evidence aside, her belief that Bullock was involved was really no more than an intuition that wouldn't go away—a hunch.

So far, the only element that didn't fit at all was Hans Mueller, the bizarre individual who had provided her with the photograph of Bullock and the Chinese girl. Maybe Mueller really was a shrink with sudden cold feet, afraid to tell her more. Bullock may well have been his client and threatened him. God, maybe they were both deranged and somehow in this together. But why?

Pam shook her head, trying for brief moments to put the nightmare of the ongoing investigation out of her mind and think about dinner. She had to eat something for strength alone, just to keep going. Maybe she would grab some Chinese food and take it back to Dougherty's place; certainly dining out alone had no appeal to her. There was also the prospect of a slight headache coming on.

The complexities of the case were enough to give the most brilliant detective a migraine in perpetuity! What would it be? A sudden gestalt jump and the lights would come on? One swift, sudden moment of understanding? But in the meantime, where and when would the madman strike again? Like some malevolent hourglass, Pam felt as if she were repeatedly being turned upside down then forced to wait for more clues to sift past her fingers.

Yesterday Detective Lieutenant Chi had telexed her the name of the Hong Kong homicide victim as well as an enlarged facsimile of the dead woman's right thumbprint. Her name was *Mai Twan*—the same woman posing with Captain Bullock in the photo! Using the FBI computer in Washington, it didn't take long for Pam to strike pay dirt. Ms Beth Twan, it appeared, had a record. She'd been in the U.S. twice in the past year and a half and on the last trip was arrested at the San Francisco airport trying to smuggle in jade jewelry. Oddly, instead of being prosecuted, she was simply deported back to Taiwan. The reason they didn't return her to Hong Kong was because of her travel documents. Mai Twan traveled on a Taiwanese passport. Why?

Pam shook her head. She understood now why Detective Chi was unaware that Mai had travelled to the States. Pamela wondered if Mai Twan's apparent one-time paramour, Captain Bullock, had somehow made a secret rendezvous with her in San Francisco. The *Abraham Lincoln* had been berthed there prior to its Far East deployment. Deciding to check the dates, she added one more notation to the growing list on her legal pad.

Pamela really needed to travel to Hong Kong to follow up on the crime there, rather than have the information fed to her second hand. She gave it serious thought, but, calculating the long hours of travel to the colony both ways, recovery time from jet lag, and three days minimum on the ground, it wouldn't be practical. More important, she'd promised Dougherty to mind the shop, to keep a tight rein here in San Diego. They needed a nerve center for the investigation, and thus far, the North Island office was it.

The phone rang shrilly, interrupting her brainstorming. She picked it up. "This is agent Bonner."

Pam's heart started to beat faster. The call was from Sean Farley, her FBI counterpart in Honolulu. Feeling expectant, she said quickly before he could go on, "Don't tell me, you found out who made that record purchase. God, I could use some positive input."

"Wishful thinking, Pamela. Sorry, I have bad news. It confirms your earlier speculation. It appears you've got a series killer on your hands."

"Sean, please. I've had a tough day, so don't waste time. What do you have?"

"Another homicide. A *real* stiff this time, virtually turned to ice in a deep-freeze warehouse. The crime is similar to the one you described in your all points wire—to a point. The tampon-sized firecracker in her snatch failed to go off. Still, I think—"

"*C'est que ca* 'snatch'?" Pam interrupted.

"Sorry, Ms Bonner, I got carried away." Farley paused then continued, "The fireworks are an identical brand. As soon as the victim thaws out, the local coroner will check out the cause of death. Right now she looks like something out of the great ice age. Under the circumstances, it won't be easy to accurately establish when the crime took place."

Pamela sighed into the phone. "Clues. Any identification at all?"

"They're working on it. Checking over the missing persons

reports, talking to the frozen food warehouse employees. Maybe we'll have something tomorrow."

She thought for a moment. "This is too important. Dougherty's staff will just have to watch the office here. I'm coming over there myself. Tell the local homicide people I'll bring along everything Todd Dougherty and I have to date. Book me a room tomorrow night in Waikiki, okay? Something reasonable or my boss will shit."

"How long you staying?"

"No more than a couple of nights. I have obligations here."

Sean Farley said on the line, "That detective in Hong Kong, Lieutenant Chi—you want I should clue him in?"

"No. I'll take care of it from here. Thanks, Sean. Good night."

Pamela replaced the phone on the hook and went over to the water cooler to get a drink. She thought about what Kenny Chi had told her. In his lengthy wire, he'd explained that the murder in Hong Kong was not only a strangulation, but the victim had also sustained a blow to the head. The ugly finale—the firecracker business—appeared identical. Now the killer had struck in Honolulu. Basically, the same MO in all three deaths. Pam went back to the desk and found Chi's cable. She read it again.

It was apparent the Hong Kong detective was determined, at any effort, to solve his case; he'd fly to San Diego immediately if necessary to pursue the investigation. In her return wire, Pamela had asked Chi to wait a few days, not only to give herself a little breathing room, but to allow the rest of the staff time to tie down several loose strings. Now, after hearing of the grisly murder in Honolulu, Pam was less inclined to delay Chi's arrival. They obviously needed to pool their resources. Instead of Detective Chi coming here, she'd propose a better arrangement, that they meet in Hawaii and compare notes with the police homicide team there.

One thing more: Before Pam could hustle out to Dougherty's pad and pack her suitcase, she had to wait for his call. He'd promised to make telephone contact right after finishing dinner with the inscrutable Captain Bullock.

While she waited, Pam picked up the phone to call for Honolulu ticket reservations. After three attempts, she found a seat on United leaving first thing in the morning. She would now contact the Chinese detective, break the news of what happened in Honolulu and tell him about her sudden travel plans. Pam hoped that Chi would be as lucky as she'd been in getting an immediate flight to Hawaii.

• • •

If the Captain's Mess was meant to impress Dougherty or tickle his vanity, it had the opposite effect. He'd definitely have preferred dinner in the officer's dirty-shirt wardroom, an informal setting where even flight coveralls were welcome. Bullock's china and spotless table linen seemed strangely out of place in the noisy, soot-covered working environment of a supercarrier warship. Dougherty smiled to himself. The immediate scene made him think of a couple of auto mechanics in a garage, rewarding themselves at the end of the day with champagne served in Baccarat flutes.

The food, however, was excellent. Swain Bullock put on an elegant show of serving the meal; obviously the effort of the stewards and his private mess cook pleased him, for he was in good spirits. Too cheerful, Dougherty thought, for a man whose wife had been buried only the morning before back in San Diego.

Time went faster aboard a carrier than Dougherty had figured. They'd already been at sea over thirty-one hours. Finishing up his stuffed pork chop with white sauce, Dougherty sat back and sipped at a glass of Perrier water. Judging from the ambience, he was sure that had they been back on shore, Bullock would next offer him a snifter of expensive cognac. From their conversation during dinner, Bullock seemed to favor classy living. Curious, since he and Maxine's base living quarters at North Island didn't reflect it. Dougherty wondered if the captain's discerning taste had been cultivated sometime after walking out on his wife Maxine.

The steward cleared away the plates and brought back creme caramel and coffee. Dougherty passed on the dessert, as did the captain. Bullock—though less than enthusiastic—invited him to smoke if he liked. Dougherty declined, finally deciding that if Pamela could kick the habit, so would he. Besides, his mind was a long way from cigarettes. "Captain, I feel intrusive. I realize I'm excess baggage on this trip and that it's not easy for either of us."

Bullock sat forward, the sagging skin under his eyes taking on extra weight. Dougherty wondered if he'd been getting enough sleep lately. The captain asked, "You mind, Lieutenant Commander, if I call you Todd?"

"No sir. Be my guest."

Bullock said seriously, "Todd, earlier you said you're convinced beyond a shadow of a doubt that my wife's killer is aboard this ship and not back in San Diego. Supposing you're right? With just under six thousand men on board, it'll be like searching for a goddamn needle in a haystack."

"At least we're at sea. And this haystack's considerably smaller than the city of San Diego or, for that matter, all of southern California."

"FBI, NIS, the local police—getting a little crowded, isn't it?" Bullock shook his head. "I'm impressed with all the attention the Government's giving to one isolated murder."

"Captain, before I didn't want to spoil your dinner by passing on the additional bad news. There's not just one crime; our quarry, it appears, is a *repeat killer*. We've learned of an apparent identical mutilation homicide in Hong Kong." Dougherty hesitated, studying the captain. "At a concurrent time when some of the personnel from the *Abraham Lincoln* were on shore leave in that city."

Bullock looked stunned, as if he'd been hit over the head. Trying to compose himself, his eyes turned flinty. "You're absolutely sure? Not a mere coincidence?"

"I spoke with the FBI woman earlier today. She's been in close touch with a homicide detective in the Crown Colony."

Bullock morosely shook his head.

Dougherty would end it there, purposely withhold the rest. This wasn't the moment to reveal what he knew about the photo Pamela had given him, the snapshot of Bullock and an attractive woman now identified to be Mai Twan—the *same woman who was murdered* in Hong Kong. For Bullock, it had either been a casual date or he had an intercontinental affair going. Dougherty would wait for all the details from Hong Kong before tipping his hand and grilling Bullock about her.

This new information was important, but it wasn't a clincher. He still didn't suspect the carrier commander of homicide; it was still too neat, as if contrived. The captain might even be royally set up. But why? There had to be an explanation. Dougherty would save the incriminating snapshot a few hours longer, wait until he or Pamela conferred with Lieutenant Chi.

"Lieutenant Commander? Todd?" Bullock was calling to him.

"Sir?"

"You seem to be caught up in a daze. Business back at North Island or some personal reflection?"

"Sorry, Captain. My frustration showing. Too much internalizing on this enigmatic case." Dougherty smiled as pleasantly as he could. "Give me three or four hours, and I hope to close in on the killer. You mentioned a *needle in a haystack*. It may not be that difficult. Matter of fact, with your medical officer's cooper-

ation and the help of a computer, I plan to break down a list of
suspects to less than two, maybe three dozen men at the most."

Bullock's face tightened. "By God, man, that's excellent.
You're making headway then. Dare I ask how you so quickly
eliminated the rest of us?"

Dougherty suppressed a smile. "Crime lab data, blood types,
even the color of hair." He didn't say what color. "Possibly even
a snapshot."

"No fingerprints?"

Dougherty shook his head. "The investigation would have been
concluded by now if we'd been that lucky." He thought for a
moment, then said abruptly, "Captain Bullock, by chance has the
ship's doctor treated you for hemorrhoids?"

"Never." Bullock knocked on his desk with his knuckle.
"Physically fit from bow to stern. Check my records if you like."

"I may do that." Dougherty quickly changed the subject. "How
many of your men will be given liberty in San Francisco,
Captain?"

"If we stay the full two and a half days, all of them. In rotating
shifts."

Dougherty nodded. "You mind going back in time? That
special R and R flight from the Philippines to Hong Kong. How
many went along on that liberty?"

For the first time Bullock looked uncomfortable. He took his
time responding. "I can't remember. More men were eligible than
came up with the money. You'll have to ask the XO. He arranged
the trip."

Dougherty nodded. "I've already done that, Captain. I'm still
waiting for a copy of those flight manifests."

A slow enlightenment seemed to creep over Bullock's face.
Smiling thinly, he said to Dougherty, "Slowly, slowly the NIS
noose tightens, is that it?"

"Slowly and I trust *noiselessly*. I hope you and your officers
will help me by keeping as mum as possible about this discussion
and my investigation. I'd like to move in on our quarry as quietly
as possible."

Bullock grinned. "Quietly? That's a laugh. You said the bastard
tried to blow you to hell and back in your Porsche. The killer
obviously knows where you live and what you look like, Lieutenant Commander. Hell, if this sailor listens to the radio, he
already knows he's failed on the bomb attempt—if in fact you
were his target. He's probably also figured it out that you've
followed him along on the carrier's deployment." Bullock thought

for a moment. "Fact is, if I were you, Todd, I'd keep an eye peeled over my shoulder at all times. You want me to have the Master at Arms assign a man to your tail?"

Dougherty shook his head. "That's all I need. Absolutely not." The steward came into the cabin and started to replenish Dougherty's coffee. "No, I've had enough. I still have a stack of personnel files to pore over before retiring, and I'll need my sleep later. Captain, before I leave, there's something else. Remember Gecko Corman?"

"Unfortunately, yes. I'd like to forget the bastard."

"Now that he's officially been placed on UA status, I'd like to look inside his personal locker. The administrative department tells me there's a combination padlock on it, and we'll need your authority to use a bolt cutter."

Bullock looked at him narrowly, then climbed to his feet. "You'll have it. What else?"

Dougherty gathered himself to leave. "Yes—the known troublemakers on the ship with brig time. Who are they? Anyone aboard with an incidence of minor theft, extortion, cheating at gambling—the petty stuff."

Bullock's smile was indulgent. "No dice. Murder may be one thing, but a sailor's hand in the cookie jar, quibbling over who grabbed the cigarettes, insubordination here and there, even sleeping on the job—are other matters. You'll have to back-up your accusations, Lieutenant Commander, and not expect carrier personnel who may have made a few mistakes to prove their innocence of this kind of monstrous charge. On my ship, it's business as usual, *innocent until proven guilty*. This is still the good old U.S.A., pal."

Dougherty backed off. He'd try again later when the captain was in a more cooperative mood. Bullock was the type who liked to show off his memory; he'd be good at remembering faces. The NIS needed his help. Dougherty headed for the exit. "Just in case, Captain, you hear of anyone on board your ship selling or horsetrading stolen car parts, please let me know."

Bullock looked genuinely puzzled. "Car parts? On a crowded nuke carrier? What the hell are you talking about?"

"Hood mascots. I've one particular ornament in mind. Off a Rolls Royce, and it's called the *Spirit of Ecstasy*. Some auto buffs call it a *Silver Lady*." Dougherty smiled at Bullock, noting that for a brief moment the captain looked strangely, suddenly old—or was that an expression of guilt? No, it had to be a look of defeat; for a second or two, the captain looked beaten. Hells bells, was there the remotest chance Pamela Bonner was right about Bullock's involvement? How could it be? *Impossible. Not in today's Navy—or even tomorrow's.*

Dougherty stepped quickly into the blue-tiled corridor and closed the door to the captain's cabin behind him.

~~~~~~ 31

Lieutenant Kenny Chi arrived at mid-morning after an all-night flight from Hong Kong. He sounded tired on the phone but agreed to join Pamela immediately at Honolulu Police Headquarters.

On the way to meet the Chinese detective, Pam stopped briefly in Waikiki at Watanabe's Music Store to see if any contact had been made with the clerk who sold the killer a dozen identical records. The saleswoman still hadn't been located; local agent Sean Farley had even talked to the missing employee's neighbors. None of them knew where the clerk was vacationing.

At Police Headquarters for the City and County of Honolulu, they met in a conference room on the second floor. The Hong Kong investigator looked to be in his late thirties; he was shorter than Pamela, slightly overweight, and had neatly-trimmed black hair parted severely in the middle of his scalp. Kenny Chi had a haughty manner and seemed to move in slow motion, except for his small charcoal eyes that constantly darted about like an alert sparrow's. Chi seemed to prefer maintaining a last-name formality during their dialogue, and, considering his aloofness, that didn't bother Pam at all.

It didn't take long to review the details of the local murder. There'd been several additional developments in the freezer homicide since Pamela first heard about the case on the telephone back in San Diego. According to a Sergeant Kailui, the strangulation victim had been identified. The green tag attached to the body in the cooler read Didi Tyler. Kailui told Pamela and Chi that the dead woman was an out-call prostitute who worked the island from Waikiki to Schofield Barracks. Didi didn't appear to have any blood enemies; she'd lived in Hawaii half a dozen years, previously being "employed" in Las Vegas.

Most of this sketchy information had come from the young prostitute's roommate, a black woman named Penny Sherman who had a prior police record, including two arrests for hustling in the bar at the Royal Hawaiian. The roommate insisted that Didi Tyler hadn't been back to the mainland since her arrival in Honolulu, and she doubted whether the murder victim had ever visited San Diego before that. Most important, Penny claimed that the roommate—who often gabbed about her tricks—never mentioned the visiting aircraft carrier *Abraham Lincoln* nor any of its crewmen. According to the Honolulu investigator, one windfall to come out of Penny's interrogation was the closing down of a part-time prostitution ring operating under the cover of Transocean Frozen Food Distributors.

For Pamela, there were a couple of noteworthy developments in this third firecracker-related homicide. After the prostitute's frozen body had thawed, the coroner determined the cause of death was strangulation—just like the victims in San Diego and Hong Kong. Second, the police found a poem written with a marking pen scrawled across the dead woman's back.

Pamela dutifully entered the morgue, trailing behind Lieutenant Chi and Sergeant Kailui. The Hong Kong detective scowled as he studied Didi Tyler's body in the refer tray.

Kailui said to them, "We were lucky." He withdrew a giant firecracker from his pocket and handed it to Pamela.

She nodded. "All too familiar." She passed it on to Chi.

He examined it quickly. "Identical. The Half Moon fireworks factory. It's tragic that the human mind can be so capricious and cruel." Chi sighed, then asked, "The fuse went out, a dud?"

The Honolulu cop nodded.

Pamela slowly shook her head. "They told me if I stay in law enforcement long enough, I'll eventually harden to all this. It's still hard to believe." She looked away from the body, her eyes roaming over the basement chamber that apparently doubled as a forensics laboratory. Nearby a flashy Porsche calendar caught her attention and held it; she couldn't help thinking back to the exploding sportscar and the helpless Duck Harris. At least Didi Tyler's body was intact and could be buried in a casket instead of a plastic bag.

Kenny Chi was speaking with the Honolulu detective, a huge, chunky Polynesian who looked like he once might have wrestled bears for five bucks a minute. Pamela wasn't listening; her blank stare alternated between the dead woman and the wall calendar. Her emotions, too, waivered—between remorse and regret. Pam figured that by now she'd be used to the highs and lows of a crime-fighting career in the FBI. Not so. As if the women being slaughtered by this butcher weren't bad enough, the warning implied in Harris's unnecessary, grisly death was a new, miserable low. There was a time in her life, right out of college, when Pam had fantasized on chucking any and all career goals and running off to Monte Carlo with a rich Arab. Right now she wished she'd pulled it off.

"*Miss Bonner?*" Kenny Chi's voice had an impatient edge to it.

She looked at him. The detective insisted on using *Miss*. Pam had tried earlier, unsuccessfully, to break him of the habit.

Small points of light appeared in Chi's intelligent, almond eyes as he asked her, "You said the killer left a calling card, some indelible message on the body?"

Pam deferred to Sergeant Kailui, who said quickly, "I was about to get to that." He summoned a pair of white-frocked attendants.

Pamela and Chi stood back as the morgue men flipped the body over as easily as a gunnysack of onions.

Chi leaned closer. He studied the verse on the victim's back for a moment, then read it aloud:

> *Each one shall in his dismal tomb be found,*
> *His flesh and outward figure reassume*
> *And hear what shall eternally resound.*

It was a while before Chi looked up and stepped away from the dead woman. The big Hawaiian detective jerked his thumb, and the morgue attendants returned the body to a face up position before sliding the drawer back into its niche.

Pamela quietly advised Chi, "I've already checked out the source. Allegorical poetry from Dante's *Inferno*—Canto Six. Are you familiar with the work, Lieutenant?"

Kenny Chi searched Pamela's eyes, silently studying her. He'd done that twice earlier, making her uneasy. The Hong Kong detective liked to stand back and think carefully before responding. Pam wasn't used to his kind of cold intelligence in southern California where a charming grin and a gift for gab were the order of the day. She was more at home with conversations where the participants smiled and poured on the oil while they thought—or plotted.

The inscrutable Chi finally replied, "No, I regret I'm not familiar with pre-Renaissance literature. Perhaps I should overcome this deficiency. You'll honor me by telling me about it."

They went back upstairs to Sergeant Kailui's office where Pamela explained as best she could. The three of them talked for another half-hour, but for Pam it was a reluctant session, and this time she didn't commit any new information to her note pad.

Kenny Chi shared a taxi with her on the way back to Waikiki. Pam planned to stay only one more night at the Moana while the Hong Kong detective was booked for two days at the Ilikai. He surprised her by announcing that since he'd come all this distance on official business with a ticket provided at government expense, he intended to take advantage of the situation. When his work was finished in Hawaii, Chi tended to take a week off and pay his own way to southern California. "A tourist, possibly my only opportunity to see your great country," he intoned. "At a pittance of the round trip cost from Hong Kong out of my own pocket."

Pam nodded, thinking if she were in his place, she'd do the same thing. She checked her watch, noting that it was going on four, and she'd promised to call Dougherty aboard the carrier at five. As the cab headed down Ala Moana Boulevard in heavy traffic, she said to Chi, "You confuse me by your closed-mouth nature, Lieutenant. Back in Kailui's office, I felt a little lonely doing all the talking."

He grinned. "You are thinking I am the silent, inscrutable Chinese, no doubt. A stereotype, Miss Bonner. For me, it's a question of *when* to speak out. Timing is everything in the investigative process. As for today, I suspect the Honolulu Police know far less than even my humble assistants. Apparently the killer was here in Hawaii for a very short time, then quickly moved on without leaving any clues. I'm afraid our only real evidence and yet-to-be-unravelled knots remain in Hong Kong and San Diego."

After a silence, Pam said firmly, "Or aboard the *Abraham Lincoln*. The murderer could make a major blunder out there."

Chi shook his head, his eyes unseeing and strangely remote. "I think not. I suspect the killer's behavior will be exemplary aboard a confining ship. Animals try to avoid sullying their nest. Unfortunately, this madman's lust to strike again will build like steam in a kettle until the carrier reaches its next port. And then—" Chi ended it there.

Pamela could tell that Kenny Chi—like most educated Chinese—was sharp as a tack. He also appeared to be a sadistic tease and enjoyed using his brilliance as a whip. She asked him, "You're convinced then, that the killer will strike next in San Francisco? Or wait until the ship reaches Bremerton?"

Chi smiled enigmatically, unwilling to commit himself. Instead, he asked, "This Captain Bullock—you're absolutely convinced that in the past there's never been a sign of psychotic collapse or trauma?"

"Lieutenant Chi, you sound more like a psychiatrist than a detective. The answer, *thus far*, is no, but we can't be sure of anything. Todd Dougherty and I both checked out his records as best we could. There could be gaps."

Chi reached into his suit pocket and withdrew the photo Pamela had sent him earlier. Studying it, he said to her, "The American naval captain looks congenial enough. Hardly the image of a megalomaniac with an insatiable hate for womanhood and an urge to kill." Chi shrugged and took on a look of grave resolve. "There are some additional facts you should know about immediately, Miss Bonner, though I'd like to share them as well with your investigative partner, this Lieutenant Commander Dougherty."

Pamela said quickly, "I'm sorry, that's impossible. At least for a couple of days. He's still at sea on the *Abraham Lincoln*. Since time is important to both of us, I suggest you trust me to relay your thoughts by wire or telephone."

Chi stared out into the traffic, thought for a moment, then looked back at her. "You're right; it's impossible for me to be in four cities at once." He again scrutinized the snapshot of Swain Bullock and Mai Twan. "This photograph you sent me—I took it to the manager of the Casino Lisboa in Macao. He recognized Captain Bullock in the photo as the same American naval officer who visited there last month with Miss Twan. Apparently the manager himself saw to their comfort in the cocktail lounge. But there is more. Mai Twan appeared to know another uniformed American in the lounge—a sailor with a saxophone who had been invited to play a few musical sets with the casino band. I don't know this other American's name, but the three of them—the seaman, Mai Twan, and Captain Bullock—later left the Lisboa together."

Pam's pulse quickened. *Dougherty's problem boy, the aviation boatswain's mate*! Pamela recited his name calmly. "Gecko Corman. He was another crewman on the *Abraham Lincoln*. He's disappeared. Go on, please."

Chi pulled out a small leatherbound notebook and jotted down Corman's name before continuing. "I'll need a photo of this sailor for the people in Macao to make an identification. There's also the possibility a certain flower seller may recall this Gecko Corman's presence near the crime site. A street vendor delivered roses to Mai Twan the day before her death; he claims a young Caucasian man purchased them. We've already checked this photo with the flower man, and the customer definitely wasn't Bullock. Could it have been the young saxophone player acting on the captain's behalf?"

Pam sighed. "Even if it was, the sailor's missing. I'm sorry, Lieutenant, it's another dead end."

Pursing his lips, Chi put the photo away. He laced his fingers together on his lap and stared out at the traffic.

Earlier they'd made plans to have dinner together at Don the Beachcomber's, at which time Pamela intended to break the news to Chi about Mai Twan's travelling on a Taiwanese passport, her detainment and immediate expulsion from the United States. Pam was still waiting for a promised wire from the Immigration and Naturalization Service office in San Francisco with backup details on the deportation. She hoped this information would be waiting for her back at the hotel or at the Honolulu FBI office. Pam finally decided she shouldn't wait until dinner to break this news to Chi. "Lieutenant, I think you should know that Mai Twan, as beautiful and exotic as Captain Bullock may have found her, was no angel with a halo."

Chi chuckled appreciatively. "I'm quite aware of that."

"But are you aware that the woman possessed a valid Taiwan passport? That she traveled twice to the United States?"

"I'm ahead of you, Miss Bonner. *Three times.* Twice to San Francisco, where the first time she was turned away, and a third time—most recently—when she went to San Diego."

"San Diego?" Pamela was surprised and let it show. "How, if her visa was revoked?"

Chi waved a scornful hand. "Unfortunately, your customs and immigration authorities didn't fingerprint her. A shame. Mai Twan is also known as Elizabeth, or Beth Twan. She has a dual citizenship with *two* legitimate passports—one from the Crown Colony, the other, by birthright, from the United States."

"But the other escapades—and the Taiwan travel document?"

"*Escapades.* Indeed, the perfect word. The third passport was counterfeit; these can be obtained easily enough for a reasonable fee from unscrupulous Kowloon printers."

Pam frowned then asked, "Your search of the woman's Victoria

Peak apartment. Any romantic correspondence at all from Swain
Bullock, or anyone else for that matter?"

"Nothing."

The taxi pulled into the Ilikai Hotel driveway and Kenny Chi
climbed out at the lobby entrance. He said to her, "Don the
Beachcomber's then. Is six-thirty satisfactory?"

She nodded. "I'll be waiting in the bar."

Chi stood poised in the taxi doorway. "Your NIS friend on the
ship—I'm most curious. You will touch base with him in the
meantime?"

"Of course," she said icily.

Chi paid exactly his half of the fare. "Tell him for me, Miss
Bonner, that on my side of the Pacific, at least, the cards look
increasingly disfavorable for this Captain Bullock. Rather than
rest on my laurels and let the FBI and NIS finish this matter, I
fully intend to keep building my own case one way or another,
until it's airtight."

Pamela looked out the taxi door at Chi. He stared back at her
with an unsmiling look of determination. The Hong Kong
detective had the singlemindedness of a metronome, she thought.
"All very good, Lieutenant Chi, I admire your perseverance. But
I doubt whether the three women clamoring from their graves for
justice will care less about the technicalities of *who* dispenses it."

"Yes, that may be true." Chi smiled enigmatically and cupped
his hand to his ear. "I, too, hear these victims crying, but even
more loudly, I hear a clock ticking. I suggest we make haste, Miss
Bonner, before more women die."

~~~~~~~ 32

The transpacific call from the carrier had been routed through a
couple of booster stations before reaching Pamela at her hotel, but
she still had difficulty hearing Dougherty's metallic voice with all
the interference. Since he'd insisted that her end of the transmission was coming in loud and clear, Pam talked at length,

explaining what she and Kenny Chi had managed to accomplish in Honolulu without him. Dougherty seemed to be listening with keen interest; at least he hadn't interrupted her.

"Stick around, Todd, there's more," she eagerly intoned. "Lieutenant Chi also checked the U.S. Legation in Hong Kong. Our military attaché there said an American sailor—he thinks it was a petty officer second class—drove Bullock's car when it went out, but a different sailor was at the wheel when the vehicle was returned. The captain switched drivers."

From the aircraft carrier's end of the transmission, Dougherty acknowledged her revelations with a crisp, "Go on, I'm listening and recording it all."

Indeed he was; Pamela found the beep alerts annoying. Trying to ignore them, she continued, speaking as slowly and distinctly as possible. "Are you sitting down, Todd? Here's the clincher. The driver who brought the car back to the attaché had a *saxophone* with him."

She heard Dougherty choke out the name Gecko Corman. Pam added, "What's more, Chi's convinced that Captain Bullock, Mai Twan, and this second sailor—obviously Corman—met at a gambling casino in Macao. They all left together and just prior to the Hong Kong crime."

Pam listened, waiting for a reaction at the other end. All she heard was heavy breathing that sounded like wind. The beep on Dougherty's recorder assured her that he was still on the line. At last he said in a serious voice, "I feel intimidated. Obviously, I need to work faster out here to hold up my end of the investigation."

"Should I meet you in San Francisco?"

"No, not yet. Fly back to San Diego and mind the store. Does Lieutenant Chi intend to stick around?"

"He plans to go on vacation, his first visit to the U.S.A."

"Good God, now? Well, make sure he stays in touch."

"I'll try." Pam hesitated. "Lieutenant Commander, is anyone else there with you?"

"Of course. I'm in the communications shack. Why?"

Pam raised her voice and said awkwardly, "Who's listening in?"

She heard Dougherty laugh. "No one. I'm holding the phone receiver to my ear, dammit. Go ahead, spill the nonsense. What do you have?"

"Miss you. Challenging case or not, I'm a little bored over here."

"Unhappy with Hawaii? What do you want, Xanadu?"

"No. To be out on that carrier nosing around. Given that impossibility, to be back in my own apartment at the end of the day—with my books, music and cat. How the hell do I know if the neighbor is feeding it properly?"

"It'll survive, Pamela. Is that all?"

"No." She stiffened. "He's guilty, Todd. I'm almost sure of it. And someone else has to be protecting him. God knows why. We've got to find out what kind of secret demons are biting at Swain Bullock's heels."

"What are you talking about?" Dougherty's voice no longer sounded cheerful, and it wasn't just the airwave static.

Pam said evenly, "Like what happened to Bullock to make him flip out. The *what, when,* and *why.*"

"Sorry, Pamela. That's your rush to judgment, not mine. Have you been sniffing glue? Better be careful dining out tonight with that Chinese gumshoe. He's apt to tell you a scorpion can be born inside a man's head if he breathes too much basil."

"You're belittling me, you flip bastard! I'm serious."

"So am I."

"Look, Todd, everything's falling into place. Weren't those your own words? At least we're doing our homework on Bullock. Can you say the same, or are you still running scared, protecting the damned Navy?"

"Try me. What have I missed?"

"Dante's *Inferno*, for one thing. All those annoying quotes the killer keeps appropriating."

"I'm plain folk, Ms Bonner, not a student of the classics. If you're such a woman of letters, give me a hint of what I need to know, and I'll pursue it."

She sighed with impatience. "Listen to me. Plainly put, the *Inferno* is the story of a traveler in Hell. My guess is that the killer's a snob. He probably believes Dante's verse is a half-sacred work, maybe even a sort of alternate Bible for his halfass, erudite mind."

There was another tiresome beep on the line followed by Dougherty coughing. "Too stuffy. His definition of himself or yours?"

"Must you be so crabbed and cynical? And turn off that damned recorder, it makes me nervous. What I'm telling you is off the record, between the two of us."

"Sorry, Pamela. Let's try again. Tell me what this *Inferno* means to you in five and ten English."

She thought for a moment. "Dark verse—call it what you will—it may be a moral pill to some people, but all it does for me is send a chill up my spine. I suggest you find a copy of the work, and check it out for yourself. Right now, I have to run. Dinner with Detective Chi."

"I'm turning green with envy."

"Good. We'll try not to solve the case without you." Pamela hung up, feeling a heated hope.

A low pressure area had moved in overnight and the morning was gray with wind-driven rain. Already the brooding reach of long hours at sea was beginning to get to Dougherty. He didn't take well to the confines of his shared cabin at all; he liked to get out, if only to the huge opening in the side of the hangar deck for fresh air. When Dougherty could stare out at the ocean instead of four walls, it seemed like a weight had been temporarily removed from his shoulders.

He stood there a long time, watching the sea kick up a fuss. Though the huge, elevated bow of the *Abraham Lincoln* was pitching only moderately in the onrushing whitecaps, the escort vessels were taking a considerable pounding. Dougherty could feel that the carrier was making less speed, apparently to accommodate them. Air operations for the day were cancelled, and the weather forecast was for continued squalls until afternoon when the narrow front was expected to move inland.

If it weren't for the low-lying clouds and on-again, off-again downpours, Dougherty would be able to see the coast of California and the Big Sur area. He knew that later in the day the carrier was scheduled to begin its submarine defense maneuvers, weather permitting. Dougherty had work to do, but the brisk air and watching the cantankerous sea did wonders for his psyche. The series of homicides had a suffocating grip on him, and breaks like this allowed him to stew in his own subconscious. As for the homicide case, he was convinced that very soon the conclusions—rational, logical, empirical—would all fall into place. Pamela Bonner's instincts were dead wrong about the *Abraham Lincoln's* commander, and Dougherty needed to straighten her out, prove she was wrong.

He'd come aboard the carrier prepared for anything, ready even to temporarily assume that reversible infinity between hunter and hunted. Pamela didn't seem to understand this unique, pragmatic relationship; her approach seemed to be clinical, a superficial overview. Not that her priorities and special female intuition weren't relevant. It was just that she was trying to tree the wrong cat. Pam was dead wrong about Swain Bullock. It didn't wash. He didn't fit, despite the mounting, uncommon occurrences stacked against him. The only explanation that made sense was that the captain was being purposely set up.

Dougherty glanced at his watch. Time to get moving. He'd asked the ship's Master at Arms and a carpenter to meet him in one of the forward bunk cubicles at ten sharp, and he didn't want to be late. Now that he had Bullock's written authorization, Dougherty intended to do some snooping through Aviation Boatswain's Mate Gecko Corman's locker.

Stepping lively to avoid a quartet of sweating joggers, Dougherty ventured across the hangar deck and descended into the labyrinth depths of the ship. The ladder he chose was crowded with work detail personnel, and he had to wait for access. Finally reaching the fourth deck, he hurried to an area called Boys' Town and an alcove where Corman had been assigned the usual enlisted man's bunk, drawer, and locker.

One of the ship's carpenters was waiting, but the Master at Arms had apparently taken off. Dougherty immediately saw why. Corman's locker had already been invaded, the combination padlock on the hasp neatly severed by a bolt cutter. The metal door was partially open and Dougherty could see the locker was empty. The confused ship's carpenter stood there with the cutting device. The man looked embarrassed. "I'm sorry, sir. I wasn't the one who opened it. I just arrived and waited for you, as instructed."

Dougherty saw red. "What the hell's going on then?"

"A couple of men assigned to the area told me that the captain came down at daybreak with his own crew. And that he took the contents away."

Dougherty shook his head. *Picked clean*, but why? "That will be all, sailor. You can go."

The ship's carpenter heaved a sigh of relief and departed. A short distance from the locker in one of the top bunk sleeping alcoves, the blue privacy curtains parted. A drowsy, off-watch sailor poked out his head. His mask of annoyance quickly disappeared when he saw all the ruckus was being caused by a lieutenant commander.

Dougherty quickly said to him, "Sorry to raise hell with your off-watch rest, sailor. But since you're up, I have a question for you."

The seaman started to crawl out of the sack, but Dougherty

gestured for him to stay put. "This won't take long. Your name and rank?"

"Aviation Boatswain's Mate Second Class Frank Hackmeyer, sir."

Dougherty studied him. "One of the green or yellow-shirts?"

"Yellow, sir."

"Like Gecko Corman. How well did you know him?"

"Well enough. We both worked the flight deck, same assignment. I hear he's officially UA and in trouble again."

"Would you say you were close friends?"

Hackmeyer frowned. "No, sir. He was a loner. When he did rap with the other guys, it was nonstop bullshit. But he did his job okay on the flight deck. And he played a mean alto sax."

Dougherty nodded. "So I hear. Tell me, Hackmeyer—you know anything about a portable radio Corman may have swapped for a Rolls Royce hood ornament?" Dougherty unfolded the catalog illustration Gecko's father had provided him back in San Diego. "A small Sony, identical to this one."

Frank Hackmeyer smiled knowingly. "You see what I mean, sir? Corman's been feeding you a line of bullshit already. As I said, we didn't talk much, but one night I saw him across the way in his bunk polishing a hood ornament. He called it a *mascot* and bragged about ripping it off some rich broad's Rolls Royce in Hong Kong. Something about revenge, if I remember right."

"What else did he say?"

"That's all. Like I say, I tried to avoid the guy, so I pulled my bunk curtains and went to sleep."

Dougherty thought for a moment. "You're sure he didn't trade his radio to get it, with some other sailor on board?"

"No, sir. The portable you described was right there in his locker this morning. The captain took it away with the rest of Corman's shit."

In the privacy of his sea cabin behind the bridge, Swain Bullock surveyed the items he'd brought up from Gecko Corman's locker. He intended to make damned sure there was nothing incriminating here before assigning one of the yeomen the job of typing up an inventory and placing the mess in storage. Todd Dougherty would be pissed at him for moving in on the locker early, but he had no choice. Bullock would merely shrug off the pre-emptive act, blaming his haste on a sudden fit of impatience. As it turned out, he was damned glad he'd arrived before Dougherty. Sometimes intuition paid off. As Bullock suspected, Gecko Corman had been using his locker for a virtual safe deposit vault.

The priceless jade had been double wrapped in protective flexible foam and a Hong Kong newspaper. The chance that the treasure would directly incriminate Bullock was remote, but it could still open up an unnecessary, nasty can of worms. The two carvings were collector's pieces and traceable. Bullock could take a chance and store them in his own sea chest until the carrier reached port, but no matter how long they were stashed, the jade could never be marketed inconspicuously.

Bullock thought about Mai Twan's sister, Yung Liu, a San Francisco prostitute. He wondered if he dared trust her to send the jade back to Mai. *No, too dangerous.* The sisters weren't on the best of terms. *Damn Gecko Corman's sticky fingers!* And damn Mai Twan for having the contraband in her apartment in the first place. Bullock suddenly flashed on the possibility the jade wasn't ripped off, that Corman may have been trying to fence it for Mai, bringing it into the states illegally. *Damn both of them.*

Bullock held up the eight-inch-high head and shoulders of a horse—a piece Mai explained had come from the Han dynasty, sometime before the birth of Christ. Only three others were known to exist, she'd boasted. The other carving was a rabbit, and if Bullock remembered correctly, it was from the more recent Ming dynasty. *Chen Yu,* the Chinese called jade. *The stone that is beautiful.* To Bullock, the priceless artifacts before him were ugly, bad omens. He considered them a kiss of death. A greedy individual might stash the carvings away, keep them at any risk, but Bullock was not motivated by greed. He was a survivalist; for the moment, monetary matters were the least of his concerns. All Bullock wanted now was a pair of shoulder boards with embroidered gold stars.

He felt sweaty as he stared at the two works of art. The fool Gecko Corman had not only contaminated the *Abraham Lincoln* by bringing the jade aboard but the ship's captain as well. Thank God, the incriminating photo of Mai and himself and the stolen Rolls hood ornament weren't in the locker. Corman had been too clever for that, hinting weeks earlier that he had them in "safekeeping."

Bullock knew that he'd survived the worst and best that could happen to him in the U.S. Navy, that he'd made the steep climb and managed it with only minor difficulty. Commanding this magnificent, nuclear-powered ship was better than being the mayor of a city with a comparable population. In fact, running the

Abraham Lincoln could be compared to being board chairman of a major American corporation.

The carrier rolled and Bullock had to steady his feet. He made up his mind quickly. *Get rid of the jade. Now.* Transporting the carvings back to Hong Kong without incriminating himself would be impossible. The pieces had to disappear—for good.

Bullock quickly wrapped the two statues in a plastic bag, secured it with a strong rubber band, and thrust it in his briefcase. Leaving the sea cabin, he stepped down the short corridor to the bridge. He entered and said to the assistant navigator, "How's the glass?"

"Rising, sir." The lieutenant looked out the rain-pelted windshield, searching the puffy gray sky for the first patch of blue. He found it and pointed. "Dutchman's breeches up ahead and five degrees to port, Captain. We should be out of it in a couple of hours."

Bullock nodded. At the moment, he wasn't concerned about improving weather; he only wanted to get to the opposite side of the bridge, out on the auxiliary conn where he could be alone for a moment. He made it without incident. At last by himself, he opened his little "bay window" that extended out over the starboard side of the ship. Bullock glared down at the sea. The wind-whipped water was an opaque gray and less than a thousand yards out the escort frigate was taking tons of it across the bow. With weather like this, Bullock knew that the men aboard the other support ships would be envious. While their own vessels tossed like corks. the *Abe Lincoln* cut easily through the storm with a steady, undulating motion.

Bullock glanced back toward the bridge. No one was watching him. If a crewman on that nearby frigate had a glass trained on the carrier, he might wonder what the captain was heaving overboard. Bullock trusted the plastic bag with the jade in it would pass for garbage. No matter, for it would sink immediately to the bottom.

He dropped the treasure into the sea. Inhaling vigorously, Bullock reclosed the window. He strolled back through the main bridge area, checking the bearing on the compass but otherwise ignoring the crewmen on duty. Now he would steel himself for the confrontation that was sure to come at any moment with the upstaged NIS investigator. Lieutenant Commander Dougherty would be pissed, but he was outranked. Under the circumstances, there wasn't a hell of a lot Dougherty could do about his disappointment. Bullock smiled with self-satisfaction and strolled back to his sea cabin.

According to that motherfucker Bullock's reprimand, Steelbinder was to be permanently assigned to the port after-steering room. He reported there as ordered, piqued and even more bent for revenge. The auxiliary control rooms for the carrier's two 65-ton rudders were located on each side of the stern, and for Steelbinder to reach this new godforsaken assignment, he had to pass through one of the latrines into a closet-like storage area, then descend a ladder into the depths of the ship. The machinery-filled compartment was the size of a small kitchen, confining enough to give its crewmen-occupants a good case of claustrophobia by the time they finished their watch.

Steelbinder would share today's duty with two other bored sailors. These men had firemen ratings and as quartermaster he'd be nominally in charge—if anything went wrong, like a disaster up on the bridge. The command would be provisional, of course, until the three of them were joined in the chamber by a chief or one of the junior operations officers. In peacetime cruising, the possibility of engaging the emergency steering mechanism was remote, for it was unlikely the command bridge would ever be disabled or severely damaged. Still, regulations required that this station and the one like it on the starboard side be manned any time the carrier was underway.

Steelbinder cursed the captain for demoting him. He was the best helmsman on the navigation staff and belonged up above during the current maneuvers. Bullock knew this. Steelbinder not only had a sharp eye for reading the compass but was good at feeling the wheel and had a sixth sense when it came to drift. The other men were sloppy; none had his alertness or visual acuity. The ship's helm was no place for gadflies or amateurs.

Up above, there'd been a break in the weather. Now, like the two other men in the steering room, he was blind to what was happening on the ocean's surface, except for the view straight ahead as seen in the TV monitor. Over the close-by rumble of the four propeller shafts, he could hear the distant roar of the steam catapults and jets screaming off the flight deck as well as the periodic announcements on the public address system. But visually, Steelbinder had no idea what was happening, none of the excitement of being up on the bridge.

Before him was the Caterpillar-sized engine that drove the rudders, and attached to it was a manually-engaged, ten-inch, polished brass wheel. Surmounting this equipment was a built-in compass and the small television monitor. The camera at the other end was stationary, capturing only the sea's surface straight ahead of the ship. There were also two sets of bridge intercom earphones, useless unless the station was activated.

With the bulkheads relentlessly closing in on them and nothing better to do, Steelbinder liked to read; the two firemen sharing the duty usually slept—albeit guardedly. However they passed the time, one of them always kept an ear tuned for the first sound of a superior's footsteps clanking down the steel ladder in the corner.

Unfortunately, today Steelbinder's new duty mates, Willy and Nipper, weren't sleeping, but playing cards and screaming epithets at each other. That, coupled with the noise of the rudder engine, made it difficult for him to concentrate on his book. He didn't like either sailor, but he'd make a half-ass effort to be reasonably civil until the watch was concluded. But the pair kept raising their voices, and his patience was wearing thin. Willy was as muscular as Steelbinder, though taller, and had a hard, pock-marked face like a concrete wall that had been raked by an automatic weapon. Steelbinder was glad to find someone with a face uglier than his own. The big fireman's work shirt was open, revealing a bare chest with a grotesque tattoo of Triton grappling with a mermaid.

Nipper, the other sailor, was elfin and wiry by comparison, with coal-black curly hair and wide-set, violet eyes. Both crewmen seemed to enjoy needling each other with irrelevant jive talk, their four-letter words fouling the compartment's air like smog.

Steelbinder slowly shook his head and tried to concentrate on his book.

"Hey, *Roscoe*!" The gruff, basso voice summoning him was Willy's. "You got plans for Halloween in the big city?"

"No. And call me R.W. I haven't decided if I'll go ashore."

"Yeah? Like you should loosen up a little, get away from your books and the weightlifting once in a while. Nipper here knows about a costume party up on Telegraph Hill. He's fixing me up with a loose lady. She's going as a stalk of wheat with a goddam

sign on her back, REAP ME." Willy guffawed at his own humor.
"You want us to line you up with something? Maybe a brainy
broad that likes to screw? Afterward, you can brag how you *left
your hard-on in San Francisco.*"

"No thanks. I'll take care of my own love life." They stared at
him as he dove back into his reading.

Willy persisted. "Hey, Steelbinder, take a gander at this." He
opened the rest of the buttons on his shirt. "How about one of
these tattoos? I got an address on Market Street where you can get
fixed up like a real macho sailor."

Steelbinder sneered, "You're full of shit, Willy. Scar up my
body with a monstrosity like that? Never."

"Oh yeah? The ladies tell me it's heroic and beautiful."

Steelbinder put a finger in the book to mark his place, folded it
shut, and glared impatiently at the sailor's tattooed chest. "Some
trollop tell you that? She's wrong, Willy. It's a sick, self-
destructive act. Read Leviticus 19:28 sometime or the Talmud.
Tattooing is associated with the cult of the dead." Hesitating, he
added with false bravado, "I think it's disgusting."

"Get off my back, man."

"Gladly. If you'll just play your cards, shut up, and let me read
in peace."

Willy and Nipper exchanged swift glances. Nipper squinted at
Steelbinder and said dully, "Kiss my ass, Steelbinder. What's so
important in that book? I hear you read about journeys through
hell. You're weird, man, real weird."

Steelbinder scowled. It would be impossible to get these two
jesters to comprehend the brilliance of Dante. No one on this ship
would ever understand what it meant to be led by the artistry and
wisdom of Virgil. He said to the two troublemakers, "For the
record, I finished Dante's *Divine Comedy* yesterday. And for the
fourth time. You should read it just once, if you're capable."

Willy grunted. Nipper shrugged and said, "What for? Do I look
the literary type?"

"No, I suppose not. Poetry is an unconscious effort of an
ordinary man to rise, if ever so briefly, above his mediocrity."

Nipper raised his middle finger. "Fuck you, egghead."

A strange, primordial impulse seized Steelbinder, an urge to
crush the two card players' brains together. A permanent lesson.
Fighting hard to suppress the impulse, he said quietly, "Hmmmm-
nnnnn. The same to you."

Nipper persisted. "So what kind of shit you reading now?"

Steelbinder shrugged. He might as well set the record straight for these semi-literate swabbies. "Yesterday it was allegory. Today, it's engineering." He held up the book in his hand, exposing the colorful dustcover of Allen Brown's *Golden Gate, Biography of a Bridge*, "I'm studying bridges—the one the carrier will pass under tomorrow morning, to be specific."

Nipper shook his head and turned back to the gin rummy game. Both men quieted down.

Returning to the book and where he'd left off before the interruption, he read again the data on the downward tonnage pressure exerted by the bridge on its piers. He learned that the two towers were hollow, honeycombed from top to bottom, and fabricated of both carbon and silicon steel.

Steelbinder computed it all in his mind. Mental challenges like this fascinated him. He quickly figured that with its own weight of 22 thousand tons, each tower of the bridge transmitted to its pier a load of 120 thousand tons. *Interesting.* But that was a *stationary load*, he mused.

He hummed aloud as his brain continued to calculate the load pressures. By comparison, the behemoth *Abraham Lincoln* had a displacement of 95,000 tons. If he were to multiply this by an onrushing, moving force of six knots—no, not enough. He'd figure the carrier's speed at twelve knots to keep ahead of the tidal current. A rough total of *twenty feet a second*. His mind was working too rapidly, getting away from him again. The fever was back, heating his blood and exciting him. He needed to *slow down*, digest one fact at a time.

He flipped back to an earlier chapter, savoring again the part where a Dr. Bailey Willis, emeritus professor of geology at Stanford, made an unpopular prognostication in 1933. The professor claimed that the foundation rock of the Golden Gate's pier on the San Francisco side "was unstable to a degree likely to damage the structure. The channel rock is serpentine and subject to landslides, as may be seen in the immediate vicinity."

Steelbinder looked up from the book, reflecting for a moment. Now completely absorbed in their game, the other two men in the steering room ignored him.

He read the next paragraph, his interest mounting. Although another geologist and bridge construction engineers refuted his warning, Professor Willis was not to be contained. He went on to insist that the Golden Gate's tower and pier "rested on a slippery incline on the edge of an abyss. There is reason to fear the concrete pier will slide down into the channel, either after long-continued movement at its base, or suddenly in an earthquake."

Steelbinder smiled as a godhead of an idea formed in his brain. Mathematics—it was all a matter of mathematical projection. Infinity. The naval architects who designed the *Abraham Lincoln* might understand this, but not the men who took her to sea. Five plus four equals nine, but nine is the cube of three. The crumbs of creation! And the power of destruction.

Steelbinder had retribution in mind—not only against the Navy, but a final tribute to Captain Bullock. There wasn't enough time between now and tomorrow morning's San Francisco arrival to properly prepare for such a plan, of course. Later—on the way out of the harbor enroute to Bremerton, he would bring it all together, striking as suddenly and as powerfully as a hell-bent windstorm. First the wall cloud, then the mezzo-cyclone, then the tornado itself; it was just a matter of timing.

Before considering the idea further, he would need paper, a pencil, and his pocket calculator. He'd also have to poke his head in the door of the navigation room—when Swain Bullock wasn't around—and study the chart of San Francisco Bay.

Steelbinder's grandfather would be pleased with the plan; perhaps it would even bring the rejected admiral peace. Yes, why not? Gerald Eisenbinder, too, would be vindicated, the ultimate revenge.

Dougherty couldn't find Dante's *Divine Comedy* in its complete form in the ship's library, but he did come up with a reference work on allegory that included some translated excerpts.

A Guide to Medieval Literature. In it, there was also an editor's introduction that attempted to decipher Dante's convoluted effort. Dougherty spent a half-hour reading about the section called the *Inferno*, but it made no impact on his weary brain; the distracting cacophony of jet aircraft landing and taking off on the flight deck above didn't help. He decided to check out the text and take it back to his cabin that was two decks farther removed from the noise.

A young yeoman assigned to library duty removed the index card from the cover pocket and gave it to Dougherty to sign. The book was still stiff with newness. Men on the *Abraham Lincoln* obviously preferred lighter fare—probably Steven King, Robert Ludlum, or Louis L'Amour. Dougherty had seen several dog-eared paperback copies of Jackie Collins's *Hollywood Husbands* on the shelf as well as an entire row of Remo Williams adventures.

Dougherty did a double-take as he signed his name. Above his signature, the only other person to have checked out the work was Captain Bullock. There was no return date column on the card or any other notation. Dougherty looked at the freckle-faced librarian, who appeared bored with his routine assignment. "Sailor, how long have you been with the *Abe Lincoln's* Administrative Department?"

"A year, sir. Six months in the library." There was a nasal quality to his voice that reminded Dougherty of Daffy Duck.

"This book. Can you tell me when the ship's CO checked it out? Or the return date?"

"No specific records are kept, Lieutenant Commander. We run a kind of informal operation here. But I think I remember roughly. It was the week the ship left Pearl, bound back to San Diego. But it wasn't—" The yeoman paused to glance at the calendar.

Dougherty impatiently drummed on the book with his fingers. "Well? Go on."

"Captain Bullock didn't check out the book himself, sir. I remember that one of the quartermasters came in to pick it up for him. A member of the navigation staff."

"You recognize this errand boy if you saw him again?"

"Of course, sir. He comes to the library often enough. Petty Officer Second Class Steelbinder. Roscoe probably reads more than anyone else on the ship."

Dougherty thought for a moment. "What other kind of books does Steelbinder read?"

"Sorry, sir. I haven't paid any attention to the titles, but they appear to be mostly technical books."

"Your records—any chance he has any books checked out right now? Under his own name?"

It took the clerk a few minutes, but he finally came up with the information Dougherty wanted. R. W. Steelbinder currently had out two nonfiction books: *Earthquake,* by A. Andrews, and *Golden Gate, Biography of a Bridge,* by Allen Brown.

34

Before boarding the United Airlines plane to Los Angeles, Pamela came close to shucking Dougherty's instructions and changing her booking to a San Francisco flight leaving an hour later. It would have been nice surprising him when the *Abraham Lincoln* pulled into port, but the bureau would have disallowed the plan on several counts. Her boss had ordered her to return to San Diego, as per Todd's arrangement, but also to stop by the L.A. office enroute to file a full update on the case. Pam shivered at the thought of the annoying paperwork that lay ahead.

She took an aisle seat in the DC-10's tourist section and buried her nose in a copy of *Modern Woman* she'd picked up at an airport newsstand. The wide-body was half-empty and minutes later lifted quickly off the ground. While most of the other passengers gawked out the left side windows paying their last respects to Diamond Head, Pam read on about the danger of repeated spermicide use.

An hour later the aircrew started the movie, a recent Clint Eastwood epic. Pamela had already seen the film so she took a Nembutal, hoping it would keep her out until the plane reached Los Angeles International. One benefit in not going up to meet Dougherty, she mused, would be the overnight comfort of her own bed and a chance to say hello to the cat. If Samantha remembered her.

Thinking about the melancholy, independent feline reminded her of the secretive Kenny Chi. The mysterious Hong Kong detective lieutenant had disappeared just before she'd checked out of her Waikiki hotel. He'd been considerate enough to leave a note, assuring Pam that he'd make contact again in about twenty-four hours—either at her Los Angeles FBI office or back at the NIS facility in San Diego. Pam suspected Chi was still trying to juggle a marginally legitimate stateside vacation at the same time as solving three homicides.

After the grisly discovery in the Honolulu freezer, Pam felt certain the killer on board the supercarrier had a compulsive need to strike each time the ship put into port. Earlier, she and Dougherty had fretted over how many deaths in other cities might well have preceded Hong Kong. Had the trail of mayhem just begun three weeks ago in the Crown Colony, or had the compulsive killings gone on for several months or years, possibly under a slightly different M.O. to avoid detection?

Right now, all Pam really cared about—*had time to care about*—was the immediate future. New attacks at San Francisco and Bremerton had to be avoided. Despite Todd dragging his feet out on the carrier, the finger of guilt still pointed to Swain Bullock. Damn the captain's sadistic soul! This modern-era Jekyll and Hyde appeared capable of anything, but why? What had gone desperately wrong, and how did this cunning malefactor slip through the Navy's touted system? Most important, what would agent Pamela Bonner use for a clincher to convince Dougherty that Bullock had in fact become unhinged? Lieutenant Chi's theorizing was no better than her own. They needed good, hard evidence—and quickly.

The flight attendants managed to disappear during the movie, and a businessman type two rows ahead of Pam jumped at the chance to go strolling after his own drinks. On each stumbling pass down the aisle, he eyed her speculatively. Pam made a point of ignoring him, moving over into an empty window seat and staring fixedly out at the clouds. The Nembutal was taking its time, so she turned her mind to case histories of other serial and series killers, thinking about the time it took to close each investigation. Some cases were wrapped in a matter of days; in others, data was assimilated excruciatingly slowly, facts needing time to bob to the surface—like quicksand giving up the dead. Too many crimes still remained unsolved for a score of years or more.

Pam recalled the complicated investigations they'd told her about at the FBI Academy. Manson, the Boston Strangler, the Green River Killer, the Night Stalker. There was also Speck, Son of Sam, and the clown who killed boys and buried them under his house. Pam's mind became fuzzy, and she gave it up. When the plane hit a nasty airpocket a few minutes later, her seat belt was loosely fastened and Pam didn't even feel the tug. She was fast asleep.

35

Breakfast had been scheduled for 6 A.M. in the captain's day cabin. In Bullock's brief scribbled invitation, he'd let Dougherty know that Rear Admiral Tanner would also be joining them. Dougherty wondered why. A little insulation against less-than-tactful, uncomfortable NIS inquiries? It didn't matter; time was running out, and Dougherty was ready to strip off the gloves; from here on in, the Secretary of the Navy himself could join in the dialogue if necessary.

Despite a few wrong turns, the investigation was in the homestretch; Dougherty could feel it. He still couldn't point his finger with certainty, but he'd made big strides in the past twelve hours, admittedly with Pam Bonner's help. Lieutenant Ingalsbe, the ship's psychiatrist, along with the medical director, Captain Bellows, had sat up with him the night before, and together they'd gone through a seven-inch stack of patient files. There were two cases of acute paranoia with repeated aggression, but both men had been transferred off in Honolulu prior to the ship going on to the Orient. There'd been no serious deranged personality problems since, at least nothing serious. The Navy doctors came up with four patients with severe hemorrhoids, but none had Type O Positive blood. All the individuals booked on the Hong Kong R and R flight were apparently in good health, and only six of them met the blood type criteria. Gecko Corman, Dougherty noted with interest, wasn't among them.

Keeping the six files out, Dougherty made photocopies of the pertinent information and took it all back to his cabin. The only problem was that none of the half-dozen men concerned had red hair. Roscoe W. Steelbinder's name was on top of one of the folders. He was also the one who checked out the text about Dante's *Inferno* from the ship's library on behalf of Captain Bullock. For this reason alone, he'd bear investigating. Steelbinder's blood type matched, but his hair was a dishwater blond color. Nor had he ever come into the dispensary complaining of hemorrhoids. Out of just under six thousand men on the *Abraham Lincoln*, the suspect list had been narrowed down to six men. The odds were definitely improving. Unfortunately, since Captain Bullock was the only one in the group who had curly red hair, he still headed the list.

Dougherty checked his watch. He finished combing his hair, straightened his collar, and left the small, two-man compartment. Since they were approaching shore, flight operations were shut down, and the ship was relatively quiet and for once easy on the ears. The more hours Dougherty spent aboard this monstrous, unyielding creature, the more satisfied he was with his unglamorous shore assignment back at North Island. In the guts of the carrier, especially, everything had a look of sameness. The omnipresent, cold fluorescent lights burned incessantly in the narrow corridors; somewhere Dougherty had read that there were over 20,000 of them on the ship. Without portholes and skylights, there was no separating day from night, and from the nuke carrier's hangar deck down, the monotonous appearance was almost suffocating. Dougherty hurried through the maze of corridors and found the ladder leading up to the island. Crossing the hangar deck, he passed a happy trio of pilots and returned their salute. He decided to put his sophomoric discontent away. Less than appreciative of his sea accommodations or not, this was the prestige world of Naval Aviation, and as inconvenient as he might find it, the supercarrier deserved his respect, not his bellyaching.

Dougherty continued up the remaining ladders to the bridge on the 08 level. Reaching it, he once more checked his watch. *Five minutes early*. Leaning against the bulwark, Dougherty paused to take in both the carrier and sea that stretched before him. The short, choppy waves were driven with whitecaps, while the wind, cool and crisp from behind the west, was stiff enough to sing in the signal halyards. The carrier was approaching the Farallon Islands and would pass them off to starboard; just beyond them loomed the California Coast, Land's End, and the Golden Gate. Dougherty saw that up forward long ranks of aircraft were tied down to the flight deck, as was the custom when entering port for purposes of showing off the ship. When the ship approached San Francisco's Embarcadero, the planes would be joined by a row of smartly uniformed personnel.

He knocked on the skipper's door at 0600 sharp. When Dougherty entered the cabin he saw that Captain Bullock's face appeared gray and serious. The stewards had set up a foldout table with three places. Bullock and Rear Admiral Tanner were just about to sit down, and they gestured for Dougherty to join them.

Bullock was first to speak. "Well, Lieutenant Commander, how goes your investigation? I trust our little fleet exercise yesterday didn't inconvenience you."

"No, sir, I welcomed the diversion. A chance to get a feel for the serious part of the Navy."

Fritz Tanner, whom Dougherty had met the second day out, smiled briefly before attacking a heap of scrambled eggs and sausage the steward placed before him. Dougherty was hungry, so he, too, retreated into silence and started to eat.

Bullock sipped his coffee and stared at them both. "The NIS investigator here thinks I'm being set up, Admiral."

Tanner nodded and replied dully, "So it appears. Let's discuss the morbid matter later. Eat before your breakfast gets cold, Captain." Tanner examined a piece of raisin toast as if it were an artifact, then slowly covered it with margarine. There was a spiteful, slow-motion manner about the rear admiral's movements that reminded Dougherty of a well-fed lizard. Tanner said to him, "So you like the feel of the seagoing Navy, is that it, Dougherty? I suggest, when we finish with this pesky San Francisco port call and get back out to sea, that you join me in Flag Plot during the second part of our exercise. You do intend to go all the way with us to Bremerton, I take it?"

"Unless I have a homicidal suspect in handcuffs before then. And thanks for the invitation to observe the exercise. I'd enjoy that."

"Good. I'll look forward to showing you around the Combat Information Center as well."

Dougherty polished off his orange juice. "Mind if I ask why the maneuver was split into two parts? Why the inconvenient shore liberty sandwiched in between?"

Bullock and Tanner exchanged wry smiles. Stroking his moustache, Tanner took his time answering Dougherty's queries. "Fleet Week in San Francisco, plus the nuisance of politics. Three Senators and a couple of members of the House are in town. They're trying to sell Congress on one more Nimitz-class nuke carrier. Accordingly, we've scheduled a VIP open house tomorrow afternoon and called in the Bay area press. For once we may get some half-ass favorable publicity."

Bullock added, "The admiral and I are obligated to put our best foot forward, no sparing the spit and polish."

And no embarrassing incidents while the ship is in port, Dougherty desperately wanted to add, but didn't.

Swain Bullock finished his coffee and nervously poured another from the thermos the steward had left on the table. He picked at his food without enthusiasm. The captain looked bored which mildly bothered Dougherty. He'd read somewhere that some psychologists believe habitual boredom conveyed a hint of cruelty.

The telephone rang, shattering the cabin's awkward silence. Bullock reached back from the table and picked it up. "This is the captain. Already? All right, tell them to keep their pants on. I'll be right out." He hung up and glanced at his watch. "Sorry gentlemen, you'll have to excuse me. The harbor pilot's coming alongside—twenty minutes early." Bullock took one more sip from his coffee, grabbed a piece of toast, and headed for the door. "Sorry, Dougherty. You have more to tell me, we can meet anytime after the ship's secured to the dock. I'll be remaining on board until tomorrow night."

Dougherty blotted his lips with a linen napkin and looked up at Bullock. "Sir, very quickly before you leave. May I ask what you've been reading lately—in your spare time?"

Bullock shot him an incredulous look then turned to Tanner. "You see, Admiral? I told you he's an odd duck. Dougherty, I'm a busy man, but for your information, the book is *Sink the Bismarck*. I'm still trying to find the goddamn time to finish it."

Dougherty leaned forward. "Captain, did you check out of the ship's library a book called *A Guide to Medieval Literature*?"

"What the hell are you talking about?"

"I'll repeat the title, sir."

Bullock cleared the breakfast steward out of the cabin with a slight gesture of his hand. "I heard you the first time. I've never borrowed a book from the carrier's library, period. I bring my own reading material aboard."

"You've never sent one of the quartermasters down to pick up a title for you?"

With a miserable grimace, Bullock replied, "Never. At no time. Somebody's being a smart-ass. You're snapping at red herrings, Lieutenant Commander. Now if you'll excuse me, I'm needed on the bridge."

Dougherty's heart skipped a beat. *R. W. Steelbinder*, the name on the library check-out card kept repeating itself in his mind. "Please, Captain, I need to ask you one more personal question *before* we reach port. Just trust my need to know, and don't get offended."

Bullock stood impatiently in the doorway. A strong draught

came into the cabin, ruffling the tablecloth and Fritz Tanner's hair. The admiral looked impatient and annoyed.

In the doorway Bullock grumbled, "You've got thirty seconds, hotshot detective."

Dougherty suddenly had a case of golfball throat, but he finally managed to ask straightforward, "Sir, I realize I asked you before about hemorrhoids."

Fritz Tanner's fork dropped in his plate.

The captain's eyes flared momentarily then seemed to shrink back into tired, pouch-like cavities. He said stonily, "God, what insolence. Captain Bellows tells me you've already examined my medical files. You're still not satisfied?"

Tanner coughed. "Gentlemen, I think that under the circumstances . . ."

Dougherty interjected, "Pardon, sir. Believe me, I'm on the captain's side; but I have a Hong Kong detective on my back who's on the opposing team and doing his damnedest to cut me off at the pass." Dougherty looked up at Bullock. "I realize you've made no complaints at the ship's dispensary. But might you have been treated by a private physician ashore?"

"Christ." Bullock shook his head. "Yes, I was, Lieutenant Commander. Twice, in San Diego. Last week. Now if you're finished with this bizarre line of inquiry, the harbor pilot's waiting for me." Instantly, the captain was gone, the steward outside closing the door after him.

Fritz Tanner pushed his chair back from the table and looked long and hard at Dougherty. "Peculiar line of questioning, my friend." Tanner sighed. "Can I safely assume you've eliminated the captain from further suspicion?"

"I didn't say that at all, Admiral. *No one* is entirely beyond suspicion. When it comes to Swain Bullock, however, well—" Dougherty thought for a moment. "Sorry, sir. It's just that I'm shaken by all the circumstantial evidence to date. Up until this morning, I was at a total loss to explain most of it. Now I have some leads; but I'll have to move fast to prove my theories. And I may need some flag rank help."

"You've got it, of course. Okay if we keep this informal and I call you Todd?"

"Fine with me, sir."

"And you can try Fritz for size. You mind telling me frankly, Todd, just what kind of man we're looking for?"

Dougherty lowered his head. "The shrinks think I'm after an acute paranoid-schizophrenic. You know the kind—a type who might paste the warning labels for all his prescriptions around the bathroom mirror like travel stickers."

Tanner risked a smile. "That hardly sounds like Swain Bullock or any other officer on the *Abe Lincoln*."

Dougherty grunted in agreement. "The psychiatrists also gave me some gobbledigook about genetic predisposition, reinforced by anti-social learning over a period of years. They suggest that the influence of immediate military service is only a minor triggering factor."

"Jesus. Gobbledigook is right. I'll tell you something, Todd. I try to read every word in the San Diego papers. Why no evidence of a struggle on the victim's part? And what about the captain's wife knowing her assailant, maybe even setting up the killer's visit?"

Dougherty grinned; everyone liked to play detective—even admirals. "I'm sorry, sir, but the facts indicate Maxine Bullock was not your average officer's wife minding the roost. She managed to get around—a lot. Let's say that with the booze and her fast-lane, kinky lifestyle, she was already embalming herself before the murder occurred. The captain had problems at home that he purposely kept buried."

Tanner grimly nodded. "From all appearances, most effectively—until the homicide."

Dougherty wanted to call the admiral Fritz, but he couldn't manage it. "Sir, you've been around him longer than anyone else since we've left port. Has Bullock confided in you at all?"

"Not a word."

"Have you noticed anything unusual, any change in his usual deportment? I'm still amazed that he went ahead with the assignment."

"As are several of us at Fleet Command." Tanner thought for a moment. "As for end results, the captain's performance thus far has been beyond reproach, though he's been noticeably irritable and lacking in patience. He seems to get put out and depressed if anything keeps his operation from running like an accurate, precision-made machine. Something else I've noticed—even when Bullock smiles, underneath he's taut as a piano wire."

"But you trust him?"

Tanner's somber eyes studied him. "Of course. Don't you?"

Dougherty exhaled sharply. "Too much so, I suspect. With the captain's hard-ass management style, efficiency seems to grip the carrier like a mechanic's vise." Dougherty's mind flashed. *Bullock isn't guilty, not even a participant. Repeat that.* Because

Dougherty wanted so much to believe, he simply believed. *Bullock just can't be involved.*

"Lieutenant Commander?"

"Sir?"

Tanner was staring at him. "How can I help you?"

Dougherty weighed what he was about to ask, once more considering the sheer nerve of it all; he had no choice. "Admiral Tanner, first, may I ask if you're being pressured to relieve the captain? From either COMNAVAIRPAC or the Pentagon?"

"No. So far the internal static is minimal. Admiral McCracken's a little miffed at your earlier wild goose chase, but I suspect he's washed his hands of the matter—for now. We're completely on our own out here."

"Good. Admiral, I'm sure you realize I can't be everywhere at once. For the record, I've narrowed down the field of murder suspects to half a dozen crewmen, not including our apparent scapegoat, the captain. One petty officer second-class heads the list, and I intend to follow this sailor the moment he steps off the ship in San Francisco." Dougherty paused. "But just for the record and to cover my ass, I'd also like to have the captain followed—as inconspicuously as possible. To be on the safe side, okay?"

Tanner shook his head. "And what's this to do with me?"

"I understand you've made table reservations for a half-dozen people tomorrow night at Ernie's Restaurant. And Captain Bullock will be present."

"My God, you know what time I visit the can, too? Yes, it's a dinner for a couple of congressmen. Shipbuilding appropriations, remember? What about it?"

"Simple enough. I'd like one of my own NIS men to be your driver for the evening. And one other thing. After dinner, if for any reason the captain decides to wander off on his own, let him have the driver. If Bullock refuses and tries to summon his own taxi, make a note of the time and the cab's license number. I can check the trip sheets later."

Tanner grimaced. "I don't like this at all, Dougherty."

"A moment ago you were calling me Todd. Sir, I'm sorry, but you did offer to help. We have an ambitious repeat killer among us, an extremely clever madman who appears to be working up a momentum. Timing is everything."

"Supposing the bastard strikes on board the carrier?"

"Highly unlikely, unless we brought some loose ladies up the gangplank to tempt him."

Fritz Tanner's face was downcast as he helped himself to a glass of water and drank it all. When he finally spoke, his voice was strained and uneven. "God in heaven, what's the military coming to? There's something worse than one man's insanity here. An element even more grave, and for that reason alone, Todd, I'll help with your dirty work. You know what really gets my hackles up? We've a damned assault here on the Navy and all it stands for. Have you given any thought at all to the rotten publicity this crisis could generate?"

Dougherty inhaled sharply. "Several sleepless nights, Admiral. The strain's already getting to me."

Tanner smiled. "At least you've a measure of sensitivity then. Good. But I'd suggest being tough at the same time, like Bullock. Build up an impenetrable shell to protect yourself when life hands you its wild cards."

"*Rotten cards*, sir. And for the moment at least, maybe you should avoid a comparison with the captain."

It was a while before Tanner spoke. "Keep me posted, Dougherty. Whatever happens, come to me first, understand? You need my help, I need yours as well. Above all, consult with me first *before* talking to the press."

Feeling anxious and tight, Dougherty finished what was left of his coffee and stood up. He looked at Tanner, groping for words to reassure the concerned rear admiral, but none came. Suddenly the investigation seemed too large for Dougherty; he felt dismal when he should be excited and smugly self-confident. Whatever the outcome of the case, he appeared to be in trouble. Was the admiral merely trying to sweep the dirt under the carpet?

Tanner saw him to the door, announcing firmly, "Don't forget, we've got to stick together on this. *For the Navy*."

Dougherty nodded. He wondered if Rear Admiral Tanner was right. *Did the Navy come first?* Dougherty had to push his next few words out against some powerful inner resistance. He said to Tanner, "For the Navy, above all, Fritz."

Steelbinder stood alone on the carrier's bow, staring out across the fog-shrouded water as if he were on lookout for the *Flying Dutchman*. Suddenly, as if by magic, the soupy haze that had nestled around the base of the Golden Gate Bridge and the Presidio lifted. Steelbinder felt the *Abraham Lincoln* increase its speed by several knots as it headed into the ship channel. He knew the supercarrier would pass swiftly beneath the world's most famous suspension bridge, for the tide was on the flood, running inbound at over nine knots.

Steelbinder had the luck to be off duty and intended to make the most of this moment. Taking in the magnificent view, he stood as far forward as he could on the carrier's bow, just behind the guard chain at the corner of the flight deck. He wondered where Dougherty's partner, the woman FBI agent, was at this very moment. Probably waiting on the San Francisco dock. Why were women always waiting for the dream that could never be? He would have to be doubly careful when he left the ship. Pamela Bonner wasn't dangerous, but she appeared to be the type to dig in her heels. And she'd be especially determined after the car bomb incident.

Steelbinder carried a white plastic bag with several objects he intended to toss overboard when he had a few moments alone on the deck. Up on the aircraft carrier's bridge—the place he rightfully belonged—the harbor pilot would be directing the replacement helmsman to steer the ship just south of the span's midcenter. Steelbinder loved to calculate. He'd already figured the overhead clearance between the ship's uppermost mast and the bridge roadway; considering today's tide, they would have twenty-one feet. Farther back on the flight deck, nattily uniformed sailors were already shuffling to their full dress assembly stations, preparing for the moment when the ship could be viewed by the entire city.

The Golden Gate Bridge loomed closer, a lady in red, regal and defiant in the autumn sun. Steelbinder had never seen the mighty span from this angle before, and he was impressed. Earlier, when he'd driven across it, he'd thought that proceeding through its twin towers was like passing through the nave of a great cathedral. Approaching the structure from seaward had an interesting dimension of its own; the famous bridge exemplified American ingenuity and achievement. It was like an exclamation point rising out of the fog.

Steelbinder squinted. He could see something else—crowds of people gathered on the Golden Gate's walkway. They appeared to be pickets, and though he couldn't read the protestors' signs from the distance, he could hear shouting. The chants became louder as the carrier drew up to the span. Some of the group dropped bulletins that rained down on the ship like confetti. One of the papers landed on the deck by his feet. Steelbinder didn't pick it up, but he caught a glimpse of a peace symbol before the wind carried it away. *Zealots*, he reasoned. More anti-nuclear-weapons activists.

Steelbinder purposefully looked south. He needed to pay attention and closely examine the tower and pier on the San Francisco side of the channel. The north pier partially straddled the Marin County beach and would be of no use for what he had in mind. Steelbinder saw what appeared to be a low, protective fender that diverted the swirling, fast-moving riptides away from the primary structure. Unfortunately, the aircraft carrier was moving by too quickly; he would have to return later by land in order to study the tower footing in closer detail.

Once beyond the bridge, several nearby sailors wandered off, and Steelbinder was momentarily alone on the bow. Seizing the moment, he reached into the plastic shopping bag at his feet. Removing his grandfather's old officer's hat, he withdrew from inside it a stack of sleeveless 45 RPM single records. He'd kept one last Midnight Admirals record for possible use in San Francisco, but the rest would have to go. It would be too dangerous keeping this inventory around him on the carrier for the rest of the deployment. *Evidence!*

Removing the 45 RPM records from the cap one at a time, Steelbinder took his time heaving them off the side of the ship. The discs caught in the wind, and like frisbees, hung momentarily suspended in space as the carrier rushed by.

Todd Dougherty stood on the catwalk beside the flight deck, sheltered from the wind and obscured from the view of the petty officer second class who stood up on the bow. Odd, Dougherty thought. Instead of taking in the stunning San Francisco skyline like the other men, the sailor ignored it, passing the time amusing himself with Frisbees—all of them apparently expendable.

"You're positive that's Steelbinder?" Dougherty asked the young seaman who had led him up here.

"Positive, sir. It's just like R.W. told me, he intended to go up on the bow to view the bridge."

Dougherty frowned with perplexity. "And play with Frisbees? Without a dog to fetch them, at that. Thanks, sailor. You can go back to your quarters."

"Sir, do me a favor? When you talk to Steelbinder, don't tell him who led you up here. He's strange, and—I don't need a hassle."

"I understand. Don't worry."

The seaman took off, and Dougherty returned his attention to the individual on the bow less than a hundred feet away. Dougherty ducked as one of the frisbees soared past him. He watched it slip into the lee of the ship, lose the wind's lift, and plummet into the bay. He also saw that it wasn't a black frisbee at all, but a 45 RPM phonograph record. Suddenly curious, Dougherty stepped quickly along the catwalk, narrowing the gap between himself and Steelbinder. He wanted a closer look at the petty officer's face to commit it to memory.

With quick, backhand movements, Steelbinder sent two more discs sailing far out over the sea. Dougherty looked on as a freak gust of wind returned one of them toward the ship. It thudded against the edge of the flight deck and dropped into the catwalk less than a dozen feet away from him. Making sure he was unobserved, Dougherty scooted over and picked it up. His body tightened when he read the label on the recording.

They were obviously watching him from the bridge. Figuring he was attracting too much attention toying with the records one at a time, Steelbinder unceremoniously dumped the rest of them into the sea. Now the admiral's hat was empty. He ran his fingers fondly over the tarnished officer's emblem and scrambled eggs on the visor, then put it back in the plastic bag. *Throw it away as well, R.W., and be done with your grandfather!* Be rid of Gerald Eisenbinder and the other *memories* once and for all. Be your own man, your own voice. Have you forgotten so soon what happened to Felicia? His mother had been treated by over a dozen psychologists, given as many psychotropic medicines, exposed to electric shock therapy, constantly locked in psychiatric wards or closets to get rid of *her memories*. All he needed to do was dispose of the hat, and there'd be no more apparitions from the past.

Steelbinder stood there on the edge of the deck, leaning forward slightly to fight the wind, thinking of the things he had to do and the order in which he must do them. With the dogs nipping so close to his heels the danger grew greater every hour. He didn't feel afraid, only challenged. The chase, in fact, excited him almost as much as his mission to clean up the underbelly of society.

Power over evil. The lofty challenge raced through his veins, making his body tingle with excitement. Steelbinder wondered if part of his strength might come from some prosaic reality of the past like his grandfather's hat. If so, it would be a mistake tossing it overboard.

Ahead of the ship, he saw the Sausalito commuter boat; beyond it, the island of Alcatraz. Now that they were in the harbor proper, the carrier had slowed, though the chill sea wind still whistled in his ears. There was another sound, too—an increasingly familiar voice calling him from the sea's depths. Steelbinder stared down at the gray-green water rushing past the ship. His subconscious wouldn't let go; it reached out to him, imparting at the same time a strange message—one of euphoria and danger.

Steelbinder loved the voice and hated it at the same time. Was he going mad, like his mother? No! Impossible. He was like his grandfather Gerald—strong, stable, honorable; he might have been every bit as successful as Rear Admiral Eisenbinder had he, too, chosen a lifelong naval officer's career.

Steelbinder turned and looked off behind the *Abraham Lincoln*. Already the escort vessels were following the carrier into San Francisco Harbor through a narrow channel. *The hole in the needle. Running the gat.* Rear Admiral Eisenbinder faced a similar situation at Pearl Harbor on the morning of December 7, 1941.

Again, he heard his grandfather's voice calling out to him. *A ship channel can make the difference in the tide of battle, Roscoe.* In Hawaii the passage had been much narrower than here, in fact, a matter of yards. It was, and still is, the only way in and out of crowded Pearl Harbor. Steelbinder recalled his grandfather's telling of that infamous day when the Japanese dive bombers and torpedo planes made their surprise attack. Battleship row was in chaos; everywhere there was billowing smoke, fire, flying splinters of steel. Death either came instantly or slowly, with excruciating pain. Zeros swept by, strafing indiscriminately at whatever moved. The *Arizona* took a bomb in her forward magazine and blew up, taking well over a thousand men to the bottom.

The major ships were sitting ducks, and although ordered to sortie, only one battleship, the *Nevada*, had enough steam to move out to sea. Steelbinder remembered these events as if they'd happened yesterday, and he'd been there himself. Indeed, when the *Abraham Lincoln* had stopped at Pearl Harbor, he'd spent a full morning wandering around Ford Island, guidebook in hand, restaging the terrible events in the theater of his mind. Steelbinder had been determined to reconstruct things exactly as his grandfather had seen them.

At 8:17 A.M. on that fateful morning four decades earlier, Rear Admiral Gerald Eisenbinder had been on duty at Naval District Headquarters. He'd watched the destroyer *Helm* make a 27 knot dash out to sea. The tricky channel's speed limit was 14 knots, but the small vessel made it, despite the determined Japanese dive bombers that swarmed overhead like gnats. Eisenbinder saw no useful purpose in letting the *Nevada* maneuver in circles around the confining harbor. Though it already had one torpedo hole below the waterline and damage topside, the determined battle-wagon, wreathed in smoke from her own guns, gradually gained speed. As the enemy planes converged on her, those on shore cheered the battleship on, including his grandfather, who ordered it to attempt a breakout.

Gerald Eisenbinder was an old reservist who'd been in the Navy since just after World War I. He had faith in the battleship's 15-inch armor plate and the *Nevada's* speed once she managed to get the rest of her boilers operating. But he failed to appreciate the skill of Japanese pilots who had been honed razor sharp from months of practice for this assignment; he'd also discounted the maneuverability and speed of their planes. From Eisenbinder's observation point, he suddenly wondered if he'd made a mistake allowing the *Nevada* to make a dash for the open sea.

If the battleship were sunk in the narrow entrance channel, the whole fleet would be bottled up for weeks, if not months. Still, Eisenbinder made no effort to change the *Nevada's* instructions. He was surprised when at the last minute the 14th Naval District Commander relieved him of his command and a new message fluttered from the signal flags on top of the base water tower. STAY CLEAR OF THE CHANNEL. The *Nevada* promptly cut its engines, turned around, and beached itself at Waipio Point.

Scapegoats had to be found for the Pearl Harbor surprise attack, and his grandfather was one of them. Rear Admiral Eisenbinder was brought before a summary court for negligence and demoted to commodore. Steelbinder wondered what would have happened if the *Nevada* had been able to make it through the channel and escape. Gerald Eisenbinder might have been a hero.

Memories of his grandfather's demise continued to thunk around in Steelbinder's mind like ricocheting bullets. Or were they real bullets from Pearl Harbor? He knew that if the recollections didn't stop soon, the headache would begin. He didn't need that, not now. Still, he couldn't compel himself to throw the admiral's hat into the sea where it rightfully belonged. Holding the plastic bag protectively, he hurried below to his quarters.

 37

Pamela missed not having children. Except for one time each year when she was tickled pink that they weren't allowed in her apartment building. Like tonight, Halloween. It was also Friday, a good time to get out on the town and try to forget the ugly investigation for a few hours. Pam considered calling some friends to suggest a quiet dinner somewhere, but it was late; they'd probably have costume party plans of their own. She decided to stay home and order in a pizza, get a good night's sleep, then spend Saturday catching up on a truckload of neglected errands.

Pam thought about her accumulated mileage to date—Los Angeles, San Diego, Honolulu, back to Los Angeles. Come Sunday night, she'd be back in the whirlwind, returning to San Diego to resume her promised vigil at Dougherty's NIS office. The more she thought about spending the weekend at home cooling her heels and keeping the cat company, however, the more she became agitated and irritable. The cat might love her for the household's return to sanity and routine, but every moment Pam stayed here she was distancing herself from the investigation. Dougherty and Chi—born sexists that they were—would probably neglect to call her, either purposely or as a matter of convenience, until after they had Swain Bullock in the ship's brig. Pam suddenly felt helpless and temporarily unable to do a damned thing about it. As much as she genuinely liked Todd, he was stifling her. And the more she thought about the situation, the more irritated she became.

The hell with Mr. Dougherty and his misplaced sense of chivalry; was he trying to protect her from anticipated violence? The same went for Kenny Chi's elusive, egotistical manner. The modern-day Charlie Chan promised to telephone her when he arrived on the West Coast, let her know his immediate itinerary and plans. All Chi had done was contact the local FBI office and leave a message where he could be reached in a bind—a San Francisco bed and breakfast hotel called The Golden Panda.

In a bind—what was that supposed to mean? Pam was in a bind right now, desperate for timely information on a difficult case. The *Abraham Lincoln* had pulled into port in San Francisco, she knew this much from the evening TV news; there'd been something about protestors marring the scene of the Bay Area's Fleet Week. Todd still hadn't called her as promised, and already it was going on six. She'd also tried four times to phone Lieutenant Chi at his hotel in San Francisco, but each time he was out.

She looked at the cat curled up on the other end of the sofa. Samantha glared back, yawned, and continued to sulk over Pam's lengthy absence. Sighing with irritation, Pam tried to decide whether to mix herself an ice cold martini. As much as she hated to drink alone, she needed to unwind; her nerves were as tight as guitar strings. There was an unfinished book on the coffee table, Zsa Zsa Gabor's seminal effort, *How to Catch a Man, How to Keep a Man, How to Get Rid of a Man*. Pam picked it up and put it back down. Arbitrarily deciding against the martini as well, she stepped over to the window and gazed down the two levels to Tiverton Avenue. She watched a group of costumed children with flashlights making the rounds of the Westwood neighborhood. *Trick or treaters*. She secretly wished she were out there with them.

On second thought, maybe not. Too many sickos around spiking chocolate creams and jellybeans with God knew what. Tonight seemed to be one time of the year borderline neurotics were licensed to peddle their wares. Unfortunately it would also be a perfect time for one full-blown psychotic to kill again—not in her immediate neighborhood, but up in the Bay Area. Considering the crisis, why was she home trying to make a silly decision over a drink, dinner, and book?

Pam watched the twinkling flashlights disappear up the street, then closed the drapery. She looked at the cat and said two words: "Sorry, kitty." Hurrying into the bedroom, she grabbed the overnight bag that was still only half unpacked from yesterday's homecoming and quickly replenished it with lingerie and toiletries. Then she called the neighbor woman and made additional arrangements for Samantha. Deciding to change purses, Pam selected a shoulder-strap, gray Gucci bag and transferred into it her gun and two extra clips of ammunition. She briefly checked herself over in the mirror, then headed for the door. Her hair was a mess, but she'd tend to it at the airport. There were still a couple of commuter flights leaving for the Bay Area, and with a little stand-by luck and her FBI identification, she was determined to get a seat on one of them.

Fleet Week being what it is in San Francisco, the *Abraham Lincoln* was given a close-in, preferential mooring at the end of combined Piers 30 and 32. It took almost two hours for the ship to secure and prepare for the open house. The plan was for guided tours scheduled between ten and six P.M. over two days.

Dougherty figured it wouldn't do any good to meet with Bullock again until he had more ironbound facts on R. W. Steelbinder. It was easy to see why the captain hadn't gone ashore the first day in port. Bullock and Admiral Tanner were both constantly surrounded by civic and federal government dignitaries yearning for the *Abraham Lincoln's* coveted VIP treatment. Lunch, tea, or dinner hosted by a supercarrier skipper or battle group admiral would be something to talk about later back home.

Dougherty managed to avoid all the public relations bullshit. After making doubly sure Steelbinder's shore liberty wasn't scheduled to begin until the second day—*Halloween of all times*—Dougherty kept to those parts of the carrier that were closed off to the public. He watched TV for a while with several pilots in the officer's dirty wardroom and caught up on paperwork in his own cabin. He also spent a couple of hours in the ship's library going through borrowers' check-out files. If this Steelbinder had a voracious reading appetite, Dougherty was determined to learn something about the quartermaster's taste in books. So much for yesterday; now it was the *Abe Lincoln's* second and final day in San Francisco.

Dougherty was growing increasingly disappointed and annoyed, for he'd still not heard from Lieutenant Kenny Chi. The Hong Kong detective, by his elusiveness, was proving more of a hindrance to the investigation than a help. As for Pamela down in L.A., Dougherty would postpone calling her until morning, just before the carrier left port. It was *Thank God it's Friday Time*, and if he buzzed her now she'd surely want to come up and spend the night with him ashore in a hotel. Under ordinary circumstances, he'd have pushed the idea himself, but not this Halloween; he had complicated plans where every second on the job counted. The likelihood was Dougherty would get little sleep in the hours ahead.

He hoped he'd licked a minor problem. Bullock was going out on the town, and an unfamiliar NIS face was needed to serve as the captain's chauffeur-escort. Calling San Diego, Dougherty instructed Sol Steinberg to get himself up to San Francisco immediately, and to bring along the Rolls Royce hood ornament. Steinberg had arrived early. He'd been quietly introduced to Admiral Tanner, whose cooperation was required if Bullock was to be surreptitiously monitored every moment he was away from the ship.

Piers 30 and 32 consisted of a landfill between two former Embarcadero wharfs. Instead of warehouses, there was a huge parking lot next to the ship. Dougherty, clad in civilian clothing, stood at the edge of the lot near the ship's personnel gangway. If he'd calculated correctly, Steelbinder would soon appear and begin his liberty.

A short distance away was a cab Dougherty had requisitioned for himself moments earlier and hired on an hourly basis. The price was exorbitant, but the older, Italian-American driver made assurances that he knew the city like the "smell of his wife's cooking." The talkative cabbie claimed to have worked for a private eye on several occasions and was up on all the tricks for discreet shadowing. Introducing himself as Dino, the boastful driver insisted he knew all the short cuts, what steep grades to avoid, which stop lights to chance running, and where to double-park with immunity.

There were actually two long lines of taxis waiting for crewmen-customers from the *Abe Lincoln*. The cabbies didn't have to wait long. At the conclusion of the watch, sailors thronged off the ship alone, in pairs, and loud-voiced gangs—mostly in civilian attire, a few in their uniforms. Many clambered into the waiting cabs, but a few chose to walk the short distance over to Market and California Streets to grab a cable car.

Dougherty checked his watch. It was almost five o'clock. Above him, extending in both directions down the pier, the *Abraham Lincoln* lay like a mountain range. There were some disruptive nuclear ship protestors on the dock, but the police, determined to keep them from spoiling the Navy's show, kept them a considerable distance from the carrier.

At last Dougherty saw his quarry, up near the hangar deck exit. Steelbinder was checking out with the chief petty officer responsible for the shore liberty tally. Steelbinder wore what looked like a pair of gray twill pants, a green turtleneck sweater, and a light yellow windbreaker with a hood folded down on the back. Dougherty made a memo to himself; dressed so casually, the crewman wasn't likely to be heading anywhere fancy.

As for Captain Bullock and Rear Admiral Tanner, it was still early and Dougherty knew that neither officer had left the carrier. A short distance from him Steinberg sat waiting in a rented Lincoln, prepared to drive the pair whenever they were ready to go. Both Dougherty and Steinberg had Motorola pack-sets inside their jackets if the need arose for communication.

Dougherty watched Steelbinder step across the long gangway and take the stairway down to the dock. The powerfully built petty officer second class carried in his hand a spiral notebook and what looked like a city map. None of the sailors coming off the ship carried overnight bags, for the word was emphatic; it was to be a very short shore leave. Everyone, without exception, was expected back on the carrier no later than 1 A.M.

Head held high like a dog taking the scent, Steelbinder stepped briskly up to the waiting line of cabs, commandeering the first one and climbing in the back. Dougherty watched the taxi pull out, but waited until it headed north along the Embarcadero before instructing his own driver to follow at a distance.

Dougherty sat forward in the seat, watching the other cab over Dino's shoulder. He and his driver were both surprised when the first taxi drove on past the usual tourist destination, Fisherman's Wharf, moving on at a fast clip down Bay Street toward the Presidio. Steelbinder's cab didn't take the bridge approach but turned off on Marine Drive, eventually winding up at Fort Point and the Military History Museum nestled under the Golden Gate Bridge superstructure. Dougherty's cab kept back, but he could see that Steelbinder had no intention of going into the museum that had apparently closed. The sun had already dropped beyond the ocean horizon, and soon it would be dark.

Dougherty watched, fascinated, as Steelbinder stepped briskly down to the edge of the water. He appeared to be studying the bridge's steel understructure and the nearest tower. For a long time he gazed at the concrete pier and the waters swirling past in great circular eddies. *A lousy place for swimming*, Dougherty reflected, as he watched his adversary plop down on a nearby bulkhead and begin taking notes. Or was he drawing a picture? For all Dougherty knew, the sailor might be writing love letters. After sitting by the channel for some fifteen minutes, all the while his cab meter still running, Steelbinder got up to leave. Overhead, the brilliant amber lights on the bridge deck had come on.

The taxi immediately whisked Steelbinder back downtown via the same route he'd come, this time making two brief stops enroute—one at Fisherman's Wharf to pick up an order of fish and chips to go, another at a nearby liquor store for what looked like a quart of beer. Steelbinder apparently finished both in the back of the cab, for when he got out at the foot of California Street by the cable car turntable, his hands were empty.

Dougherty took off his tie and crammed it in the pocket of his tweed jacket. If the hunted chose to go casual tonight, so would the hunter. Dougherty's driver said into the rear-view mirror, "I think your friend's about to go for a ride on that cable car. If I follow too far behind we could lose him if he suddenly hops off while it's moving."

Dougherty considered the possibility. The cable cars only did nine miles per hour and Steelbinder looked fleet-footed enough. "Look, cabbie—I'm sorry, *Dino*. There's a fat tip waiting when we wrap this up if you don't lose me. I'm riding on that cable car with him. Just keep your eye on that yellow jacket of his, okay? Try to stay within hailing distance, that's all I ask."

"Whatever, pal. If you want me to park the wheels and join you in a two-man alternating screen on foot, let me know."

Dougherty climbed out of the cab, turned, and looked narrowly at the cabbie. "I'm impressed. You formerly a cop?"

"Naw. I got a daughter down in Hollywood writing detective stuff for TV. I get to read the scripts before they get on the tube."

"Fine. Dino, if I signal, come up fast and pick me up."

The cabbie nodded. Dougherty took his time strolling over to the cable car. The gripman and several bystanders were pushing it around on the turntable. Steelbinder watched, but made no effort to help. Dougherty boarded on the opposite side of the car from his quarry and stood, holding onto the rail. Steelbinder sat, staring up the hill and craning his neck to look up at the glittering skyscrapers.

38

As the cable car began its clattery run up California Street, Dougherty found himself wishing that he'd obtained help to tail Steelbinder. Neglecting to call the local FBI personnel may have turned out to be an error, for San Francisco was an unfamiliar town, and if anything went wrong, Pamela would never forgive him. And in more ways than one.

The cabbie was probably right. In a congested metropolitan area like this, a three-man, radio-equipped shadow team was the only way to go. Dougherty could only pray that his quarry in the front of the cable car didn't suspect he was being tailed and take countermeasures.

The cable car, having only begun its run, was uncrowded. Dougherty glanced around him. The gripman wore a Hopalong Cassidy hat and neckerchief over his uniform in deference to Halloween—a night when anything could happen, Dougherty reflected. The unpredictable was already hanging over him like a poised, sharp guillotine, ready to plummet at any moment. Whatever lay ahead in the next few hours, Dougherty was as ready as he'd ever be. His small pack-set radio didn't include the local San Francisco police frequency, but it would at least bring Sol Steinberg running if necessary, and messages could be relayed to the proper authorities. At least there was the .38 special tucked in the holster under his jacket. Dougherty figured he was ready for anything—even a wild goose chase.

As the cable car rattled past Montgomery Street, the city's "Grand Canyon" of financial skyscrapers, Steelbinder rose slightly from his bench seat. Dougherty watched him closely, fully prepared to jump off himself, but the sailor sat back down. But moments later when the gripman braked at Grant Avenue, Steelbinder suddenly bounded from his seat and headed off into the clutter and noise of Chinatown. Dougherty followed, checking back to make sure Dino the cabbie was still trailing them at a discreet distance. The night was cooler than Dougherty had figured, and he now wished he'd worn a sweater under his sports jacket. Elbowing his way through several Halloween revelers, Dougherty remembered that surveillance was a skill like anything else, and it needed to be practiced. He knew that heading up a fleet NIS operation from a comfy North Island desk was one thing, but shagging ass on the street while remaining unobtrusive was another. It had been a while since Dougherty had played point man, and he hoped he hadn't become too rusty. *Don't press*. He kept repeating the rules in his mind. *Don't move in close unless you're ready to make contact*.

Steelbinder in his bright yellow jacket was easier to follow than Dougherty figured. Tall and big shouldered, the curly-haired blond man walked with a determined step, unlike the bug-eyed tourists strolling leisurely along Grant Avenue sidewalks. Tonight almost half the pedestrians, even entire families, wore bizarre costumes. Many of the children carried candlelit, papier-maché jack o'lanterns. Steelbinder kept moving, pausing only a couple of times to look in the fascinating windows of the Chinese shopkeepers. At the corner of Clay Street, he paused as if undecided whether to turn down the hill toward Kearny. He finally continued on down Grant Avenue, turning into a tea room at mid-block.

Dougherty followed him up to the tea room's entry but didn't go inside. He didn't have to. Steelbinder had taken a small marble-top table near the window where he could observe the colorfully-dressed crowd on the sidewalk. Dougherty kept moving, hoping he hadn't been spotted; Steelbinder was preoccupied with a waiter. Crossing the street, Dougherty took up a vantage behind a loitering group of masked teenagers. From there he watched his mark sip tea and open the fortune cookies. Steelbinder, apparently dissatisfied with what he'd read, summoned the Chinese waiter, who moments later brought out a plate with at least a half-dozen more.

Dougherty waited patiently, as did his taxi driver, who had found a place to park in a loading zone halfway up the block. Even after the waiter cleared away the dismantled, uneaten fortune cookies, Steelbinder took his time, ordering more tea. Finally, he paid his tab and came back outside, looking up and down the sidewalk in both directions before again proceeding north on Grant. This time Dougherty kept pace with him by following on the opposite side of the street. They'd gone a full block when Steelbinder, without hesitating, reversed himself and headed back to Clay. *Retracing his route to check for followers*, Dougherty figured, glad now he hadn't crossed over. But at the corner his quarry turned down into a park-like playground and disappeared. Dougherty doubled back himself and hurried to the same intersection where he was suddenly confronted by Dino in his taxi.

The cabbie shouted to him, "Todd, c'mere!"

When Dougherty hurried over to the cab's window, Dino pointed. "He's headed into the parking structure. If there's no car waiting for him inside, I'll lay you any odds he'll wind up on the bridge."

Dougherty grew impatient. "What bridge?"

"The overpass going into the Hyatt Hotel. Get over to it, and you'll find him."

"Thanks. Dino, wait for me outside the lobby entrance." Dougherty took off. He ran to the hotel, slowing only to pass through the thick-carpeted foyer. Avoiding the elevators, he took the stairwell to the next level three at a time, then took off again. He didn't pause to catch his breath until he'd reached the middle of the overpass walkway.

Dougherty's heart pounded as he looked around him. No sign whatever of Steelbinder. Proceeding over to the parking structure, Dougherty checked out the stairway leading to the street. The landing appeared empty. He kept going down. As he rounded a blind corner at the bottom of the staircase, a hand darted out and tapped him firmly on the shoulder. Dougherty jumped.

"Sir, I don't mean to give you a bad time, but why are you following me?" The voice was Steelbinder's.

Dougherty cursed inwardly as he turned. He stared into the chunky sailor's misshapen face, amazed at how menacing and ugly it was close up. Dougherty was so near he could smell mint on Steelbinder's breath. Startled as he was and a little embarrassed, it took several seconds for Dougherty to regain his composure and take command of the situation. He finally asked, "You're R.W. Steelbinder . . . from the *Abraham Lincoln's* quartermaster staff?"

The man confronting him edged back only slightly, shifting on his feet, and stared back with nervous, flashing eyes. *Cruel eyes*, Dougherty decided.

Steelbinder said frostily, "You know that well enough. I mean, yes, sir."

Dougherty blew out a gust of air. So much for playing the undercover game. He said flatly, "I'm Lieutenant Commander Dougherty, Naval Investigation Service."

His opponent sneered, "I'm already aware of that, sir. May I ask why you're skulking about, following me?"

Dougherty dodged the question by asking one of his own. "You knew my identity? Who else aboard the carrier knows?"

"The entire ship, I suspect. Sorry, Lieutenant Commander, but the *Abe Lincoln* is a far smaller community than you think. Scuttlebutt moves at light speed from stem to stern."

Dougherty felt outflanked. Rubbing his chin to hold back a grin, he admitted, "I suspect you're right."

Steelbinder continued to stare at him.

Dougherty cleared his throat and bluntly asked, "Mind if I ask what the hell you were up to yesterday morning—out on the bow of the carrier?"

"Taking in the view, like everyone else."

"And tossing a pile of records into the bay?"

Steelbinder thought for a moment, then grumbled, "Just having some fun, sir. No harm meant. They sank immediately."

"I wasn't concerned with polluting the bay. You said *fun*. The wind blew one of those records damn near into my lap. 'Many A Time the World Comes Short of Thought' by the Midnight Admirals. Were they all identical? And where did you get them?"

Steelbinder appeared agitated. Smoothing down the sides of his curly blond hair, he said hesitantly, "All different. Worn out and scratched discs I found in the ship's trash. My guess is they were left over from when they had juke boxes in the cafeterias. Got too noisy so the captain killed the idea." He paused, then added sarcastically, "The captain killed a lot of good things, sir."

Dougherty waited until a chattering Oriental couple had passed by them and gone up the stairs, then said, "That kind of rotten music, I sympathize with Bullock. How familiar are you with this heavy metal group—the Midnight Admirals?"

Shrugging, Steelbinder put on an odd mask of innocence. "I'm vaguely familiar with them, yes. But they're not one of my favorites. My own heavies happen to be Beethoven and Mozart."

Dougherty slowly shook his head. "I understand you're one of the ship's best helmsmen. The navigation officer praises your performance."

"I try, sir."

"Seamanship, just like anything else, can be an art."

Steelbinder let out a small bark of laughter. "Yes, sir. And I recognize the quote."

"Great. I thought I was being original."

"The Greek Admiral Thucydides, sir. He wrote *History of the Peloponnesian War*. The captain likes to quote from him when he addresses the crew."

Dougherty looked at Steelbinder narrowly. "I understand you're an avid book reader. You consider yourself a student of warfare?"

"No, Lieutenant Commander. Just interested, shall we say, in *acute conditioned violence*—shall we say the mind of the warrior. Have we talked enough? I'd like to go now and preferably without being followed. I can save you time by providing my itinerary for the evening if it will help."

Dougherty stiffened with annoyance. "Answer a couple more questions, and I'll back off. This intellectual bent of yours—does it extend to old literature? Specifically, late medieval, pre-renaissance poetry?"

"No, I'm afraid not." Steelbinder's eyes sparkled.

Dougherty stared at him, wishing he had a truth serum or lie detector machine along. "The ship's librarian tells me you checked out a book that included pre-renaissance poetry. Like Dante's *Divine Comedy*. Ring a bell?"

Flushing slightly, Steelbinder grew more annoyed. "It was for the captain. Sir, he often sent me down from the bridge on a variety of errands."

I'll bet, mused Dougherty. "In this case, Bullock denies it."

Steelbinder's cruel eyes rounded. "Hmmmmm-nnnnn. I thought he might. Pardon, sir, but the skipper's an extremely complicated man. He tends to be forgetful." Steelbinder paused, stared at Dougherty for several moments, then as an afterthought, intoned, "The captain can also be spiteful. Are you through with me, Lieutenant Commander? I am on authorized liberty."

Dougherty was troubled but tried not to let it show. He said quickly, "I understand you acted as Captain Bullock's chauffeur in Hong Kong."

"Sir, I'd prefer not to talk about that. I'm already in enough trouble with the skipper."

"At the time you were replaced by another driver—Aviation Boatswain's Mate Gecko Corman, correct?"

Steelbinder exhaled sharply and retreated into a defiant silence.

Dougherty tried again. "You know where this Corman is now? Or why he disappeared?"

"No, sir. And respectfully, I believe this interrogation is out of order."

"Feeling intimidated are you, Steelbinder?"

"Captain Bullock has instructed me not to discuss the matter."

Liar, liar, liar, Dougherty growled to himself.

Steelbinder made a show of checking his watch then said

smoothly, "I intend to catch a foreign film down the street. If you want to come along and watch my every move, suit yourself. But unless you plan to haul me in for breaking some naval regulation, I'd like to conclude this conversation—*sir*."

Dougherty said dryly, "No charges. Not yet anyway."

Steelbinder stepped briskly away, pausing and glancing back when he reached the end of the playground. Pulling the hood of his jacket over his head, he walked swiftly downhill toward Kearny Street.

Dougherty contained his temper and made a half-hearted attempt to follow the sailor on foot. Suddenly changing his mind, he hailed Dino's cab instead and slumped into the rear seat. Dougherty's mind raced as he considered the new rules to the game and his options.

It turned out Steelbinder told him the truth about one thing: he did go into a movie house, the Bella Union on Kearny Street. The theater showed oriental flicks. Dougherty tapped his driver on the shoulder. "You think he understands Chinese? And is there a back door to the place?"

Dino shrugged. "They usually have English subtitles. Lots of action in Oriental films. You should see one yourself sometime. As for the exits, we can drive around back and check it out."

"Hold up a minute." Dougherty enjoyed the warmth of the cab and wondered if there'd be any point, now that he'd been recognized, in keeping up with the sailor. The other side of the coin was that he couldn't simply hand over the city to a possible killer. Dougherty dug into his wallet and handed the cab driver five bucks. "Do me a favor. Go in there and see if he's actually interested in the damn film. And try not to be conspicuous."

"I'll need another buck for popcorn."

"Forget it. Get moving."

Dino smiled shrewdly and climbed out of the cab. "Hell, this reminds me of the time they caught Dillinger at the Biograph. You want me to stay with your man for the entire show?"

"No. Come back out and let me know what's going on. But count all the exits."

Dino swaggered across the street and disappeared into the theater.

While waiting, Dougherty kept checking his watch. The cabbie was gone less than fifteen minutes, but it seemed like a half-hour.

At last Dino slipped back behind the wheel. "He's in the tenth row, middle section. It's an early show, and there's less than a dozen other people in the auditorium."

Dougherty nodded slowly, but couldn't resist the riposte, "You were gone long enough; the two of you enjoy the flick?"

"Sorry." Dino tugged his earlobe and grinned. "Like I say, plenty of fast-paced excitement in Chinese films."

"What about the exits? Could he go out the back way by a fire door?"

"Yeah. One on each side of the stage."

Dougherty ran it all quickly through his mind and decided he had to take the chance; sitting in the back of the darkened theater he might go unnoticed. He couldn't lose Steelbinder now. "Dino, wait here, and try not to fall asleep." Climbing out of the cab, Dougherty headed across the street to the Bella Union.

Foreign films of any kind fascinated Steelbinder, and he'd almost allowed himself to get caught up in this Chinese feature. *No, not tonight, Roscoe; there isn't time*. He had far more eye-popping entertainment planned for this Halloween.

Steelbinder watched with interest as a short, older man padded down the theater's aisle as far as the front row, turned, then walked back up, glancing right and left as if counting the house. Steelbinder figured right away that the individual was a bogus bill; he wasn't even dressed the part. Theater managers didn't wear wool plaid shirts; they wore ties, many of them a black tux. The snooper had to be one of Dougherty's stooges.

Steelbinder nursed his patience until the spook finally left the auditorium, then scurried down the aisle and parted the curtains under the fire exit sign. Confronted by a staircase, he bounded to the top, reaching a formidable steel door with a push bar lock. He pushed. The door's lock mechanism screamed an alarm, but it didn't matter; by the time the theater attendants came backstage, he'd be long gone.

Steelbinder sprinted down the dark alley, his mind calculating. So Dougherty knew more than he'd figured. Was the woman sleuth out here somewhere as well, dogging him in the darkness? Steelbinder knew now that an avalanche had been set in motion, and there was no use trying to outrun it. Survival was dependent on vigilance; keeping out of its direct path, jumping quickly to one side or the other. Like a ski patrolman who knew how to set a *controlled* avalanche, Steelbinder would focus his destruction on one part of the slope while he remained safely on another.

Trying not to attract unnecessary attention, Steelbinder slowed his pace to cross Jackson Street before heading into the alley on the opposite side. He needed to get to an address in nearby North

Beach and wanted to be there early, before Swain Bullock arrived. This time Steelbinder would be prepared. If everything went according to schedule, there would be plenty of time to set up his trap and carefully consider all the parameters. No more fuck-ups like in Honolulu.

A blinking neon sign on the side street off Grant Avenue caught his attention and held it. Steelbinder felt an odd sensation. Mesmerized, he edged down the hill until he was directly under the writhing, oscillating green dragon that marked the entry to a chop suey house. The neon creature had hideous flashing eyes and reminded him more of a monstrous snake than a dragon.

There were a few technicolor nightmares of childhood that Steelbinder could never forget, and the writhing creature on this sign reminded him of one oft-repeated dream in particular: the frightful times he'd seen Satan as an enormous cobra slithering over the foot of the bed, glaring down at him. When Roscoe did terrible things during the day as he often did, at night the ceiling-high snake would only sway gently back and forth and smile. But if Steelbinder behaved himself or even thought kind, peaceful things, the huge cobra would writhe, hiss, spread its shield, and bear down on his face. Sometimes Roscoe buried his head in the pillow, hiding. Other times he would wake up sweating profusely, reeking with anxiety and hurting from a horrible headache.

Steelbinder continued to stare hypnotically at the gruesome electronic monster. Drawn to it, his heart pounded and he grew angry. If he had a stepladder, he'd climb up and tear off its green neon tubes one by one. Steelbinder wasn't about to be influenced again by giant snakes; being controlled by his vexatious grandfather was enough!

Trembling slightly, he removed from his jacket pocket the four-inch-long superfirecracker he'd brought along for tonight's *rite of passage*. Staring at its red and black filigree wrapping and turning it over in his hand, he considered putting it to good use now. Could he throw it at the offensive, glittering neon that threatened him, timing the pitch to destroy the snake—or dragon? *Was there a difference?* The blinking, slithering creature was hideous; it vexed his sensibilities, and he was losing control. He had to do something. He could feel the blood beginning to boil in his veins.

Suddenly, he heard his grandfather's soothing voice calling to him: *Calm down, Roscoe. You're safe*. Forget the snake. It will let you pass by unharmed. The two of us have prodigious plans for tonight. Don't spoil them by premature indiscretions. *Think, Roscoe! Think!* Then the voice passed away, replaced by an all too familiar spasm in the back of the neck.

Steelbinder let out a long sigh. Retrieving the bottle of Valium from his pocket, he swallowed one tablet without water. The doorman to the Chinese restaurant was eyeing him suspiciously, so he walked on. As usual, he would heed the Midnight Admirals' and his grandfather's advice. Hadn't they become one and the same? Though Steelbinder wanted to cop one more look at the terrible neon dragon, he fought the temptation, instead quickening his pace toward North Beach.

~~~~~~~ 39

The whore house wasn't much different from the ones he'd seen in Hong Kong. Kenny Chi realized now that he wouldn't get to Hollywood or Disneyland this weekend, not with all the loose ends here in San Francisco. Conjecture on the Mai Twan homicide had been one thing, but now odd new information was coming into focus. Chi had one consolation: It was looking better all the time that he'd be able to submit the Hawaii-West Coast portion of the trip as a reimbursable travel expense. Had he known before the valuable information this Yung Liu had to tell him, he might have stayed at the Fairmont or Four Seasons instead of the modest bed and breakfast inn just eight blocks away in North Beach.

He asked the young Chinese prostitute, "Are you afraid?"

Yung Liu looked at him through veiled eyes. "No. Should the captain try anything with me, I have a gun under the mattress."

Chi waved his hand. "No. I need *both* Mai's killer and Swain Bullock alive, not dead. You must rely on my protection. I'll be outside on the fire escape landing."

"But the police—shouldn't we call them?"

"To this place? If you wish to remain employed by Madame Fong, I think not. Besides, I need additional evidence before bringing the local authorities into the case."

Yung Liu Twan squirmed in her chair. "Then perhaps I should

be afraid. You saw what happened to my sister's body, Lieutenant."

Kenny Chi sighed and wrinkled his nose. The slattern's room smelled of transitory love, clove cigarettes, and cheap perfume. He asked her firmly, "Why didn't you return to Hong Kong for Mai's funeral?"

"I was frightened."

"Of Captain Bullock or the killer? They'd both flown back to their ship in Manila."

"No. I was afraid I would not be readmitted to this country. There was also the matter of airfare."

"How old are you, Yung Liu?"

"Twenty-two."

Chi shook his head in disbelief. She looked younger, like a mere teenager. He suspected the prostitute was lying, but it didn't matter. Chi looked around him. He'd seen more than his share of Chinese cat houses before, and this one in San Francisco had nothing unique going for it. Yung Liu's private room had an embossed tin ceiling, blue velour wallpaper, a large mirror, and a gold-framed oil painting. A mass-produced, airbrushed Tibetan mountain landscape. Stomach art, Chi thought. Over Yung Liu's large circular bed was a row of brass track lights pointed at random around the room. A stereo cabinet, sink, and pair of velvet-covered chairs completed the room's furnishings. Chi had chosen the chair nearest the fire escape window where his eyes could alternate between Yung Liu and the lights of Russian Hill. He'd only meant to question the girl for fifteen minutes, and already he'd been here over a half-hour. It was time to leave. If what the young woman had told him were true, the chances were excellent that Captain Bullock would be paying her a visit at any time.

"Please, Lieutenant. Don't send me back to Hong Kong."

He considered her. "If you cooperate, that won't be necessary. I'll only need a deposition with your notarized signature." Chi shook his head. "It's a shame that Mai Twan's driver and houseboy lied to my investigators."

"I'm sorry. He was protecting me."

"And inadvertently, Mai's murderer." Chi felt genuinely sorry for the young prostitute. The light from the overhead track lights fell like a benediction over her half-closed eyes. Yung Liu had unusually high cheekbones, wide-set, charcoal eyes, and an overgenerous mouth with a lower lip made even more pronounced by a nervous habit of running the tip of her tongue across its glistening surface. Staring out the window, she said to him, "What happened to my sister was terrible, but I must now go back to work, or the Madame will penalize me. You do understand?" She stood up, tightening her gold-embroidered robe as she padded to the door.

Chi removed the miniature Sony cassette recorder from his jacket pocket and handed it to her. "As I explained earlier, the tape is set to go. Merely push the red button at the appropriate time." What Chi didn't tell Yung Liu was that the tape unit was specially fitted with a tiny transmitter mike enabling him to listen from outside the building. He'd be ready to move if she were in jeopardy. Chi was determined to play down the danger part of it lest she might not cooperate. He asked her, "You're sure you understand the procedure? Shall I show you again?"

"No, that won't be necessary. I understand." She took the tape player and hid it within the leaves of the oregon grape plant Chi had brought her for this purpose.

Chi asked, "And the fire escape. You won't forget to release the ladder and lower it for me?"

"I promise to take care of it." Yung Liu gestured toward the door. "Now you must leave."

Chi followed her out into the hallway, where they were greeted by a woman with an estrogen-less baritone voice. "Time is money, and Halloween is one of my busiest nights," said Madame Fong. She smiled at Chi and said haughtily, "You want to stay longer, you feed the meter."

Chi nodded. He turned back to Yung Liu and whispered, "I'll return later for the tape."

The young woman waited until Madame Fong had retreated back down the stairs, then smiled and said to Chi, "You're sure the captain will show up tonight?"

"Yes. It's his last opportunity. The carrier sails in the morning. I merely put myself in his shoes. Curiosity and guilt, Yung Liu, are terrible demons." Chi hesitated, then said solemnly, "You'll eventually have to tell your story to the local police. I suggest we take care of that tomorrow."

She nodded.

He smiled at her and hurried downstairs, tipping Madame Fong generously as he went out the front door. Moments later on the street, Chi again studied the darkened North Beach neighborhood, determined to find a safe haven from which to comfortably observe the comings and goings at Madame Fong's house of ill repute. If Swain Bullock didn't make an appearance tonight, Chi would feel the fool. The weather was chilly, and Chi pulled up his jacket collar as he walked down to the 7-Eleven store on the corner. He ordered a hot tea in a large styrofoam cup and took it back with him to one of the apartment entries directly across from Madame Fong's whorehouse. Retreating into the shadows of the wooden stairway, he sat down to nurse the tea while he waited.

The dinner in the private wine cellar at Ernie's restaurant had gone pleasantly enough, though after an hour's time Captain Bullock had to fight hard against boredom. The conversation had been mostly grousing over monies spent on new supercarriers with no funding for equally advanced aircraft to equip them. Bullock had heard it all before, too many times, but knew that when a naval officer is a guest of San Francisco's mayor, a Congressman member of the House Military Appropriations Committee, and a U.S. Senator from California, one is obliged to listen and dutifully answer the endless questions. Rear Admiral Tanner also appeared palled by the drift of the conversation; he, too, worked hard at a contrived diplomacy.

Finally there was an embarrassingly long lull in the dinner dialogue. Fritz Tanner broke the silence, commenting to the mayor, "Surprised us to see all the pickets yesterday protesting our arrival. Hell, I'd have thought Fleet Week was almost sacred around here—the local economy being so dependent on the military installations. How many facilities you have?"

Mayor Stortini grinned. "Too many to count if we expand the boundary of our so-called metropolitan area. As for the pickets, it's this trendy anti-nuke thing. Nothing serious, Admiral. Mostly noise."

Bullock sat forward. "On an aircraft carrier, noise gets to be a way of life."

Senator Norris held his glass of Pinot Noir in both hands, glancing over it first at Tanner, then at Bullock. "I hate to pass on the bad news, gentlemen, but my friends in the news media tell me you're in for more harassment. Your opponents apparently plan a spectacular show of force tomorrow morning."

The mayor coughed into his napkin to hide his embarrassment. He explained awkwardly, "Radicals—out for national attention. Probably convinced they'll get some TV time by focusing on America's newest nuclear-powered carrier."

Bullock looked at Stortini critically. "I think you'd better level with us, Mayor. What do you know?"

Stortini frowned. "We suspect they'll try to mess things up at the pier before you depart, then assemble on the Golden Gate Bridge and attempt to shut down traffic. Police intelligence indicates they intend to dump both flowers and red paint down on your deck. To simulate blood."

Fritz Tanner shook his head and said solemnly, "Over my dead body."

Congressman Anderson nodded. "Mine as well."

The mayor raised his hand. "Easy, gentlemen. The State Patrol will let 'em have their signs and flowers, but they'll promptly pull in anyone carrying paint or obstructing bridge traffic."

Bullock was wide awake now, exchanging swift looks of concern with Tanner. He couldn't believe what he was hearing. This was the nineteen eighties, not the sixties. Even before leaving San Diego, they'd both had reservations over releasing to the press the hour of the *Abraham Lincoln's* arrival in San Francisco or its subsequent departure time. Suddenly this concern had been validated. Bullock did some fast calculating.

Fine, then. If the troublemakers planned to lay a publicity mine before him, and if it was set to go off at nine, Bullock would avoid it easily enough. The carrier could pull out early under the cover of darkness before the city got out of bed. But Bullock would be damned if he'd tell this to the talkative politicians confronting him. He'd discuss the plan with Tanner later when they were back on the ship. If the other vessels in the fleet complement couldn't pull their act together and depart early with the *Abraham Lincoln*, they could leave at their scheduled time and endure the damned demonstration. Bullock would rendezvous with them a few hours later, just outside the Golden Gate.

Prudently, Senator Norris changed the subject, bringing up the escalating cost of the Service Life Extension Program at the Newport News shipyard. Tanner listened, but Bullock wearily glanced at his watch. The others ordered dessert and coffee, but he declined. Bullock instead pushed back his chair from the table. "Gentlemen, will you excuse me temporarily? I have an important phone call to make."

Fritz Tanner frowned and looked at him uncertainly. Bullock walked slowly out of the private dining room and went up to the lounge, but he ignored the pay phone. Instead he reached into his pocket and withdrew a pen and leatherbound memo pad. He wrote swiftly:

Gentlemen: Regret that I have an unexpected problem back on the ship. Please carry on without me. Sincere thanks for your hospitality.

Signing the note, Bullock handed it to the waiter, instructing him to deliver it down to the private dining room. He also gave the waiter a ten dollar bill for showing him through the kitchen to the restaurant's rear door.

It was a heady time for Detective Kenny Chi. If Swain Bullock showed up, he'd be able to wrap this case on his own, without the FBI woman's help. Pamela Bonner and the NIS officer were still convinced they were hunting down just one man—a straightforward series murderer. Chi debated whether to return the FBI woman's phone call tonight. He could definitely use Pamela's help tomorrow afternoon when he'd meet with the local police. With the FBI on Chi's side, he'd be able to cut through some of the red tape at San Francisco Police Headquarters. Chi made up his mind. He'd summon Pamela at her Los Angeles apartment tonight, no matter what the hour, as soon as he was certain Swain Bullock was back aboard the carrier.

Chi put aside his tea and sat up attentively as another taxi, one of several in the past half hour, pulled up in front of Madame Fong's. It was a busy night. This time a familiar face emerged from the cab—the same individual in the snapshot with Mai Twan. *Captain Swain Bullock.* The American naval officer looked different in civilian clothing, but the thick, curly red hair, snappy gait and self-assured manner were just as Yung Lui Twan had described the man. Chi watched Bullock adjust his tie, glance cautiously up the street in both directions, then step quickly into the Castle of Ecstasy.

The two of them stood on the sidewalk outside Ernie's.

"Damn and double damn." Dougherty glanced at Sol Steinberg, unimpressed with his assistant's flimsy excuse for allowing Bullock to elude him. "Who told you to sit in the car and wait? You should have kept watch from the restaurant's lobby or just outside that dining room."

Steinberg looked back at him like an abused puppy. "Sorry, Lieutenant Commander, I tried, but one of the waiters gave me the boot. Insisted a chauffeur couldn't loiter inside."

Dougherty nodded. "Forget it. My own damn fault. I should have asked Admiral Tanner to set you up inside the restaurant. How long has Bullock been gone?"

"A half-hour, maybe longer."

"And what about the rear admiral?"

Steinberg gestured toward the restaurant entry. "Tanner's

pissed. He went back in to get his hosts. You want for me to send them off in a cab so the two of us can take the car?"

"I'd never hear the end of it." Dougherty cursed softly. "Take them all home, then meet me back at the carrier. Without some lead, we'd never find Bullock or Steelbinder on the streets; this town's too big. But we can do one thing while they're away from the ship. Providing Rear Admiral Tanner cooperates."

"What's that?"

"I'm going through Swain Bullock's cabin with a fine tooth comb. You do the same with Steelbinder's personal locker."

Steinberg felt better; it showed on his face. "Under the circumstances, I think the admiral will be glad to authorize it, sir. He's miffed as hell that Bullock outsmarted him."

 **40**

The moment she stepped off the plane at San Francisco Airport, Pam headed for a pay phone. She called the *Abraham Lincoln* and a petty officer answered on the quarterdeck, explaining that Lieutenant Commander Dougherty had left the ship for the evening. Disappointed, Pam hung up, deciding to try back later after booking a hotel. She hurried out of the airport terminal and hailed a Yellow cab, instructing the driver to take her to the Golden Panda Inn, a small hotel somewhere in Chinatown or North Beach. The cabbie insisted he'd been driving in San Francisco for more than a dozen years and had never heard of it.

"Just go. We'll look it up in the yellow pages when we get downtown."

The driver obeyed. Except for his chattering on the radio asking his dispatcher to look up the address, they drove the Bayshore into town in silence.

Twenty minutes later Pamela paid the taxi fare and climbed out in front of a four-storey brick building on Broadway. She'd halfway expected the Golden Panda to be one of the city's architectural prizes, possibly a residential Victorian converted into a bed and breakfast inn. Though the blue awning and gleaming

brass nameplate were new, to Pamela's dismay the hotel looked
suspiciously like a recently refurbished flophouse. She hurried
inside and approached a registration desk that was nearly swallowed by a jungle of ficus plants. The lobby smelled of fresh
paint, and the furniture looked new as did the carpet. A few of the
potted plants still had gay bows on them. Pam guessed the Golden
Panda had only recently opened for business.

Pam asked the young Oriental at the desk to ring Kenny Chi's
room. The clerk shook his head, insisting that Chi had gone out
earlier and still hadn't returned. He glanced at her overnight bag.
"You'll be wanting a room for yourself, or will you be joining Mr.
Chi?"

She gave him a steely look. "We're not together." Usually
when Pam stayed in San Francisco, she treated herself to the
Marriott or the Mark Hopkins. It was getting late and might get
later before Kenny Chi showed his face, and she was determined
to sit in this lobby all night, if necessary, to intercept the elusive
Chinese detective.

"Yes," she finally told the desk clerk. "I'll take a single room,
preferably on the south side. The porter can take my bag up, but
I'd like to wait down here for my friend."

"As you wish." He examined her Visa card, comparing it with
her name as she signed it on the register. "Miss Bonner, then. May
I bring you out some coffee or tea?"

"No cocktail lounge?"

"I'm sorry, no."

"Make it tea, please." Pam strolled over to a nearby overstuffed
sofa and oozed into it. Nearby was a convenient stack of
magazines and a copy of the *Chronicle*. Pam settled in; it was a
good place to keep an eye on the lobby door.

Bullock double-checked the address, then pushed the button to
the right of the intricately carved oak door. From somewhere
within, he heard a very un-Chinese chime that sounded like the
first bar of "Belly up to the Bar, Boys."

Madame Fong herself admitted Bullock with a silly little
curtsey, steering him immediately into a spacious, plush-carpeted
parlor expensively outfitted with period furniture. The room was
occupied by several attractive women—mostly Oriental. A haunt-
ingly beautiful Eurasian girl glanced up from a magazine, taking
Bullock in from head to toe. Other lovelies idly lounged about
watching a big-screen television, its volume turned down. A
sultry black woman in a silver lamé gown stood combing her hair

before a huge, gilt-framed mirror surmounted by carved gilt cherubs.

Bullock looked each of the women over appreciatively, but indicated no interest, instead handing Madame Fong a slip of paper with a name on it.

The older woman put on a pair of rhinestone-trimmed eye-glasses and read Bullock's memo. "Yung Liu Twan? Yes, of course. One of our younger hostesses." The madam went over to a nearby house phone, spoke quietly and briefly, then returned to Bullock. "A splendid choice, sir. She's lovely. Have you been here with us before?"

Bullock shook his head.

"Ah, then, the arrangements. We accept all major credit cards, but offer a twenty per cent discount for cash.

"Fine. What's the tab?"

Madame Fong's mannish voice lowered to a whisper. "Fifty, one hundred, two hundred—the options are discreetly left up to the customer. You understand the variables, of course?"

The black woman by the mirror sang out, "Different strokes for different folks."

Bullock smiled and handed Madame Fong a fifty dollar bill. She looked disappointed but quickly tucked it in her bosom.

Yung Liu floated into the parlor. Clad in a yellow robe slit just above the knee, her costume included a pearl necklace, matching earrings, and red satin shoes. The Chinese girl suddenly grew rigid when she saw Bullock but almost as quickly relaxed, smiled dutifully, and took him by the hand. Bullock smelled her perfume and decided he liked it, though he'd come here on business, not to screw. Wordlessly, Yung Liu led him upstairs.

Madame Fong checked her watch, scribbled the time in a small notebook, then watched the prideful, red-haired customer climb the open staircase with Yung Liu. When the couple had disap-peared down the second floor hallway, she hastened to an inconspicuous closed door at one side of the reception parlor Opening it, she went inside a dimly lit room.

Steelbinder's spirits soared. *At last.* As expected, Bullock had taken the bait! Steelbinder had waited quietly in the darkened room, staring into the reception parlor through the large one-way mirror for over forty-five minutes, and finally his patience had been rewarded. *The Preview Room for Voyeurs*, Madame Fong had called this special chamber. Judging from some of the seedier patrons who had earlier shared it with him prior to making their selections, Steelbinder considered it a *Holding Tank for Degenerates*. Unsavory experience that it was, the clandestine room had saved him valuable time. Swain Bullock, once more, had proved utterly predictable. Equally important, Steelbinder now knew *which* prostitute was Yung Liu Twan. A perfect setup.

Madame Fong came up to him in the darkness. Before she could speak, he announced, "You needn't be concerned, Madame. I've decided. I want to observe that last couple."

She frowned at him and huffed, "You can't be serious. You passed over some of our most interesting customers—and my best girls, like Molly and Denise. Not to mention Cobra Woman and that bondage customer. Instead You want to observe that stuffy man with inexperienced little Yung Liu? What kind of voyeur are you?"

"I'm just a beginner."

"Don't say later I didn't warn you. Madame Fong likes her customers to get their money's worth."

Steelbinder grew impatient. "I'll be quite satisfied."

"Supposing all they do is talk, he just cries on her shoulder? Take it from me, it happens often enough."

"I'll take that chance. Could we please go up now?"

Madame Fong shrugged. "Remember, no refunds. You can still wait a little longer, see what else comes in. God knows the ghouls we'll get on Halloween."

Steelbinder said sharply, "No. Take me upstairs."

"All right, all right." They left the preview room. She quickly escorted Steelbinder to the second floor, showing him to another darkened chamber that abutted Yung Liu's room. Madame Fong pointed to his shoes. "Remove them," she whispered. "Absolute silence is a house rule. The walls are thick enough, and the girls are instructed to play their stereos, but unfortunately the one-way mirror conducts sound."

Steelbinder nodded. Slipping off his shoes, he ventured into the dim room and gently closed the door after him.

Swain Bullock sat down on the edge of the moon-shaped bed, felt the simulated fur, and watched Yung Liu fuss with a green plant. As if purposely avoiding him, she strolled over to the window and opened it just a crack.

She asked, "Would you like to have a drink brought up?"

Bullock said quickly, "No. Is that the only greeting you have for me? We need to talk."

"Of course. What else?"

He gestured toward one of the velvet chairs, and she sat. "Do you know what happened to my wife?"

"Yes. The firecracker murder. It was on television here. You want me to say I'm sorry?"

"Not if you don't want to."

She looked at him. "I don't."

"You're the only one I can trust, Yung Liu."

She looked away, avoiding his gaze. "No. You shouldn't have come. I don't want to become involved. And it is dangerous for you. Supposing the police or the FBI have followed you?"

Bullock stiffened in his resolve, remembering that the young woman before him was every bit as stubborn as her older sister Mai. He lowered his eyes and said quietly to her, "The jade is gone, Yung Liu. At the bottom of the sea. I won't be involved; I should have sent it back to Mai, but there wasn't time." Bullock paused. "I loved Mai very dearly, but she would have destroyed me, Yung Liu. I have a career, but she persisted, growing angry and impossible. Can you tell me why?"

The prostitute found a package of clove cigarettes on a nearby table, lit one, and blew a long column of smoke toward Bullock. "Now? What does it matter, Captain? You have your nerve coming here."

Bullock leaned forward, staring at her. "I have to know what happened, *after I left her*. Under the circumstances, I'm reluctant to write or telephone to Hong Kong."

"I can see why. There is blackmail, then?"

Bullock slowly nodded. Getting to his feet, he went over to the mirror. Frowning, he rubbed his cheeks and felt for a beard. He studied his face, wondering now if he'd made a mistake coming here. When he spoke again, his voice was uneven. "You're my only link with the past, Yung Liu. I need your help. You've got to tell me what happened after I left." He turned to face her. "You know everything, I can see it in your eyes."

"Yes, I know, but no thanks to you."

"She told you about our argument?"

"No, but I'm aware of it."

"I'm sorry it had to end that way, a terrible fight. But Mai and her houseman both theatened me if I didn't cooperate."

"Threatened? I don't understand."

"To inform my wife. Or worse, go to the Navy."

Yung Liu merely shrugged and blew more smoke in his direction. "Love is blind. You were both blind. Mai loved you, but she also loved money; she always has. You were a fool not to see this. Perhaps she only needed you to move the jade across the Pacific. You had every right to refuse, but that was no justification to push her off the balcony."

Startled, Bullock said sternly, "I didn't push her. She fell down the steps. You know everything that happened, all of it?"

"Of course. The houseboy Sam Loo wrote me a lengthy letter. Last week."

"Then you're in this ugly jade racket with them."

"No." Yung Liu abruptly stood up. "I'm not. Mai never trusted me with her business. Would I work in this fleabag if I were with them? We didn't get along. Still, she was my sister."

Bullock thought for a moment. "I don't understand. The houseboy was away during my visit."

Yung Liu took a long drag off her cigarette, frowned, then put it out in an ashtray. "So you and others were led to believe. My sister was very cautious and secretive. Sam always remained in the apartment next to hers, available in case she needed him. Before you, there were other sailors and sometimes trouble. Sam Loo was not only Mai's chauffeur and partner-in-crime, but also a bodyguard."

Bullock's spirits sagged. "Don't tell me. She probably had an affair going with him as well?"

"No. Toward the end, only with you."

Bullock stopped pacing the floor. "*The end*? I don't understand." He watched Yung Liu go over to the window and look out at the lights of the city.

Finally she said to him, "Why did you come here? I think you lie to me."

Bullock shook his head and spoke with aggrieved emphasis. "I need your help. If you know everything, you must tell me what happened that day, after I summoned the ambulance."

"You didn't summon an ambulance, Captain. Remember? You only called the police—*later*, at your convenience." She studied him, then said dully, "Why did you push my sister down the stairs, Captain? Why didn't you go for a doctor or stay with her?"

Bullock sighed, shook his head, then let it all out. "Unkind words led to an argument; an argument to a fight. She said she was going to call my wife, right there on the spot, long distance. I tore the phone out of the wall. The next thing I knew she was throwing heavy pottery. I ran out on the balcony and she followed. Mai shoved, and I shoved back. When she let loose with a haymaker, I ducked."

"Excuse me, but what is this *haymaker*?"

Bullock demonstrated with his fist and arm. "When I dodged her swing, Mai went flying down the brick staircase. I found her unconscious on the landing and carried her back to her bed. No telephone, so I ran down the block to where my driver was asleep in the car."

"In my sister's car—the Rolls Royce."

"She insisted I use it while we were in the city. The driver took me down the hill to a police call box."

"You asked the police to take care of it. Then the two of you abandoned the car and left the scene."

"It was one of those panic situations. I later regretted it. I was worried about my wife back in San Diego, my Navy career. I'm up for an important flag rank promotion."

"But you told Mai your marriage was on the rocks."

"Maybe it was—but I still panicked. If Mai's all right now, what difference does it make?"

Yung Liu looked at him hatefully. "So confused you went back to your hotel and left the next day on a plane back to Manila, completely putting her out of your mind?"

Bullock swallowed hard then stiffened, annoyed that a mere hooker was pushing him. "This bodyguard-houseman of hers—Sam Loo. If he was next door, he obviously took care of her."

Yung Liu scowled. "No. He said he ran out to get a doctor himself, but, when he returned, Mai's apartment was swarming with police. With several pieces of misappropriated jade on the premises, he promptly left town for several days."

Bullock shrugged. "Which only proves he's in it with her, all the way."

"His alibis worked well, Captain Bullock. Like *yours*."

"You're avoiding something, Yung Liu. Where's Mai Twan now? In jail?"

She glared icily at him. "*My sister is dead.*"

The Chinese girl might as well have hit Bullock in the stomach with a sledge hammer. He slumped back down on the bed. "Dead? What the hell are you talking about?"

"Mai was *killed*, Captain. And you had a hand in it."

"What kind of bullshit is this?" Bullock jumped to his feet.

"After the houseboy's letter, I believed you were a mad killer—of both Mai and your wife. Now I realize that if you'd had true ulterior motives, you would have absconded with the jade and not come here."

"Jade? For Chrissakes, I've already thrown two priceless pieces overboard! Can't you see that Mai and her syndicate were using me, setting up the entire U.S. Navy in a major smuggling operation? I could have gone to prison!"

"You still may, Captain." She looked at him coyly. "As I said, love is blind. You are successful in your way, yet you condemn my sister's cleverness. Two entirely different worlds, Captain Bullock. As Confucius would say, 'The superior man understands what is right; the inferior man merely understands what will sell.'"

"Nice touch, Yung Liu. Men come up here to get laid, and, for a bonus, you give them a fortune cookie. Any other advice?"

She sighed. "I am sorry for you, so I'll overlook your sharp tongue. Do you want to know the circumstances of Mai's death or not?"

Bullock quickly nodded.

Yung Liu took a deep breath. "Exactly the terror that happened to your wife in San Diego. Strangulation, assault, all this finalized by a gruesome firecracker mutilation."

Bullock's legs felt rubbery. He sat back down, placing his head in his hands to steady himself. His mind was spinning—out of control. *Another mutilation, this one in Hong Kong!* How could he dare tell Dougherty or the FBI woman about this one? One wrong word at the wrong moment, and he'd only sink into the quagmire deeper.

His brain flashed on the obvious: there were only two fellow *Abraham Lincoln* crewmen who he'd introduced to Mai Twan. *Gecko Corman and Roscoe Steelbinder.* Both had driven her car; both knew where she lived on Victoria Peak. He was already convinced that one of them had stolen the hood ornament from the Rolls Royce. The sailors' names repeated themselves in Bullock's brain. Never would it have occurred to him that the San Diego homicide was related to his other problem in Hong Kong. It had to be Gecko Corman. Why else had the yellow shirt suddenly deserted and disappeared? Blackmail was one thing, but *murder*?

"Are you all right, Captain Bullock?"

Yung Liu looked over at him through lidded, unsympathetic eyes. She stood in front of the fire escape window, her hands behind her. Bullock wondered if he were being paranoid, or had she tapped softly on the glass with her fingers?

She said to him, "I think you should go now. You've already said too much. But as for this firecracker incident, there's something else you should know." She reached in her robe pocket and withdrew a news clipping, handing it to him.

It was a piece from Hong Kong's English language

newspaper—a report on a Victoria Peak homicide investigation. Mai Twan's murder!

Yung Liu explained, "Take it along and read it carefully, Captain. You'll see that my sister was dead before this firecracker madman found her, that she died of a concussion from the fall. If this is so, you let her die, Captain. Murder, manslaughter, call it what you will. So go now, please. If there is some mad vulture on your trail, picking at the scraps and attempting to frame you, I can't worry about this. Perhaps I don't care. Maybe I hope this crazy eventually kills you as well. Leave me now, and don't bother our family again, please."

Bullock stared at her in disbelief. All this had to be a nightmare, some outlandish, grotesque fantasy. But why would she lie? He scanned the news article and saw to his amazement that it was all true. What would it be? A charge of manslaughter? Assault, complicated by hit and run? Bullock's heart thumped wildly in his chest. Suddenly his panicky concern was interrupted by a sound outside the window—*footsteps on creaking metal steps.*

Someone had been out there listening, watching them. Why? Pushing Yung Liu aside, he leaped for the window, threw the latch, and thrust it upward. Bullock crawled outside. The steel-grated landing was empty, but below him a shadowy figure slithered down the steep staircase to the street.

Bullock told himself fiercely, *Go after the snoop.* Find out what he wants. You may have to fight the bastard, but what the hell, you're already swimming with sharks in water over your head. But Bullock's mind was also urging restraint. It was impossible to think clearly after the shocker Yung Liu had given him. Glancing at her one more time, he took a deep breath and plunged down the fire escape steps.

By the time he reached street level, the eavesdropper had disappeared up the darkened alley. Bullock started to follow but changed his mind. It could be a deliberate trap. Considering for a moment, he decided to head for familiar territory. Going in the opposite direction, he found a cab at the corner and instructed the driver to take him back to the ship.

41

Watching silently from behind the one-way mirror, Steelbinder couldn't believe his good fortune. Captain Bullock, in his blind eagerness to track down an eavesdropper and bail out of Yung Liu's room, had left a trail of fingerprints on the window lock mechanism, the frame itself, and possibly the fire escape handrails. Excellent! The only part that bothered Steelbinder was *who* might have been outside the window. Possibly a false alarm?

He mulled it over in his mind. Besides himself, the only other person aware of Swain Bullock's relationship with the Hong Kong woman was Gecko Corman, but he was dead. Steelbinder considered what he'd just overheard, the harlot telling Bullock about Mai Twan's houseboy not being on leave after all. Might Sam Loo have witnessed the crime in Hong Kong? Had he come to San Francisco and stood guard outside Yung Liu's window? No, that lazy miscreant wouldn't have sent her a letter if he'd planned on coming to America. The snooper outside had to be someone from the cathouse checking up on the young prostitute, or a neighborhood voyeur.

Steelbinder watched through the mirror as Yung Liu swept across the room to close and relock the window. She then went over to the bed, wearily sat, and took her time lighting a cigarette. Steelbinder trembled slightly as a familiar power slowly, surely took hold of his body. As always , half his mind grappled with the reins, trying to keep the other half from stampeding. It never seemed to work, for it was impossible to stop the red fury once it started to pound in his veins.

While Captain Bullock had been in the adjoining room Steelbinder had sat hushed, looking on with interest and growing anticipation. Now he was restless and eager to get on with it; already, his forehead was covered with sweat and there was a familiar tingle in his groin. There'd be no necktie party this time. He would have to improvise. The window drapery cord would suffice.

Yung Liu sat on the bed, her legs crossed. Impatiently puffing her Krakatoa cigarette, she slowly looked up, focusing directly on the one-way mirror. He swallowed hard and edged back. The whore was smiling as if she was undressing him!

Abruptly, Yung Liu got up from the bed and came over to the glass. She gently tapped on it, beckoning to Steelbinder with a curved finger that he should come in and join her. How did she know he was behind the mirror, watching all the while? Had he made a noise or had the madam somehow alerted her?

Steelbinder bent down and put on his shoes. "Hmmmmm-nnnn," he mumbled. *Yung Liu was inviting him in?* Why was everyone being so cooperative, making his task so wonderfully simple? Well, their error. I'll soon see about this harlot's fearlessness and nonchalance. Withdrawing a pair of pre-talcumed rubber gloves from his jacket pocket, Steelbinder quickly slipped them on, then eased open the viewing chamber's door and glanced up and down the hallway to make sure he was unobserved. Stepping over to Yung Liu's door, he rapped softly. While he waited he thought about a line from Shakespeare: *The devil hath power to assume a pleasing shape.* It was hard to believe the young Chinese libertine was so trusting, inviting an unknown entity—a face behind a mirror at that— into her room. If she only knew she was summoning her own swift demise!

Steelbinder was glad for the relative simplicity of the scenario, especially after the complicated logistics required of him down in San Diego. Meeting Maxine Bullock outside that popular military bar the night before her eradication had not been without risk; he could have been spotted. But in the end, the scheme had worked perfectly, as would this one. This whore-bitch would be a mere token, for there were so many, but he was making progress. A beginning. The best part of all was shifting the blame, ostracizing his arch-enemy, Captain Bullock, seeing him wind up behind bars.

Yung Liu came to the entry. Steelbinder impatiently brushed her aside and entered her room, closing the door after him. The chamber stank from clove cigarettes and her perfume. The young prostitute studied his face, obviously disappointed. *Women always were.* She stepped back slightly, either taken aback by his ugliness or the cruel, hypnotic stare he had for her. She finally brightened, but it was only a facade. She said, "I suppose you were disappointed. Madame Fong should have provided you with a much better peep show. I'm afraid you witnessed only a personal tiff, which I hope you'll put out of your mind." Pausing, she smiled seductively. "Perhaps I can help you forget, at no extra charge? Though if I make you happy, you might consider a decent gratuity."

Steelbinder smiled inwardly. *The bitch is about to die, and she has the gall to ask for a fat tip!* Continuing to stare at her, his pulse quickened. "You knew I was in there?" he asked, keeping his voice to a coarse whisper. "I tried to be silent."

"I sometimes sense when there are customers behind the mirror." Yung Liu giggled. "But not in your case. What gave you away was a circle of condensation on the surface of glass. You stood too close." She winked at him, then tittered, "With your mouth open. You were breathing hard—for me?"

Glancing at his watch, he said to her, "How much time before the madam returns?"

"Since my last customer left early—and by the window—you've got fifteen minutes. Considerably longer if you go back downstairs and make additional financial arrangements."

Steelbinder frowned with annoyance. Wordlessly, he went over to the fire escape window and jerked the drapery closed. He turned and pointed to the circular bed and its fur spread. "I'm allergic to fur. Please remove it."

Yung Liu sighed and did as he asked.

While her back was turned to him, Steelbinder took out his Swiss army knife and severed a yard-long section of the drapery cord, quickly stashing it inside his windbreaker pocket.

When the sheets were bared and Yung Liu turned back to him, her face bore a puzzled, wary look. Eyebrows furrowing, she asked, "Your hands. Do you always wear rubber gloves? I mean, if you have a skin problem, I'd like to know."

Ignoring her, Steelbinder reached into the capacious pocket of his jacket and withdrew a forty-five record. Pulling the disc out of its paper sleeve, he asked thickly, "You do like rock music? Something by the Midnight Admirals?"

"Whatever you wish. But I'd be happier if you took off your coat and shirt. Have you some kind of rash? What about herpes?"

Annoyed, he glared at her. "I'm in perfect health. Far too clean for you, I suspect." He went over to the stereo player and fumbled with the control mechanism.

"You're a cocky bastard. Don't press your luck if you expect a good time." She came over to help him, and together they got the music going. "Heavy metal," she said with a frown, turning the volume down slightly. Steelbinder turned it back up.

Yung Liu slowly shook her head.

"They're a talented group. You'll see. It is the only rock group I trust with my writing."

"*Your writing*? You help with their music?"

He looked at her hatefully. "Soon, they'll discover the brilliance of my lyrics."

She shook her head and changed the subject. "Your rubber gloves—God, what next? I'm surprised you didn't bring in a wetsuit or a duffel bag full of toys. One character came in here earlier wearing a gorilla mask."

"What do you expect on Halloween?" Steelbinder went over to examine the bed. The sheets were a delicate pink with tiny red rosebuds that from a distance looked like polka dots. The pattern made him dizzy. "The bedding is clean? Do you change the sheets between customers?"

"Always. Madame Fong's has a classy reputation."

Steelbinder straightened out some of the wrinkles in the sheet, then turned back to her and unzipped his pants. His brain flashed back over the past month. Now that he was ready, the technicolor memories of the other indulgences became erotically sweet, adding to his anticipation of what lay ahead. He wheezed slightly as he stepped toward her.

"Take off your coat," Yung Liu instructed.

"No," he said firmly.

She stared back at him, not with professional nonchalance, but this time with obvious abject fear. Steelbinder was glad for this and smiled. It was as if the young hooker guessed from his eyes and heavy breathing that he wasn't just another seducer, but someone who wanted more than she was able to give.

"What's your name?" she asked stupidly, stalling for time.

Steelbinder didn't reply, instead inching toward her and repeatedly flexing his muscular shoulders under the windbreaker. He glared at her but said calmly, "You shouldn't have let the captain get away scot-free, my dear, if he's guilty of manslaughter. And that's only part of it. There's also the little matter of an attempted murder on the ship."

"What are you talking about?" Yung Liu asked, her voice breaking.

"Simple enough. Swain Bullock was being blackmailed by one of the crewmen. The captain tried, unsuccessfully, to silence him. It wasn't important. I took care of the job for him. Now I enjoy pulling the captain's strings at whim. He's my puppet. Can you understand that, Yung Liu?"

"No. I don't understand you at all."

"Then listen closely. Life is a continual battle between the spirit and wicked flesh. I have been spiritualized by God to triumph over the flesh—through my deeds humanity will be able to reach eternal felicity in the afterworld."

Frantic now, she edged away from him. "Why are you telling me this?"

"Like Dante, I have the power to transport you to another world and spiritualize you." Steelbinder went over to the door, threw the deadbolt and smiled dangerously. He started flexing his muscles again. "Now you won't die in total ignorance." He was fully prepared to pounce, cover the woman's mouth with his powerful hand if she screamed, but Yung Liu surprised him by merely sitting down on the bed and taking on a vampish pose. It was as if she'd heard it all before, that he was engaged in Halloween theatrics, and she was determined to call his bluff. No! She was reaching for something, under the side of the mattress. Whatever the whore creature was after, it wouldn't matter; she'd never find it.

Steelbinder leaped, his iron hands clutching the drapery cord, stringing it taut, flinging it forward, down and around. Cinching it up before she could let out a sound. Deftly twisting. Squeezing, and relishing every moment of it. Sealing her lungs tight and choking off the air.

For several seconds, he watched the young woman's arms flail on the bed and her face turn a ghastly off-blue. The twitching part of it always reminded Steelbinder of his childhood, the headless chickens flapping their wings after his grandmother wrung their necks. Gazing down into the prostitute's bulging, staring eyes he almost had an orgasm and had to think of other things in order to throttle back. *Not now, Roscoe, save the best until later*. Again he thought of Dante, the words from the *Inferno* he'd committed to memory. One canto in particular fitted the occasion perfectly:

> *Many are the animals that with her wed,*
> *And there shall yet be more, until the hound*
> *Shall come and in her misery strike her dead.*

When the hooker was absolutely still, Steelbinder undressed her. As he suspected, she wore nothing under the yellow silk robe. He was surprised to find her breasts so small and undeveloped, and wondered how old his victim might be. As with the others, Steelbinder spread-eagled the body across the bed. Hurriedly, he removed his jacket, sweater and T-shirt, but left his pants and shoes on. Standing before the mirror, where he could watch both his own body and the dead woman's, he masturbated, all the while flexing his deltoids and pectorals. It flashed on him that someone in turn might be observing his performance from the other side. He quickly dismissed the likelihood, for there were several minutes remaining of his allotted time.

When his narcissistic scene was concluded and the flood of pleasure had ebbed, he felt different sensations take over. First remorse, then anger, and finally a mood of reprisal. It was time to go to work. He put his shirt and the windbreaker jacket back on. Patting the pockets, he found the small plastic box, withdrawing from it a tuft of curly red hair. He scattered several strands on the sheets and pillow beside Yung Liu's body. Next, he carefully implanted the firecracker in the woman's mound, just as he'd done with the other victims. This time, lighting the fuse and immediately leaving the room wouldn't work. *He needed to buy time,* precious minutes to get away from the building in order to shift the blame. When the firecracker went off the whorehouse was sure to respond like an overturned hornet's nest.

Steelbinder found an ash tray and eased it between the dead prostitute's legs. Taking out the birthday candle he'd brought along, he melted some wax, then secured it upright in the ash tray. This time, as another precaution, he'd inserted a *double* four-inch fuse in the superfirecracker. He took his time, pushing the dead woman's pubic hairs aside as he carefully wound the fuse around the base of the birthday candle.

Satisfied with the improvised fuse delay, Steelbinder went over to the stereo player and tried, unsuccessfully, to get the record to repeat automatically. No luck. Mumbling some pithy observations, he abandoned the idea of music. Like a concerned stage manager prior to a curtain, he rechecked the scene carefully to make sure everything was in its proper place. Then he reopened the draperies and the fire escape window, just a crack. Going back to Yung Liu's body, he lit the small candle carefully with her Bic lighter. He then left the room, closing the door behind him before stripping off the rubber gloves and cramming them in his jacket pocket.

Humming softly and smiling to himself, Steelbinder slipped downstairs, then calmly walked over to where Madame Fong waited by the front door. She glanced at her watch and said cynically, "You still have ten minutes. The couple didn't excite you at all?"

Steelbinder thought quickly. "No. You were right. Unfortunately, that customer appears to know your girl too well. All they do is talk—and fight. They're still at it. I don't find old lover's quarrels sexually stimulating."

The older woman pursed her lips and thought for a moment. "Well, I did warn you. No refunds, but you're welcome to go back in the holding tank, see what else comes in."

Impatient, Steelbinder smiled at her. "No, thank you."

"Take my advice. " She gave him a friendly poke in the ribs. "Give up this voyeur nonsense. You have to learn to physically express yourself!"

Steelbinder nodded. "I just may do that. It's Halloween, and the evening is young."

Hurrying out of the whorehouse, Steelbinder was glad for the invigorating night air. He felt refreshed and completely satisfied. But he didn't have time to rest—not yet. He had to get back immediately, prepare for his big encore on the *Abraham Lincoln*—the big finish for Swain Bullock and the U.S. Navy.

It was still reasonably early, but Pamela's continuing travel and long workdays had finally taken their toll. She'd fallen asleep in the Golden Panda's lobby.

Lieutenant Chi had slipped in the front entry, and now his familiar voice at the desk, inquiring for messages, brought her wide awake. When the desk clerk gestured in her direction, Kenny Chi came over immediately, offering her his usual annoying smile. She noticed that the pants of his light gray business suit were soiled, as if he'd been crawling on his knees in a filthy attic or garage. Chi bowed slightly and said to her, "Miss Bonner. Indeed, this is a surprise. We meet earlier than expected. I was about to call your apartment in Los Angeles, hoping to convince you to fly up here tomorrow."

She looked at him seriously. "Do you intend to solve this case entirely on your own, Lieutenant Chi?"

Chi stiffened and took on his usual inscrutable air. "On the contrary. Now that you're here. . . ."

"Please, don't apologize," she rapidly interjected. "It appears you're not the only one winging it alone. I've telephoned the quarterdeck of the *Abraham Lincoln* and our friend Todd Dougherty is also out on the city. Where is he?"

"I'm afraid I have no idea."

"Odd. Considering the evidence to date, I'd have thought you'd both be trailing the captain. You have all the priorities. What do

I have to do, Lieutenant? Go out there and pound the streets myself to find Swain Bullock?"

"Patience, Miss Bonner, please." Chi gave her a patronizing smile. "Each of us have our own ways of doing things. Rare plants scattered in among common ones do better, often producing twice as many seeds. Do you know why?"

She looked at him, annoyed.

Chi extrapolated: "They do not compete. To better understand this, as detectives we should avoid being like birds that are tuned to eating red insects. We'll miss the purple and green bugs because we don't understand their nature. The man we're after is cunning, Pamela, *multi-hued*. He may be highly disturbed, but he's also a kind of genius. Swain Bullock, in my opinion, doesn't fit that description. He may be ambitious, smart and resourceful but hardly brilliant."

"I'm too tired for cleverness, Lieutenant."

Chi gestured toward one of the lobby sofas, and they both sat. Loosening his tie, he looked at her and said firmly, "I fear your suspicions regarding the captain are ill-founded, Miss Bonner. Indeed, it appears Swain Bullock is in considerable trouble, but he is not a pathological maniac."

Startled, she stared at Chi. "*Considerable trouble?* Would you mind qualifying?"

"Mai Twan has a sister here in the city. I'll take you to meet her tomorrow. She has a tape recording for us you'll find most interesting. And an important deposition to make."

Pam exhaled sharply. Had she been drowning in instinct, all wrong? "Lieutenant Chi, I won't sleep tonight unless you tell me now. If Bullock's not the repeat murderer, why are you pursuing him?"

The Chinaman pondered for a moment. "A matter of manslaughter. I hope to prove my point tomorrow. You must trust me."

Pam was fully awake now, a little beside herself. "You're being very smug, Lieutenant."

"Miss Bonner, tonight Captain Bullock left an elegant dinner early to go to a house of ill repute. He booked a room but only *talked* with one of the prostitutes—a woman who happens to be Mai Twan's sister. I assure you this young working lady was safe and very much alive when Bullock left her. I followed him back to the ship. The captain committed no crime in San Francisco." Chi got up from the couch and checked his watch. Noting that Pam was staring at his dirty trousers, he grinned. "The fire escape landing outside of Madame Fong's was a bit filthy, as you can see. Excuse both my appearance and fatigue, please. I now suggest we both get a good night's sleep so our heads will be clear for tomorrow."

Chi's words leavened Pamela's feeling of abandonment; as close now as she was to the action here in San Francisco, she felt drained and defeated, with no notion of what to do next. She said to the detective, "You've forgotten the murderer! He's out there then, free to strike when and where he likes. *Probably tonight.*"

Kenny Chi shrugged and said absently, "And precious little either of us can do about it until we have a suspect and a decent lead. Or he makes his move. Let's trust your friend Todd Dougherty is making progress aboard the carrier. We'll talk with him first thing in the morning."

"Sooner than that, I hope." Pam felt anxious and tight. "I left a message for him to call, whatever the hour."

"Fine. Good night, Miss Bonner. If you manage to reach him, I suggest we meet for an early breakfast."

Pam answered in a compressed voice, "The carrier's leaving tomorrow morning, and Dougherty may want to stay with it."

Detective Chi thought for a moment. "Then it's all the more important that the two of us resolve matters here in the city. If need be, we can hire a helicopter and catch up with Captain Bullock later." Chi sighed. "Good night, Pamela."

Pam nodded without enthusiasm. There was an uneasy silence as she watched Kenny Chi pad off to the elevator. She sat there for a long moment after he'd gone. Behind the registration desk, the switchboard buzzed. The night clerk answered the phone, then looked her way. "Pamela Bonner? You have a call." He gestured toward a nearby telephone.

Hurrying over to pick it up, she answered with an edgy, "Hello."

"Pamela? Sorry it took so long to get back. What the hell are you doing in San Francisco?" The voice was Dougherty's, and it sounded as beat as she felt.

"It's a weekend, my own time. Any objections?"

"None," he conceded. "Other than I miss you. Happy Halloween."

"Todd, we have to talk."

"That's an understatement." He paused. "Mind if I come by and spend half the night with you? I'm getting a little claustrophobic in my sea cabin."

"*Half the night*? Sounds a little like wham, bam, thank you, ma'am, to me."

Dougherty explained: "Sorry. Three or four hours is all I can spare. Looks like Captain Bullock's pulling a fast one on the news media. We're pulling out at five in the morning."

Her voice betraying emotion, she said to him, "I take it you're not finished? You have to stay with the ship?"

"Yes. You want me to come over or not?"

"Of course. Todd, I've talked with Lieutenant Chi. He's been following Swain Bullock all night."

"That's the first good news in the past few hours."

"The captain's clean. Nothing happened."

"I figured as much. It's what I've been trying to tell you for three days. He's a set-up, Pam. Twenty minutes ago I found another of those records by the Midnight Admirals. I'm certain it was planted in Bullock's day cabin."

"My god, you broke in while he was out?"

"No. Admiral Tanner let me in."

Pam's heart quickened. "Todd, tell me. You must have narrowed the list of suspects down by now. Give."

"I need more time—a matter of hours. We'll talk about it when I get there. This Golden Panda Hotel allow visitors in your room after ten p.m.?"

"Don't sweat it. I'll pay for a double and leave your hall pass at the front desk. Bye."

~~~~~42

Dougherty paused on the carrier's gangway, shivering in the predawn chill as he gazed back at the city. In the hills above the Embarcadero most of San Francisco still slept, oblivious to the carrier's burst of departure activity. Aware that the checklist for getting a ship the size of the *Abraham Lincoln* underway—even under Condition Four Peacetime Cruising—was like the countdown for a space shot, Dougherty reported back aboard a full hour before the moved-up embarkation time. Had he been an actual member of the crew, he'd have left the warmth of Pamela's bed at the Chinatown hotel even earlier. Dougherty stifled a yawn as he stepped out on the quarterdeck and saluted the Junior Officer of the Day. "I report my return, sir."

"Very well, Lieutenant Commander. Admiral Tanner left a message. He'd like to see you in his quarters—anytime after 0730."

Nodding, Dougherty headed for the escalator leading below. Several masters at arms passed by him, routinely searching the vessel for stowaways. Crew members, a few still buttoning their shirts, hurried to their at-sea watch stations. Dougherty reflected on what Pamela had relayed to him, before and after they'd made love. As soon as possible he needed to confront Captain Bullock, but he suspected this would be impossible until after the super-carrier had cleared port. Dougherty felt certain the homicidal madman who had the Navy by the balls was one of two enlisted men—Gecko Corman or R.W. Steelbinder. Both had the same blood type, though virtually nothing else in common. Unfortunately Aviation Boatswain's Mate Corman wasn't aboard the carrier. That shifted the focus to Petty Officer Second Class Steelbinder. If the sailor were clean, why would he have purposely eluded Dougherty in Chinatown?

The circumstantial evidence was growing, but the hard stuff still wasn't there. And Dougherty still had no surefire scheme to get it. The investigation was taking too long. God forbid, Pamela had even suggested calling the behavioral science types back in. What really worried Dougherty was what might have occurred during that hairy interval—the hour and a half time period between when he'd lost Steelbinder at the Belle Union Theater and when the quartermaster had nonchalantly reported back aboard the ship. Thankfully, Dougherty wouldn't have to go tomorrow to the San Francisco authorities, nosing around to make sure there were no unexplained Halloween mutilation murders. Pamela had promised to take care of that discomfiting chore for him.

He shuddered at the thought of a killing earlier tonight in the city—and for more than one reason. A swarm of local homicide detectives meant more bureaucracy to fight, having to go back, spending valuable time retracing the case from the beginning. There'd be the inevitable arguments over federal versus local jurisdiction, having to quote from the Universal Code of Military Justice, enforcing the authority of the Attorney General of the United States. The frustrating protocols would never end, and the investigation was already costing the taxpayers an arm and a leg.

At least he could take comfort that R.W. Steelbinder, for the moment, was safely ensconced in his bunk, asleep. Dougherty had checked earlier and learned the quartermaster wouldn't go on duty until 0800, when he would have the forenoon watch down in the aft steering room.

Reaching his own cabin, Dougherty opened the door and turned on the lights. His civilian tech rep roommate had left the ship in San Francisco, and Sol Steinberg had replaced him, appropriating the upper bunk. Steinberg rolled over, blinked his eyes, and said to Dougherty, "What's the hell's happening out there? All that noise—doesn't anyone ever sleep on this ship?"

Shrugging, Dougherty closed the cabin door. "We're getting underway four hours early. You clear it with the OD to stay aboard until Bremerton?"

Steinberg nodded. "Have a good time with the FBI woman?"

"What the hell's that supposed to mean?" Dougherty peeled off his shirt and pants and crawled in the lower bunk.

From above him, another query: "What did she learn from that Chinese detective?"

"Pamela's convinced that Kenny Chi's on to something important. I think she's also a little green with envy."

"First Fed woman agent I've ever met who's got both brains and sexy looks to spare. Tough luck you couldn't spend the entire night."

"Steinberg?"

"Yeah?"

"Leave Pam out of it." Dougherty's tone sharpened. "And don't press your luck because you're a goddamn civilian. You're in officer's country now, so let's show a little respect. For the record, I'm getting to like this shipboard protocol."

Above him, a clearing of the throat, followed by, "*Yes, sir, Lieutenant Commander*. But what do we do now?"

Dougherty closed his eyes. "We take it a step at a time. But with Bullock preoccupied sneaking us out of town early and Steelbinder getting his beauty sleep, I plan to get a few well-earned nods while I can. Wake me up at 0600." Dougherty shifted his brain into neutral and immediately drifted off to sleep.

Steelbinder didn't need the attenuated buzzer on his wrist watch to waken him at three. He'd been restless and oozing with anticipation, unable to sleep for the last half hour. Rolling out of the bunk, he grabbed his toiletry kit and headed for the latrine. A half hour later he was showered and dressed, leisurely sipping coffee from one of the vending machines.

Steelbinder skipped breakfast, hurrying up to the 08 level to report to the Quartermaster of the Watch. He would explain that he'd made arrangements to swap aft-steering-room duty shifts with one of the other helmsmen who claimed to be under the weather. Steelbinder knew the other man wasn't sick, merely an opportunist glad at the chance to sleep in. The sailor had figured Steelbinder had a screw loose for suggesting the switch. 0800 was a far more civilized hour to go to work than 0400, especially after a night of shore liberty.

To report to the QOW, Steelbinder had to enter the bridge area where the captain was already at work. He observed his arch-foe without being obvious. As stoic as ever, Bullock seemed no worse for wear, considering the bad news and emotional wear and tear he'd endured just a few hours earlier at the Chinese whore house. Bullock ignored Steelbinder, continuing to confer with the harbor pilot and navigator.

After getting the QOW's approval of the duty swap, Steelbinder left the bridge by way of the navigation room. He paused at the plotting table, permitting his eyes to roam over National Ocean Service Chart Number 18650, San Francisco Bay from Candlestick Point to Angel Island. Making sure he was alone in the room, he grabbed the three-arm plastic protractor. It took less than a minute to determine the course the Abraham Lincoln would be obligated to take once it rounded Alcatraz Island and entered the Westbound Ship Traffic Lane through the Golden Gate. 255 degrees magnetic. He reset the protractor and turned one of its arms. He calculated that a thousand yards out from the center span of the bridge, the ship would need only to turn twenty-five degrees for a rendezvous with disaster.

Committing the critical figures to memory, he strolled leisurely out of the chart room just as the assistant navigator entered. As Steelbinder expected, the lieutenant JG paid no attention to him. All qualified helmsmen were encouraged to study charts and books on navigation in their spare time, and Steelbinder's was a familiar face.

He sprinted down the island ladders, then headed aft along the hangar deck toward the carrier's stern. On the way he did some fast calculating. He knew that Captain Bullock's plan to embark four hours early in the darkness wasn't without minor complications. At five in the morning the tide would be at full ebb, running out through the Golden Gate at six knots. The *Abraham Lincoln*, to maintain comfortable steerage, would probably be doing 12 knots, which meant it would pass under the bridge at 18 knots. Roughly translated, he estimated the ship's speed at 600 yards per minute, 30 feet per second.

Reaching the vertical ladder to the steering chamber, Steelbinder started down, hand over hand. He knew that since the ship was in port, there'd be no midwatch to relieve; he and two assistants would be the first to stand the duty. The other men, a machinist and fireman, were already present. They didn't acknowledge his arrival by introducing themselves, for both were slouched on the floor against the bulkhead, sound asleep.

Steelbinder made no effort to wake them, in fact hoping they'd both stay that way for another hour. He didn't blame them for cat napping, for he, too, hated this boring assignment. To keep occupied and maintain a degree of sanity, all a man could do down here was sleep, read, or play cards. It would probably take a full-blown war alert to bring this and hundreds of other aft-steering rooms on U.S. Navy ships into optimum readiness.

Ignoring his sleeping companions, Steelbinder started down his personal checklist. The first task was to temporarily disable the squawk box system. *Do it now, while the other crewmen dozed.* Stepping quickly to the other end of the compartment, he used his army knife to disconnect the copper leads to the ceiling-mounted speaker. Communication with the bridge would now be confined to the 1JV telephone circuit, and he'd made sure earlier there would only be one headset in the chamber. As standby helmsman, he had first claim to it. The other two crewmen would have to speculate on what was happening topside.

"Where's Frenchie?" A groggy voice with a Brooklyn accent. One of his fellow duty men had awakened.

Steelbinder said to him, "We've swapped duties. I'm R.W. Go back to sleep if you want. I'll keep an eye on the ladder."

"Yeah? I might do that. Thanks."

"Don't mention it." Steelbinder smiled. He waited a few moments, then once more examined the two important pieces of equipment and their control mechanisms that would enable him—however briefly—to play God and be complete master of the carrier. Ninety seconds at the most—less than two minutes—was all the time he needed. The bridge control switch, shiny brass and oval-shaped, just large enough to fit in the palm of the hand, was at the top of an electrical panel behind the rudder engine.

Steelbinder smiled to himself as he recalled an incident he'd been warned about much earlier, a time when a crewman on the carrier *Ranger* had hung his jacket on a similar switch, inadvertantly throwing it clockwise. Immediately, the bridge helm was disconnected and the aft-steering room enabled; all hell broke loose for *ten minutes* before sanity prevailed and one of the engineers corrected the trouble. In the meantime the ship had swung in a helpless circle until the engines were stopped and reversed. Steelbinder wouldn't need *ten minutes* for what he had in mind, not in the narrow Golden Gate channel.

The other mechanism that was critically important to him was the auxiliary steering system itself, a wheel-like unit surmounting the ship's rudder that could be manually engaged by a slight shift of gears. The bridge would never know if the enabling device was activated unless notified on the 1JV or a troubleshooter was sent down here to investigate. An indicator on the bridge would alert the helmsman and captain to the position of the port side rudder, but they'd be helpless to correct its movement.

Satisfied with the equipment and the procedure he was committed to follow, Steelbinder once more checked his watch. Calmly, he sat down to wait. Both of his duty companions were snoring now. Good. The less conversation in the confining compartment, the better.

Overhead on the TV monitor, he could see crewmen scurrying over the bow, making last-minute checks on the aircraft tie-downs. He'd give anything for a second camera on the bridge, focusing on the captain when the time came. Swain Bullock was doomed, along with his ship. If the captain still thought the way to a flag promotion was to dish out hell with mustard and horseradish, he was in for a tremendous surprise. Steelbinder, together with his grandfather, was about to destroy Swain Bullock's career forever. The captain's piss and vinegar and all the Navy traditions in the world wouldn't save him now.

It all depended on timing, of course. Steelbinder knew that the *Abraham Lincoln* had twice the destructive force of any battle fleet sent out in World War II. In less than half an hour, if his damage estimates were accurate, all this weaponry would be rendered useless for weeks, possibly even months. Ship repairs took time. Equally important, and certainly more spectacular, would be the indeterminate fate of the Golden Gate Bridge itself. Would the 1930's geologist's prediction prove true? Even if the rock formation under the bridge pier held, what would be the cataclysmic effect on the steel tower itself when struck by the onrushing 93,000 ton supercarrier?

If Steelbinder were asked to describe the exhilaration and

euphoria he felt at this moment, he'd be at a loss for words. How dare Todd Dougherty, Pamela Bonner, and a few Navy quacks join forces against him! *Preposterous*! A Faustian rogue, a professional executioner, a philosopher, a tormented genius, a perfectionist—perhaps he was all of these. How dare Dougherty and his minions consider him deranged, a genetic misfit or like his mother, Felicia. *He wasn't like her at all!* Steelbinder had taken after his grandfather. Together they would continue to write the music of the times. If some here-today, gone-tomorrow rock group didn't play it, what did it matter? There would be others in the hereafter. He and his grandfather were timeless, embodying the cusp between illusion and disillusion!

Captain Bullock kept·a close eye on the bridge crew but had otherwise retreated into silence. When the carrier had cleared Alcatraz Island and turned to port, the harbor pilot set a temporary new course, straight down the bay toward the three white and two green lights that marked mid-span on the Golden Gate Bridge. The pre-dawn darkness was clear, free of fog, with a half moon on the western horizon. There was only a light breeze, and the water was calm, but the tide was flowing swiftly toward the sea and the long silhouette that was the *Abraham Lincoln* ran faster to keep ahead of it. Up ahead, the carrier's destroyer and frigate escort was already beyond the bridge and fanning out, starting their routine sonar pinging.

Bullock was glad to get away from San Francisco and the rotten headache the port call had brought him. No matter the gravity of the problem, however, he prided himself in being able to stow away troubles the moment he stepped back on the ship. There was nothing he could do about the Hong Kong tragedy now, so there was no use dwelling on it. He'd deal with the situation later, after delivering the nuke carrier to the Bremerton drydock. There would be time enough to think about it then.

Bullock could at least take pleasure that he'd avoided the major demonstrations set for the Embarcadero pier and the deck of the Golden Gate Bridge. Come daybreak, the motley crowd of protestors, along with the broadcast and print media, would be in for one hell of a surprise. Bullock glanced out the bridge window, checking the eastern horizon. Dawn was still forty-five minutes away. Another ten minutes and they would be out in the Pacific Ocean. Turning to the harbor pilot, he asked, "How's she responding?"

The pilot, a wiry, middle-aged Greek-American, looked over

the helmsman's shoulder, studying the bearing on the gyrocompass and the rudder indicator. "A little sluggish on the starboard corrections, Captain. Since we have the bay to ourselves, I'd suggest a few more knots speed."

The third mate stood ready at the engine telegraph, eyes flicking nervously between the harbor pilot and Bullock in his throne-like chair at the side of the bridge.

Bullock stared out into the night and the string of amber lights ahead that marked the Golden Gate's roadway. He gave the command to increase the carrier's speed from 12 knots to 16. The quartermaster of the watch noted the time, 0525, and entered the new engine command in the log. The *Abraham Lincoln's* combined speed, tide included he noted, would now be a fast 22 knots.

~~~~~~ 43

Steelbinder put on the communications headset. Huddled in the aft-steering room, he felt the increased vibration of the propellor shafts as the carrier increased speed. He figured the ship was carrying about three degrees of right rudder to hold her course, but all he could see in the overhead TV monitor was the bow of the carrier and the gentle curve of lights that was the bridge drawing closer and closer. The only way he would know the moment when the ship was within a thousand yards of the bridge was when the harbor pilot made a required change of course for the straight shot down the channel.

Finally the helmsman up above turned the wheel, and moments later, the carrier heeled, ever so slightly, to port. Steelbinder's heart pounded in his chest as he counted the seconds, ready to flip the rudder relay switch.

Now! He quickly threw it to the off position, relieving the bridge of all control of the port rudder. He then dove for the auxiliary steering mechanism, quickly engaged the ratchets, and turned the ten-inch brass wheel. The rudder and compass gradually responded. The carrier's hull came around even faster than he'd hoped.

Steelbinder glanced at the second hand of his watch. Timing and the vessel's forward momentum would determine his success. He was wise in disconnecting the squawk box. The cursing and frantic shouting coming over the 1JV telephone circuit were tough enough on his ears. Steelbinder ignored the QOW's urgent summons from above.

Suddenly, a second, more authoritative voice came through the earphones. "We have an emergency situation here," it crowed. "No response whatever on the port rudder! Port after-steering room, do you acknowledge? I repeat, after-steering room . . ."

Now another voice—young and anxious to be of service— interrupted. "Starboard room manned and ready, sir."

Again, the OD on the bridge: "Not you. Shut up, Fletcher. We're trying to raise Steelbinder. You asleep down there, Roscoe? What the hell's going on, quartermaster?"

Steelbinder added to the confusion by remaining silent, as planned. In the 1JV earphones he heard in the background more confusion, cursing on the bridge, the captain shouting to stop all engines.

Too late, fool. Steelbinder checked the second hand on his watch, then said into the intercom mouthpiece, "This is Petty Officer Second Class Steelbinder. Sorry, but there was a malfunction on the line, but I can hear you clearly now." Taking a deep breath, he lied again, "Having difficulty engaging the emergency steering, but I'm trying." In fact, he was having no trouble at all; the auxiliary system worked perfectly, and the supercarrier was turning precisely as he wanted toward its doomsday course. He only needed a *few more seconds*.

Steelbinder knew that upstairs they were trying desperately to regain control by over-correcting with the starboard rudder. With the ship's forward momentum, it wouldn't be enough. Next, Captain Bullock would use the engines on one side or the other, but it didn't matter; there wasn't enough time. Eyes on the TV monitor, Steelbinder threw his own helm farther to the left. The compass needle moved again, edging inexorably southward, approaching 255 degrees.

Steelbinder's frantic movements and shouting into the intercom had finally awakened the nearby machinist's mate. The sailor stumbled to his feet and said to him, "What the hell's going on?"

"Control malfunction up at the helm. Check out that faulty squawk box. And wake your pal. Have him climb out of here and find one of the engineers—fast."

The machinist's mate was groggy and too stunned to question

Steelbinder's instructions. He did as he was told, finding the loose wire on the loudspeaker intercom and repairing it. The second crewman hurriedly left the compartment. Had either man ventured up beside him and peered into the small overhead TV monitor, they'd have seen that *Abraham Lincoln* was rapidly closing on the Golden Gate's south tower.

"General Quarters! Condition Zebra!"

The bridge was in chaos. Swain Bullock was incredulous over what was happening to his ship. Not bothering to consult with the harbor pilot, he'd taken over command of the off-course super-carrier immediately. The vessel's sudden, uncontrolled yaw to port had at first been partially corrected, but now the helm had lost all control. The *Abraham Lincoln* continued to wander off course, striking out in a diagonal line across the ship channel. There was no traffic, but the huge carrier was now on a dead-run toward one of the bridge towers!

Bullock screamed for full speed astern, but he knew it was an empty gesture; the screws would require precious seconds to first come to a halt. Even then, there was the ship's 22 knot forward momentum. 93,000 tons of it. Bullock didn't want to think about the mathematical certainties, there wasn't time. No time for anything! Why weren't the rudders responding? His tortured gaze went from the rapidly closing bridge to the helmsman.

"Hard to starboard!" Bullock shouted again, uselessly. The bridge wheel was already over all the way, and still the compass turned in the opposite direction. 253, 254, 255. In a fraction of a second, Bullock's entire Navy career flashed before him then disappeared in a whiff of smoke. Was this scene of helplessness to be his horrible destiny? The Golden Gate tower loomed closer. He wanted to be sick, but there wasn't even time for that. As the concrete pier and soaring steel tower bore down on them, Bullock instinctively drew back from the bridge widows, bracing himself against the gyrocompass.

Steelbinder could hear all four screws finally spin backward, digging great voids in the water of San Francisco Bay. He smiled, keenly aware that it was too late; the vessel's fate was sealed. The awakened fireman had repaired the squawk box, and now he, too, could hear the amplified bedlam carried down from the helm.

Steelbinder no longer needed the compass. His tortured gaze was riveted to the TV monitor. Plunging ahead, the broad, scythe-like bow of the carrier was about to strike the bridge tower head-on.

The curious fireman came up beside Steelbinder and glanced up at the TV. The color rapidly drained from his face, and he instinctively drew back, bracing himself for the impact. Steelbinder, too, held on.

The supercarrier struck hard. Both of them were hurled to the deck by a shock that thundered from stem to stern. After a few moments, Steelbinder gathered himself together and stood up, gloating. Had he been alone in the chamber, he would have cheered. *Mission accomplished.* He'd caught the captain asleep with his main sheet belayed. *There was no excuse for a collision at sea.* Captain Swain Bullock, as far as the Navy was concerned, had run out of past, present, and future.

Steelbinder squinted at the TV monitor. Something was wrong, not quite right with the results of the crash. Puzzled, he shook his head in disbelief. The bridge was still there—defiant, unmoving, as if defying him! Intact, as solid as ever! The ship was at a standstill, even though the propeller shafts were still struggling in reverse.

On the TV screen he could see the shocked crewmen on the flight deck pick themselves up and run forward to check the damage. They were nuzzled right up against the tower. One F-14A had apparently broken away from its deck tie-downs and hung precariously over the bow.

Making sure the other man in the compartment didn't see him, Steelbinder went over to the rudder relay switch and covertly flipped it back to the correct "on" position. As before, he used a handkerchief to muffle the pronounced click and to avoid leaving fingerprints. Then he went over by the exit ladder, sat down on the deck, and waited for the inevitable arrival of an angry engineering officer.

The Golden Gate Bridge was apparently still intact. Why? The carrier had to have sustained major damage. Steelbinder could still hear the engines straining in reverse, yet the ship hadn't budged. He guessed the bow was caught up on the bridge footing. Was it possible that he'd miscalculated the tower set-back and the bow's overhang by only a matter of inches?

Steelbinder's curiosity was getting the better of him. If they didn't come down that ladder soon, he would leave his post, go up and . . . *wait, pay attention!* A voice was summoning him on the intercom! He'd almost forgotten he still had the 1JV unit on his head; in the earphones his name and rank were being repeated for the third time. It was the head navigator, ordering him to report to the command bridge on the double. Shrugging, he took off the headset and handed it to the confused fireman. "Your show now. They want me topside." Smiling secretly, Steelbinder climbed the ladder out of the chamber.

The general quarters alarm sounded, but before Dougherty could sleepily crawl down from his bunk, he was suddenly thrown out by a sudden, horrendous impact. Instinctively, he knew one of two things happened: the ship had either been torpedoed or run into something solid. Being an optimist abut the chances of war, Dougherty hoped it was the latter. He picked himself up off the floor, rubbed a bruised shoulder, and hurriedly dressed.

Sol Steinberg had somehow managed to stay in his top bunk, but now he, too, was throwing on a shirt. "Jesus! What happened?" he asked.

Dougherty checked his watch. It wasn't even five-thirty yet. "We've either run aground or hit a ship." He knew they still had to be in San Francisco Bay. The wall speaker crackled again; this time it was an urgent-voiced OD summoning key personnel to the bridge. Dougherty heard a half-dozen names and was surprised to hear that the last one was Petty Officer Second Class Roscoe W. Steelbinder.

"Steinberg, get up to the bridge. Stay in the background, but find out what's going on. And take your radio-pack with you to keep in touch."

His assistant asked him, "You're not going up on deck?"

"Later. Right now I intend to take advantage of the confusion. You may have checked out Steelbinder's bunk area earlier, but I want to nose around myself. With all this hell breaking loose, now's the perfect time." Dougherty pocketed his own radio, and both men hurriedly left the compartment. At the end of the corridor, they took ladders in opposite directions.

Dougherty slid down to the next deck and crossed to the opposite side of the ship. The passageways were crowded with crewmen, most of them hurrying to muster. The men looked more confused than afraid. Dougherty assumed the ship wasn't in serious trouble—unless a nuclear war was underway and they were about to be vaporized. As for navigational calamities, he knew that with two-thousand-plus watertight compartments to rely on, the *Abraham Lincoln* was virtually unsinkable. The supercarrier took up a lot of water and had probably run aground in the bay. As curious as Dougherty was over what happened, right now he was worried about his murder suspect, R.W. Steelbinder.

Earlier, Steinberg had explained that among the quartermaster's belongings, he'd spotted a U.S. passport. Steinberg admitted that he'd been pressed for time during the illegal search and in his haste hadn't examined the inside of the travel document, nor had he gone through a stack of business envelopes nearby that may have been important. It now occurred to Dougherty that Steelbinder, as a Navy crewman, didn't need a civilian passport for his travel to Hong Kong. His green military I.D. card would have sufficed.

Dougherty felt in his pocket for the key the ship's locksmith had fabricated for him earlier. Like Steinberg, he'd have to work illegally, and quickly, before being discovered. Predictably, the cubicle of bunks was empty. The crew was either at emergency stations or up on deck, gawking.

Steelbinder's vertical locker contained civilian apparel—the same clothes he'd worn ashore earlier. Methodically going through the pockets of the yellow windbreaker, Dougherty found a plastic bottle of pills, half-full. *Valium*. It was filled by a Honolulu pharmacy, but the name on the label wasn't Steelbinder's. The prescription belonged to Didi Tyler—*the deep-freeze prostitute*. Dougherty stared at the label, feeling a sudden elation.

Steelbinder was no longer just a primary suspect; he was guilty in big neon letters. Dougherty was reluctant to put the pill bottle back, but he had no choice; he'd repeat the search later, legally, with a warrant or signed orders. The only other item in the jacket pocket was a ticket stub from the Belle Union Theater. *Unimportant*. Closing and relocking the cabinet, he went over to the capacious drawer under Steelbinder's bunk. The second key required a little jostling, but finally the clasp gave.

Just as Steinberg had reported, the quartermaster's belongings were meticulously organized. The toiletries bag was on top, in it a package of Preparation H suppositories. Dougherty looked for the items that had most surprised Steinberg—the tattered admiral's hat and pressed officer's khakis. They were gone. Had Steelbinder removed them sometime in the past four hours? Dougherty felt a stab of panic. What was the madman up to now?

At least the U.S. passport and envelopes were still here. Dougherty examined the passport, discovering that it wasn't Steelbinder's at all, but belonged to a *Beth Twan*. He instantly recognized the picture under the embossed seal. It was the same Chinese woman in the photo Pamela had given him days earlier:

the snapshot of Swain Bullock and Mai Twan in front of a Rolls
Royce! Beth and Mai had to be the same person. Dougherty noted
the passport had been diagonally rubber-stamped across the first
page with the word DUPLICATE. Suddenly, as if to complicate
matters for him even more, a photo fell out of the passport. It, too,
was a duplicate—the same picture of the captain and Mai by the
Rolls.

It didn't make sense. Why had Steelbinder been so thorough
about everything else, yet so sloppy about stashing the incriminating passport and snapshot? Had he planned to put them to some
diabolical use here on the ship? Dougherty opened the fat business
envelopes to discover four packets of color prints. Gecko Corman's name was on the processing labels. There were fifty or sixty
photos of classic automobile hoods, each shot favoring the
radiator cap ornament. *Quality photographic work*, Dougherty
noted. He thumbed through the pictures, pausing to admire one
particular mascot on the front of a 1920 Mercer. Todd wanted
desperately to learn more about Steelbinder, but these photos—
apparently belonging to Gecko Corman—only added to his
confusion. Dougherty next examined a manila folder. Nothing but
old bills and a San Diego storage unit agreement. Taking out his
memo pad, he made a note of the address.

There was something else in the folder—a dog-eared piece of
paper that had turned brittle and yellow with age. He carefully
unfolded the document and looked it over. It was a Navy order—
an old one—dated February 12, 1942. A summary court-martial
conducted during the war at Pearl Harbor, Hawaii. Dougherty
read on. The name Rear Admiral Gerald Eisenbinder meant
absolutely nothing to him, but whoever the poor bastard, he'd
been demoted to Commodore and forced into an early retirement.

Dougherty put the documents and the classic auto photos back,
exactly where he found them. Staring at the drawer, he weighed
the possibilities. Steelbinder had to be involved in some horse
trading, and Gecko Corman was involved. Dougherty was about
to close the drawer when another object caught his eye—
something Steinberg hadn't mentioned after his first go-around.
Using his handkerchief, Dougherty lifted the small, clear plastic
box by its edges. Inside were several tufts of curly red hair.

"Lieutenant Commander Dougherty, please report immediately
to the flight deck." The metallic voice coming from the nearby
squawk box was Sol Steinberg's. The NIS assistant had somehow
managed to borrow the priority, all-ship MC circuit. Assuming the
summons was important, Dougherty hastily put Steelbinder's

belongings back as he'd found them and locked up. He headed topside, sprinting up the escalator steps.

Dougherty walked out on the flight deck but immediately braked to a halt, doing a double-take, like everyone else, at the mind-boggling sight of the Golden Gate Bridge square in the aircraft carrier's lap. An urgent chattering came from his Motorola pack-set. Dougherty put the radio to his ear and turned down the volume.

Steinberg announced, "Sorry, Lieutenant Commander, to bug you down below on the ship's squawk box, but these walkie-talkies are useless inside the steel hull. I'm up here on the signal bridge."

Dougherty looked up, found his assistant, and nodded. He said into the radio, "What do you have up there? How did it happen?"

"The captain's raising hell, trying to find out. The helmsman from the aft-steering room on the port side is still missing. I'm afraid it's your diabolical friend Steelbinder."

Dougherty tasted bile in his throat. "Tell Bullock I've seen the evidence. Roscoe's our man. And he's not in his cubicle; I just came from there."

Steinberg pointed forward. "Probably out on the bow with the other rubbernecks."

Instinctively, Dougherty felt for the gun that wasn't there. Instead of a shirt uniform, he should have worn a jacket with a holster underneath. No time to go all the way back down and fetch either now. "Steinberg, I'm going out and look around. Keep a watch up on the 08 level in case he shows up. No telling what he might try with the captain."

"Be careful, Todd. The bastard knows what you look like. Remember what he did to Harris."

"Yeah, I remember. Ten-four." Dougherty started across the darkened deck. Damage control parties were already stringing power lines and preparing to hook up portable lights over the damaged bow.

Dougherty looked up, shaking his head in disbelief. They were two leviathans, one-on-one. A mighty supercarrier interlocked with a giant suspension bridge was an awesome sight, one he wasn't likely to forget. For a brief moment Dougherty forgot the killer at hand, his mind preoccupied with the import of the collision itself.

44

Dougherty stepped forward cautiously, keeping to the shadows of the jet aircraft that lined both sides of the flight deck. He was convinced that what had happened to the carrier was more than bad luck; Roscoe Steelbinder had to have had a hand in this.

Dougherty edged closer to the forward lip of the flight deck, the wide section of the bow extending from the forecastle. Beside him, one of the chiefs shouted for a yellow shirt to fetch a tow tractor. A damage control party was struggling in the darkness to secure the F-14A that hung precariously overboard. Dougherty's eyes scanned methodically over the men around him. He felt like an arson investigator at a fire, hunting for some mischievous firebug who might have pissed or come in his pants from the excitement.

The steel tower of the suspension bridge was so close Dougherty could almost reach out and touch it from the carrier. Just three more feet and the carrier's overhanging deck would have struck it. The area was a beehive of officers who had come out to investigate, but in the darkness it was difficult to make out faces. Suddenly, Dougherty caught a glimpse of an admiral's star on a shirt collar. Rear Admiral Tanner? No, this individual was tall and broad-shouldered; Fritz Tanner was short and pear-shaped. *The uniform in Steelbinder's locker*! Dougherty's heart did a burial-at-sea drum roll as he edged closer then halted. Even in the darkness, he was certain that it was Steelbinder underneath the tarnished scrambled eggs and lightning bolts on that officer's cap! The bogus admiral carried a fire axe and had a canvas bag of signal flares strapped over his shoulder.

Dougherty's breath quickened as he moved in closer. He saw that Steelbinder was behaving erratically—teeth set, lips twitching like an animal's. The man looked angry and out of control, likely to try anything.

Suddenly Steelbinder loped off into the shadows, hunkering around the far side of the damaged F-14A. Dougherty warily followed after him, trying to get as close as he could. He watched Steelbinder creep up to the precariously hanging jet and measure it with his eye—first one of the aircraft's wings, then the Golden Gate's concrete pier just below, then the wing again. No, it wasn't the wing itself that had caught his eye, but the fighter's *fuel tanks*!

Dougherty groaned. One slash with the axe through the Tomcat's aluminum skin and the deck would be awash with JP-4 fuel. The volatile spill would flow over the forward lip of the carrier, raining down on the bridge pier and tower! One match was all that it would take to get an inferno going.

Dougherty bolted, screaming at the same time. "Stop that man with the axe!"

He was too late. Steelbinder managed to take a mortal whack at the underside of the Tomcat's wing. Fuel gushed out on the deck and cascaded over the carrier's bow.

Eager for a chance to play hero and not the least intimidated by Steelbinder's admiral's uniform, a half-dozen sailors took off after him. Steelbinder cursed them soundly, flung the axe overboard, and started running—the wrong way. Trapped, he had nowhere to go but the end of the flight deck. Confronting Steelbinder was the waist-high chain temporarily strung out across the bow to prevent ship's personnel from accidentally slipping over the brink.

Frantic, Steelbinder unhooked the chain, heaving a section of it over the bow several feet upwind from the spilled fuel. Before Dougherty and the others could reach him, he'd crawled over the curved lip of the deck and begun hand-over-handing it down to the concrete pier directly below. The drop was less than fifteen feet.

Dougherty paused, then pushed the other sailors aside. "Stay on the carrier! The engines are still straining in reverse, and the hull could slip off that pier at any moment." Dougherty started down the chain. Below him, having reached the dubious safety of the pier, Steelbinder was casting about for his next move. He glanced up at Dougherty then disappeared around the base of the reddish-orange, monolithic tower that occupied most of the concrete pier.

Dougherty followed. After slithering down the chain to the pier himself, he saw the reason the *Abraham Lincoln's* protruding flight deck had not crashed into the Golden Gate's tower. Dougherty stared with amazement at the lower part of the supercarrier's bow, noting that the bottom of the tower was surrounded by an oval-shaped concrete fence—or fender—to keep back the angry sea and tides. Inside this barrier was a small moat of placid water. The carrier's bow had struck the eight-feet-thick outer wall, and a section of it had collapsed, along with it a few watertight compartments of the ship. Already a damage control specialist was being lowered over the side on a bos'n's chair, inspecting the grotesquely twisted steel with a powerful searchlight. The aircraft carrier's bow seemed to be hung up on the shattered concrete barrier.

Dougherty quickly put the *Abraham Lincoln's* problems aside and concentrated on his own challenge. Avoiding the rain of jet fuel, he edged along the side of the pier, his back pressed against the cold steel rivets of the tower. He found a door marked ELEVATOR, but it was locked. Dougherty hesitated, weighing the danger of moving on, turning the nearby corner.

He called out, "Steelbinder! You're wasting time! We both know you're trapped, so give it up now."

The response was a long laugh—contemptuous and unsettling. "We've only begun to play hide and seek, Lieutenant Commander. Why not invite Captain Bullock down here to join us? Or is he too preoccupied with his ailing ship?" Steelbinder's voice echoed against the carrier and back across the moat; Dougherty could only make a vague guess where his opponent was hiding. Was he behind the nearest leg of the tower or the far one?

Dougherty bolted across the fifty feet of clear area between the two huge steel uprights. Somewhere above him, on the bridge roadway, he heard sirens. Soon the entire city and half of Marin County would be alerted to the accident. Up on the carrier's deck, a damage control crew was washing down the bow with high-pressure hoses. A couple of crewmen had rigged up a powerful light, shining it in Dougherty's direction. Instead of improving the situation, it blinded him.

He shouted up to them, "No! Turn it the other way, over to the right!"

The men complied. As the beam swept across the pier, Dougherty saw a figure force open a small door in the side of the tower. Caught in the light, Steelbinder briefly glared at Dougherty with cold, predatory eyes, then disappeared inside the steel structure.

Dougherty grimaced at his lack of foresight. Besides the elevator, of course there had to be a *staircase*. The bridge's riveted towers weren't solid steel, but hollow, completely honeycombed from bottom to top. He spoke impatiently into his pack-radio: "Come in, Steinberg. You there? Sol, I need you, dammit."

"Ten-four. I'm here, boss. Go ahead."

"I've found Steelbinder, and I'm going after him inside the bridge tower."

"You want me to join you with a couple of masters at arms?"

"No. You might not make it back before sailing time. Besides, this isn't our turf. Out here I need some civilian authorities. And it sounds like a few of them have arrived upstairs."

"About this *sailing time*—so far it doesn't look like we're going anywhere. Over."

"You will. The tide's about to change and come roaring back in. If I know Bullock, he won't stick around here to lick his wounds. Steinberg, get over to the ship's radio shack and contact the FBI. Alert them to meet me up on the roadway, near the south tower. Over."

"Lieutenant Commander, you forgetting something? Ms Bonner's in town. Your partner, remember?"

"Go ahead, roust her out of bed. A hotel called the Golden Panda. You reading all this?"

"Yeah. I'll get on it right away. Ten-four."

Clipping the radio back on his belt, Dougherty stealthily approached the swinging steel door to the tower. Amber light from within streaked out on the pier and water below. Cautiously, an inch at a time, he looked inside, but to his disappointment saw no convenient staircase leading upward—only a dimly lit shaft the circumference of a phone booth with a steel ladder extending into infinity. Dougherty could see a blurred image far above him and hear Steelbinder's feet clunking on the steel rungs. The chamber smelled damp and musty.

He shouted upward. "It's a dead end, Roscoe! They'll be waiting for you on the bridge roadway! You're trapped."

"Never! And stop calling me Roscoe. As of now, it's Rear Admiral Steelbinder. You didn't hear of my promotion, Lieutenant Commander?" Steelbinder's laugh echoed down the shaft.

Gritting his teeth, Dougherty warily started up the rungs of the ladder. He wondered how many there would be and whether the madman above him would stop at the roadway level or continue all the way to the top of the tower. *Admiral*! Dougherty grumbled the word to himself, then shouted, "You're a demented, sadistic butcher, Steelbinder. That's all you deserve to be called."

"Better save your breath, Dougherty! It's a prolonged climb." A lengthy pause, followed by, "What's in this pursuit for you? Another stripe? A promotion, like Captain Bullock expects?" Steelbinder hesitated again, apparently to catch his breath. Above Dougherty, the footsteps on the ladder also stopped. Then again the cocksure voice: "You want stars for your collar, too? Here, Dougherty, take mine! I have no further use for them!"

Dougherty heard a small clattering sound. One of the brass collar emblems stung as it bounced off his head. The second star missed him. Both plummeted to the bottom of the shaft. Dougherty leaned as best he could to one side of the ladder in case Steelbinder dropped something heavier and deadlier.

"Why the flag-rank masquerade, Steelbinder?"

"All the world's a stage, Dougherty! You should know that! You really should have brought Pamela along. She seemed to be quite taken up with my acting ability a few days back. Perhaps I have a better handle on Ms Bonner than you do, my friend."

"Leave the woman out of it." Dougherty paused to catch his breath. The dank steel walls closed in on him, and he didn't rest for long. He swore again and resumed his climb.

Again he heard Steelbinder's voice: "Hmmmmm-nnnn. You and your ilk will never understand a creative force like me, because you lack the capacity to understand. Listen to me carefully, Mr. Investigator, and not your shrink friends. I suspect they think I'm just another creature molded by a state where the virus of schizophrenia and violence are routine. Hardly. R. W. Steelbinder has risen above the rabble."

The clanking footsteps above Dougherty stopped. Steelbinder's voice resumed, "Ah! What have we here? I'm sorry, Lieutenant Commander, but our delightful conversation must be terminated. It appears I've found an exit door. And another light switch. Perhaps you would prefer to climb in the dark."

The lights in the shaft abruptly went out. Dougherty tried to climb faster, groping in the blackness, but he was running out of steam.

Suddenly a deafening pistol report reverberated down the shaft. With it came a flashing hot projectile that missed Dougherty's shoulder by inches. All he could do was flinch, press himself against the ladder, and feel the searing heat as the flare shot past.

Dougherty was lucky, for his left shirtsleeve and his shoes were soaked with jet fuel. The star shell struck the bottom of the honeycombed shaft and burned intensely. Squinting against the brilliant green light, Dougherty held his breath and double-timed it up the remaining rungs of the ladder. Luck was still with him; with the exits closed at the top of the shaft and the door below left open, the acrid smoke was drawn out at pier level.

Dougherty found the metal door Steelbinder had evidently escaped through, pushed it open, and stepped out on the bridge's pedestrian walkway. He expected to see his quarry darting away along the span, but instead Dougherty was confronted by two members of the Golden Gate's security patrol. "Which direction did the other naval officer go?" he asked them breathlessly.

The two guards looked at each other. Shrugging, one said to Dougherty, "You're the only one to come out of there."

Dougherty snapped, "Impossible. I followed him."

The second guard shrugged. "We were about to take the elevator down to investigate the collision damage."

Dougherty glanced back inside the shaft, then closed the door to hold down the smoke. He'd blundered. There was only one place Steelbinder could have gone—straight up into the darkness. Dougherty took out his radio pack-set. "Steinberg, come in, please."

"Yeah, chief. I'm standing by. Over."

"Look, let me know fast. How many cartridges do one of those emergency flare kits contain? Don't ask why, just find a signalman and get back to me. Ten-four."

Less than a third of the way up the shaft, Steelbinder came upon a hatch he could only assume was some kind of fire block. He threw the hatch open, scurried through, then closed it behind him. He sat in the dark to catch his breath, glad to be rid of the acrid smoke from the flare below. Lighting a match, he saw the hatch had no lock mechanism and could be easily opened from either side. He couldn't stay here; despite the darkness, he had to keep moving, struggle all the way to the top of the tower.

Steelbinder thought about the remaining three flare cartridges in his kit. He was determined not to waste them. When he reached the top of the tower he'd fire one down at the bow of the carrier itself, into the volatile JP-4 fuel leaking onto the Golden Gate's tower and pier. Another flare would be fired into the night sky when the press media arrived. Very important that they see clearly what he and his grandfather had wrought in all its perspective. Though he'd miscalculated the strength of the concrete fender surrounding the pier, half a spectacle was better than none at all. Steelbinder could at least add a little color to the collision drama by getting a conflagration going. And what better place to conduct this *fantastico finale* than from the top of one of the Golden Gate's seven-hundred-feet high towers?

As a precaution he would save the last flare for his own protection. If Todd Dougherty or anyone else chose to follow him up here, there would be no more near-misses. By waiting and firing at close range, he could burn a hole right through any opponent's body.

Steelbinder continued the monotonous climb. Hand over hand. One foot, then the other. Rivulets of sweat coursed off his forehead, but he was in excellent shape and his pumped-up biceps handled the strain easily. His chest expanded and contracted rhythmically, taking in big lungfuls of air with virtually no effort. Every fifty feet or so Steelbinder paused on the rungs to light a match and listen carefully. It didn't do any good to look down, for there was only blackness. So far, so good. No one followed; *they knew he had the flare pistol*. The clammy, rivet-studded shaft grew eerily silent; this high up even the sound of the bridge's roadway traffic had quieted.

With the periodic pauses, it took him almost ten minutes to reach the top. A small doorway led out to a precarious, windy perch he would share with the cable saddles and a rotating red aerobeacon. Steelbinder pushed his grandfather's hat down farther on his forehead and surveyed the lofty realm. Once he got used to the height and the shrieking wind, it would be the perfect place to play king of the mountain! In every direction, the view was beyond superlatives.

To Steelbinder, the best view of all, of course, was the *Abraham Lincoln*, stretched out below him. Immobile and canted at an angle to the bridge, the helpless carrier had come alive with work lights on its deck. The waters off the stern were unruffled now, the vessel's giant screws apparently stilled while waiting for the tide to change. Steelbinder cursed the 1930's geologist whose earth movement prophecies now seemed unfounded. Far from undergoing death throes, the Golden Gate's south tower, pier, and span itself seemed as stout as ever.

Steelbinder couldn't see underneath the warship's overhanging flight deck, but from the reflections on the water he suspected an emergency repair crew was at work with cutting torches. Probably trying to clear away sections of steel hung up on the Golden Gate's concrete fender.

Steelbinder pulled out his flare gun, pushed in another cartridge, and studied the supercarrier. His enthusiasm for starting a conflagration on the ship's bow ebbed, for he could see a tractor had pulled the damaged Tomcat back on deck and fire control crews were washing down the area with high-pressure water hoses. *Too late*. There wouldn't be enough jet fuel let to set off a campfire, let alone an inferno! Steelbinder cursed as he searched for another target of opportunity. He desperately needed to think.

Sitting down under the flashing red aerobeacon to get out of the wind, he scanned the eastern horizon and the 180-degree panorama of lights that was San Francisco Bay. San Francisco and Oakland were the brightest jewels of all—standing out like diamond-studded carpets under the night sky. Off in the distance, another helicopter was heading this way, and already there were sirens and a string of red blinking lights on the bridge's approach road. Heading down mid-channel was a fast-moving boat, probably the local Coast Guard cutter. *Let them all come! The more the merrier.*

Steelbinder was startled by a jarring ring that sounded like a schoolhouse firebell. It was coming from an oval-shaped steel box near the hatch to the accommodation ladder. On the other side of it was a larger door he hadn't noticed before, apparently the elevator access. Steelbinder climbed to his feet and ventured over to the telephone box. Throwing it open, he stared irritably at the handset as it rang several more times. He finally jerked it from the hook. Cautiously, he said, "Yes?"

"Look, wiseass. This is Bridge Security. You mind identifying yourself before the wind up there blows you into oblivion?"

"Try Rear Admiral R. W. Steelbinder on for size."

"Sure, pal. Whatever you say. There's a naval officer down here who claims you're dangerous, that you're armed."

Steelbinder laughed. "Indeed. When the press arrives, I may demonstrate my weaponry. Unless you force me to use it on you in the meantime."

"Look, Mr. Steelbinder . . ."

"That's *Admiral Steelbinder*, please."

"We don't give a shit who you are or what you're running from. It's our job to just get you off the bridge—no harm to you or anyone else, okay? So be a good boy and cooperate. Come down now, quietly, before our A-team gets here."

Steelbinder huddled over the phone box to shield it from the wind. "Bring whatever professional assistance you require. All I ask is that you give the press decent seats up front."

"Look, pal, do us a favor? In another twenty minutes the morning rush traffic begins. Steelbinder? You still there?"

"I'm listening."

"I've got a job to do, all right? If you're planning to jump, asshole, how about making it easier? Like giving me some information first? Social security number and next of kin? You have any phone numbers we can call, how about friends in the Bay area?"

Steelbinder said angrily, "Stop your blathering and put Lieutenant Commander Dougherty on the wire."

A lengthy pause, followed by, "Okay, Roscoe. I'm here, now what?" Dougherty's voice could barely be heard over the din of the nearby traffic.

"Talk louder, Dougherty! Tell me, how many of you down there? What are my odds?"

"Steelbinder, get it through your head. It's over!" Dougherty's voice came in loud and clear. "Besides the bridge security types, you've got a couple of California Highway Patrolmen to contend with and more on the way. Try their patience too long, and they'll send in a sharpshooter in a helicopter."

"That's laughable, Dougherty. No, you'd never permit that. You need me to talk. I'm the only one who can tell you the truth about Captain Bullock. The Navy comes first, Lieutenant Commander. Have you forgotten?" Steelbinder smiled to himself as he heard cursing and an argument at the other end of the line. Jurisdiction, quibbling over authority? Let them battle over procedure; he had all the time in the world.

While Steelbinder held the receiver to his ear and waited, his mind began to wander. In the past hour he'd handled everything a task at a time, a minute at a time. He'd come to no conscious decision to stay up here, to die on the bridge; it was just something his mind grasped instinctively and accepted. Staring down at the damaged supercarrier, he felt grandly triumphant but at the same time saddened. The games with Swain Bullock specifically and the U.S. Navy in general were drawing to a close. Finished.

For Steelbinder, too, the rotting reins of a military career, the restraints confining him to rationality that had first parted in Hong Kong—it was over. Playing Captain Bullock for the patsy had been a thrilling challenge, but now it was time to pay the piper and move on to bigger things. Was that fear he felt ballooning in his stomach? No, never fear! Think of the future, not of the past and present! Above all, *he would not retreat*.

Perhaps he'd abandoned the aircraft carrier too hastily. Even if he managed to squeeze out of this, he'd have to run and keep running—a fugitive. His earthly world would come apart, and he'd be helpless. No! Rather than face the hounds alone, he would be better off joining Gerald Eisenbinder. *You could even change your name again, R.W.! Go back to Eisenbinder*. Together, he and his grandfather could accomplish anything. Steelbinder listened hard for the old man's words of wisdom, but with the wind howling over the top of the tower, it was difficult, very difficult to hear the familiar voice from the sea.

"Steelbinder! You still there?" It wasn't his grandfather but Dougherty shouting again in the telephone earpiece. This time he ignored the NIS man until the muddiness in his head lifted. Finally, he said, "You're after the wrong man, Dougherty. Captain Bullock's the killer you're after. Consider all the evidence!"

"Yeah? Then what are you doing up there, running away?" Dougherty's unctuous voice oozed contempt.

"Fresh air and the view, what else?"

"What else, phoney admiral, is a bloody list of homicides that would make Jack the Ripper envious."

Steelbinder laughed and said into the handset, "You think I'm a fool? You can't prove I'm involved in those crimes."

"You think not? What happens when we send your photo to that music store clerk in Honolulu for identification? What about that dead call girl's prescription bottle in your jacket pocket? Mai Twan's passport and locks of Captain Bullock's red hair in your personal locker? There's more, Roscoe. You're the right blood type. Ever hear of genetic fingerprints? And we've got a detective from Hong Kong tracing down the source of those superfirecrackers. It's cut and dried, Roscoe. Come down and let me read you Miranda. Confess now, and save us time and trouble."

"Never. Why the grandstand play on behalf of some seedy whores, Lieutenant Commander? A few less swashbuckets and society . . ."

Dougherty didn't let him finish. "You rotten scumbag. As if defenseless women weren't enough, you're a cop killer, too. Already slipped your mind that you blew to hell my assistant, Duck Harris? He was also my friend. Sorry, Steelbinder, in my book, there's no place for you among civilized men. If I were the judge, I'd fry you first and listen to the prosecution later."

"Stop being so theatrical, Dougherty. I'd spit down on your bad performance if it weren't for this strong wind. And I also spit in the eye of two thousand years of your kind of civilization—a world of spineless men made silly by wine, women, and song. Before I hang up on your own swansong, I require one item, which I'm sure one of the patrol cars can supply. A portable amplifier—one of those bullhorns. Send it up in the elevator— *without* any company. I'll expect it before the news media arrives."

"Fuck yourself, Roscoe." Dougherty hung up first.

45

A San Francisco police squad car was dispatched to give Pamela Bonner and Kenny Chi a swift ride from Chinatown out to the bridge. Once dressed and down in the hotel lobby, however, the Hong Kong detective balked. Chi glanced nervously at his watch and said to the uniformed sergeant who was to escort them, "Please, officer. It's very important. In light of what's happened, I must make a short stop enroute."

Pamela was still struggling into her coat as she followed them out the door to the street. The cop held the car door open for her, at the same time giving Chi an unsympathetic look. "Ask your partner here. She's the one in a life or death panic to get out to the Golden Gate."

Chi hastily slid into the back seat beside Pamela. "We need to stop at Madame Fong's—the house of prostitution I mentioned earlier."

"What?" She stared at him. "Not now, for God's sake. Todd Dougherty may be in trouble."

"There's some timely evidence I must collect. We may need it."

The cop behind the wheel turned and looked at Chi shrewdly. "You know about Madame Fong's? Plenty of trouble there tonight."

Chi sat forward. "What kind of trouble?"

Up front on the passenger side, the sergeant slammed the door and nodded to the driver. The patrol car took off, red light swirling. The driver glanced at Chi in the rear-view mirror and continued, "The grisliest murder of the year, that's all. One of the Chinese hookers. Homicide's still investigating."

Chi sat back in the seat and swore softly in Cantonese.

The sergeant up front turned and studied him. "Madame Fong's have anything to do with this crackpot out on the Golden Gate?"

Chi looked at Pamela.

Immediately, she said to the driver, "If it's only a few blocks away, leave my associate off. He can grab a cab and join me later on the bridge."

The driver nodded, and moments later they screeched to a halt in front of Madame Fong's. Three other police vehicles lined the curb. Chi got out, wished Pamela luck, and dashed toward the building. Behind him, the squad car bearing the FBI woman turned on its siren and raced up Broadway.

Chi had to look up to present his bona-fides to the San Francisco detective in charge. Lieutenant Burke Morgan was a six-feet-four, barrel-chested Irish-American with flushed jowels and curly silver hair. Morgan listened patiently, but it took five minutes of fast explaining before Chi was allowed to go upstairs. A rattled and weary-eyed Madame Fong supported his story, assuring the San Francisco homicide cop that Kenny Chi had in fact been among Yung Liu's visitors earlier in the evening. But she was surprised to discover now that he, too, was a detective.

To Chi, his San Francisco counterpart was a stereotype—the typically aggressive, burned-out detective he'd seen more times than he cared to remember on American cops-and-robbers television. There seemed to be an endless flood of these cardboard stereotype programs imported to Hong Kong. Burke Morgan was not only surly, but pig-headed and egotistical, and Chi didn't expect to learn much from the man. It didn't matter; nothing mattered now but the tape cassette. As they climbed the staircase, he asked Morgan, "How long ago did the crime occur?"

"Just after eleven. They're still working on the body—or what's left of it—down at the morgue. You want to go down and check it out?"

Chi declined. They went down the hall, and Morgan nodded to the patrolman guarding Yung Liu's room. The cop opened the door and stepped briskly to one side. Lieutenant Morgan let Chi pass through first.

There was no chalk marking up the carpet—it wasn't necessary. The circle of spattered blood expanding out from the bedding to the walls and ceiling made the location of the body patently clear. For Chi, the scene was disturbingly familiar. Quickly, he scanned the room. Even without the young slattern's body, the scene was a pluperfect hell. Chi exhaled wearily and looked at his watch. "I assume you went over the room in minute detail earlier?"

The San Francisco detective hunched his shoulders and nodded.

Chi noted that the bushy Oregon grape was intact on the corner table, exactly as he'd left it earlier. He strolled over to it, trying to be as casual as possible. Chi deliberately focused on the large mirror on the opposite wall, hoping to draw Morgan's attention away from the plant. "That mirror—I assume it's one of those two-way affairs?"

Morgan nodded. "Kinky, you get the picture." He glanced only momentarily at the mirror, not enough time for Chi to plunge his hand into the ivy and retrieve the miniature recorder. Chi decided to try again, hoping this time to get Morgan to venture over to the fire escape window. "How about outside? Can the window be opened? Any leads there?"

Morgan smiled. "Matter of fact, yes. Oddly, there were prints enough out on the landing, but not even a partial in here. We're running them through the FBI computer."

"How about the neighbors across the way?"

Morgan studied him. "You're Chinese, Lieutenant. Maybe you should tell me. This is a tough, clannish part of the city. Chinatown's not your usual talkative neighborhood, never has been. Cat house or not, the neighbors are a flinty lot, hardened by the circumstances. Tough to open up, like shucking oysters."

Chi nodded; he knew his own people well enough. He was virtually on top of the plant now, leaning over it.

Morgan gave him a wry smile and said abruptly, "That was your recorder, I take it? Kinda figured it didn't belong to the fish."

Chi made no bones about searching the ivy now. The bug wasn't there. He turned back to the San Francisco homicide cop and saw him withdraw the miniature Sony from his jacket pocket. Morgan extended it toward Chi. "It's already been dusted for prints—yours, I assume. And we've taken the liberty of copying the tape."

Grinning, Chi said, "Then at the moment, I fear you know far more than I do."

"Not really. Two male voices in the room. The first one was a cocky individual the victim kept calling captain. Plenty to do about illegal jade; some other gobbledigook about causing her sister's homicide in Hong Kong. Yung Liu's second visitor was the killer. The pervert didn't say a hell of a lot, but Christ, what he did say will flip your stomach. It's all there, including sound effects. You want to listen to the tape here or go downtown where we can be more comfortable? I'm hoping, Lieutenant Chi, you can explain some of this."

Chi sighed, "What about the firecracker fragments? You do have them?"

Morgan nodded, his face turning grimmer by the minute.

Turning the miniature recorder over in his hands, Chi asked,

"Lieutenant Morgan, tell me. Is it possible you haven't been outside to your car for the past half hour? Have you been listening to the police frequency?"

"No. I've been busy in here. I can handle one crisis at a time. Why do you ask?"

"I think, Lieutenant, you'll want to drive me out to the Golden Gate Bridge. We can listen to this tape together enroute, and I'll try to answer your questions as best I can."

"Why the bridge? That's state territory, out of my jurisdiction."

Chi smiled. "Obviously, mine as well, Detective Morgan. But I suspect the man who committed this homicide—as well as others—is the same person who caused a Navy aircraft carrier to crash into the Golden Gate's south tower."

Burke Morgan's jaw dropped.

"Thirty-five minutes ago, to be exact," Chi added. "Now shall we get moving?"

46

Barriers had been set up on one side of the Golden Gate's roadway. The California Highway Patrol worked quickly to divert traffic away from the curb lane, reserving it for emergency vehicles only.

Pamela climbed out of the police car and took in the tumult around her. Racing over to the handrail, she glanced downward, stunned at the sight of the brilliantly illuminated *Abraham Lincoln* nosed up against the bridge pier. The supercarrier was so close it seemed she could reach out and touch it. She hurried over to an agitated group of individuals a short distance away. Spotting Todd Dougherty among them, she immediately went up to him. He gently took her aside, out of hearing range of the others, but instead of a kiss, he squeezed her hand.

"Better late than never," he admonished. "Our man has made his move. It's Steelbinder."

"Where is he now?"

Dougherty looked pale and a little edgy. He pointed straight up.

"On top and armed with a Very pistol. He's got four flares left, se don't get any heroic ideas."

"You reek of oil."

"Aviation fuel. I'll explain later." Dougherty gestured toward the nearby tower. "There's a steel ladder inside. I tried to follow him up, but one of his flare shells missed me by inches. An closer and I'd have been welded to the rungs."

She walked with him around the base of the monolithic, an deco structure, trying to avoid a TV camera crew that had talked their way past the police. Two CHP officers hustled the reporter back down the bridge walkway, then roped off the area.

Pam said to Dougherty, "No crewmen from the carrier up here to give you a hand? Not very courteous of Captain Bullock."

Dougherty grinned. "Out of his jurisdiction now. Besides treeing a cat is what I get paid for, Ms Bonner. The captain has better things to do—or haven't you looked beneath the bridge?"

"I have, and I still wonder about the son-of-a-bitch."

He stared at her. "Haven't given up on trying to crucify Bullock, have you? Even now, after all this?"

"I'm sorry, Todd. According to Kenny Chi, your hero's not ou of the woods. Not by a long shot." Pam's alert eyes lef Dougherty, noting that the door to the tower elevator had been unlocked and remained open. Inside on the floor of the three feet-square lift someone had left a bullhorn.

Dougherty said to her, "I suggest that while Bullock frets over the carrier, we concentrate on Steelbinder. Women will sleep better when we put him away."

She looked at Dougherty askance. "Don't I wish. Unfortunately, it's a thin, almost invisible line. Others will step over it Our friend Roscoe Steelbinder is just one of many." Pam knew al too well that even though they might slam this one troublemaker behind bars, only a fraction of the world's misfits were incarcerated. It was a myth that struggling, highly-disturbed people couldn't function in the real world; many did, despite great inner turmoil and homicidal tendencies. Coping had its limits. Pam shook her head, feeling a measure of defeat. "Sorry, Todd. We just happened to draw the short straw on this one. A matter of bad luck."

"Fine. Let's hope I reach retirement status before my luck runs out again."

Pam held a hand over her brow and looked up toward the top of the darkened tower. "What do you intend to do now? Just outwait him?"

"You have a better idea? He's trapped; time's on our side, not his. The worst that could come of it is he might jump. Or we eventually let a sharpshooter pick him off."

"He has no gun?"

Dougherty frowned. "Just the signal pistol. It's enough."

She held Dougherty's glance. "I want to hear what he has to say—before we get into a life and death confrontation. Lieutenant Chi claims there's more to Steelbinder's crimes than meets the eye."

"Probably so. But what do you suggest? Steelbinder asked for a bullhorn to be sent up, but the bridge's security chief is against it. Claims that if we turn this thing into a circus, he'll have to close down traffic." Dougherty glanced at his watch. "Look over there at the inbound lanes. Ten minutes ago that was a trickle of cars; the morning rush into the city has already begun, and it's going to get worse."

Pam stared at the traffic then turned back toward the elevator. One of the state patrolmen, she noted, was closely guarding it. "Todd, we need a confession, not the last big tantrum, suicide. If Steelbinder wants to purge his system, I say let him have the damned bullhorn. Crowd problems down here or not, as long as he's talking, he's not shooting flares. *Or jumping.*"

Dougherty frowned. "What kind of spectacle do you want? Some chest-pounding in front of the TV cameras, coming off like Kong on top of the Empire State Building? Forget it."

"No. I just want to hear what Roscoe has to say. Call it intuition, but I've a feeling he won't hurt me. He doesn't need a bullhorn; he needs a spokesperson." Pam hesitated. "I think I can communicate with him. I did before."

"What are you talking about?" He stared at her

"I'm convinced Dr. Hans Mueller and Roscoe Steelbinder are one and the same."

"Oh, God, now you tell me."

"Todd, I wasn't sure. Anyway, he was probably scared off when I brought you into the picture. He could have snuffed me that night in La Jolla but he didn't."

Dougherty shifted uncomfortably. "Great. You want him to make an embarrassing statement, all you have to do is reach inside that tower elevator, push the control button, and step aside. The bullhorn goes up, and you keep Steelbinder happy. But just try convincing or getting past that beefy state cop over there."

Pam asked, "What kind of embarrassing speech do you think Steelbinder would make?"

"Who knows? That's the problem. Remember your history, like what happened when that sadist Marquis de Sade was in the Bastille? He improvised a megaphone and urged the crowd to storm the damned prison."

Pam thought for a moment. "It's worth the risk. We need to communicate with him to unravel the rest of the case. I intend to send that elevator up—if you'll set up a distraction."

Dougherty cocked his head and looked at her askance. "You've picked a helluva time to try to find out *What Makes Sammy Run.*"

Pam went closer to Todd as if to whisper, but kissed his earlobe instead. He seemed surprised and let it show. Smiling, Dougherty strolled over to the bridge rail and summoned the CHP officer by the elevator to join him. The state cop obliged.

Pamela didn't hear Dougherty's contrived banter; she was preoccupied in her dash for the lift. Instead of pausing before the door to activate the controls as he expected, on impulse she jumped inside the elevator and leaned hard on the control button.

The door thudded shut before Dougherty and the cop could race over to stop it. Pam heard pounding, followed by cursing and her name being shouted. Then there was only the sound of the squeaking lift mechanism and the guide tracks in the steel shaft. The small car was cold and damp, and a sign warned against carrying more than three people. Pam smiled, for three thin people would have been a crowd.

Pam had plenty of time to contemplate as the elevator crept up the inside of the tower. It occurred to her, too late, that fear might be in order, that possibly she wasn't being brave at all, but foolish. And the small gun in her purse gave her no special sense of bravado. Removing the Erma Escam .22 from her shoulder bag, she placed it in the waist pocket of her woolen jacket.

Above all, she had to put fear out of her mind. She'd talked her way out of tough spots before. Remain calm, work the eye contact carefully, she kept reminding herself. It was probably some past reading, a lengthy article on men who hated women that gave her the sudden gutsy strength to confront Steelbinder face-to-face. If *misogyny* had its peculiar ground rules, she'd learn to play by them, storm the ramparts later at an opportune moment.

The elevator finally clunked to a halt at the top of the tower. Pam took in a deep breath. Picking up the bullhorn, she held it out before her like a peace offering and opened the elevator door.

Immediately the wind snatched at her hair and a glaring white light from a TV helicopter blinded her. Then the chopper and its high-intensity floodlight circled around to the other side of the tower, and she could see him standing less than a dozen feet away, glaring at her, pointing the Very pistol. She recognized him immediately, even under the admiral's hat he wore recklessly tilted to one side. Steelbinder's feet were spaced evenly apart, and he repeatedly flexed his muscular shoulders. His wide-set eyes flashed under the brilliant white light, making him look like an android on amphetamines. Overhead, the circling news helicopter, caught in the intermittent, blood-red glow of the tower's powerful aerobeacon, looked alien as well, like an object from a science fiction movie. Pam's confidence disintegrated in the noise and confusion, yet she knew she couldn't just stand there speechless.

She shouted over the roar of the helicopter, "You once sent me a gift, Roscoe! Or should I call you *Dr. Hans Mueller*—the fan at my lecture? I'm returning the favor!" Pam stepped slowly forward, extending the bullhorn before her like a peacepipe.

Steelbinder studied her for a moment then waved his gun arm threateningly. "Stop playing games with me, Ms Bonner. First throw your handbag into the elevator. Use it to block the door so the car can't be summoned back down! Then you may hand over the bullhorn, but very carefully. And you may call me R.W., but not Roscoe."

Pamela obeyed. Steelbinder grabbed the portable amplifier, retreated a short distance away, and looked fiercely at the TV news helicopter as if it were an offensive insect. Angered, he aimed the Very pistol at the aircraft and fired. Pam flinched with horror as she watched the green flare rocket upward. Luckily, it was deflected by the wind and wash of the chopper's rotors. The panicky pilot immediately banked away, leaving the immediate area and maneuvering instead in a wide circle closer to the Marin shoreline. After witnessing Steelbinder's attack on the press helicopter, Pam changed her mind about drawing him out with sweet talk. *Timing was everything*. Steelbinder hurried to reload the clumsy flare pistol, but when he turned back to face Pamela, he found himself staring into the barrel of her Erma Escam. He smiled contemptuously at her small handgun. "You can't be serious, coming up here to confront me with that toy?" Unafraid, he swaggered closer.

"It will stop you well enough if you come any nearer."

Hesitating a few feet away, he hunched his powerful shoulders and studied her through narrow eyelids.

Pam's mouth suddenly went dry. For a moment she felt surreal and dopey; she had to fight back a strange, sudden urge to pull the trigger, to once and for all be rid of this malevolent creature and everything he stood for. Her mind blurred back on Maxine Bullock's mutilated body and the woman on the Honolulu morgue tray. The recollections sharpened in focus. Most vivid of all, Pam saw again the horror of the explosion in front of her on the San Diego roadway, what appallingly little had been left of Duck Harris.

Steelbinder slowly shook his head. "Temptations, temptations! I wouldn't try it, Pamela dear. If we both fired at the same time, this flare gun would surely blow what was left of you right off the top of the tower." The wind increased, and Steelbinder's free hand grabbed for his hat. He shouted, "Provided the wind up here doesn't do the job first! It appears we have an interesting standoff, Ms Bonner. What now?"

Collecting herself and trying to remain calm, Pamela let out a long breath. "You wanted a bullhorn. Now you have a choice. Talk to them down there or talk to me. Just get it off your chest, Roscoe. I need to know about Captain Bullock. The loose ends."

"Hmmmmm-nnnn. Where's your pen? No lecture notes this time?"

"No notes this time, *Dr. Hans Mueller*. Just start talking."

"You look uncomfortable, Pamela. You're not fond of high places?"

"Why did you come up here? It's a dead end."

"You might call it behavioral research." He smiled evilly. "No, a better phrase, perhaps, is *fulfilling one's destiny*."

"Of course. I suppose you're rewriting behavioral psychology? Trying to give meaning to your empty, miserable life?"

Steelbinder pursed his lips. "My life? Miserable? Hardly, my dear. Examine the record; it's been one accomplishment after another. Look down below you. It's a clear night with perfect visibility. Do you believe that Navy supercarrier struck the bridge by accident?"

"I'm not impressed. You need help, Roscoe. Professional help."

"For what purpose? I once had you convinced that I was a *professional*—with a Beverly Hills office to boot. You're laughable, Pamela. And so full of bravado, attempting to intimidate me with that gun."

Pam was about to reply when she was startled by a bell ringing. A *telephone*? The shrill sound came from a metal box close to Steelbinder.

He let it ring twice, then groped inside, knocked the receiver off the hook and let it hang on its cord.

She said astringently, "That call might be important."

"For me, no. But you're welcome to pick it up if you choose." He stepped to one side. "Go ahead, enter a plea for help if you think it'll do you any good."

Pam stared at the receiver several seconds, trying to decide what to do. It might be Todd, trying to let her in on a plan. Wary and taking her time, she edged closer to the metal box. As she bent over to snatch up the receiver, her eyes left Steelbinder for just a fraction of a second. The slight distraction proved her undoing.

His foot shot up in a blur. Pam tried, too late, to dodge his karate-like kick, but was unsuccessful. The gun was knocked from her hand and she watched, helplessly, as it skittered along the top of the tower and slid off into eternity. Steelbinder calmly took the telephone out of her hand and ripped its connecting cord out of the box. Smiling with satisfaction, he threw the entire unit over the edge of the tower.

47

"Sit down," he commanded. "There on the steel deck."

Pamela's nerves were screaming. She did as she was told.

"So you believe I need treatment, Pamela?" Steelbinder smiled a little too cheerfully. "Your kind will never understand tormented genius." He gestured toward the base of the tower. "Down below, that warship and the men on it. The Navy doesn't understand."

"Spare me the tears," she prodded, "who would ever comprehend you?"

"The poet Dante Alighieri, for one. And my grandfather—yes, he understands perfectly." Steelbinder looked at her seriously, then let out an unsettling, contemptuous laugh. "You appear confused. Obviously, you don't enjoy fine literature. How about music? Are you fond of the rock group called the Midnight Admirals? Very talented artists, ahead of their time. Like me, Pamela."

"Everyone to his or her taste."

Steelbinder's voice softened. "Did you listen to the records I left behind and carefully study the words? Were you impressed?"

"Yes, I listened. Several times. I was sickened."

"Useless, useless. You try my patience like the others. An unfortunate waste when no one grasps my commission. Pamela, look over there at the horizon. The mid-watch is over; soon the stars will fade from the sky. Life on earth, in all the cosmos, regulates itself so perfectly, don't you agree? We're both helpless, Pamela. There's no stopping all the beautiful ongoing energy. You've only made a fool of yourself by interfering."

Pam stared at him, feeling disoriented and helpless. "I try to make that energy run a little smoother by enforcing the laws of society. And I'm proud of it." So damned trite, but she couldn't think of anything else to say, certainly nothing profound that would move the irrational beast before her.

The smile abruptly left Steelbinder's face, as if the time for playing cat and mouse were over. He said dourly, "Remember my earlier advice, Pamela? Wake not the sleeping wolf, lest it attack you? You should have stayed out of my affairs, but you didn't heed my warning. Why not? Is it because you have some inner need to leap into the murky water with me? Yes, that must be it."

Pam shuddered; she wasn't about to dignify his ludicrous question with a reply.

"Pamela, you truly amuse me. Do you really think it would do any good to lock me up for life? And as for society's morbid acts of retribution like the death penalty . . . yes, I know some of you call it a deterrance. Ah, when I think of the spectacle! Even if you were to hang, gas, or electrocute me, it wouldn't be over. Surely you've heard of reincarnation?"

"Roscoe, please—"

"There you go again, calling me Roscoe."

"I don't care any longer what I call you."

"Have you heard of reincarnation, Pamela? *Have you?*"

"I put as much stock in reincarnation as I do flying saucers."

"A fatuous comparison, my dear."

"Roscoe, it's cold up here, and you're trying my patience. All right, go ahead. If you could come back, who or what would you like to be?"

He gazed at her predatorily. "Several interesting people, but if I had to choose only one, a lycanthrope."

"A what?"

"A werewolf, Pamela."

She grimaced. "And use the moon as a sexual traffic light?

Would you mind terribly telling me why, Roscoe?" While waiting for his response, she remembered a study determining that lycanthropic psychosis at full moons can be quite real, even though the physical transformation part is nonsense. *Keep him talking, Pamela. Stall for time.*

The hand with the Very pistol in it remained steady on her, but Steelbinder gestured grandly with the bullhorn as he spoke. "The perfect reincarnation. It would combine the best of both worlds—refined culture and raw instinct. Two separate, opposing souls are better to deal with the world's problems than one."

Pam didn't respond.

Keeping a wary eye on her, Steelbinder edged closer to the dizzying edge of the tower to survey the gathering crowd below. "Hmmmmm-nnnnn," he mumbled. "Two souls committed to the tenebrous Golden Gate waters will be much better than one. We're going to leap together, Pamela. But from the far side of the tower where we can avoid hitting the carrier. It's wonderfully practical—a perfect way to say goodbye to the past and greet the auspicious future. You're not afraid are you, Pamela? What better way to teach reincarnation than demonstrating?"

"Change the subject, please."

"Did you know the top of this tower is 746 feet above the water? A leap from here will be a springboard into eternity with definite advantages. Certainly less bloody than a bullet to the brain and none of the repellant body spasms and defecating associated with poison. The jump is swift and sure, and from this added height, our earthly bodies should hit the water at over ninety miles an hour."

Pam put her hands over her ears. "Stop! I won't listen."

Steelbinder calmly continued: "Unfortunately, it's still too dark up here for our friends below to properly witness the event. Hurtling through the air at high speed, they may not see us. I'll have to properly light up the sky for the occasion. As you know, I'm very fond of fireworks, Pamela."

"So it appears." Watching Steelbinder's every move, Pam felt as if her brain and body were in slow motion. The wind had eased up a bit, and it was no longer necessary for them to shout at each other. Pam could do easily without another flare. The darkness had been a blessing, partially shielding her from the precarious height and having to look down. The bloody visions of what Steelbinder had done to the others passed out of her mind, replaced now by the grim prospects for her own survival. She started to tremble. *You should have shot him while you had the chance, Pamela Bonner*! All she could think of now was the water far below—how inky, cold, swift, and deep it was reported to be.

Pam made up her mind. Less than a dozen feet separated her from the elevator. Somehow, she had to reach it. If he dragged her over to the edge of the tower she might lose her equilibrium, even fall of her own accord!

Steelbinder had been curiously silent for a long time, as if undecided what to say over the bullhorn. Twice he raised it to his lips, and twice he put it back down.

"Silence becomes you, Roscoe. You may have me temporarily helpless, but your self-centured child's world is over for good. Why drag it out with laughable speeches? And I don't think you'll jump. That's the big attention-getting finale for people who've led drab, unexciting lives. All the spectacular—though I admit infamous—things you've done, throwing in the towel by suicide just wouldn't fit. There's nothing down there for you but dark, gloomy water."

"You're wrong, Pamela. Very wrong. It's not suicide, but a springboard into the supramundane world. I know from family experience; my grandfather proved it to me. I'd always planned to join him later, so why not now? He wants to meet you too, Pamela." Steelbinder's tortured gaze swept around the horizon. The sky beyond Richmond and Berkeley was turning gray with light.

Pam thought for a moment, then asked, "Where's Gecko Corman, Roscoe? What happened to him?"

Steelbinder pointed beyond the Golden Gate, out to sea. "Ashes to ashes, what else? Crematory dust, by now probably scattered in the ocean."

Pamela pressed her interrogation. "Who were the others? We know about Hong Kong, Honolulu, San Diego. How many more?"

"You need to catch up, Pamela. Your fellow investigators were unable to follow me last night. A shame. Do you think I could pass up a draggle-tail in San Francisco—especially on Halloween?"

Pam swallowed hard, remembering what the police had told her about Madame Fong's and Kenny Chi's plea to stop there. She felt a sudden pang of guilt for having slept through the incident. Losing control, she shook her head and angrily shouted, "You sick son-of-a-bitch, *how many more?* Go ahead, spit out the rest of your poison!"

"Poison? Hardly. A whore is a whore. I feel no shame, only

keen satisfaction." He shrugged. "There were three more. All perfect crimes. New York, Los Angeles, and Miami."

"And that's it? No one else?"

Steelbinder raised an eyebrow and stared at her. "Well, why not? If we're going to jump together, you're entitled to know it all. My *grandmother* was first on the list. By substituting medicines, I expedited her death. *Euthanasia*, Pamela. I was obeying my grandfather; he ordered me to do it, of course." Steelbinder's mouth twisted slightly, as if undecided whether to grimace or grin. Abruptly, he changed the subject. "Pamela, look down below. The television crews. I believe they're ready for us."

Pam shook her head. She suddenly found herself pleading. "Forget the bullhorn and the theatrics, R.W., please. We'll take the elevator down, and you can talk to them quietly, as long as you want. I'll help you. There'll be TV camera close-ups. A chance for millions to see you across the nation."

He frowned. "My Phantom-of-the-Opera face in a television close-up? Hardly. You're making light of me." Steelbinder stood there motionless, watching her for what seemed an eternity. Finally he ranted, "The final six lines to Dante's *Divine Comedy*—the cantos from the *Inferno*. Can you remember the words, Pamela?"

"We've had enough of your haunted, medieval mind, Roscoe. Why did you frame Captain Bullock?"

Steelbinder didn't respond; instead he leaned over the handrail and bellowed to the crowd below on the bullhorn: "Hear me, you cretins! Hear the words of Dante Alighieri!

> *But my own wings were not for such a flight*
> *Except that, smiting through the mind of me,*
> *There came fulfillment in a flash of light."*

To make his point, Steelbinder raised his Very pistol and fired. A green flare lit up the sky. He immediately struggled to reload the signal gun with another flare shell but not fast enough. Seizing the moment, Pamela was on her knees, scuttling for the elevator doorway. He shouted at her and cursed, but she shut out the words, hearing only her heart hammering in her chest.

The elevator door shut all too slowly. At the same time Steelbinder's signal pistol resounded. The flare hit the closed door.

Pam's emotions somersaulted as she waited for the car to descend. *Move, damn it!* She tapped the down button again, but nothing happened. She pushed again, harder, and continued to lean her entire body against it. From outside she heard Steelbinder raving on the bullhorn, more Dante:

> Here vigor failed the lofty fantasy:
> But my volition now, and my desires
> Were moved like a wheel revolving evenly
> By love that moves the sun and starry fires.

"To which, in my own words, I say to all of you, a simple, unadorned goodbye."

The elevator jerked and finally started down. Pam started breathing again. It took forever to descend, but when the door slid open at road level, Dougherty's arms were there to hold her. The press moved in, and she was temporarily blinded by camera flashes. When she finally could see into his eyes, he was scowling.

"You okay?"

Pam nodded. "It wasn't Steelbinder who gave me the rubbery knees. I don't like high places."

Dougherty risked a smile. "You're brave but also a little crazy."

"Fanny Hurst once said, 'A woman has to be twice as good as a man to go half as far.' What do we do now?"

"He has one flare left. We try to get him to fire it then move in with a helicopter."

"That may not be necessary, Lieutenant Commander." The low-pitched voice of authority came from a California Highway Patrol captain who had come up behind Pamela.

She and Dougherty faced him, surprised by what he held in his hand. *Steelbinder's flare gun.* The trigger on the Very pistol was on safety, and it still contained an unspent flare shell.

The CHP officer explained, "One of my men saw it strike the windshield of a passing car. A Navy officer's cap came floating down a few moments later, but the wind blew it over the bridge rail. We think he jumped."

Pam looked at Dougherty, waiting.

He said to the highway cop, "I'm going up. There's room in the lift for two more."

The captain's eyes sparkled with bravado. "Count me in." He drew his gun.

Pam shrugged and headed back to the elevator, but Dougherty jerked her aside. He said firmly, "Acrophobia, remember? This time you stay here. Let the rest of us have a turn."

Before she could object, a highway patrolman with a shotgun joined the CHP captain in the elevator. Dougherty slid inside with them and the door closed in Pamela's face. All she could do now was swallow her pride and face the semicircle of reporters closing in around her.

~~~~~~~~ **48**

The first thing Dougherty saw when the elevator door opened was one of the carrier's rescue helicopters circling overhead. The Sikorsky circled slowly, directing its high-intensity quartz spotlight on top of the tower.

The three of them stepped out on the steel deck, guns drawn. Dougherty saw no sign of Steelbinder. The brilliantly illuminated area was empty, but they had to be sure. The Highway Patrol captain set off to check the cable saddle on the right side, while Dougherty and his shotgun escort investigated the one on the left. Other men were stationed down at roadway level watching the ladder shaft and exit, so there was no chance Steelbinder could escape that way.

The huge steel saddles and cables were covered with dew and Dougherty had to watch his footing. He scrambled to the top where he could hang on to a waist-high safety line. There was no one on the other side of the saddle. Ditto for the other end of the tower.

Dougherty was about to climb back down when he did a double-take; a few feet away he spotted an officer's shirt and slacks, neatly folded with a pair of shoes on top to keep them from blowing away. The same set of khakis Steelbinder had worn earlier? Dougherty scanned the sloping bridge cables in both directions. No one out there. Handing the clothing down to the other men, he climbed off the saddle, found the entry to the ladder shaft, and flashed a light inside. Empty.

The Highway Patrol captain, confident that their quarry had in fact leaped, tucked his pistol back in its holster. "Gentlemen, it appears our so-called *Bridge of Sighs* has claimed another victim."

"Without leaving a farewell note?" asked the assistant with the shotgun.

Dougherty shrugged. "He said everything he had to say to the FBI woman. She was up here with him long enough."

The CHP captain shielded his eyes from the rotating red aerobeacon and said to Dougherty, "All that double-talk on the bullhorn. Make any sense to you?"

"Dante's allegory? Afraid not. My partner was convinced there was something to it. The damned poetry was probably like this case. It had to be opened farther and farther until it was fully exorcised." Dougherty glanced up at the hovering Navy Sikorsky, then down to the carrier. He spoke into his pack-set radio: "Steinberg, you still standing by?"

"Yeah, boss. You're coming in clear."

"Get word to the chopper that Steelbinder jumped. Tell the pilot to search the water around the pier for a body. The tide's coming in, so try the Bay side. We're closing up shop here."

"Yes, sir, right away." Steinberg sounded elated. "Don't expect too much, boss. I hear only a small percentage of victims are recovered in this channel."

"We'll try anyway. Ten-four." Dougherty put the radio away. He looked up at the annoying aerobeacon, momentarily mesmerized by the 360-degree sweep of its red warning signal. His mind flashed that it was trying to tell him something. *An omen.* Pamela was right. In the future there would be others ready to replace Roscoe W. Steelbinder. They were probably already there, germinating in some hotbed of perversity. And as for this case, it really wasn't fully exorcised. Not quite. There was still the matter of Swain Bullock.

The Officer of the Day hurried up to the captain. "The rescue helicopter reports that it's unable to find a trace of Steelbinder's body, sir."

Bullock nodded. "Turn the search over to the Coast Guard, and have the Sikorsky crew return to the carrier. And bring those men in the whale boat back on board as well."

"The damage crew has already returned, Captain. And the detail topside reports that everything's secure on the flight deck."

Bullock checked his watch, wondering how long it would take the engineering officer to finish sounding the inside of the hull and return with a report. In the meantime, all Bullock could do was pace from one end of the *Abraham Lincoln's* command bridge to the other. Beyond the starboard side windshield he could see the lights of the fishing fleet putting to sea. The harbor pilot had gone to the Communications Room, alerting the boats by radio to hug the other side of the channel, keep moving, and stay clear of the disabled carrier. The Bay Area Coast Guard cutter was on the scene, fighting the tides and trying to maneuver in a tight circle several hundred yards astern of the *Abraham Lincoln*.

Each minute of waiting was killing Bullock. The armpits of his neatly pressed khaki shirt were ringed with sweat. Admiral Tanner, too, had gone down into the *Abraham Lincoln's* hull to check on the progress of Damage Control and the Sounding and Security Watch.

At last Tanner and Commander Jabbits, the ship's engineering officer, returned to the bridge. Both men appeared out of breath from the long climb. Expectant, Bullock went up to them. Fritz Tanner stepped aside, watchful and waiting, aware that it was Jabbits's place to report directly to the ship's commander.

"The forward peak tank's dry as a bone, Captain. Three holding compartments have taken on water, but most of the damage is under the stem, starboard side of the double bottom. One of the longitudinal frames is bent like an accordian and hung up on the pier, but the rest of the bow is as strong as ever. The hull will probably hold any oncoming sea short of a full gale."

"Thank God." Bullock took off his hat and wiped his sweating forehead with a handkerchief. He turned to the Navigator. "How much longer until the tide turns?"

"Ten minutes ago, sir. It's already started in."

Bullock looked at his watch, then asked the engineering officer, "Jabbits, you think it's safe to give it hell again, all engines astern?"

The commander frowned and thought for a moment. "Six inches more of water would make a big difference. In another half hour, we'll probably float free."

"That's the second time you've used the word *probably*, Commander. Stop equivocating."

The engineering officer stiffened.

Rear Admiral Tanner edged Jabbits aside and faced Bullock. "Do whatever you feel is necessary, Captain. It's your ship."

Bullock quickly considered his options. In another half hour, it would be daylight and traffic on the bridge would be jammed. It was bad enough this incident—he avoided the words mishap or accident—had occurred in the darkness. Bullock made up his mind. The carrier needed to make its getaway now, before the goddamn demonstrators arrived and the news media made everything worse. Bullock could already visualize the twisted facts of the collision. He would pour on the power now. The ship might take a few yards of concrete fender with it, but that was someone else's problem. The Navy could settle up on the liabilities later.

Bullock dismissed Jabbits and summoned the OD, "All engines astern! Standard speed."

The command was repeated and sent down on the engine telegraph. Seconds later the supercarrier trembled as the four powerful screws strained in reverse. Nothing happened, so Bullock increased the revolutions.

Suddenly there was a bristling screech of steel as the ship broke free from the pier. Around Bullock, the men on the bridge cheered, including Rear Admiral Tanner. Everyone smiled except Bullock. The harbor pilot immediately took charge of the helm and strove to get the supercarrier back out to mid-channel.

Bullock pulled Fritz Tanner aside. "Since my next decision involves the fleet, I'll need your concurrence, Admiral."

Tanner shot him a puzzled look. "I'm listening. What are the options?"

"The major drydocks in the Bay area are occupied which leaves the following choices: we can go back to Piers 31-32, anchor out in the bay over by Alcatraz, or proceed to sea. The carrier can still do fifteen knots and get us to Bremerton. Maybe even eighteen knots for short periods to conduct air operations. But with the damage we've sustained, no high speed maneuvers like you'd originally intended. Frankly, sir, I'd like to get the hell out of here, dump the sub-coordinated maneuvers, and get this ship into the hospital in Bremerton—where it belongs."

Tanner thought for a moment. "Reasonable enough. If Naval District COM-TWELVE wants to blow steam at us for leaving the scene of an accident, they can fly their investigation team out to the carrier."

"Thanks, sir, for your support. Now if you'll excuse me." Bullock scanned the bridge. Besides the Harbor Pilot, there was another civilian present that concerned him. Up until now, Todd Dougherty's NIS assistant had been useful to Bullock. Sol Steinberg with his walkie-talkie had managed to keep him apprised of what was happening up on the Golden Gate and the disposition of the ship's crazed quartermaster, Roscoe Steelbinder. Bullock went up to the NIS intermediary. "Convey my best wishes to Lieutenant Commander Dougherty, Mr. Steinberg.

He's done an excellent job. As of now, however, he's on his own. I assume with all those screaming sirens up on the bridge roadway, he'll have more than enough paperwork to handle."

"Apparently so, sir."

"The suicide leap was a goddamn shame. I'd have liked to keelhaul this Steelbinder myself rather than let him take the easy way out."

Rear Admiral Tanner swiftly added, "Count your blessings. He's saved the taxpayers the cost of prosecution."

The OD came up to Bullock. "Captain? I have something of interest." He held up a soaking wet officer's cap, its visor replete with scrambled eggs and lightning bolts—all considerably tarnished. "One of the boatswain's mates fished it out of the water, sir."

Sol Steinberg stepped forward. "That's the hat, Captain. The one Steelbinder had in his locker."

Bullock and Tanner both shook their heads. Smiling, Bullock handed the hat to Steinberg. "You can keep it. A souvenir of the deployment." He put a hand on Steinberg's shoulder. "Now that your work is complete, you can go ashore with the harbor pilot."

"No, sir," said Steinberg awkwardly. "Lieutenant Commander Dougherty insists I should remain aboard the carrier. I'm to go all the way to Bremerton with you and keep in touch with him."

Bullock's spirits ebbed; he'd crossed one hurdle only to be confronted by another. Working hard to bite back his annoyance, he stared at the NIS civilian. Bullock watched with concern as Steinberg, nursing his pack-set against one ear, stepped outside the carrier's bridge. Once more the small two-way radio began to chatter frantically.

~~~~~~ 49

The carrier was over sixty miles up the coast when the CH-46 Sea Knight made its approach downwind. Dougherty had managed to appropriate the twin-rotor chopper from the Naval Air Station at Alameda. The Sea Knight was noisy, and he found it impossible to communicate with Pamela and Lieutenant Chi, who sat opposite him in the cargo area. The U.S. Navy called these passenger or cargo transfers out to sea a "pony express" run, and their comings and goings were usually taken for granted. They did require the ship captain's approval, however, and Bullock was apparently taking his sweet time about giving them clearance to land.

Annoyed, Dougherty put on the intercom phones and listened to the chopper's pilot communicating with the *Abe Lincoln's* air operations center.

"Repeat, this is Sea Knight Delta-five-niner, still standing by out here. You intend for us to follow you all the way to Bremerton?"

"Hold on, we're still waiting for your green deck."

"What's the big holdup?"

"Argue with the ship's CO, not me. Was that message traffic for three PAX? Over."

"Repeat, one NIS officer and two civilians."

Dougherty tore off the earphones, glanced at Pamela, and slowly shook his head. She smiled back, taking it all in stride.

For the past half-hour Dougherty had been considering how best to approach Captain Bullock, even the advantages of jumping up the ladder, asking Rear Admiral Tanner to listen to the Hong Kong detective's story and the tape cassette first. Pamela was against that. Chi suggested they leave Bullock alone with the tape and the three of them return later. Whatever course they took, the closing-in procedure would leave Dougherty with distaste. He'd just as soon spill a sack of vipers on the table linen of the Officer's Wardroom.

Unfortunately, Petty Officer Second Class Roscoe W. Steelbinder's demise didn't dictate a happy ending for Swain Bullock; the captain was still in serious trouble. A ship collision was an unforgivable blot on a captain's record.

Even if he survived that investigation, there was the Hong Kong mess—Bullock's voice on the tape at Madame Fong's, spilling his guts out to Yung Liu before her murder at Steelbinder's hands. The bizarre truth had come to the surface, and Dougherty wondered whether Bullock would put up a legal fight or live with it. Whatever happened, would the captain's superiors and the men serving under him understand the thin line between damnation and redemption? Dougherty wondered about a conviction. What would the captain's guilt signify?

Dougherty looked out the perplex window as the chopper

executed a wide turn then went into a side-slipping plunge toward the moving carrier. Even before the CH-46 had settled down on the flight deck, a green shirt bounded forward with tie-down chains.

When Dougherty, Pamela, and Chi stepped out of the helicopter, they were greeted by the Junior Officer of the Day and Sol Steinberg. Dougherty instructed the Sea Knight's crew to wait. If everything went according to plan, they'd be leaving the carrier in less than an hour—hopefully with Captain Bullock in tow.

Dougherty gave the customary boarding salutes and introduced his two civilian companions. The JOD asked Pamela and the Hong Kong detective to sign in on his clipboard, then shouted to Dougherty, "The captain's busy on the bridge, sir, but he'll see all of you in his office in twenty minutes! Do you need an escort?"

"I know the way! Thank you, Lieutenant." Dougherty watched the JOD depart. He waited for the chopper's rotors to wind down a little more, then said to Steinberg, "We need to get into Steelbinder's locker again to round up that passport and other evidence."

"Already took care of it, boss. After the bridge collision. The ship's master at arms has everything secured." Steinberg reached into his jacket pocket and withdrew a shiny silver object. "Except this. I had it in my own cabin."

Lieutenant Chi's eyes widened as he took the Rolls Royce hood ornament into his hands. Chi examined its damaged base, nodded, and handed it to Pamela. She put the mascot in her purse.

Dougherty said to Steinberg, "Have the master at arms hustle all the evidence down to the captain's office, but wait outside until we call you in."

Steinberg departed.

Kenny Chi seemed mesmerized by the activity on the flight deck. Dougherty knew the planned ASW exercise had been cancelled, and already the supercarrier's air squadrons were dispersing, flying back to their land bases. The waist catapult was set up to fire off a couple of Tomcats and the three of them were in the way. Dougherty directed Pamela and Chi over to the safety of the island, away from the jet blast. Deck personnel gaped at the unusual sight of a woman on board during sea operations. Enjoying the attention, Pamela smiled back.

Dougherty led the way down the ladder to the 03 level and a companionway that was reasonably quieter. As they passed through the blue curtains marking off command country, Dougherty ran into Rear Admiral Tanner. They exchanged salutes.

"Sir!"

"Relax, Lieutenant Commander. I wanted to intercept your little lynching party before you confront Captain Bullock."

"Sir," Dougherty protested, "We're neither judge nor jury. Just a trio of investigators with a job to do."

Tanner waved his hand. "Interrogation then. I understand. I also understand that Swain Bullock hasn't turned out to be one of your favorite ship commanders." Tanner looked over Dougherty's shoulder. "Is this the FBI woman you've told me about?"

Pam extended her hand. "I'm Pamela Bonner, Admiral." She stepped to one side. "And this is our visitor from Hong Kong, Lieutenant Detective Kenny Chi."

Tanner's eyes narrowed. "I'm impressed. International expertise as well, then. The plot must be truly convoluted when we have to call in the Inspector Clouseaus and Charlie Chans of the world."

Chi wasn't amused. "I'm afraid this Charlie Chan detective is a clumsy American stereotype we Chinese do not appreciate."

Dougherty cleared his throat.

Fritz Tanner smiled. "Perhaps we'd best get to business. I hope you can all appreciate the legal complexities regarding the bridge accident this morning. Accountability being what it is in the Navy, I'd like the ship's legal officer to sit in when we confer with Captain Bullock. Would you object?"

Pamela politely interjected, "Pardon, sir. We're not here regarding the carrier's collision with the Golden Gate Bridge."

Tanner looked troubled. "The matter of his wife's homicide again? When do we let that wound heal of its own accord?"

Kenny Chi stiffened. "When our investigation is concluded, sir."

"Please, Admiral," Dougherty begged, "Just give us a half hour alone with the skipper before you and the counsel join us."

Tanner thought for a moment then said to Dougherty, "When you need me, I'll be up on the flag bridge. I smell bad news, Lieutenant Commander. Accordingly, I intend to grab some fresh air while I can." He stepped briskly down the corridor.

An orderly admitted them to the handsome office the *Abraham Lincoln's* captain used for formal administrative duties. They all declined coffee, and the aide departed. Chi and Dougherty immediately sat in the white contour chairs surrounding Swain Bullock's desk, but Pamela strolled the room's perimeter, taking in the wall memorabilia.

Ignoring them both, Kenny Chi brought out his miniature

recorder. He checked the cassette and placed it before him on the captain's desk as if the unit were a prize of war.

The three of them didn't have to wait long. Almost immediately Bullock strode into the room. The captain's face belied his erect, quick-stepped manner; he looked drawn and tired, his eyes red-lined. The Bullock whirlwind seemed to have lost some of its punch, Dougherty thought. Like himself, the captain had been up all night.

Bullock sat behind his huge desk, studying each of them in turn. When he saw Chi's recorder, his jaw tightened. "The three of you asked for an informal meeting. Let's keep it that way." He pushed the small Sony back toward Chi. "We keep this conversation off the record, or we don't meet at all. Which will it be?"

Kenny Chi picked up the cassette unit and said boldly, "I'm sorry, Captain. Of course we do not intend to record this conversation. I only intend to play a tape for you." Chi afforded Bullock a wooden smile. "You apparently know the others, so permit me to introduce myself. I'm Lieutenant Chi of the Royal Hong Kong Police." Chi hesitated. "Since I'm officially a guest in your country, I believe I'll defer now to the Naval Investigation Service."

Dougherty was surprised. He'd halfway hoped the Chinese detective would do the most of the interrogating—and uncomfortable finger pointing. Dougherty hadn't prepared an opening statement about Hong Kong, and he found himself groping for the right words. He hesitated too long, and Bullock jumped on him.

"Lieutenant Commander Dougherty appears to be tongue-tied." Bullock scowled and checked his watch. His manner, as usual, was hard as a nutmeg. "Ms Bonner, you didn't come along just for the ride. Perhaps you have something enlightening to tell me?"

Pamela sat forward, her face reddening. "Todd Dougherty is in the Navy, sir, and subject to all its diplomatic proclivities. I can be more frank and say what I wish." She hesitated. "I don't like you, Captain, and have no need to be polite or deferential. While my associates here seem to be content at sniffing at success, I assure you I intend to go for it all the way." Tossing her head, she stared at Bullock with an air of saucy triumph. "Sorry to be so blunt, Captain, but if you're so intent on saving time, just listen to Lieutenant Chi's tape cassette."

Dougherty swiftly interjected, "You'll have to excuse Ms Bonner's manners, sir. She's not without prejudice. I'm afraid that from the beginning she's been convinced you're a modern-day Captain Bligh and some kind of sexist troll."

Bullock laughed, but it was a forced laugh that quickly evaporated. "Intemperate ship masters went out with Victorian literature. I suspect the FBI woman's problem is that she simply can't fathom the psychological and biological imperatives in dealing with men at sea. A naval ship commander these days is an effective leader because of MBO—that's management by objective—and setting a strong example."

"*Example, Captain*?" Pamela's icy query hung in the air.

Bullock glared at her. "Don't be so petty and sardonic, Ms Bonner. Sarcasm coming from a woman is most deadly." He smiled to the others then added with disdain, "If it were up to me, every woman would be a wonderfully soft, mysterious cat."

Pamela winced. "You're only slightly effective at being nominally macho, Captain." She rose to her feet and approached his desk. Bullock drew back slightly as she reached into her handbag and withdrew a shiny silver object. With considerable emphasis, she placed the Rolls *Spirit of Ecstasy* hood ornament in front of him then calmly went back to her seat.

Dougherty swiftly interjected, "You do recognize it, Captain?"

Detective Chi followed the conversation, his alert eyes moving from one face to the next. Now he, too, stared at Bullock, waiting for the captain's head of steam to fizzle out.

Dougherty added in a compressed voice, "I'm afraid there's much more. You needn't say anything now. I suggest you just listen to the tape, please."

With difficulty Bullock rose from his chair. Knuckles pressed against the desk and his feet in a kind of boxer's stance, he said, "The tape recording. It's undoubtedly a fabrication, a part of Roscoe Steelbinder's ill-fated frame-up. Where did you get it, in Hong Kong?"

"No," Dougherty replied. "Back in San Francisco."

Bullock looked puzzled.

Chi said firmly, "Sit back down, Captain. It's your voice, last night."

Pamela added, "At an establishment called Madame Fong's. I'm sure it will all come back to you."

Bullock's eyes were transparent and bulging, their black target centers suddenly shrinking. He slumped down into his chair as Kenny Chi punched the play button on the recorder.

Dougherty made sure Chi played the entire tape, including Steelbinder's subsequent arrival on the scene. Bullock avoided their eyes while he listened. His hard, heady manner was a thing of the past now. Trembling and fidgeting with several paper clips on his desk, he appeared as nervous as a highly trained greyhound or thoroughbred racehorse. Dougherty waited for the sickening sound of the firecracker before going over and turning off the cassette. The *Abraham Lincoln's* captain looked as if he wanted to be sick.

As a footnote, Dougherty said dully to Bullock, "Unfortunately for all of us, the San Francisco Police duplicated this tape."

Swain Bullock shook his head like a pilot who had just pulled out of a dive too fast.

There was a knock on the cabin door and Dougherty went over to open it. Steinberg and the ship's Master at Arms stood in the corridor, each of them cradling a cardboard box. Dougherty gestured with his hand for them to stand pat for a moment and closed the door. Returning to the desk, he explained to Bullock, "More evidence we intend to place on the table. Frankly, Captain, I'd prefer to do it back at Alameda rather than here on the carrier. San Francisco homicide has agreed to meet us there. They'll have a barrage of questions as well. Under the circumstances, why air our dirty laundry in front of your fellow crewmen? Or Rear Admiral Tanner?"

Bullock's eyes and the changing color of his face told the story—incredulity, disbelief, anger, and finally, sheer horror at what was taking place. "My uniform," he said dully. "I'll have to change into a fresh uniform." Bullock's sense of logic, for the moment, had apparently gone into a state of shock. He sputtered, "The admiral—does Fritz Tanner have to hear that tape?" Bullock sounded as if he were being choked.

Dougherty glanced at Chi and Pamela, saw them both shrug. He said to the captain, "Not right away, if you cooperate with us. I can't make any guarantees about next week."

Bullock stared at his desk. "No alternatives, none whatsoever?"

Pamela leaned forward. "Being a hard-ass, fighting son-of-a-bitch, you probably wouldn't like them. A dissolute ship captain giving up his wanton ways, retiring early from the Navy and becoming a respectable, quiet, private citizen? More than likely on probation."

"Madness. You're all mad." Bullock dismally added, "You expect me to pass up an admiral's star?"

Dougherty stared at him but said nothing.

"How much time do I have?" the captain asked.

"Whatever you require," Dougherty replied. "But keep in mind that we have a borrowed chopper, and it's double-parked on your flight deck."

Bullock nodded. "I need ten minutes to confer with Admiral Tanner, another ten to pick up my overnight bag. You think you can have me back on the ship by tomorrow afternoon?"

Detective Chi coughed. Pamela and Dougherty looked at one another. Chi finally responded, "I suspect that will depend entirely on what you tell us."

"Yes, of course."

50

They waited in the helicopter, holding their ears and wincing every time another F-14A rocketed off the waist catapult. Pamela, Steinberg, and Detective Chi sat huddled in the back of the Sea Knight, while Dougherty, concerned over what might be holding the captain up, paced the flight deck outside. Bullock had already run twenty minutes over the time he'd requested. Dougherty shielded his eyes against the sun and stared up at the bridge on the 08 level, but still saw no sign of the supercarrier's skipper.

Checking his watch again, Dougherty shouted to the others inside the chopper, "Sit tight. If I don't rattle his cage, we'll never get out of here." Dougherty ran across the flight deck to the island and took the steep steps to the bridge two at a time. He paused before the door to Swain Bullock's at-sea cabin to catch his breath before knocking. The compartment door opened abruptly before he could raise a clenched hand.

The captain stood there in a pilot's G-suit and tightly laced boots. In one hand he cradled a shiny black helmet marked with his initials and an eagle rank emblem, in the other a handsome leather carry-on bag. Mouth open, Dougherty stared at Bullock.

Before he could say anything, Bullock explained to him in a somber voice, "Relax, Lieutenant Commander. I'm not about to give you the slip by boarding a space shuttle. If you and your friends insist, however, that I go back to Alameda Naval Air Station, I intend to get there on my own. *Without* a well-meaning but embarrassing escort." Bullock paused to rub his chin. "Besides, I'm behind on my flying time."

"Sir? Isn't this out of order? I don't understand."

"You don't have to as long as I have the admiral's blessing."

Taken aback, Dougherty suddenly found himself wondering if the *Abraham Lincoln's* master was somehow different, beyond ordinary legislation. They walked together outside, then paused as the captain leaned on the bulwark and surveyed his domain—as if for the last time. Bullock gave what appeared to be a prearranged hand signal to one of the yellow shirts standing near an A-4 Skyhawk up forward. From the burst of activity around the training and support jet, Dougherty guessed it was being made flight ready for the captain.

Bullock said flatly, "Cheer up, Dougherty. I'll be on the ground, waiting for you at Alameda. I suggest looking at it this way: from experience you should know scuttlebutt travels at damn near light speed on this ship. The men feed on speculation, too often the wrong kind. After what happened back at the Golden Gate, if I were to be summarily jerked off the carrier, escorted by you on that chopper . . ." Bullock straightened his shoulders and pushed out his jaw. "Well, Lieutenant Commander, it would be worse than merely losing the crew's respect. I'd be the laughing stock of the *Abraham Lincoln*. And I suspect the entire Navy, for that matter. For the sake of morale, we can't allow that, can we?"

Dougherty smiled in spite of himself. "I wouldn't worry, sir. The men might assume you're going ashore on business."

Bullock glared at him. "My ass. By now every sailor on this ship knows you're an NIS investigator."

"It's still a little irregular, sir."

"*Highly irregular*, but eminently practical. Forget me for a moment, Dougherty. It's a matter of what's best for the Navy. Incidentally, that A-4's cockpit is a little cramped, so I trust you won't mind taking my overnighter with you in the chopper?" With a waggish grin, Bullock dropped the carry-on bag in front of Dougherty. "No hard feelings about the investigation." Bullock offered him a handshake.

Dougherty, feeling an uncomfortable premonition, hesitantly shook the extended hand, noting its coldness. Before he could say anything, the captain turned and stepped briskly away. After only a few feet, Bullock hesitated and looked back at him thoughtfully. "You've done an exemplary job, Dougherty. I'm impressed. Tell me, are you familiar with Thucydides, admiral of the Athenian fleet?"

Dougherty frowned with impatience. "To an extent, sir."

Swain Bullock's eyes looked distant, as empty as clear gray

glass. "One of his more significant quotes was, 'What I fear now is not the enemy's strategy, but my own mistakes.' " Bullock held his stare briefly then moved quickly toward the ladder leading to the flight deck.

Dougherty watched Bullock depart. Shrugging, he picked up Bullock's luggage and started to follow but was suddenly restrained by a firm hand on his elbow. "Wait, Lieutenant Commander. I'd like a few words. We've plenty of time."

Dougherty turned and saluted Rear Admiral Tanner. "Sir?"

"Relax, please. Odd, don't you think, that the captain should quote from a man who made a mess of the greatest of the Greek wars?"

Dougherty nodded. An out-of-focus memory struggled to the surface and sharpened. *Thucydides.* "Wasn't he the one who spent twenty years in exile? Admiral, if I might add, it's also odd that the captain refuses to accompany us off the ship. I'm in an awkward position."

Fritz Tanner held his glance. "A man going into harm's way should have the right to decide how to get there." The admiral studied him. "Do you like the Navy, Dougherty?"

"I love it, sir. It's my life."

"So do I," Tanner said shortly. "So do I."

Dougherty waited for the din of another catapult launch to subside then added, "Though I sometimes wish that instead of flying a desk I could be jockeying one of those Tomcats or involved in a little fleet action." Even as he fantasized, Dougherty continued to stare admiringly at the orchestration taking place on the flatiron-sized deck below. The flight area was one one-hundredth the space of an airport but just as busy, and the coordinated movements never failed to impress him. Observing it all, he understood clearer than ever the justification for the rituals, repeated drills, and the discipline. Also the reasons for his officer's stripes, the countless traditional things that made the Navy an autocratic beast, but at the same time made it function as perfectly as possible.

Tanner nudged Dougherty to regain his attention. "Unwind, Lieutenant Commander. You're doing an important job. All of us sometimes get an itch to ride someone else's bicycle." Tanner pointed off the port side to the other ships accompanying the carrier. A submarine had just started to dive.

Tanner observed, "Look at that smug bastard out there. The skipper of that Trident sub is the Navy's new elite. War ever breaks out, a carrier captain or tired old battle group commander like myself—we're just functionaries, off to one side of the chain of command. The word to fire goes from the White House directly to that submarine. I get an information *copy* of the dispatch. The Navy's changed, Dougherty. The surface sailors may do the housekeeping, but all the action's underwater or up in the sky."

Dougherty listened, but his eyes were now focused down on the flight deck. He watched Swain Bullock climb into the cockpit of the A-4 Skyhawk. Dougherty said, "Is that why even a supercarrier captain keeps his aviator's wings polished and does a little flying now and then? Sorry, Admiral, but I'd feel much better if Bullock would at least let me accompany him."

Another Tomcat was on the catapult and Tanner was forced to shout back. "Impossible! The Skyhawk holds only the pilot!"

Dougherty waited until the waist launch was completed and the F-14A had banked off to the left. "Very convenient for the captain. What about the *Abe Lincoln*? You trust the XO to take the carrier the rest of the way in to Bremerton?"

Below them the flight deck was relatively quiet again. Tanner smiled. "Between the two of us, I suspect we'll manage. You forgetting I commanded the *Carl Vinson* before getting a fat stripe and a star?"

Dougherty uncomfortably shifted his feet. "Sir, do you really expect Captain Bullock to get out of this without any powder burns on his uniform?"

Fritz Tanner took a deep breath and let it out. "No. Sadly, I don't. But I pray the Navy itself gets a fair shake. Maybe that's up to you, Dougherty. We've proved we can clean up our own house in jig time. I'm sorry, I should say *you* proved that. I'm afraid it's a cold, indifferent world out there, Lieutenant Commander; one in which stubborn idealists like the two of us grow old all too quickly."

Pilot "Squeegee" Liddell and Radar Intercept Operator "Hambone" Greco sat in their twin-engine Tomcat, engines idling, ready to taxi into position on the waist catapult. A brisk wind blew over the *Abraham Lincoln's* bow while overhead the sky was blue from horizon to horizon. Both men were in a good mood. With the fleet exercise cancelled and perfect flying weather ahead, they'd be back at Miramar in San Diego in just over half an hour.

Squeegee stared toward the bow in amazement. He watched Swain Bullock lower the plastic canopy on the A-4 and begin taxiing into position for launch from the starboard bow catapult. Squeegee said into the hot mike to his RIO: "Hambone, am I

seeing things, or is the old man himself taking that Skyhawk up
for a spin?"

"Roger. First time I've seen him put in flight time at sea, but
why not? Can't blame him. He's entitled to a flying fix like the
rest of us."

"Stop jiving me, man. I say you're about to lose a wager. Or
has our earlier bet slipped your mind?"

"Don't rub it in. I already figured I'd blown that ten bucks
when the captain slammed us into the goddamn bridge."

"That was *twenty bucks*, asshole, providing Bullock doesn't
make admiral lower-half. I think this is bye-bye to old hardass."

Squeegee strained to one side of his seat, trying to see forward
along the flight deck. He caught a glimpse of a purple shirt
holding up a board for Bullock, telling him the A-4's total takeoff
weight. Squeegee wondered where the captain intended to take the
trainer at its limited speed. Whatever the destination, as soon as
their own Tomcat was airborne, he and Hambone would enjoy
overtaking Bullock, passing the A-4 up like Grandpa in the slow
lane.

The bow catapult's blast deflection plate came up, obscuring
their view of the Skyhawk. All Squeegee could see now were the
heat waves generated above the carrier deck as Bullock ran up the
Skyhawk's throttle.

Pamela grew impatient as she waited with Chi and Steinberg in
the rear of the Sea Knight. Dougherty had still not returned. Not
understanding the obvious change in plans, she stared in wonderment out the helicopter's side window as Captain Bullock, alone
in the A-4 trainer, prepared to catapult off the carrier. Before
climbing aboard the jet, he'd stopped by the Sea Knight and
confronted her briefly, explaining that he'd rendezvous with them
later; that Todd Dougherty would be down from the bridge shortly
to explain everything. Before Pam could question Bullock, he'd
sauntered off in his usual cocky manner. The helicopter's pilot had
closed the door after him to shut out some of the deafening flight
deck noise.

Kenny Chi shook his head and said to her, "Supposing our
cunning captain flies off somewhere, parachutes out of the plane,
and disappears?"

Pam shook her head. "Possible, but not probable. He's not the
type to run." She pointed outside. Bullock's jet was ready for
takeoff.

The light on the carrier's island turned green and the launch
officer arched over and touched the deck.

51

Wham! A massive jolt of steam from the below-deck piston activated the catapult, hurling Bullock's A-4 at 150 miles an hour toward the front of the carrier.

Pamela was hunched next to Steinberg, staring out the same plexiglas port. She felt him suddenly grow tense. Pam too, sensed something was wrong with the launch. She'd watched several aircraft take off in the last half hour; each time she'd gasp as they'd sink slightly once off the catapult, then heave a sigh of relief as engine thrust took over and the plane gained aerodynamic lift. But this time the sound was different— ominously different.

The A-4's engine had apparently gone dead a fraction of a second before Bullock reached the bow of the carrier. "Flame out!" Steinberg screamed in her ear. He threw open the helicopter door, and they all leaped out on the flight deck in time to see Bullock's Skyhawk mushing downward, tail low, heading toward the water less than 300 yards directly in front of the onrushing carrier. Pam pressed her hands against the sides of her head, aware that if the jet went in it would sink like a rock. Bullock had mere seconds to eject before it was too late. "Pull up! Pull up!" she shouted futilely. She should have cried *eject*. The A-4 was completely without power.

"Plane in the water!" boomed the carrier's loudspeaker. "Plane in the water!" All activity on the flight deck came to an immediate standstill. Personnel gaped or ran forward.

Bullock didn't eject.

The Skyhawk hit the sea tail first, hurtling huge roostertails of water into the air as it flipped end over end twice before plunging under the waves. A klaxon sounded on the carrier. Bullock's jet would probably sink quickly, but even if it floated for a short period, there wasn't time for the carrier to turn out of the way or slow its forward momentum. Standard procedure was for the ship to make a tight turn and return to the area.

Pam swallowed hard. Instinctively needing to touch someone,

she grabbed for Chi's and Steinberg's hands and squeezed hard. There was nothing more to see up forward, so Pamela numbly sat down in the helicopter's hatch and looked toward the carrier's island.

Striding toward her with a carry-on bag was Todd Dougherty. He shook his head in utter defeat. Suddenly, one of the lead yellow shirts hot-footed across the deck toward him. Before Dougherty could climb inside the Sea Knight with Pamela, the deck crewman shouted, "Lieutenant Commander, the Admiral wants you on the Intercom!" He offered Dougherty his own mouse ear helmet with its hot mike and earphones.

Dougherty put it on.

"Dougherty, we've got a problem!" Tanner's clipped voice.

Dougherty groaned. "I have eyes, Admiral. What can I say? Any chance for rescue or recovery?"

"The plane guard chopper's already in the air. That's not why I need you. Take a look up forward . . . at that first Tomcat parked on the starboard side."

Dougherty glanced toward the bow of the ship. Some three hundred feet away, he saw an F-14A being prepared for taxi and takeoff. It was still secured to the deck, with the pilot and RIO aboard, the canopy raised. But a yellow shirt stood poised on the fighter's wing. Oddly, the man appeared to be tossing off a salute to Dougherty.

Suddenly, a familiar voice disrupted the intercom. "Dougherty, my friend! I wouldn't want you and Pamela to leave right away. I'll need that helicopter. Captain Bullock's sudden demise leaves me in a compromising spot."

Dougherty's stomach pushed up in his throat. The voice was unmistakably *Roscoe Steelbinder's*.

Again, Fritz Tanner on the intercom: "Sorry, Dougherty. He's got a hand grenade in his hand and is threatening to toss it into the cockpit of that Tomcat."

Dougherty looked closer. He saw the object in Steelbinder's hand and how he'd blocked open the canopy of the F-14A with a monkey wrench. Helpless, the two-man flight crew sat waiting and watchful. Dougherty's lungs heaved. "Steelbinder, I have to give you credit. How did you get off the Golden Gate tower alive?"

"Studied books in the library, Dougherty, what else? Remember the old video game called Pac-Man? The bridge towers are honeycombed with horizontal passages and have alternate ladders down to the piers. The difficult part was the cold swim back to the ship. A short one, thanks to Captain Bullock. The lines extending down from the whaleboat davit were no problem at all for a man in prime physical condition. Are you still there, Admiral?"

Tanner's grim voice: "I'm listening, you prick."

"Unfortunately, one of the boatswain's mates discovered me as I climbed off the davit on to the deck. You'll find him bound and gagged in one of the paint lockers. I would have thrown him overboard, but the whaleboat was returning down below."

While Steelbinder rambled, Dougherty quickly whispered the bad news to Pamela. Then he said into the intercom mouthpiece, "Thanks for being charitable, Roscoe, but get down to basics. What do you want?"

In the distance Steelbinder clasped the frag grenade with both hands, demonstrating how he might pull the pin reflexively if a sniper tried to take a shot at him. He said to Dougherty on the intercom, "Now that I've taken proper care of Captain Bullock, I want very little. It's amazing the damage two quarters taped inside a Skyhawk's engine do when they become dislodged. Now then, is Pamela with you, Dougherty?"

"She's here. Get on with it."

"I'll need two parachutes placed inside that Sea Knight. Then I want a blue shirt with a tractor to tow the helicopter down the flight deck to within twenty feet of where I'm standing. As close to this Tomcat as possible, understand?"

Dougherty waited for more.

"You're too quiet, Lieutenant Commander. Are you taking all this down?"

"I'm listening, you asshole."

"Have Flight Operations line up those parachutes. I suggest no monkey business, as one of them will be for Pamela. Inconvenient, I realize, but someone has to be a hostage. One more request. Make sure the helicopter's fuel tanks are topped off."

Rear Admiral Tanner suddenly interjected, "Steelbinder! Supposing I call your bluff and refuse to cooperate?"

"I'm growing impatient, gentlemen. You wouldn't want anything to happen to this flight crew, would you? Not to mention losing yet another multi-million-dollar airplane?"

Dougherty thought quickly. "Roscoe, I need time. Just don't lose control, okay? I'm going to give these mouse ears to Pamela while I go try to round up those parachutes." Before handing over the helmet-enclosed earphones, he whispered in her ear: "Have him recite *The Divine Comedy* backwards if necessary, but keep him occupied."

She nodded and put on the intercom unit.

Dougherty took off, darting to the other side of the helicopter where he was out of Steelbinder's line of sight. Dougherty beckoned to a nearby flight deck crew. Wearing intercom headsets of their own, they knew what was going on. Dougherty went up to a purple shirt, grabbing his slate and a piece of chalk; he scribbled quickly in large bold letters, then gestured toward the F-14A on the nearby waist catapult. The fighter's engines were still idling, but since the carrier had gone into emergency status and turned away from the wind, the plane was unable to take off.

The purple shirt scampered over to the jet and flashed Dougherty's message to the pilot, indicating with a finger to his lips that the Tomcat crew should stay off the hot mike. At the same time a green shirt disconnected the catapult launch bar under the aircraft.

Pilot Squeegee Liddell understood what he had to do. Ordinarily, he'd taxi his fighter back to the stern and park it with the rest of his squadron. The three words on the purple shirt's slate, however, meant it had to appear he was headed for a tie-down up by the bow. Squeegee prayed his RIO in the back of the cockpit understood the danger confronting them. As a precaution to make sure the gabby Hambone didn't break silence and give away the plan, Squeegee turned off the hot mike circuit.

He pushed the throttles, applying the right brake at the same time. The Tomcat's twin engine alternately roared and screamed as he pulled out onto the center deck area. Squeegee glanced up to the walkway behind the command bridge. Rear Admiral Tanner was watching him with a confounded look. Beside him the XO and Air Wing Commander were waving their arms, trying to signal him back. Squeegee swallowed hard and ignored them.

As he taxied on by the helicopter he saw the NIS commander nod with approval. Up ahead on the right was the troubled F-14A, its plexiglas canopy hinged open, the deranged sailor with the grenade standing defiantly on the wing and threatening the crew.

Squeegee stared straight ahead, purposely avoiding eye contact with the yellow shirt they'd called Steelbinder and worse names on the intercom. Appearance would count for everything; he had to make it look like a routine aircraft relocation. Until the very last moment.

Now! Squeegee tromped hard on the left pedal, applying the brake for a tight turn in the center of the deck. At the same instant, he rammed the engine throttles forward to eighty percent.

Cyclones of white flame belched from the Tomcat's twin

exhausts. Squeegee flashed on the repeated warnings in flight school: at 80% thrust all personnel within 250 feet had damn well better be chained down to the deck.

Roscoe Steelbinder was unsecured and in a precarious spot. He didn't even have time to jump across the wing and grab hold of the cockpit cowling. Instantly caught up in the rank-smelling jet blast, he was propelled off the Tomcat's wing like a leaf in the wind.

Steelbinder half tumbled, half flew across the flight deck, then out and beyond the carrier's six-feet-wide safety net. Arms flung out like a skydiver, Steelbinder seemed to hover in the air for brief seconds before plummeting into the sea beside the carrier. The grenade, too, was propelled overboard. The force of Squeegee and Hambone's exhaust blast was so great it sprung the canopy of the tied-down F-14A.

The victim might have stood a chance if the *Abe Lincoln* hadn't been executing an emergency turn to port. But with the carrier's stern kicking out to the right, Steelbinder was swiftly drawn into the side of the ship and sucked downward into the four massive props. Up on the bridge, the XO called for all engines to be stopped. Fitz Tanner came up beside the acting ship's commander and slowly shook his head.

Down on the flight deck, a purple shirt passed his blackboard around for his buddies to read what Todd Dougherty had written on it. The slate read simply: BLOW HIM AWAY.

~~~~~ 52

The supercarrier drifted for almost an hour while the area was searched for the two victims. The rescue helicopter finally reported back the grisly news that parts of Steelbinder's body had been recovered, but there was no sign of Bullock. Earlier, the Skyhawk's tail empennage had been spotted tossed up in the carrier's wake, but the wreckage sank before it could be retrieved.

Dougherty was silent like the others. Pamela, Lieutenant Chi, and Steinberg had joined him in the *Abraham Lincoln's* chart room, where they waited for a statement from Rear Admiral

Tanner. Dougherty guessed that Bullock went straight to the bottom of the Pacific strapped in the seat of his plane.

The Navy record books would call the captain's jet crash a *mishap*. By law, the carrier's accident investigation team would meet within hours, but Dougherty knew all they could do was speculate on why Bullock didn't pull the seat eject handle. As for Steelbinder being blown overboard, Dougherty would take full responsibility for that incident.

At last a desolate looking Fritz Tanner came in from the command bridge. He seemed at a complete loss for words.

Breaking the ice, Pamela said softly to him, "Have we learned anything at all from all this, Admiral?"

Tanner held her curious gaze. "I'm sorry," he said dully. "I wonder if the moment deserves eulogies or any other kind of speech."

Lieutenant Chi asked somberly, "Could the captain have saved himself?"

Tanner stared at Chi. "Bullock could have ejected, but he didn't. Who knows what went on in the man's mind at that critical moment?"

Pamela exchanged ironic glances with Dougherty then said to Tanner, "Are you implying he had no intention of flying to Alameda to face the music?"

Tanner shrugged. "I didn't say that, but who knows? An officer's career in the Navy is a game of following rules, Ms Bonner. Pocketing one's personal opinions and many personal convictions. Above all, it's a matter of honor." Tanner pursed his lips unhappily. "It wasn't so much the case of Bullock dishonoring the Navy, but dishonoring himself. And I suspect he couldn't live with that."

Chi and Pamela retreated into silence.

Tanner looked at Dougherty through narrow eyelids. "What's it going to be, Lieutenant Commander? Do we keep riding this uncomfortable investigation or bury it for the good of all concerned? It appears this is an NIS decision, not a line matter. Right now, Dougherty, you're carrying a bigger load with your two and a half stripes than I am with a couple of stars."

Tanner's words hung in the air, and Dougherty felt cornered. It was no use heaving on the prosecution line any longer, but before he could intelligently answer the admiral he needed to confer with the Hong Kong detective. The tension in the chart room increased measureably.

Kenny Chi cleared his throat. "It's obvious that with all the principal actors in this tragedy deceased, there's no one to prosecute. As for that duplicate tape at San Francisco Police Headquarters, I now suspect it's doomed for the old business file." Chi let out a sigh. "Between the two of us, Lieutenant Commander, I'd like nothing better than to resume my California vacation."

Dougherty felt suddenly overcome with relief; it was like the desert when the rains came.

Pamela asked eagerly, "The investigation is closed then?"

Dougherty nodded. He turned to Tanner, "If the rear admiral concurs that Bullock is military history, I'm willing to leave it that way."

Tanner risked a smile. "Who am I to question U.S. Navy history? It's unpatriotic."

From next door in the command bridge Dougherty heard the XO shouting. "Engines all ahead one third." The sea search was obviously concluded.

Dougherty was about to lead the others down to the waiting helicopter, but Tanner beckoned to him. "Lieutenant Commander, I have a suggestion. The *Abraham Lincoln* will take another two days to reach Bremerton. For the official log, you might like to remain aboard until the accident inquiry team concludes its findings. As for your investigative partner here, Captain Bullock told me she was highly determined to experience life aboard a carrier at sea." Tanner turned to Pamela. "Since we're no longer conducting exercises, Ms Bonner, I see no reason why you shouldn't remain aboard for the rest of this ferry mission. Our wounded ship is a far cry from a comfy love-boat, but we just happen to have available the captain's cabin with its private bath."

Dougherty smiled. He wanted to get back to San Diego, but he did need the results of the aircraft accident investigation—as would Pamela, to summarize her own report. He looked at her, "How about it? Officially, for the record, we'd be wrapping up the case. Off the record, it's a two-day enforced reprieve before going back to the grind."

"What about your office at North Island?"

"Steinberg will return and cover for me."

She thought for a moment, then smiled. "If I have one weakness, it's curiosity. Not to mention a stubborn determination to penetrate any and all sexist strongholds. You're on, Gentlemen."

The admiral turned to Kenny Chi. "You're welcome to tag along, Detective. We'll give you a first class tour of the ship."

Chi shook his head. "Thank you, Admiral. The sooner I clear the air with San Francisco's homicide people, the faster I get down to Disneyland and Hollywood."

Tanner frowned. "Hollywood?"

"Yes." Chi grinned. "The place where they made your wonderful *Charlie Chan* movies, remember?"

Chi and Steinberg said goodbye and headed for the flight deck and the waiting helicopter.

Fritz Tanner smiled at Pamela. "Ms Bonner, I suspect you've been putting up with Todd Dougherty's good offices long enough. All naval officers are not as incorrigible as Dougherty, you know. Will you join my staff for dinner tonight? Stop pouting, Lieutenant Commander. You may come along as well."

Pam hesitated, but Dougherty was in a decisive mood. "Yes, sir," he answered for her. "We'll both be there."

"At six, then, my flag quarters mess."

Dougherty nodded and led Pamela outside. They watched Steinberg and Chi climb aboard the Sea Knight and the big rotors start to turn. Moments later the helicopter was given a takeoff clearance, and it left the carrier, moving off to the southeast. They watched it disappear toward the California coast, barely visible through the haze some twenty miles distant. Below them, flight crews tramped back to their duty stations. As soon as the carrier was brought into the wind, they'd resume launching the rest of the aircraft. Dougherty winked at Pam. "May I escort you down to the captain's suite?"

She smiled at him. "Could we go over to the other side of the carrier first?"

Dougherty shrugged. "Why not? Any particular reason?"

She didn't respond. A few moments later they were on the opposite side of the island, by themselves on a catwalk extending out over the sea. Pamela's hair fluttered in the wind as she reached in her purse and withdrew the shiny Rolls hood ornament. She examined the mascot with a look of disapproval. "Back there I almost felt sorry for Swain Bullock, especially when his Hong Kong chauffeurs ganged up on him."

Dougherty looked away, staring at the distant horizon. "The captain bought his troubles; he demanded too much of himself and life in general. The other two saw opportunity knocking. Bullock was shrewd enough to recognize the bad seed in Steelbinder and replaced him, only to get another lemon in Gecko Corman. They both had it in for the captain, in different ways."

Pam tossed the *Spirit of Ecstasy* mascot into the sea. "It's turned out to be a bad luck charm."

Dougherty smiled and stared at her. "After we unwind from all this, what's next for excitement?"

"Mmmmm. I'll have to think about it. Nothing cheap. We could try making love—the romantic kind."

"You're more sentimental than I had you figured."

Pam thought for a moment. "You know what Roscoe Steelbinder told me up on top of the tower? About reincarnation, how he was determined to come back, one way or another?"

"No. And I'm not sure I want to hear about the future."

"Fine, then consider the past. Andy, have you ever thought what it would be like to go back in time, just temporarily?"

"Frankly, no." Dougherty felt the carrier pick up speed preparatory to begin launching planes.

The wind increased, ruffling Pamela's hair. She pulled several strands out of her face, smiled, and said, "Wouldn't it be great if we could just *sample* some wild adventure and then return to normalcy—or whatever we are today?"

"Like *Fantasy Island*. You sound as crazy as Steelbinder. Okay, who in the past would you like to be?"

"I'm trying to decide between Cleopatra and Claudius's wife Messalina."

Dougherty looked at her askance. "I'll bite. Why?"

She winked at him. "Both were legendary nymphomaniacs."

"Now I know you're a yo-yo. I prefer you like you are. Kicked-back, selective, passionate, but on the job . . ."

She held his arm. "Go ahead, finish. A feminist hothead?"

"No. Just assertive . . . and cunning. You know what you want and don't mince words." Dougherty held her closer. "I like your style—and your bizarre sense of humor. Maybe it's time we decided whether we want a fling or a commitment."

She studied him, straightening his collar and toying with his oak leaf insignias. Draping both arms loosely over his shoulders, she asked, "What do I have to do to convince the shy gentleman? Come on like that woman doctor in New York who tried to kidnap a male doctor and make him a 'love slave'?"

Dougherty steered her back inside, toward the ship's ladder. "I suggest we see if the captain's suite has a door with a dead-bolt on it."

~~~~~~ Epilogue

The barge was anchored some thirty feet out in the Hudson River, providing a comfortable moat between the rock concert performers and the disruptive audience. The late summer festival was being compared to Woodstock, but it was closer to New York City. The crowd would have been far larger except for the ominous weather forecast. Already ugly black thunderheads scudded toward the riverbank site, threatening both the open stage and the crowds along the grassy slope. The heavy metal rock group concluding its second number was called The Midnight Admirals.

Bowing to the applause, the sweating lead guitarist swaggered forward with a microphone. "I'm hearing two kinds of thunder out there! As long as the applause and cheering drowns out that nasty stuff upstairs, we'll keep on playing, okay? Hell, if you're not sissies, neither are we!"

There was some half-hearted cheering from the audience.

"For our next number, we're doing a little departure from our usual gig. How many sailors and ex-sailors out there today?"

A couple hundred voices hooted back, and the lead guitarist was impressed. "New London? Norfolk? Brooklyn Navy Yard? San Diego? *All right*! You'll like this next number. It's about an old Navy salt who spends all his years at sea then refuses to retire when he reaches the end of the line! He ends it all by climbing into his admiral's barge and setting the damn thing on fire! A Viking's funeral—you still with me?"

There were cheers and assorted catcalls, these punctuated by another loud growl of thunder overhead. The group's bass player briefly grabbed the mike from his partner. "Better let them in on how we came by the music, big mouth!"

"Nah! The motherfuckers wouldn't believe it! Okay, it came with the fan mail! Some talented Navy swabbie named R. W. Steelbinder wrote the lyrics. How's that for dedicated fans?

Thanks, R.W.! Not bad stuff, either." The musician scanned the crowd. "You want us to kick ass with it?"

Applause, a few whistles. Squeals from the younger women. Some of the crowd, intimidated by the threatening sky, began to file out. The dedicated remained, though a little edgy.

"Eyes front, folks, for a little demonstration of a Viking funeral." The surly lead guitarist pointed to the moat in front of him where a stagehand prepared to push off a small wooden dinghy. Propped up on its seat was a mannequin dressed as a parody of a turn-of-the-century Navy admiral. The stagehand used lighter fluid to set the effigy and the boat afire.

The Midnight Admirals started to play. The amps and drums were deafening, the lead guitarist's words barely audible:

> *Two score years before the mast, zam!*
> *A dozen more in cruisers fast, zam!*
> *Damn the torpedoes and full speed ahead!*
> *One old warrior hates to lose, zam!*
> *Send the bastard out just one last cruise . . .*

The lightning bolt hit then, striking one of the lofty spotlight platforms off to the left of the barge. The stunned crowd stared open-mouthed as the scaffold crashed into the river. Luckily, the light platform was unoccupied. Following the electrical flash, the heavens seemed to break loose all at once, sending down a torrent of rain that quickly turned to pea-sized hail. Urged on by the stinging pellets, the crowd dispersed.

Women screamed. Children wailed. Several concertgoers panicked and were trampled in the rush to the exit. On stage the Midnight Admirals did what they could to protect their equipment and cowered under plastic tarps. The storm didn't abate but grew worse.

As for the Viking funeral rite, the fierce blaze consuming the boat and its occupant fizzled out under the downpour. The charred remains of the dummy toppled to one side of the dinghy, but the admiral's hat—surprisingly unscathed by the flames—fell into the water. Despite the hailstorm, the hat rode easily on the surface like a cork, drifting out of the moat and into the Hudson River proper. Even then it stubbornly refused to sink, instead bobbing lightly downstream, out of the storm, bound for New York Bay, possibly even the open sea.

ABOUT THE AUTHOR

Douglas Muir resides in Newport Beach, California. He has degrees from the University of Washington and UCLA and was an award-winning film and television writer-director before turning to full-time novel writing. Among his numerous credits is the acclaimed *Undersea World of Jacques Cousteau*.

Muir's prior books include *Tides of War* and *Red Star Run*. He is currently at work on a new adventure novel.